Edition de Luxe

THE WORKS
OF
MATTHEW ARNOLD
IN
FIFTEEN VOLUMES
VOLUME VII

'*O quam magna multitudo dulcedinis Tuæ, Domine, quam abscondisti timentibus Te!*' PSALM xxxi. (xxx. in Vulgate) 19.

"*La tendance à l'ordre ne peut-elle faire une partie essentielle de nos inclinations, de notre instinct, comme la tendance à la conservation, à la reproduction?*"
SENANCOUR.

'And as it is owned the whole scheme of Scripture is not yet understood, so, if it ever comes to be understood, it must be in the same way as natural knowledge is come at: by the continuance and progress of learning and of liberty, and by particular persons attending to, comparing, and pursuing intimations scattered up and down it, which are overlooked and disregarded by the generality of the world. Nor is it at all incredible that a book which has been so long in the possession of mankind should contain many truths as yet undiscovered. For all the same phenomena and the same faculties of investigation, from which such great discoveries in natural knowledge have been made in the present and last age, were equally in the possession of mankind several thousand years before.' BUTLER.

'If a great change is to be made, the minds of men will be fitted to it, the general opinions and feelings will draw that way. Every fear, every hope, will forward it; and then they, who persist in opposing this mighty current, will appear rather to resist the decrees of Providence itself, than the mere designs of men. They will not be resolute and firm, but perverse and obstinate.'

LITERATURE & DOGMA

AN ESSAY
TOWARDS A BETTER
APPREHENSION OF THE BIBLE

BY

MATTHEW ARNOLD

AMS PRESS
NEW YORK

Reprinted from the edition of 1903-04, London
First AMS EDITION published 1970
Manufactured in the United States of America

International Standard Book Number:
Complete set: 0-404-00450-4
Volume 7: 0-404-00457-1

Library of Congress Catalog Card Number: 72-113544

AMS PRESS, INC.
New York, N.Y. 10003

PREFACE

An inevitable revolution, of which we all recognise the beginnings and signs, but which has already spread, perhaps, farther than most of us think, is befalling the religion in which we have been brought up. In those countries where religion has been most loved, this revolution will be felt the most keenly; felt through all its stages and in all its incidents. In no country will it be more felt than in England. This cannot be otherwise. It cannot be but that the revolution should come, and that it should be here felt passionately, profoundly, painfully; but no one is on that account in the least dispensed from the utmost duty of considerateness and caution. There is no surer proof of a narrow and ill-instructed mind than to think and uphold that what a man takes to be the truth on religious matters is always to be proclaimed. Our truth on these matters, and likewise the error of others, is something so relative that the good or harm likely to be done by speaking ought always to be taken into account. 'I keep silence at many things,' says Goethe, 'for I would not mislead men, and am well content if others can find satisfaction in what gives me offence.' The man who believes that his truth on religious matters is so absolutely the truth, that say it when, and where, and to whom he will, he cannot but do good with it, is in our day almost always a man whose truth is half blunder, and wholly useless.

To be convinced, therefore, that our current theology is false, is not necessarily a reason for publishing that conviction. The theology may be false, and yet one may do more harm in attacking it than by keeping silence and waiting. To judge rightly the time and its conditions is the great thing ; there is a time, as the Preacher says, to speak, and a time to keep silence. If the present time is a time to speak, there must be a reason why it is so.

And there *is* a reason ; and it is this. Clergymen and ministers of religion are full of lamentations over what they call the spread of scepticism, and because of the little hold which religion now has on the masses of the people,—the *lapsed masses*, as some call them. Practical hold on them it never, perhaps, had very much, but they did not question its truth, and they held it in considerable awe. As the best of them raised themselves up out of a merely animal life, religion attracted and engaged them. But now they seem to have hardly any awe of it at all, and they freely question its truth. And many

PREFACE

of the most successful, energetic, and ingenious of the artisan class, who are steady and rise, are now found either of themselves rejecting the Bible altogether, or following teachers who tell them the Bible is an exploded superstition. Let me quote from the letter of a working-man,—a man himself of no common intelligence and temper,—a passage that sets this forth very clearly. 'Despite the efforts of the churches,' he says, 'the speculations of the day are working their way down among the people, many of whom are asking for the *reason* and *authority* for the things they have been taught to believe. Questions of this kind, too, mostly reach them through doubtful channels ; and owing to this, and to their lack of culture, a discovery of imperfection and fallibility in the Bible leads to its contemptuous rejection as a great priestly imposture. And thus those among the working class who eschew the teachings of the orthodox, slide off towards, not the late Mr. Maurice, nor yet Professor Huxley, but towards Mr. Bradlaugh.'

Despite the efforts of the churches, the writer tells us, this contemptuous rejection of the Bible happens. And we regret the rejection as much as the clergy and ministers of religion do. There may be others who do not regret it, but we do. All that the churches can say about the importance of the Bible and its religion we concur in. And it is the religion of the Bible that is professedly in question with all the churches when they talk of religion and lament its prospects. With Catholics as well as Protestants, and with all the sects of Protestantism, this is so ; and from the nature of the case it must be so. What the religion of the Bible is, how it is to be got at, they may not agree ; but that it is the religion of the Bible for which they contend they all aver. 'The Bible,' says Dr. Newman, 'is the record of the whole revealed faith ; so far all parties agree.' Now, this religion of the Bible we say they cannot value more than we do. If we hesitate to adopt strictly their language about its *all*-importance, that is only because we take an uncommonly large view of human perfection, and say, speaking strictly, that there go to this certain things,—art, for instance, and science, which the Bible hardly meddles with. The difference between us and them, however, is more a difference of theoretical statement than of practical conclusion. Speaking practically, and looking at the very large part of human life engaged by the Bible, at the comparatively small part unengaged by it, we are quite willing, like the churches, to call the Bible and its religion *all*-important.

All this agreement there is, both in words and in things, between us and the churches. And yet, when we behold the clergy and ministers of religion lament the neglect of religion and aspire to restore it, how must we feel that to restore religion as they understand it,

PREFACE

to re-inthrone the Bible as explained by our current theology, whether learned or popular, is absolutely and for ever impossible!—as impossible as to restore the feudal system, or the belief in witches. Let us admit that the Bible cannot possibly die; but then the churches cannot even conceive the Bible without the gloss they at present put upon it, and this gloss, as certainly, cannot possibly live. And it is not a gloss which one church or one sect puts upon the Bible and another does not; it is the gloss they *all* put upon it, and call the substratum of belief common to all Christian churches, and largely shared with them, even by natural religion. It is this so-called axiomatic basis which must go, and it supports all the rest. If the Bible were really inseparable from this and depended upon it, then Mr. Bradlaugh would have his way and the Bible would go too; since this basis is inevitably doomed. For whatever is to stand must rest upon something which is verifiable, not unverifiable. Now, the assumption with which all the churches and sects set out, that there is 'a Great Personal First Cause, the moral and intelligent Governor of the Universe,' and that from him the Bible derives its authority, cannot at present, at any rate, be verified.

Those who 'ask for the *reason* and *authority* for the things they have been taught to believe,' as the people, we are told, are now doing, will begin at the beginning. Rude and hard reasoners as they are, they will never consent to admit, as a self-evident axiom, the preliminary assumption with which the churches start. But this preliminary assumption governs everything which in our current theology follows it ; and it is certain, therefore, that the people will not receive our current theology. So, if they are to receive the Bible, we must find for the Bible some other basis than that which the churches assign to it, a verifiable basis and not an assumption ; and this, again, will govern everything which comes after. This new religion of the Bible the people may receive ; the version now current of the religion of the Bible they never will receive.

Here, then, is the problem : to find, for the Bible, a basis in something which can be verified, instead of in something which has to be assumed. So true and prophetic are Vinet's words : 'We *must*,' he said, 'make it our business to bring forward the rational side of Christianity, and to show that for thinkers, too, it has a right to be an authority.' Yes, and the problem we have stated must be the first stage in the business. With this unsolved, all other religious discussion is idle trifling.

This is why Dissent, as a religious movement of our day, would be almost droll, if it were not, from the tempers and actions it excites, so extremely irreligious. But what is to be said for men, aspiring to deal with the cause of religion,

PREFACE

who either cannot see that what the people now require is a religion of the Bible quite different from that which *any* of the churches or sects supply ; or who, seeing this, spend their energies in fiercely battling as to whether the Church should be a national institution or no ? The question, at the present juncture, is in itself so absolutely unimportant! The thing is, to recast religion. If this is done, the new religion will be the national one ; if it is not done, separating the nation, in its collective and corporate character, from religion, will not do it. It is as if men's minds were much unsettled about mineralogy, and the teachers of it were at variance, and no teacher was convincing, and many people, therefore, were disposed to throw the study of mineralogy overboard altogether. What would naturally be the first business for every friend of the study ? Surely, to establish on safe grounds the value of the study, and to put its claims in a new light where they could no longer be denied. But if he acted as our Dissenters act in religion, what would he do ? Give himself, heart and soul, to a furious crusade against keeping the Government School of Mines!

Meanwhile, however, there is now an end to all fear of doing harm by gainsaying the received theology of the churches and sects. For this theology is itself now a hindrance to the Bible rather than a help. Nay, to abandon it, to put some other construction on the Bible than this theology puts, to find some other basis for the Bible than this theology finds, is indispensable, if we would have the Bible reach the people. And this is the aim of the following essay : to show that, when we come to put the right construction on the Bible, we give to the Bible a real experimental basis, and keep on this basis throughout ; instead of any basis of unverifiable assumption to start with, followed by a string of other unverifiable assumptions of the like kind, such as the received theology necessitates.

And this aim we cannot seek without coming in sight of another aim, too, which we have often and often pointed out, and tried to recommend : *culture*, the acquainting ourselves with the best that has been known and said in the world, and thus with the history of the human spirit. One cannot go far in the attempt to bring in, for the Bible, a right construction, without seeing how necessary is something of culture to its being admitted and used. The correspondent we have above quoted notices how the lack of culture disposes people to conclude at once, from any imperfection or fallibility in the Bible, that it is a priestly imposture. To a certain extent, this is the fault not of people's want of culture, but of the priests and theologians themselves, who for centuries have kept assuring men that perfect and infallible the Bible is. Still, even without this confusion added by his

PREFACE

theological instructors, the *homo unius libri*, the man of no range in his reading, must almost inevitably misunderstand the Bible, cannot treat it largely enough, must be inclined to treat it all alike, and to press every word.

For, on the one hand, he has not enough experience of the way in which men have thought and spoken, to feel what the Bible-writers are about; to read between the lines, to discern where he ought to rest with his whole weight, and where he ought to pass lightly. On the other hand, the void and hunger in his mind, from want of aliment, almost irresistibly impels him to fill it by taking literally and amplifying certain data which he finds in the Bible, whether they ought to be so dealt with or no. Our mechanical and materialising theology, with its insane licence of affirmation about God, its insane licence of affirmation about a future state, is really the result of the poverty and inanition of our minds. It is because we cannot trace God in history that we stay the craving of our minds with a fancy-account of him, made up by putting scattered expressions of the Bible together, and taking them literally; it is because we have such a scanty sense of the life of humanity, that we proceed in the like manner in our scheme of a future state. He that cannot watch the God of the Bible, and the salvation of the Bible, gradually and on an immense scale discovering themselves and *becoming*, will insist on seeing them ready-made, and in such precise and reduced dimensions as may suit his narrow mind.

To understand that the language of the Bible is fluid, passing, and literary, not rigid, fixed, and scientific, is the first step towards a right understanding of the Bible. But to take this very first step, some experience of how men have thought and expressed themselves, and some flexibility of spirit, are necessary; and this is culture. Much fruit may be got out of the Bible without it, and with those narrow and materialised schemes of God and a future state which we have mentioned; *that* we do not deny, but it is not the important point at present. The important point is, that the diffusion everywhere of some notion of the processes of the experimental sciences,—processes falling in, too, very well with the hard and positive character of the life of 'the people,'—the point is that this diffusion does lead 'the people' to ask for the *ground* and *authority* for those precise schemes of God and a future state which are presented to them, and to see clearly and scornfully the failure to give it. The failure to give it is inevitable, because given it cannot be; but whereas in the training, life, and sentiment of the well-to-do classes there is much to make them disguise the failure to themselves and not insist upon it, in the training, life, and sentiment of the people there is next to

PREFACE

nothing. So that, as far as the people are concerned, the old traditional scheme of the Bible is gone; while neither they nor the so-called educated classes have yet anything to put in its place.

And thus we come back to our old remedy of *culture*,—knowing the best that has been thought and known in the world; which turns out to be, in another shape, and in particular relation to the Bible: *getting the power, through reading, to estimate the proportion and relation in what we read.* If we read but a very little, we naturally want to press it all; if we read a great deal, we are willing not to press the whole of what we read, and we learn what ought to be pressed and what not. Now this is really the very foundation of any sane criticism. We have told the Dissenters that their 'spirit of watchful jealousy' is wholly destructive and exclusive of the spirit of Christianity. They answer us, that St. Paul talks of 'a godly jealousy,' and that Jesus Christ uses severe invectives against the Scribes and Pharisees. The Dissenters conclude, therefore, that their jealousy is Christian, because covered by Jesus Christ's use of invective.

Now, there can be no doubt whatever, that in his invectives against the Scribes and Pharisees Jesus abandoned the mild, uncontentious, winning, inward mode of working (*He shall not strive nor cry!*) which was his true characteristic, and in which his charm and power lay; and that there was no chance at all of his gaining by such invectives the persons at whom they were launched. The same may be said of the cases where St. Paul lets loose his 'godly jealousy,' and employs objurgation instead of the mildness which was Jesus Christ's true means, and which Paul,—though himself no special adept at it,—nevertheless appreciated so worthily, and so earnestly extols. St. Paul certainly had no chance of convincing those whom he calls 'dogs,' the 'concision,' utterers of 'profane and vain babblings,' by such a manner of dealing with them.

What may, indeed, fairly be said is, that the Pharisees against whom Jesus denounced his woes, or the Judaisers against whom Paul fulminated, were people whom there could be no hope of gaining; and that not *their* conversion, but a strong impression on the faithful who read or heard, was the thing aimed at, and very rightly aimed at. And so far at any rate as Jesus Christ's use of invective against the Pharisees is concerned, this may be quite true; but what a criticism is that, which can gather hence any general defence of jealousy and objurgation as Christian! For, in the first place, such weapons can have no excuse at all except as employed against individuals who are past hope, or against institutions which are palpably monstrosities. They can have

PREFACE

none as employed against institutions containing more than half a great nation, and therefore a multitude of individuals good as well as bad. And therefore we see that Jesus Christ never dreamed of assailing the Jewish Church; all he cared for was to transform it, by transforming as many as were transformable of the individuals composing it. In the second place, when such means of action have a defence, they are defensible *although* violations of Jesus Christ's established rule of working, never commendable as exemplifications of it. Mildness and sweet reasonableness is the one established rule for Christian working, and no other rule has it or can it have. But, using the Bible in the mechanical and helpless way in which one uses it when one has hardly any other book, men fail to see this, clear as it is. And they do really come to imagine that the Dissenters' 'spirit of watchful jealousy' may be a Christian temper; or that a movement like the Liberation Society's crusade against the Church of England may be a Christian work. And it is in this way that Christianity gets discredited.

Now, simple as it is, it is not half enough understood, this reason for culture: namely, that to read to good purpose we must read a great deal, and be content not to use a great deal of what we read. We shall never be content not to use the whole, or nearly the whole, of what we read, unless we read a great deal. Yet things are on such a scale, and progress is so gradual, and what one man can do is so bounded, that the moment we press the whole of what any writer says, we fall into error. He touches a great deal : the thing to know is where he is all himself and his best self, where he shows his power, where he goes to the heart of the matter, where he gives us what no other man gives us, or gives us so well. In his valuable *Church History*, Dr. Stoughton says of Hooker : ' The Puritan principle of the authority and unchangeableness of a revealed Church-polity Hooker substantially admits. Although this deep thinker sometimes talks perilously of altering Christ's laws, he says : " In the matter of external discipline itself, we do not deny but there are some things whereto the Church is bound till the world's end."' Dr. Stoughton does not see that to use his Hooker in this way is entirely fallacious. Hooker, this 'deep thinker,' as Dr. Stoughton truly calls him, one of the four chief names of the English Church, is great by having, signally and above others, or before others and when others had not, the sense, in religion, of *history* and of historic development. So, too, Butler is great by having the sense of philosophy, Barrow by having that of morals, Wilson that of practical Christianity. But if Hooker spoke, as he did, of Church-history like a historian, and exploded

PREFACE

the Puritan figment, due to a defective historic sense, of a revealed Church-polity, a Scriptural Church-order,—if Hooker did this, this was so new that he could not possibly do it without reservations, limitations, apologies. He could not help saying : 'We do not deny there may be *some* external things whereto the Church is eternally bound.' But he is truly himself, he is the great Hooker, the man from whom we learn, when he shatters the Puritan figment, not when he uses the language of compliment and ceremony in shattering it.

In like manner that eloquent orator, Mr. Liddon, looking about him for authorities which commend the Athanasian Creed, finds Hooker commending it, and quotes him as an authority. This, again, is to make a use of Hooker which has no soundness in it. Hooker's greatness is that he gives the real method of criticism for Church-dogma, the *historic* method. Church-dogma is not written in black and white in the Bible, he says : it has to be collected from it ; it is, as we now say, a development from it. This and that dogma, says Hooker, 'are in Scripture nowhere to be found by express literal mention, only deduced they are out of Scripture by collection.' And he assigns the one right criterion for determining whether a dogma is justly deduced, and what Scripture means, and what is its true character : the criterion of *reason*. He assigns this with splendid boldness: 'It is not the word of God itself,' says he, 'which doth, or possibly can, assure us that we do well to think it his word'; no, it is reason, much-reviled reason. Surely this is enough for a sixteenth-century divine to give us in theology,—the very method of true science! without our expecting him to make the full application of it, without expecting him to say that the Church-dogmas of his time, the dogma of the Athanasian Creed among the rest, which were not seriously in question yet, on which the Time-Spirit had not then turned his light, were *false* developments; without wondering at his saying, that *they* were developments 'the necessity whereof is by none denied'! This is all that Hooker's warranty of the Athanasian Creed really comes to, or can come to. To fix the method by which that Creed must finally be judged was the main issue for him; to *judge* the Creed by that method was a side-issue, whereon he never really entered nor could enter, but treated the thing as already settled. Therefore Hooker is no real authority in favour of the Athanasian Creed; though we might think he was, if we read him without discrimination. And to read him with discrimination culture is necessary.

Luther, again, Mr. Liddon cites as a witness on the question of the Athanasian Creed; and he might as well cite him as a witness on the question of the origin of species. Luther's

PREFACE

greatness is in his revival of the sense of conscience and personal responsibility, and in the fresh vigorous power which this sense, joined to his robust mother-wit, gave him in using the Bible. He had enough to do in attacking Romish developments from the Bible, which by their practical side were evidently, to a plain moral sense and a plain mother-wit, *false* developments, without attacking speculative dogma, which had no visible bad effects on practice, which had all antiquity in its favour, on which, as we say, the Time-Spirit had not then turned his light, of which,—so Luther might say, like Hooker,—'the necessity was by none denied.' All this high speculative dogma he could not but affirm, and the more emphatically the more he questioned lower practical dogma. But his affirmation of it is not one of those things we can use; and whoever reads in the folios of Luther's works without passing lightly over very much, and, amongst it, over this, reads there ill. And without culture, without the use of so many books that he can afford not to over-use and misuse *one*, ill a man is likely to read there.

We can hardly urge this topic too much, of so great a practical importance is it, and above all at the present time. To be able to control what one reads by means of the tact coming, in a clear and fair mind, from a wide experience, was never perhaps so necessary as in the England of our own day, and in theology, and in what concerns the Bible. In every study one has to commence with the facts of that study. To get the facts, the data, in most matters of science, but notably in theology and Biblical learning, one goes to Germany. Germany, and it is her high honour, has searched out the facts and exhibited them. And without knowledge of the facts, no clearness or fairness of mind can in any study do anything; this cannot be laid down too rigidly. Now, English religion does not know the facts of its study, and has to go to Germany for them. This is half apparent to English religion even now, and it will daily become more and more apparent. And so overwhelming is the advantage given by knowing the facts of a study, that a student, who comes to a man who knows them, is tempted to put himself into his hands altogether; and this we in general see English students do, when they have recourse to the theologians of Germany. They put themselves altogether into their hands, and take all that they give them, conclusions as well as facts.

But they ought not to use them in this manner; for a man may have the facts and yet be unable to draw the right conclusions from them. In general, he may want *power;* as one may say of Strauss, for instance, that to what is unsolid in the New Testament he

PREFACE

applies a negative criticism ably enough, but that to deal with the reality which is still left in the New Testament, requires a larger, richer, deeper, more imaginative mind than his. But perhaps the quality specially needed for drawing the right conclusion from the facts, when one has got them, is best called *perception*, justness of perception. And this no man can well have who is a mere specialist, who has not what we call *culture* in addition to the knowledge of his particular study; and so many theologians, in Germany as well as elsewhere, are specialists! After we have got all the facts of our special study, justness of perception to deal with the facts is still required, and is, even, the principal thing of all.

But in this sort of tact, the German mind, if one may allow oneself to speak in such a general way, does seem to be even by nature somewhat wanting. In the German mind, as in the German language, there does seem to be something *splay*, something blunt-edged, unhandy and infelicitous,—some positive want of straightforward, sure perception, which tends to balance the great superiority of the Germans in special knowledge, and in the disposition to deal impartially with knowledge. For impartial they are, as well as learned; and this is a signal merit. While M. Barthélemy St.-Hilaire cannot translate Aristotle without intermixing platitudes in glorification of the French gospel of the Rights of Man, while one English historian writes history to extol the Whigs and another to execrate the Church, German workers proceed in a more philosophical fashion. Still, in quickness and sureness of perception, —in tact,—they do seem to fall somewhat short.

Of course in a man of genius this shortcoming is much less observable; but even in Germans of genius there is something of it. Goethe even, for instance, had less of quick, keen tact, one must surely own, than the great men of other nations whom alone one can cite as his literary compeers: Shakespeare, Voltaire, Cicero, Plato. Whether it be, as we have elsewhere speculated,[1] from race; or whether this quickness and sureness of perception comes, rather, from a long practical conversance with great affairs, and only those nations which have at any time had a practical lead of the civilised world, the Greeks, the Romans, the Italians, the French, the English, can have it; and the Germans have till now had no such practical lead, though now they have got it, and may now, therefore, acquire the practical dexterity of perception; however this may be, the thing is so, and a learned German has by no means, in general, a fine and practically sure perception in proportion to his learning.

[1] *On the Study of Celtic Literature*, pp. 79, 80.

PREFACE

Give a Frenchman, an Italian, an Englishman, the same knowledge of the facts,—removing from him, at the same time, all such disturbing influence as political partisanship, ecclesiastical antipathies, national vanity,—and you could, in general, trust his perception more than you can the German's. This, I say, shows how large a thing criticism is; since even of those from whom we take what we now in theology most want, knowledge of the facts of our study, and to whom therefore we are, and ought to be, under deep obligations, even of them we must not take too much, or take anything like all that they offer; but we must take much and leave much, and must have tact enough to know what to take and what to leave. And an Englishman with the necessary knowledge has in other respects the training likely to give this tact; but without knowledge and culture we cannot have it.

For a right understanding of the Bible itself, the discriminative experience, so much required in all our theological studies, is particularly indispensable. And to our popular religion it is especially difficult; because we have been trained to regard the Bible, not as a book whose parts have varying degrees of value, but as the Jews came to regard their Scriptures, as a sort of talisman given down to us out of Heaven, with all its parts equipollent. And yet there was a time when Jews knew well the vast difference there is between books like Esther, Chronicles, or Daniel, and books like Genesis or Isaiah. There was a time when Christians knew well the vast difference between the First Epistle of Peter and his so-called Second Epistle, or between the Epistle to the Hebrews and the Epistles to the Romans and to the Corinthians. This, indeed, is what makes the religious watchword of the British and Foreign School Society: *The Bible, the whole Bible, and nothing but the Bible!* so ingeniously (one must say) absurd; it is treating the Bible as Mahometans treat the Koran, as if it were a talisman all of one piece, and with all its sentences equipollent.

Yet the very expressions, *Canon of Scripture*, *Canonical Books*, recall a time when degrees of value were still felt, and all parts of the Bible did not stand on the same footing, and were not taken equally. There was a time when books were read as part of the Bible which are in no Bible now; there was a time when books which are in every Bible now, were by many disallowed as genuine parts of the Bible. St. Athanasius rejected the Book of Esther, and the Greek Christianity of the East repelled the Apocalypse, and the Latin Christianity of the West repelled the Epistle to the Hebrews. And a true critical sense of relative value lay at the bottom of all these rejections. No one rejected Isaiah or the Epistle to the Romans. The books rejected

PREFACE

were such books as those which we now print as the Apocrypha, or as the Book of Esther, or the Epistle to the Hebrews, or the so-called Epistle of Jude, or the so-called Second Epistle of St. Peter, or the two short Epistles following the main Epistle attributed to St. John, or the Apocalypse.

Now, whatever value one may assign to these works, no sound critic would rate their intrinsic worth as high as that of the great undisputed books of the Bible. And so far from their finally getting where they now are after a thorough trial of their claims, and with indisputable propriety, they got placed there by the force of circumstances, by chance or by routine, rather than on their merits. Indeed, by merit alone the Book of Esther could have no right at all to be now in our Canon while Ecclesiasticus is not, nor the Epistle of Jude and the Second Epistle of Peter rather than the First Epistle of Clement. But the whole discussion died out, not because the matter was sifted and settled and a perfect Canon of Scripture deliberately formed; it died out as mediæval ignorance deepened, and because there was no longer knowledge or criticism enough left in the world to keep such a discussion alive.

And so things went on till the Renascence, when criticism came to life again. But the Church had now long since adopted the Vulgate, and her authority was concerned in maintaining what she had adopted. Luther and Calvin, on the other hand, recurred to the old true notion of a difference in rank and genuineness among the Bible-books. For they both of them insisted on the criterion of internal evidence for Scripture : 'the witness of the Spirit.' How freely Luther used this criterion we may see by reading in the old editions of his Bible his prefaces, which in succeeding editions have long ceased to appear. Whether he used it aright we do not now inquire, but he used it freely. Taunted, however, by Rome with their divisions, their want of a fixed authority like the Church, Protestants were driven to make the Bible this fixed authority ; and so the Bible came to be regarded as a thing all of a piece, endued with talismanic virtues. It came to be regarded as something different from anything it had originally ever been, or primitive times had ever imagined it to be. And Protestants did practically in this way use the Bible more irrationally than Rome practically ever used it ; for Rome had her hypothesis of the Church Catholic endued with talismanic virtues, and did not want a talismanic Bible too. All this perversion has made a discriminating use of the Bible-documents very difficult in our country ; yet without it a sound criticism of the Bible is impossible ; and even, as we say, the very word *Canon*, the *Canon of Scripture*, points to such a use.

But, indeed, there is hardly any great thing

PREFACE

perverted by men which does not in some sort thus indicate its own perversion. The idea of the infallible Church Catholic itself, as we have elsewhere said,[1] is an idea the most fatal of all possible ideas to the concrete, so-called infallible, Church of Rome, such as we now see it. The infallible Church Catholic is, really, *the prophetic soul of the wide world dreaming of things to come ;* the whole human race, in its onward progress, discovering truth more complete than the parcel of truth any momentary individual can seize. Nay, and it is with the Pope himself as with the Church Catholic. That amiable old pessimist in St. Peter's Chair, whose allocutions we read and call them impotent and vain,—the Pope himself is, in his idea, the very Time-Spirit taking flesh, the incarnate ' *Zeit-Geist* ' ! O man, how true are thine instincts, how over-hasty thine interpretations of them !

But to return. Difficult, certainly, is the right reading of the Bible, and true culture, too, is difficult. For true culture implies not only knowledge, but right tact and justness of judgment, forming themselves by and with knowledge ; without this tact it is not true culture. Difficult, however, as culture is, it is necessary. For, after all, the Bible is *not* a talisman, to be taken and used literally ; neither is any existing Church a talisman, whatever pretensions of the sort it may make, for giving

[1] *St. Paul and Protestantism*, p. 144.

the right interpretation of the Bible. Only true culture can give us this interpretation; so that if conduct is, as it is, inextricably bound up with the Bible and the right interpretation of it, then the importance of culture becomes unspeakable. For if conduct is necessary (and there is nothing so necessary), culture is necessary.

And the poor require it as much as the rich; and at present their education, even when they get education, gives them hardly anything of it. Yet hardly less of it, perhaps, than the education of the rich gives to the rich. For when we say that culture is: *To know the best that has been thought and said in the world*, we imply that, for culture, a system directly tending to this end is necessary in our reading. Now, there is no such system yet present to guide the reading of the rich any more than of the poor. Such a system is hardly even thought of; a man who wants it must make it for himself. And our reading being so without purpose as it is, nothing can be truer than what Butler says, that really, in general, no part of our time is more idly spent than the time spent in reading.

Still, culture is indispensably necessary, and culture is *reading*; but reading with a purpose to guide it, and with system. He does a good work who does anything to help this: indeed, it is the one essential service now to be rendered to education. And the plea that this or that man has no time for culture will vanish as soon

PREFACE

as we desire culture so much that we begin to examine seriously our present use of our time. It has often been said, and cannot be said too often : Give to any man all the time that he now wastes, not only on his vices (when he has them), but on useless business, wearisome or deteriorating amusements, trivial letter-writing, random reading, and he will have plenty of time for culture. '*Die Zeit ist unendlich lang,*' says Goethe ; and so it really is. Some of us waste all of it, most of us waste much, but all of us waste some.

CONTENTS

CHAP.		PAGE
	INTRODUCTION	1
I.	RELIGION GIVEN	10
II.	*ABERGLAUBE* INVADING	61
III.	RELIGION NEW-GIVEN	79
IV.	THE PROOF FROM PROPHECY	107
V.	THE PROOF FROM MIRACLES	116
VI.	THE NEW TESTAMENT RECORD	148
VII.	THE TESTIMONY OF JESUS TO HIMSELF	181
VIII.	THE EARLY WITNESSES	250
IX.	*ABERGLAUBE* RE-INVADING	276
X.	OUR 'MASSES' AND THE BIBLE	312
XI.	THE TRUE GREATNESS OF THE OLD TESTAMENT	340
XII.	THE TRUE GREATNESS OF CHRISTIANITY	365
	CONCLUSION	384

LITERATURE AND DOGMA

INTRODUCTION

MR. DISRAELI, treating Hellenic things with the scornful negligence natural to a Hebrew, said the other day in a well-known book, that our aristocratic class, the polite flower of the nation, were truly Hellenic in this respect among others,—that they cared nothing for letters and never read. Now, there seems to be here some inaccuracy, if we take our standard of what is Hellenic from Hellas at its highest pitch of development. For the latest historian of Greece, Dr. Curtius, tells us that in the Athens of Pericles 'reading was universally diffused'; and again, that 'what more than anything distinguishes the Greeks from the barbarians of ancient and modern times, is the idea of a culture comprehending body *and soul* in an equal measure.' And we have ourselves called our aristocratic class *Barbarians*, which is the contrary of Hellenes, from this very reason: because, with all their fine, fresh appearance, their open-air life, and their love of field-sports, for reading and thinking they have in general no great turn. But no doubt Mr. Disraeli was thinking of the primitive Hellenes of north-western Greece, from among whom the Dorians of Peloponnesus originally came, but who themselves remained in their old seats and did not migrate and develop like their more famous brethren. And of these primitive Hellenes, of Greeks like the Chaonians and Molossians, it is probably a very just account to give, that they lived in the open air, loved field-sports, and never read. And, explained in this way, Mr. Disraeli's parallel of our aristocratic class with what he somewhat misleadingly calls the old Hellenic race, appears ingenious and sound. To those lusty northerners, the Molossian and Chaonian Greeks—Greeks untouched by the development which contradistinguishes the Hellene from the barbarian,—our aristocratic class, as he exhibits it, has a strong resemblance. At any rate, this class,—which from its great possessions, its beauty and attractiveness, the admiration felt for it by the Philistines or middle class, its actual power in the nation, and the still more considerable destinies to which its politeness, in Mr. Carlyle's opinion, entitles it, cannot but attract our notice pre-eminently,—shows at present a great and genuine disregard for letters.

And perhaps, if there is any other body of

INTRODUCTION

men which strikes one, even after looking at our aristocratic class, as being in the sunshine, as exercising great attraction, as being admired by the Philistines or middle class, and as having before it a future still more brilliant than its present, it is the friends of physical science. Now, their revolt against the tyranny of letters is notorious. To deprive letters of the too great place they have hitherto filled in men's estimation, and to substitute other studies for these, is the object of a sort of crusade with a body of people important in itself, but still more important because of the gifted leaders who march at its head.

Religion has always hitherto been a great power in England; and on this account, perhaps, whatever humiliations may be in store for religion in the future, the friends of physical science will not object to our saying that, after them and the aristocracy, the leaders of the religious world fill a prominent place in the public eye even now, and one cannot help noticing what their opinions and likings are. And it is curious how the feeling of the chief people in the religious world, too, seems to be just now against mere letters, which they slight as the vague and inexact instrument of shallow essayists and magazine-writers; and in favour of dogma, of a scientific and exact presentment of religious things, instead of a literary presentment of them. 'Dogmatic theology,' says the *Guardian*, speaking of our existing dogmatic theology,—'Dogmatic theology, *that is, precision and definiteness* of religious thought.' 'Maudlin sentimentalism,' says the Dean of Norwich, 'with its miserable disparagements of any *definite* doctrine; a *nerveless* religion, without the *sinew* and *bone* of doctrine.' The distinguished Chancellor of the University of Oxford thought it needful to tell us on a public occasion lately, that 'religion is no more to be severed from dogma than light from the sun.' Every one, again, remembers the Bishops of Winchester[1] and Gloucester making in Convocation their remarkable effort 'to do something,' as they said, 'for the honour of Our Lord's Godhead,' and to mark their sense of 'that infinite separation for time and for eternity which is involved in rejecting the Godhead of the Eternal Son.' In the same way: 'To no teaching,' says one champion of dogma, 'can the appellation of Christian be truly given which does not involve the idea of a Personal God.' Another lays like stress on correct ideas about the Personality of the Holy Ghost. 'Our Lord unquestionably,' says a third, 'annexes eternal life to a right knowledge of the Godhead,'—that is, to a right speculative, dogmatic knowledge of it. A fourth appeals to history and human nature for proof that 'an undogmatic Church can no more satisfy the

[1] The late Bishop Wilberforce.

INTRODUCTION

hunger of the soul, than a snowball, painted to look like fruit, would stay the hunger of the stomach.' And all these friends of theological science are, like the friends of physical science, though from another cause, severe upon letters. Attempts made at a literary treatment of religious history and ideas they call 'a subverting of the faith once delivered to the saints.' Those who make them they speak of as 'those who have made shipwreck of the faith'; and when they talk of 'the poison openly disseminated by infidels,' and describe the 'progress of infidelity,' which more and more, according to their account, 'denies God, rejects Christ, and lets loose every human passion,' though they have the audaciousness of physical science most in their eye, yet they have a direct aim, too, at the looseness and dangerous temerity of letters.

Keeping in remembrance what Scripture says about the young man who had great possessions, to be able to work a change of mind in our aristocratic class we never have pretended, we never shall pretend. But to the friends of physical science and to the friends of dogma we do feel emboldened, after giving our best consideration to the matter, to say a few words on behalf of letters, and in deprecation of the slight which, on different grounds, they both put upon them. But particularly in reply to the friends of dogma do we wish to insist on the case for letters, because of the great issues which seem to us to be here involved. Therefore of the relation of letters to religion we are going now to speak ; of their effect upon dogma, and of the consequences of this to religion. And so the subject of the present volume will be *literature and dogma*.

II

It is clear that dogmatists love religion ;—for else why do they occupy themselves with it so much, and make it, most of them, the business, even the professional business, of their lives ? And clearly religion seeks man's salvation. How distressing, therefore, must it be to them, to think that 'salvation is unquestionably annexed to a right knowledge of the Godhead,' and that a right knowledge of the Godhead depends upon reasoning, for which so many people have not much aptitude ; and upon reasoning from ideas or terms such as substance, identity, causation, design, about which there is endless disagreement ! It is true, a right knowledge of geometry also depends upon reasoning, and many people never get it ; but then, in the first place, salvation is not annexed to a right knowledge of geometry ; and in the second, the ideas or terms such as *point*, *line*, *angle*, from which we reason in geometry, are terms about which there is no ambiguity or disagreement.

INTRODUCTION

But as to the demonstrations and terms of theology we cannot comfort ourselves in this manner. How must this thought mar the Archbishop of York's enjoyment of such a solemnity as that in which, to uphold and renovate religion, he lectured lately to Lord Harrowby, Dean Payne Smith, and other kindred souls, upon the theory of causation! And what a consolation to us, who are so perpetually being taunted with our known inaptitude for abstruse reasoning, if we can find that for this great concern of religion, at any rate, abstruse reasoning does not seem to be the appointed help; and that as good or better a help,—for indeed there can hardly, to judge by the present state of things, be a worse,—may be something which is in an ordinary man's power.

For the good of letters is, that they require no extraordinary acuteness such as is required to handle the theory of causation like the Archbishop of York, or the doctrine of the Godhead of the Eternal Son like the Bishops of Winchester and Gloucester. The good of letters may be had without skill in arguing, or that formidable logical apparatus, not unlike a guillotine, which Professor Huxley speaks of somewhere as the young man's best companion;—and so it *would* be, no doubt, if all wisdom were come at by hard reasoning. In that case, all who could not manage this apparatus (and only a few picked craftsmen can manage it) would be in a pitiable condition.

But the valuable thing in letters,—that is, in the acquainting oneself with the best which has been thought and said in the world,—is, as we have often remarked, the judgment which forms itself insensibly in a fair mind along with fresh knowledge ; and this judgment almost any one with a fair mind, who will but trouble himself to try and make acquaintance with the best which has been thought and uttered in the world, may, if he is lucky, hope to attain to. For this judgment comes almost of itself ; and what it displaces it displaces easily and naturally, and without any turmoil of controversial reasonings. The thing comes to look differently to us, as we look at it by the light of fresh knowledge. We are not beaten from our old opinion by logic, we are not driven off our ground ;—our ground itself changes with us.

Far more of our mistakes come from want of fresh knowledge than from want of correct reasoning ; and, therefore, letters meet a greater want in us than does logic. The idea of a triangle is a definite and ascertained thing, and to deduce the properties of a triangle from it is an affair of reasoning. There are heads unapt for this sort of work, and some of the blundering to be found in the world is from this cause. But how far more of the blundering to be found in the world comes from people fancying that

INTRODUCTION

some idea is a definite and ascertained thing, like the idea of a triangle, when it is not; and proceeding to deduce properties from it, and to do battle about them, when their first start was a mistake! And how liable are people with a talent for hard, abstruse reasoning, to be tempted to this mistake! And what can clear up such a mistake except a wide and familiar acquaintance with the human spirit and its productions, showing how ideas and terms arose, and what is their character? and this is letters and history, not logic.

So that minds with small aptitude for abstruse reasoning may yet, through letters, gain some hold on sound judgment and useful knowledge, and may even clear up blunders committed, out of their very excess of talent, by the athletes of logic.

CHAPTER I

RELIGION GIVEN

WE have said elsewhere[1] how much it has contributed to the misunderstanding of St. Paul, that terms like *grace, new birth, justification,*—which he used in a fluid and passing way, as men use terms in common discourse or in eloquence and poetry, to describe approximately, but only approximately, what they have present before their mind, but do not profess that their mind does or can grasp exactly or adequately,—that such terms people have blunderingly taken in a fixed and rigid manner, as if they were symbols with as definite and fully grasped a meaning as the names *line* or *angle*, and proceeded to use them on this supposition. Terms, in short, which with St. Paul are *literary* terms, theologians have employed as if they were *scientific* terms.

But if one desires to deal with this mistake thoroughly, one must observe it in that supreme term with which religion is filled,—the term

[1] *Culture and Anarchy*, p. 151.

God. The seemingly incurable ambiguity in the mode of employing this word is at the root of all our religious differences and difficulties. People use it as if it stood for a perfectly definite and ascertained idea, from which we might, without more ado, extract propositions and draw inferences, just as we should from any other definite and ascertained idea. For instance, I open a book which controverts what its author thinks dangerous views about religion, and I read : 'Our sense of morality tells us so-and-so; our sense of God, on the other hand, tells us so-and-so.' And again, 'the impulse in man to seek God' is distinguished, as if the distinction were self-evident and explained itself, from 'the impulse in man to seek his highest perfection.' Now, *morality* represents for everybody a thoroughly definite and ascertained idea :—the idea of human conduct regulated in a certain manner. Everybody, again, understands distinctly enough what is meant by man's perfection :—his reaching the best which his powers and circumstances allow him to reach. And the word 'God' is used, in connection with both these words, morality and perfection, as if it stood for just as definite and ascertained an idea as they do ; an idea drawn from experience, just as the ideas are which they stand for ; an idea about which every one was agreed, and from which we might proceed to argue and to make inferences, with the certainty that, as in the case of morality and perfection, the basis on which we were going every one knew and granted. But, in truth, the word 'God' is used in most cases as by no means a term of science or exact knowledge, but a term of poetry and eloquence, a term *thrown out*, so to speak, at a not fully grasped object of the speaker's consciousness, a *literary* term, in short; and mankind mean different things by it as their consciousness differs.

The first question, then, is, how people are using the word; whether in this literary way, or in a scientific way. The second question is, what, supposing them to use the term as one of poetry and eloquence, and to import into it, therefore, a great deal of their own individual feelings and character, is yet the common substratum of idea on which, in using it, they all rest. For this will then be, for them, and for us in dealing with them, the real sense of the word; the sense in which we can use it for purposes of argument and inference without ambiguity.

Strictly and formally the word 'God,' we now learn from the philologists, means, like its kindred Aryan words, *Theos*, *Deus*, and *Deva*, simply *shining* or *brilliant*. In a certain narrow way, therefore, this is the one exact and scientific sense of the word. It was long thought, however, to mean *good*, and so Luther took it to mean *the best that man knows or can know;* and in this sense, as a matter of fact and history, mankind constantly use the word. This is the common substratum of idea on which men in general, when they use the word *God*, rest; and we can take this as the word's real sense fairly enough, only it does not give us anything very precise.

But then there is also the scientific sense held by theologians, deduced from the ideas of substance, identity, causation, design, and so on; but taught, they say, or at least implied, in the Bible, and on which all the Bible rests. According to this scientific and theological sense, —which has all the outward appearances, at any rate, of great precision,—God is an infinite and eternal substance, and at the same time a person, the great first cause, the moral and intelligent governor of the universe; Jesus Christ consubstantial with him; and the Holy Ghost a person proceeding from the other two. This is the sense for which, or for portions of which, the Bishops of Winchester and Gloucester are so zealous to do something.

Other people, however, who fail to perceive the force of such a deduction from the abstract ideas above mentioned, who indeed think it quite hollow, but who are told that this sense is in the Bible, and that they must receive it if they receive the Bible, conclude that in that case they had better receive neither the one nor the other. Something of this sort it was, no doubt, which made Professor Huxley tell the London

School Board lately, that 'if these islands had no religion at all, it would not enter into his mind to introduce the religious idea by the agency of the Bible.' Of such people there are now a great many; and indeed there could hardly, for those who value the Bible, be a greater example of the sacrifices one is sometimes called upon to make for the truth, than to find that for the truth as held by the Bishops of Winchester and Gloucester, if it is the truth, one must sacrifice the allegiance of so many people to the Bible.

But surely, if there be anything with which metaphysics have nothing to do, and where a plain man, without skill to walk in the arduous paths of abstruse reasoning, may yet find himself at home, it is religion. For the object of religion is *conduct*; and conduct is really, however men may overlay it with philosophical disquisitions, the simplest thing in the world. That is to say, it is the simplest thing in the world as far as *understanding* is concerned; as regards *doing*, it is the hardest thing in the world. Here is the difficulty,—to *do* what we very well know ought to be done; and instead of facing this, men have searched out another with which they occupy themselves by preference,—the origin of what is called the moral sense, the genesis and physiology of conscience, and so on. No one denies that here, too, is difficulty, or that the difficulty is a proper object for the human faculties to be exercised upon; but the difficulty here is speculative. It is not the difficulty of religion, which is a practical one; and it often tends to divert the attention from this. Yet surely the difficulty of religion is great enough by itself, if men would but consider it, to satisfy the most voracious appetite for difficulties. It extends to rightness in the whole range of what we call *conduct;* in three-fourths, therefore, at the very lowest computation, of human life. The only doubt is whether we ought not to make the range of conduct wider still, and to say it is four-fifths of human life, or five-sixths. But it is better to be under the mark than over it; so let us be content with reckoning conduct as three-fourths of human life.

And to recognise in what way conduct is this, let us eschew all school-terms, like *moral sense,* and *volitional,* and *altruistic,* which philosophers employ, and let us help ourselves by the most palpable and plain examples. When the rich man in the Bible-parable says: 'Soul, thou hast much goods laid up for many years; take thine ease, eat, drink, and be merry!'[1]—those *goods* which he thus assigns as the stuff with which human life is mainly concerned (and so in practice it really is),—those goods and our dealings with them,—our taking our ease, eating, drinking, being merry, are the matter of *conduct,* the range where it is exercised.

[1] Luke xii. 19.

Eating, drinking, ease, pleasure, money, the intercourse of the sexes, the giving free swing to one's temper and instincts,—these are the matters with which conduct is concerned, and with which all mankind know and feel it to be concerned.

Or, when Protagoras points out of what things we are, from childhood till we die, being taught and admonished, and says (but it is lamentable that here we have not at hand Mr. Jowett, who so excellently introduces the enchanter Plato and his personages, but must use our own words): 'From the time he can understand what is said to him, nurse, and mother, and teacher, and father too, are bending their efforts to this end,—to make the child *good*; teaching and showing him, as to everything he has to do or say, how this is right and that not right, and this is honourable and that vile, and this is holy and that unholy, and this do and that do not';—Protagoras, also, when he says this, bears his testimony to the scope and nature of *conduct*, tells us what conduct is. Or, once more, when M. Littré (and we hope to make our peace with the Comtists by quoting an author of theirs in preference to those authors whom all the British public is now reading and quoting),—when M. Littré, in a most ingenious essay on the origin of morals, traces up, better, perhaps, than any one else, all our impulses into two elementary instincts, the instinct of self-preservation and the reproductive instinct,—then we take his theory and we say, that all the impulses which can be conceived as derivable from the instinct of self-preservation in us and the reproductive instinct, these terms being applied in their ordinary sense, are the matter of *conduct*. It is evident this includes, to say no more, every impulse relating to temper, every impulse relating to sensuality; and we all know how much that is.

How we deal with these impulses is the matter of *conduct*,—how we obey, regulate, or restrain them; that, and nothing else. Not whether M. Littré's theory is true or false; for whether it be true or false, there the impulses confessedly now are, and the business of conduct is to deal with them. But it is evident, if conduct deals with these, both how important a thing conduct is, and how simple a thing. Important, because it covers so large a portion of human life, and the portion common to all sorts of people; simple, because, though there needs perpetual admonition to form conduct, the admonition is needed not to determine what we ought to do, but to make us do it.

And as to this simplicity, all moralists are agreed. 'Let any plain honest man,' says Bishop Butler, ' before he engages in any course of action' (he means action of the very kind we call *conduct*), 'ask himself: Is this I am going about right or is it wrong? is it good or is it evil? I do not in the least doubt but that this question would be answered agreeably to truth and virtue by *almost any fair man in almost any circumstance.*' And Bishop Wilson says: 'Look up to God' (by which he means just this: Consult your Conscience) 'at all times, and you will, *as in a glass,* discover what is fit to be done.' And the Preacher's well-known sentence is exactly to the same effect: 'God *made man upright;* but they have sought out many inventions,'[1]—or, as it more correctly is, '*many abstruse reasonings.*' Let us hold fast to this, and we shall find we have a stay by the help of which even poor weak men, with no pretensions to be logical athletes, may stand firmly.

And so, when we are asked, what is the object of religion?—let us reply: *Conduct.* And when we are asked further, what is conduct?— let us answer: *Three-fourths of life.*

II

And certainly we need not go far about to prove that conduct, or 'righteousness,' which is the object of religion, is in a special manner the object of Bible religion. The word 'righteousness' is the master-word of the Old Testament. *Keep judgment and do righteousness! Cease to do*

[1] Ecclesiastes vii. 29.

evil, learn to do well![1] these words being taken in their plainest sense of conduct. *Offer the sacrifice,* not of victims and ceremonies, as the way of the world in religion then was, but: Offer the sacrifice of *righteousness!*[2] The great concern of the New Testament is likewise righteousness, but righteousness reached through particular means, righteousness by the means of Jesus Christ. A sentence which sums up the New Testament and assigns the ground whereon the Christian Church stands, is, as we have elsewhere said,[3] this: *Let every one that nameth the name of Christ depart from iniquity!*[4] If we are to take a sentence which in like manner sums up the Old Testament, such a sentence is this: *O ye that love the Eternal, see that ye hate the thing which is evil! to him that ordereth his conversation right shall be shown the salvation of God.*[5]

But instantly there will be raised the objection that this is morality, not religion; morality, ethics, conduct, being by many people, and above all by theologians, carefully contradistinguished from religion, which is supposed in some special way to be connected with propositions about the Godhead of the Eternal Son, or propositions about the personality of God, or about election or justification. Religion, however, means simply

---

[1] Isaiah lvi. 1; i. 16, 17. [2] Psalm iv. 5.
[3] *St. Paul and Protestantism*, p. 147. [4] 2 Timothy ii. 19.
[5] Psalm xcvii. 10; l. 23.

either a binding to righteousness, or else a serious attending to righteousness and dwelling upon it. Which of these two it most nearly means, depends upon the view we take of the word's derivation; but it means one of them, and they are really much the same. And the antithesis between *ethical* and *religious* is thus quite a false one. Ethical means *practical*, it relates to practice or conduct passing into habit or disposition. Religious also means *practical*, but practical in a still higher degree; and the right antithesis to both ethical and religious, is the same as the right antithesis to practical : namely, *theoretical*.

Now, propositions about the Godhead of the Eternal Son are theoretical, and they therefore are very properly opposed to propositions which are moral or ethical; but they are with equal propriety opposed to propositions which are religious. They differ in kind from what is religious, while what is ethical agrees in kind with it. But is there, therefore, no difference between what is ethical, or morality, and religion? There *is* a difference; a difference of degree. Religion, if we follow the intention of human thought and human language in the use of the word, is ethics heightened, enkindled, lit up by feeling; the passage from morality to religion is made when to morality is applied emotion. And the true meaning of religion is thus, not simply *morality*, but *morality touched by emotion*.

I RELIGION GIVEN

And this new elevation and inspiration of morality is well marked by the word 'righteousness.' Conduct is the word of common life, morality is the word of philosophical disquisition, righteousness is the word of religion. Some people, indeed, are for calling all high thought and feeling by the name of religion; according to that saying of Goethe: 'He who has art and science, has also religion.' But let us use words as mankind generally use them. We may call art and science touched by emotion *religion*, if we will; as we may make the instinct of self-preservation, into which M. Littré traces up all our private affections, include the perfecting ourselves by the study of what is beautiful in art; and the reproductive instinct, into which he traces up all our social affections, include the perfecting mankind by political science. But men have not yet got to that stage, when we think much of either their private or their social affections at all, except as exercising themselves in conduct; neither do we yet think of religion as otherwise exercising itself. When mankind speak of religion, they have before their mind an activity engaged, not with the whole of life, but with that three-fourths of life which is *conduct*. This is wide enough range for one word, surely; but at any rate, let us at present limit ourselves in the use of the word *religion* as mankind do.

And if some one now asks: But what *is* this

application of emotion to morality, and by what marks may we know it?—we can quite easily satisfy him; not, indeed, by any disquisition of our own, but in a much better way, by examples. 'By the dispensation of Providence to mankind,' says Quintilian, 'goodness gives men most satisfaction.'[1] That is morality. 'The path of the just is as the shining light which shineth more and more unto the perfect day.'[2] That is morality touched with emotion, or religion. 'Hold off from sensuality,' says Cicero; 'for, if you have given yourself up to it, you will find yourself unable to think of anything else.'[3] That is morality. 'Blessed are the pure in heart,' says Jesus Christ, 'for they shall see God.'[4] That is religion. 'We all want to live honestly, but cannot,' says the Greek maxim-maker.[5] That is morality. 'O wretched man that I am, who shall deliver me from the body of this death!' says St. Paul.[6] That is religion. 'Would thou wert of as good conversation in deed as in word!'[7] is morality. 'Not every one that saith unto me, Lord, Lord, shall enter into the kingdom of Heaven, but he that doeth

---

[1] 'Dedit hoc Providentia hominibus munus, ut honesta magis juvarent.' [2] Proverbs iv. 18.
[3] 'Sis a venereis amoribus aversus; quibus si te dedideris, non aliud quidquam possis cogitare quam illud quod diligis.'
[4] Matthew v. 8.
[5] θέλομεν καλῶς ζῆν πάντες, ἀλλ' οὐ δυνάμεθα.
[6] Romans vii. 24.
[7] εἴθ' ἦσθα σώφρων ἔργα τοῖς λόγοις ἴσα.

the will of my Father which is in Heaven,'[1] is religion. 'Live as you were meant to live!'[2] is morality. 'Lay hold on eternal life!'[3] is religion.

Or we may take the contrast within the bounds of the Bible itself. 'Love not sleep, lest thou come to poverty,' is morality; but, 'My meat is to do the will of him that sent me, and to finish his work,' is religion.[4] Or we may even observe a third stage between these two stages, which shows to us the transition from one to the other. 'If thou givest thy soul the desires that please her, she will make thee a laughing-stock to thine enemies;'[5]—that is morality. 'He that resisteth pleasure crowneth his life;'[6]—that is morality with the tone heightened, passing, or trying to pass, into religion. 'Flesh and blood cannot inherit the kingdom of God;'[7]—there the passage is made, and we have religion. Our religious examples are here all taken from the Bible, and from the Bible such examples can best be taken; but we might also find them elsewhere. 'Oh that my lot might lead me in the path of holy innocence of thought and deed, the path which august laws ordain, laws which in the highest heaven had their birth, neither did the race of mortal man

---

[1] Matthew vii. 21. [2] ζῆσον κατὰ φύσιν.
[3] 1 Tim. vi. 12. [4] Prov. xx. 13; John iv. 34.
[5] Ecclesiasticus xviii. 31. [6] Ecclesiasticus xix. 5.
[7] 1 Corinthians xv. 50.

beget them, nor shall oblivion ever put them to sleep; the power of God is mighty in them, and groweth not old!' That is from Sophocles, but it is as much religion as any of the things which we have quoted as religious. Like them, it is not the mere enjoining of conduct, but it is this enjoining touched, strengthened, and almost transformed, by the addition of feeling.

So what is meant by the application of emotion to morality has now, it is to be hoped, been made clear. The next question will probably be: But how does one get the application made? Why, how does one get to feel much about any matter whatever? By dwelling upon it, by staying our thoughts upon it, by having it perpetually in our mind. The very words *mind*, *memory*, *remain*, come, probably, all from the same root, from the notion of staying, attending. Possibly even the word *man* comes from the same; so entirely does the idea of humanity, of intelligence, of looking before and after, of raising oneself out of the flux of things, rest upon the idea of steadying oneself, concentrating oneself, making order in the chaos of one's impressions, by attending to one impression rather than the other. The rules of conduct, of morality, were themselves, philosophers suppose, reached in this way;—the notion of a whole self as opposed to a partial self, a best self to an inferior, to a momentary self a permanent self requiring the restraint of impulses a man would naturally have indulged;—because,

RELIGION GIVEN

by *attending* to his life, man found it had a scope beyond the wants of the present moment. Suppose it was so; then the first man who, as 'a being,' comparatively, 'of a large discourse, looking before and after,' controlled the native, instantaneous, mechanical impulses of the instinct of self-preservation, controlled the native, instantaneous, mechanical impulses of the reproductive instinct, had morality revealed to him.

But there is a long way from this to that habitual dwelling on the rules thus reached, that constant turning them over in the mind, that near and lively experimental sense of their beneficence, which communicates emotion to our thought of them, and thus incalculably heightens their powers. And the more mankind attended to the claims of that part of our nature which does *not* belong to conduct, properly so called, or to morality (and we have seen that, after all, about one-fourth of our nature is in this case), the more they would have distractions to take off their thoughts from those moral conclusions which all races of men, one may say, seem to have reached, and to prevent these moral conclusions from being quickened by emotion, and thus becoming religious.

III

Only with one people,—the people from whom we get the Bible,—these distractions did not happen.

The Old Testament, nobody will ever deny, is filled with the word and thought of righteousness. 'In the way of righteousness is life, and in the pathway thereof is no death'; 'Righteousness tendeth to life'; 'He that pursueth evil pursueth it to his own death'; 'The way of transgressors is hard';—nobody will deny that those texts may stand for the fundamental and ever-recurring idea of the Old Testament.[1] No people ever felt so strongly as the people of the Old Testament, the Hebrew people, that conduct is three-fourths of our life and its largest concern. No people ever felt so strongly that succeeding, going right, hitting the mark in this great concern, was *the way of peace*, the highest possible satisfaction. 'He that keepeth the law, happy is he; its ways are ways of pleasantness, and all its paths are peace; if thou hadst walked in its ways, thou shouldst have dwelt in peace for ever!'[2] Jeshurun, one of the ideal names of their race, is the *upright;* Israel, the other and greater, is the *wrestler with God*, he who has known the

---

[1] Prov. xii. 28; xi. 19; xiii. 15.
[2] Prov. xxix. 18; iii. 17. Baruch iii. 13.

contention and strain it costs to stand upright. That mysterious personage by whom their history first touches the hill of Sion, is Melchisedek, the *righteous* king. Their holy city, Jerusalem, is the foundation, or vision, or inheritance, of that which righteousness achieves, —*peace*. The law of righteousness was such an object of attention to them, that its words were to 'be in their heart, and thou shalt teach them diligently unto thy children, and shalt talk of them when thou sittest in thine house, and when thou walkest by the way, and when thou liest down, and when thou risest up.'[1] That they might keep them ever in mind, they wore them, went about with them, made talismans of them. 'Bind them upon thy fingers, bind them about thy neck: write them upon the table of thine heart!'[2] 'Take fast hold of her,' they said of the doctrine of conduct, or righteousness, 'let her not go! keep her, for *she is thy life!*'[3]

People who thus spoke of righteousness could not but have had their minds long and deeply engaged with it; much more than the generality of mankind, who have nevertheless, as we saw, got as far as the notion of morals or conduct. And, if they were so deeply attentive to it, one thing could not fail to strike them. It is this: the very great part in righteousness which

---

[1] Deuteronomy vi. 6, 7. [2] Prov. vii. 3; iii. 3.
[3] Prov. iv. 13.

belongs, we may say, to *not ourselves*. In the first place, we did not make ourselves and our nature, or conduct as the object of three-fourths of that nature; we did not provide that happiness should follow conduct, as it undeniably does; that the sense of succeeding, going right, hitting the mark, in conduct, should give satisfaction, and a very high satisfaction, just as really as the sense of doing well in his work gives pleasure to a poet or painter, or accomplishing what he tries gives pleasure to a man who is learning to ride or to shoot; or as satisfying his hunger, also, gives pleasure to a man who is hungry.

All this we did not make; and, in the next place, our dealing with it at all, when it is made, is not wholly, or even nearly wholly, in our own power. Our conduct is capable, irrespective of what we can ourselves certainly answer for, of almost infinitely different degrees of force and energy in the performance of it, of lucidity and vividness in the perception of it, of fulness in the satisfaction from it; and these degrees may vary from day to day, and quite incalculably. Facilities and felicities,—whence do they come? suggestions and stimulations,— where do they tend? hardly a day passes but we have some experience of them. And so Henry More was led to say, that 'there was something about us that knew better, often, what we would be at than we ourselves.' For instance: every one can understand how health and freedom from pain may give energy for conduct, and how a neuralgia, suppose, may diminish it. It does not depend on ourselves, indeed, whether we have the neuralgia or not, but we can understand its impairing our spirit. But the strange thing is, that with the same neuralgia we may find ourselves one day without spirit and energy for conduct, and another day with them. So that we may most truly say: 'Left to ourselves, we sink and perish; visited, we lift up our heads and live.'[1] And we may well give ourselves, in grateful and devout self-surrender, to that by which we are thus visited. So much is there incalculable, so much that belongs to *not ourselves*, in conduct; and the more we attend to conduct, and the more we value it, the more we shall feel this.

The *not ourselves*, which is in us and in the world around us, has almost everywhere, as far as we can see, struck the minds of men as they awoke to consciousness, and has inspired them with awe. Every one knows how the mighty natural objects which most took their regards became the objects to which this awe addressed itself. Our very word *God* is a reminiscence of these times, when men invoked 'The Brilliant on high,' *sublime hoc candens quod invocent omnes Jovem*, as the power representing to them that which transcended the limits of their narrow

---

[1] 'Relicti mergimur et perimus, visitati vero erigimur et vivimus.'

selves, and that by which they lived and moved and had their being. Every one knows of what differences of operation men's dealing with this power has in different places and times shown itself capable; how here they have been moved by the *not ourselves* to a cruel terror, there to a timid religiosity, there again to a play of imagination; almost always, however, connecting with it, by some string or other, conduct.

But we are not writing a history of religion; we are only tracing its effect on the language of the men from whom we get the Bible. At the time they produced those documents which give to the Old Testament its power and its true character, the *not ourselves* which weighed upon the mind of Israel, and engaged its awe, was the *not ourselves* by which we get the sense for *righteousness,* and whence we find the help to *do right*. This conception was indubitably what lay at the bottom of that remarkable change which under Moses, at a certain stage of their religious history, befell the Hebrew people's mode of naming God.[1] This was what they intended in that name, which we wrongly convey, either without translation, by *Jehovah,* which gives us the notion of a mere mythological deity, or by a wrong translation, *Lord,* which gives us the notion of a magnified and non-natural man. The name they used was: *The Eternal*.

---

[1] See Exodus iii. 14.

RELIGION GIVEN

Philosophers dispute whether moral ideas, as they call them, the simplest ideas of conduct and righteousness which now seem instinctive, did not all grow, were not once inchoate, embryo, dubious, unformed.[1] That may have been so; the question is an interesting one for science. But the interesting question for conduct is whether those ideas are unformed or formed *now*. They are formed now; and they were formed when the Hebrews named the power, out of themselves, which pressed upon their spirit: *The Eternal*. Probably the life of Abraham, *the friend of God*, however imperfectly the Bible traditions by themselves convey it to us, was a decisive step forwards in the development of these ideas of righteousness. Probably this was the moment when such ideas became fixed and ruling for the Hebrew people, and marked it permanently off from all others who had not made the same step. But long before the first beginnings of recorded history, long before the oldest word of Bible literature, these ideas must have been at work. We know it by the result, although they may have for a long while been but rudimentary. In Israel's earliest history and earliest literature, under the name of Eloah, Elohim, *The Mighty*, there may have lain and matured, there did lie and mature, ideas of God more as a moral power, more as

---

[1] 'Qu'est-ce-que la nature?' says Pascal: '*peut-être une première coutume*, comme la coutume est une seconde nature.'

a power connected, above everything, with conduct and righteousness, than were entertained by other races. Not only can we judge by the result that this must have been so, but we can see that it was so. Still their name, *The Mighty*, does not in itself involve any true and deep religious ideas, any more than our name, *The Shining*. With *The Eternal* it is otherwise. For what did they mean by the Eternal; the Eternal *what?* The Eternal *cause?* Alas, these poor people were not Archbishops of York. They meant the Eternal *righteous*, who loveth *righteousness*. They had dwelt upon the thought of conduct and right and wrong, till the *not ourselves* which is in us and all around us, became to them adorable eminently and altogether as *a power which makes for righteousness;* which makes for it unchangeably and eternally, and is therefore called *The Eternal*.

There is not a particle of metaphysics in their use of this name, any more than in their conception of the *not ourselves* to which they attached it. Both came to them not from abstruse reasoning but from experience, and from experience in the plain region of conduct. Theologians with metaphysical heads render Israel's *Eternal* by *the self-existent*, and Israel's *not ourselves* by *the absolute*, and attribute to Israel their own subtleties. According to them, Israel had his head full of the necessity of a first cause, and therefore said, *The Eternal;* as, again, they imagine him looking out into the world, noting everywhere the marks of design and adaptation to his wants, and reasoning out and inferring thence the fatherhood of God. All these fancies come from an excessive turn for reasoning, and a neglect of observing men's actual course of thinking and way of using words. Israel, at this stage when *The Eternal* was revealed to him, inferred nothing, reasoned out nothing; he felt and experienced. When he begins to speculate, in the schools of Rabbinism, he quickly shows how much less native talent than the Bishops of Winchester and Gloucester he has for this perilous business. Happily, when *The Eternal* was revealed to him, he had not yet begun to speculate.

Israel personified, indeed, his Eternal, for he was strongly moved, he was an orator and poet. *Man never knows how anthropomorphic he is,* says Goethe, and so man tends always to represent everything under his own figure. In poetry and eloquence man may and must follow this tendency, but in science it often leads him astray. Israel, however, did not scientifically predicate *personality* of God; he would not even have had a notion what was meant by it. He called him the maker of all things, who gives drink to all out of his pleasures as out of a river; but he was led to this by no theory of a first cause. The grandeur of the spectacle given by the world, the grandeur of the sense of its all being *not ourselves*, being above and beyond ourselves and immeasurably dwarfing us, a man of imagination instinctively personifies as a single, mighty, living and productive power; as Goethe tells us that the words which rose naturally to his lips, when he stood on the top of the Brocken, were: 'Lord, what is man, that thou mindest him, or the son of man, that thou makest account of him?'[1] But Israel's confessing and extolling of this power came not even from his imaginative feeling, but came first from his gratitude for righteousness. To one who knows what conduct is, it is a joy to be alive; and the *not ourselves*, which by bringing forth for us righteousness makes our happiness, working just in the same sense, brings forth this glorious world to be righteous in. That is the notion at the bottom of a Hebrew's praise of a Creator; and if we attend, we can see this quite clearly. Wisdom and understanding mean, for Israel, the love of order, of righteousness. Righteousness, order, conduct, is for Israel at once the source of all man's happiness, and at the same time the very essence of *The Eternal*. The great work of the Eternal is the foundation of this order in man, the implanting in mankind of his own love of righteousness, his own spirit, his own wisdom and understanding; and it is only as a farther and natural working of this energy that Israel conceives the establishment of

[1] Psalm cxliv. 3.

order in the world, or creation. 'To depart from evil, *that* is understanding! Happy is the man that findeth wisdom, and the man that getteth understanding. *The Eternal by wisdom hath founded the earth, by understanding hath he established the heavens*';[1] and so the Bible-writer passes into the account of creation. It all comes to him from the idea of righteousness.

And it is the same with all the language our Hebrew religionist uses. God is a father, because the power in and around us, which makes for righteousness, is indeed best described by the name of this authoritative but yet tender and protecting relation. So, too, with the intense fear and abhorrence of idolatry. Conduct, righteousness, is, above all, a matter of inward motion and rule. No sensible forms can represent it, or help us to it; such attempts at representation can only distract us from it. So, too, with the sense of the oneness of God. 'Hear, O Israel! The Lord our God is one Lord.'[2] People think that in this unity of God,—this monotheistic idea, as they call it,—they have certainly got metaphysics at last. They have got nothing of the kind. The monotheistic idea of Israel is simply *seriousness*. There are, indeed, many aspects of the *not ourselves*; but Israel regarded one aspect of it only, that by which it makes for righteousness. He had the advantage, to be sure, that with this

[1] Prov. iii. 13-20.   [2] Deut. vi. 4.

aspect three-fourths of human life is concerned. But there are other aspects which may be set in view. 'Frail and striving mortality,' says the elder Pliny in a noble passage, 'mindful of its own weakness, has distinguished these aspects severally, so as for each man to be able to attach himself to the divine by this or that part, according as he has most need.'[1] That is an apology for polytheism, as answering to man's many-sidedness. But Israel felt that being thus many-sided degenerated into an imaginative play, and bewildered what Israel recognised as our sole *religious* consciousness,—the consciousness of right. 'Let thine eyelids look right on, and let thine eyelids look straight before thee; turn not to the right hand nor to the left; remove thy foot from evil!'[2]

For does not Ovid say,[3] in excuse for the immorality of his verses, that the sight and mention of the gods themselves,—the rulers of human life,—often raised immoral thoughts? And so the sight and mention of *all* aspects of the *not ourselves* must. Yet how tempting are many of these aspects! Even at this time of day, the grave authorities of the University of Cambridge

---

[1] 'Fragilis et laboriosa mortalitas in partes ista digessit, infirmitatis suae memor, ut portionibus coleret quisque, quo maxime indigeret.'—*Nat. Hist.* ii. 5.   [2] Prov. iv. 25, 27.
[3] Tristia ii. 287 :—
    'Quis locus est templis augustior? haec quoque vitet
        In culpam si qua est ingeniosa suam.'
See the whole passage.

are so struck by one of them, that of pleasure, life and fecundity, — of the *hominum divomque voluptas, alma Venus,*—that they set it publicly up as an object for their scholars to fix their minds upon, and to compose verses in honour of. That is all very well at present; but with this natural bent in the authorities of the University of Cambridge, and in the Indo-European race to which they belong, where would they be now if it had not been for Israel, and for the stern check which Israel put upon the glorification and divinisation of this natural bent of mankind, this attractive aspect of the *not ourselves?* Perhaps going in procession, Vice-Chancellor, bedels, masters, scholars, and all, in spite of their Professor of Moral Philosophy, to the temple of Aphrodite! Nay, and very likely Mr. Birks himself, his brows crowned with myrtle and scarcely a shade of melancholy on his countenance, would have been going along with them! It is Israel and his *seriousness* that have saved the authorities of the University of Cambridge from carrying their divinisation of pleasure to these lengths, or from making more of it, indeed, than a mere passing intellectual play; and even this play Israel would have beheld with displeasure, saying: *O turn away mine eyes lest they behold vanity, but quicken Thou me in thy way!*[1] So earnestly and exclusively were Israel's regards bent on one aspect of the *not*

[1] Psalm cxix. 37.

ourselves: its aspect as a power making for conduct, righteousness. Israel's *Eternal* was the Eternal which says: '*To depart from evil*, that is understanding! Be ye *holy*, for I am *holy!*' Now, as righteousness is but a heightened conduct, so holiness is but a heightened righteousness; a more finished, entire, and awe-filled righteousness. It was such a righteousness which was Israel's ideal; and therefore it was that Israel said, not indeed what our Bibles make him say, but this: 'Hear, O Israel! *The Eternal is our God, The Eternal alone.*'

And in spite of his turn for personification, his want of a clear boundary-line between poetry and science, his inaptitude to express even abstract notions by other than highly concrete terms,—in spite of these scientific disadvantages, or rather, perhaps, because of them, because he had no talent for abstruse reasoning to lead him astray,—the spirit and tongue of Israel kept a propriety, a reserve, a sense of the inadequacy of language in conveying man's ideas of God, which contrast strongly with the licence of affirmation in our Western theology. 'The high and holy One that inhabiteth eternity, whose name is holy,'[1] is far more proper and felicitous language than 'the moral and intelligent Governor of the universe,' just because it far less attempts to be precise, but keeps to the language of poetry and does not essay the

[1] Isaiah lvii. 15.

language of science. As he had developed his idea of God from personal experience, Israel knew what we, who have developed our idea from his words about it, so often are ignorant of: that his words were but *thrown out* at a vast object of consciousness, which he could not fully grasp, and which he apprehended clearly by one point alone,—that it made for the great concern of life, *conduct*. How little we know of it besides, how impenetrable is the course of its ways with us, how we are baffled in our attempts to name and describe it, how, when we personify it and call it 'the moral and intelligent Governor of the universe,' we presently find it not to be a person as man conceives of person, nor moral as man conceives of moral, nor intelligent as man conceives of intelligent, nor a governor as man conceives of governors,—all this, which scientific theology loses sight of, Israel, who had but poetry and eloquence, and no system, and who did not mind contradicting himself, knew. 'Is it any pleasure to the Almighty, that thou art righteous?'[1] What a blow to our ideal of that magnified and non-natural man, 'the moral and intelligent Governor'! Say what we can about God, say our best, we have yet, Israel knew, to add instantly: 'Lo, these are *parts* of his ways; *but how little a portion is heard of him!*'[2] Yes, indeed, Israel remembered that far better than our bishops do. 'Canst thou by searching find

[1] Job xxii. 3.   [2] Job xxvi. 14.

out God; canst thou find out the perfection of the Almighty? It is more high than heaven, what canst thou do? deeper than hell, what canst thou know?'[1]

Will it be said, experience might also have shown to Israel a *not ourselves* which did not make for his happiness, but rather made against it, baffled his claims to it? But no man, as we have elsewhere remarked,[2] who simply follows his own consciousness, is aware of any *claims*, any rights, whatever; what he gets of good makes him thankful, what he gets of ill seems to him natural. His simple spontaneous feeling is well expressed by that saying of Izaak Walton: 'Every misery that I miss is a new mercy, and therefore let us be thankful.' It is true, the *not ourselves* of which we are thankfully conscious we inevitably speak of and speak to as a man; for 'man never knows how anthropomorphic he is.' And as time proceeds, imagination and reasoning keep working upon this substructure, and build from it a magnified and non-natural man. Attention is then drawn, afterwards, to causes outside ourselves which seem to make for sin and suffering; and then either these causes have to be reconciled by some highly ingenious scheme with the magnified and non-natural man's power, or a second magnified and non-natural man has to be supposed, who pulls the contrary way to the first. So arise Satan and

---

[1] Job xi. 7, 8.   [2] *Culture and Anarchy*, p. 181.

his angels. But all this is secondary, and comes much later. Israel, the founder of our religion, did not begin with this. He began with experience. He knew from thankful experience the *not ourselves* which makes for righteousness, and knew how little we know about God besides.

IV

The language of the Bible, then, is literary, not scientific language; language *thrown out* at an object of consciousness not fully grasped, which inspired emotion. Evidently, if the object be one not fully to be grasped, and one to inspire emotion, the language of figure and feeling will satisfy us better about it, will cover more of what we seek to express, than the language of literal fact and science. The language of science about it will be *below* what we feel to be the truth.

The question, however, has arisen and confronts us: what *was* the scientific basis of fact for this consciousness? When we have once satisfied ourselves both as to the tentative, poetic way in which the Bible-authors used language, and also as to their having no pretensions to metaphysics at all, let us, therefore, when there is this question raised as to the scientific account of what they had before their minds, be content with a very unpretending answer. And in this way such a phrase as that which we have formerly used concerning God, and have been much blamed for using,—the phrase, namely, that, 'for science, God is simply *the stream of tendency by which all things fulfil the law of their being,*'—may be allowed, and may even prove useful. Certainly it is inadequate; certainly it is a less proper phrase than, for instance: 'Clouds and darkness are round about him: righteousness and judgment are the habitation of his seat.'[1] But then it is, in however humble a degree and with however narrow a reach, a *scientific* definition, which the other is not. The phrase, 'A Personal First Cause, the moral and intelligent Governor of the universe,' has also, when applied to God, the character, no doubt, of a scientific definition; but then it goes far beyond what is admittedly certain and verifiable, which is what we mean by scientific. It attempts far too much. If we want here, as we do want, to have what is admittedly certain and verifiable, we must content ourselves with very little. No one will say, that it is admittedly certain and verifiable, that there is a personal first cause, the moral and intelligent governor of the universe, whom we may call *God* if we will.

[1] Ps. xcvii. 2. It has been urged that if this personifying mode of expression is more proper, it must also be more scientifically exact. But surely it must on reflection appear that this is by no means so. Wordsworth calls the earth 'the mighty mother of mankind,' and the geographers call her 'an oblate spheroid'; Wordsworth's expression is more proper and adequate to convey what men feel about the earth, but it is not therefore the more scientifically exact.

RELIGION GIVEN

But that all things seem to us to have what we call a law of their being, and to tend to fulfil it, is certain and admitted; though whether we will call this *God* or not, is a matter of choice. Suppose, however, we call it *God*, we then give the name of *God* to a certain and admitted reality; this, at least, is an advantage.

And the notion of our definition does, in fact, enter into the term *God*, in men's common use of it. To please God, to serve God, to obey God's will, means to follow a law of things which is found in conscience, and which is an indication, irrespective of our arbitrary wish and fancy, of what we ought to do. There *is*, then, a real power which makes for righteousness; and it is the greatest of realities for us.[1] When St. Paul says, that our business is 'to serve the spirit of God,' 'to serve the living and true God';[2] and when Epictetus says: 'What do I want?—to acquaint myself with the true order of things, and comply with it,'[3] they both mean, so far, the same, in that they both mean we should obey a tendency, which is *not ourselves*,

---

[1] Prayer, about which so much has often been said unadvisedly and ill, deals with this reality. All good and beneficial prayer is in truth, however men may describe it, at bottom nothing else than an energy of aspiration towards the eternal *not ourselves* that makes for righteousness,—of aspiration towards it, and of co-operation with it. Nothing, therefore, can be more efficacious, more right, and more real.

[2] Philippians iii. 3 (in the reading of the Vatican manuscript); 1 Thessalonians i. 9.

[3] τί βούλομαι; καταμαθεῖν τὴν φύσιν καὶ ταύτῃ ἕπεσθαι.

but which appears in our consciousness, by which things fulfil the real law of their being.

It is true, the *not ourselves*, by which things fulfil the real law of their being, extends a great deal beyond that sphere where alone we usually think of it. That is, a man may disserve God, disobey indications, not of our own making, but which appear, if we attend, in our consciousness, —he may disobey, I say, such indications of the real law of our being, in other spheres besides the sphere of conduct. He does disobey them, when he sings a hymn like : *My Jesus to know, and feel his blood flow*, or, indeed, like nine-tenths of our hymns,—or when he frames and maintains a blundering and miserable constitution of society,—as well as when he commits some plain breach of the moral law. That is, he may disobey them in art and science as well as in conduct. But he attends, and the generality of men attend, only to the indications of a true law of our being as to *conduct;* and hardly at all to indications, though they as really exist, of a true law of our being on its æsthetic and intelligential side. The reason is, that the moral side, though not more real, is so much larger ; taking in, as we have said, at least three-fourths of life. Now, the indications on this *moral* side of that tendency, not of our making, by which things fulfil the law of their being, we do very much mean to denote and to sum up when we speak of *the will of God*, *pleasing God, serving God.* Let us keep firm footing on this basis of plain fact, narrow though it may be.

To feel that one is fulfilling in any way the law of one's being, that one is succeeding and hitting the mark, brings us, we know, happiness; to feel this in regard to so great a thing as conduct, brings, of course, happiness proportionate to the thing's greatness. We have already had Quintilian's witness, how right conduct gives joy. Who could value knowledge more than Goethe? but he marks it as being without question a lesser source of joy than conduct. Conduct he ranks with health as beyond all compare primary. 'Nothing, *after* health and *virtue*,' he says, 'can give so much satisfaction as learning and knowing.' Nay, and Bishop Butler, at the view of the happiness from conduct, breaks free from all that hesitancy and depression which so commonly hangs on his masterly thinking. 'Self-love, methinks, should be alarmed! May she not pass over greater pleasures than those she is so wholly taken up with?' And Bishop Wilson, always hitting the right nail on the head in matters of this sort, remarks that, 'if it were not for the practical difficulties attending it, *virtue would hardly be distinguishable from a kind of sensuality.*' The practical difficulties are indeed exceeding great. Plain as is the course, and high the prize, we all find ourselves daily led to say with the *Imitation:* 'Would that for one single day we had lived in this world as we ought!' Yet the course is so evidently plain, and the prize so high, that the same *Imitation* cries out presently: 'If a man would but take notice, what peace he brings to himself, and what joy to others, merely by managing himself right!' And for such happiness, since certainly we ourselves did not make it, we instinctively feel *grateful;* according to that remark of one of the wholesomest and truest of moralists, Barrow: 'He is not a man, who doth not delight to make some returns thither whence he hath found great kindness.' And this sense of gratitude, again, is itself an addition to our happiness! So strong, altogether, is the witness and sanction *happiness* gives to going right in conduct, to fulfilling, so far as conduct is concerned, the law indicated to us of our being. Now, there can be no sanction to compare, for force, with the strong sanction of happiness, if it be true what Bishop Butler, who is here but the mouthpiece of humanity itself, says so irresistibly: 'It is manifest that nothing can be of consequence to mankind, or any creature, but happiness.' But we English are taunted with our proneness to an unworthy eudæmonism, and an Anglican bishop may perhaps be a suspected witness. Let us call, then, a glorious father of the Catholic Church, the great Augustine himself. Says St. Augustine: 'Act we *must* in pursuance of what gives us most delight; *quod amplius nos delectat, secundum id operemur necesse est.*

And now let us see how exactly Israel's perceptions about God follow and confirm this simple line, which we have here reached quite independently. First: 'It is *joy* to the just to do judgment.'[1] Then: 'It becometh well the just to be *thankful*.'[2] Finally: 'A *pleasant* thing it is to be thankful.'[3] What can be simpler than this, and at the same time more solid? But again: 'The statutes of the *Eternal* rejoice the heart.'[4] And then: 'I will give thanks unto thee, O *Eternal*, with my whole heart; at midnight will I rise to give thanks unto thee because of thy righteous judgments!'[5] And lastly: 'It is a good thing to give thanks unto the *Eternal*; it is a good thing to sing praises unto our *God!*'[6] Why, these are the very same propositions as the preceding, only with a power and depth of emotion added! Emotion has been applied to morality.

God or *Eternal* is here really, at bottom, nothing but a deeply moved way of saying *conduct* or *righteousness*. 'Trust in *God*' is, in a deeply moved way of expression, trust in the law of conduct: 'delight in *the Eternal*' is, in a deeply moved way of expression, the happiness we all feel to spring from conduct. Attending to

---

[1] Prov. xxi. 15.   [2] Ps. xxxiii. 1.
[3] Ps. cxlvii. 1.   [4] Ps. xix. 8.
[5] Ps. cxxxviii. 1; cxix. 62.   [6] Ps. xcii. 1; cxlvii. 1.

conduct, to judgment, makes the attender feel that it is joy to do it. Attending to it more still, makes him feel that it is the commandment of the Eternal, and that the joy got from it is joy from fulfilling the commandment of the Eternal. The thankfulness for this joy is thankfulness to the Eternal; and to the Eternal, again, is due that further joy which comes from this thankfulness. 'The fear of the Eternal, that is wisdom; and to depart from evil, that is understanding.'[1] '*The fear of the Eternal*' and '*To depart from evil*' here mean, and are put to mean, and by the very laws of Hebrew composition which make the second phrase in a parallelism repeat the first in other words, they *must* mean, just the same thing. Yet what man of soul, after he had once risen to feel that to depart from evil was to walk in awful observance of an enduring clue, within us and without us, which leads to happiness, but would prefer to say, instead of ' to depart from evil,' 'the fear of the Eternal'?

Henceforth, then, Israel transferred to this Eternal all his obligations. Instead of saying: 'Whoso keepeth the commandment keepeth his own soul,'[2] he rather said, 'My soul, wait thou only upon *God*, for of him cometh my salvation!'[3] Instead of saying: 'Bind them (the laws of righteousness) continually upon thine

---

[1] Job xxviii. 28. [2] Prov. xix. 16.
[3] Ps. lxii. 5, 1.

heart, and tie them about thy neck!'[1] he rather said, 'Have I not remembered *Thee* on my bed, and thought upon *Thee* when I was waking?'[2] The obligation of a grateful and devout self-surrender to the Eternal replaced all sense of obligation to one's own better self, one's own permanent welfare. The moralist's rule: 'Take thought for your permanent, not your momentary, well-being,' became now: 'Honour the *Eternal*, not doing thine own ways, nor finding thine own pleasure, nor speaking thine own words.'[3] That is, with Israel *religion* replaced *morality*.

It is true, out of the humble yet divine ground of attention to conduct, of care for what in conduct is right and wrong, grew morality and religion both; but, from the time the soul felt the motive of religion, it dropped and could not but drop the other. And the motive of doing right, to a sincere soul, is now really no longer his own welfare, but *to please God*; and it bewilders his consciousness if you tell him that he does right out of *self-love*. So that, as we have said that the first man who, as 'a being of a large discourse, looking before and after,' controlled the blind momentary impulses of the instinct of self-preservation, and controlled the blind momentary impulses of the sexual instinct, had *morality* revealed to him; so in like manner we may say, that the first man who was thrilled

[1] Prov. vi. 21. [2] Ps. lxiii. 7.
[3] Isaiah lviii. 13.

with gratitude, devotion and awe at the sense of joy and peace, not of his own making, which followed the exercise of this self-control, had *religion* revealed to him. And, for us at least, this man was Israel.

Now here, as we have already pointed out the falseness of the common antithesis between *ethical* and *religious*, let us anticipate the objection that the religion here spoken of is but natural religion, by pointing out the falseness of the common antithesis, also, between *natural* and *revealed*. For that in us which is really natural is, in truth, *revealed*. We awake to the consciousness of it, we are aware of it coming forth in our mind; but we feel that we did not make it, that it is discovered to us, that it is what it is whether we will or no. If we are little concerned about it, we say it is *natural;* if much, we say it is *revealed*. But the difference between the two is not one of kind, only of degree. The real antithesis, to natural and revealed alike, is *invented, artificial*. Religion springing out of an experience of the power, the grandeur, the necessity of righteousness, is revealed religion, whether we find it in Sophocles or in Isaiah. 'The will of mortal men did not beget it, neither shall oblivion ever put it to sleep.' A system of theological notions about personality, essence, existence, consubstantiality, is *artificial* religion, and is the proper opposite to *revealed;* since it is a religion which comes forth in no one's consciousness, but is invented by theologians,—able men with uncommon talents for abstruse reasoning. This religion is in no sense revealed, just because it is in no sense natural. And revealed religion is properly so named, just in proportion as it is in a preeminent degree natural.

The religion of the Bible, therefore, is well said to be *revealed*, because the great natural truth, that '*righteousness tendeth to life*,'[1] is seized and exhibited there with such incomparable force and efficacy. All, or very nearly all, the nations of mankind have recognised the importance of conduct, and have attributed to it a natural obligation. They, however, looked at *conduct*, not as something full of happiness and joy, but as something one could not manage to do without. But: 'Sion heard of it and *rejoiced*, and the daughters of Judah were *glad*, because of thy judgments, O Eternal!'[2] Happiness is our being's end and aim, and no one has ever come near Israel in feeling, and in making others feel, that *to righteousness belongs happiness!* The prodigies and the marvellous of Bible-religion are common to it with all religions; the love of righteousness, in this eminency, is its own.

[1] Prov. xi. 19.   [2] Ps. xcvii. 8.

V

The real germ of religious consciousness, therefore, out of which sprang Israel's name for God, to which the records of his history adapted themselves, and which came to be clothed upon, in time, with a mighty growth of poetry and tradition, was a consciousness of *the not ourselves which makes for righteousness*. And the way to convince oneself of this is by studying the Bible with a fair mind, and with the tact which letters, surely, alone can give. For the thing turns upon understanding the manner in which men have thought, their way of using words, and what they mean by them. And by knowing letters, by becoming conversant with the best that has been thought and said in the world, we become acquainted not only with the history, but also with the scope and powers, of the instruments men employ in thinking and speaking. And this is just what is sought for.

And with the sort of experience thus gained of the history of the human spirit, objections, as we have said, will be found not so much to be refuted by reasoning as to fall away of themselves. It is objected: 'Why, if the Hebrews of the Bible had thus eminently the sense for righteousness, does it not equally distinguish the Jews now?' But does not experience show us, how entirely a change of circumstances may change a people's character; and have the modern Jews lost more of what distinguished their ancestors, or even so much, as the modern Greeks of what distinguished theirs? Where is now, among the Greeks, the dignity of life of Pericles, the dignity of thought and of art of Phidias and Plato? It is objected, that the Jews' God was not the enduring power that makes for righteousness, but only their tribal God, who gave them the victory in the battle and plagued them that hated them. But how, then, comes their literature to be full of such things as: 'Shew me thy ways, O Eternal, and teach me thy paths; let *integrity and uprightness* preserve me, for I put my trust in thee! if I incline unto *wickedness* with my heart, the Eternal will not hear me'?[1] From the sense that with men thus guided and going right in goodness it could not but be well, that their leaf could not wither and that whatsoever they did must prosper,[2] would naturally come the sense that in their wars with an enemy the enemy should be put to confusion and *they* should triumph. But how, out of the mere sense that their enemy should be put to confusion and *they* should triumph, could the desire for goodness come?

It is objected, again, that their 'law of the

[1] Ps. xxv. 4, 21; lxvi. 18. [2] Ps. i. 3.

Lord' was a positive traditionary code to the Hebrews, standing as a mechanical rule which held them in awe; that their 'fear of the Lord' was superstitious dread of an assumed magnified and non-natural man. But why, then, are they always saying: '*Teach* me thy statutes, *Teach* me thy way, *Show* thou me the way that I shall walk in, *Open mine eyes, Make me to understand* wisdom *secretly!*'[1] if all the law they were thinking of stood, stark and written, before their eyes already? And what could they mean by: 'I will *love* thee, O Eternal, my strength!'[2] if the fear they meant was not the awe-filled observance from deep attachment, but a servile terror? It is objected, that their conception of righteousness was a narrow and rigid one, centring mainly in what they called *judgment*: 'Hate the evil and love the good, and establish *judgment* in the gate!'[3] so that 'evil,' for them, did not take in all faults whatever of heart and conduct, but meant chiefly oppression, graspingness, a violent mendacious tongue, insolent and riotous excess. True; their conception of righteousness *was* much of this kind, and it was narrow. But whoever sincerely attends to *conduct*, along however limited a line, is on his way to bring under the eye of conscience all conduct whatever; and already, in the Old Testament, the some-

---

[1] Ps. cxix. 12; lxxxvi. 11; cxliii. 8; cxix. 18; li. 6.
[2] Ps. xviii. 1.   [3] Amos v. 15.

what monotonous inculcation of the social virtues of judgment and justice is continually broken through by deeper movements of personal religion. Every time that the words *contrition* or *humility* drop from the lips of prophet or psalmist, Christianity appears.

It is objected, finally, that even their own narrow conception of righteousness this people could not follow, but were perpetually oppressive, grasping, slanderous, sensual. Why, the very interest and importance of their witness to righteousness lies in their having felt so deeply the necessity of what they were so little able to accomplish! They had the strongest impulses in the world to violence and excess, the keenest pleasure in gratifying these impulses. And yet they had such a sense of the natural necessary connection between conduct and happiness, that they kept always saying, in spite of themselves: *To him that ordereth his conversation right shall be shown the salvation of God!*[1]

Now manifestly this sense of theirs has a double force for the rest of mankind,—an evidential force and a practical force. Its evidential force is in keeping before men's view, by the example of the signal apparition, in one branch of our race, of the sense for conduct and righteousness, the reality and naturalness of that sense. Clearly, unless a sense or endowment of human nature, however in itself real and

[1] Psalm l. 23.

beneficent, has some signal representative among mankind, it tends to be pressed upon by other senses and endowments, to suffer from its own want of energy, and to be more and more pushed out of sight. Any one, for instance, who will go to the Potteries, and will look at the tawdry, glaring, ill-proportioned ware which is being made there for certain American and colonial markets, will easily convince himself how, in our people and kindred, the sense for the arts of design, though it is certainly planted in human nature, might dwindle and sink to almost nothing, if it were not for the witness borne to this sense, and the protest offered against its extinction, by the brilliant æsthetic endowment and artistic work of ancient Greece. And one cannot look out over the world without seeing that the same sort of thing might very well befall conduct, too, if it were not for the signal witness borne by Israel.

Then there is the practical force of their example; and this is even more important. Every one is aware how those, who want to cultivate any sense or endowment in themselves, must be habitually conversant with the works of people who have been eminent for that sense, must study them, catch inspiration from them. Only in this way, indeed, can progress be made. And as long as the world lasts, all who want to make progress in righteousness will come to Israel for inspiration, as to the people who have had the sense for righteousness most glowing and strongest; and in hearing and reading the words Israel has uttered for us, carers for conduct will find a glow and a force they could find nowhere else. As well imagine a man with a sense for sculpture not cultivating it by the help of the remains of Greek art, or a man with a sense for poetry not cultivating it by the help of Homer and Shakspeare, as a man with a sense for conduct not cultivating it by the help of the Bible! And this sense, in the satisfying of which we come naturally to the Bible, is a sense which the generality of men have far more decidedly than they have the sense for art or for science. At any rate, whether this or that man has it decidedly or not, it is the sense which has to do with three-fourths of human life.

This does truly constitute for Israel a most extraordinary distinction. In spite of all which in them and in their character is unattractive, nay, repellent,—in spite of their shortcomings even in righteousness itself and their insignificance in everything else,—this petty, unsuccessful, unamiable people, without politics, without science, without art, without charm, deserve their great place in the world's regard, and are likely to have it more, as the world goes on, rather than less. It is secured to them by the facts of human nature, and by the unalterable constitution of things. 'God hath given commandment to bless, and he hath blessed, and we cannot reverse it ; he hath not seen iniquity in Jacob, and he hath not seen perverseness in Israel ; the Eternal, his God, is with him !'[1]

Any one does a good deed who removes the stumbling-blocks out of the way of feeling and profiting by the witness left by this people. And so, instead of making our Hebrew speakers mean, in their use of the word God, a scientific affirmation which never entered into their heads, and about which many will dispute, let us content ourselves with making them mean, as matter of scientific fact and experience, what they really did mean as such, and what is unchallengeable. Let us put into their 'Eternal' and 'God' no more science than they did :— *the enduring power, not ourselves, which makes for righteousness.* They meant more by these names, but they meant this ; and this they grasped fully. And the sense which this will give us for their words is at least solid ; so that we may find it of use as a guide to steady us, and to give us a constant clue in following what they say.

And is it so unworthy ? It is true, unless we can fill it with as much feeling as they did, the mere possessing it will not carry us far. But matters are not at all mended by taking their language of approximate figure and using it for the language of scientific definition ; or by crediting them with our own dubious science, deduced from metaphysical ideas which they

[1] Numbers xxiii. 20, 21.

never had. A better way than this, surely, is to take their fact of experience, to keep it steadily for our basis in using their language, and to see whether from using their language with the ground of this real and firm sense to it, as they themselves did, somewhat of their feeling, too, may not grow upon us. At least we shall know what we are saying; and that what we are saying is true, however inadequate.

But is this confessed inadequateness of our speech, concerning that which we will not call by the negative name of the unknown and unknowable, but rather by the name of the unexplored and the inexpressible, and of which the Hebrews themselves said: *It is more high than heaven, what canst thou do? deeper than hell, what canst thou know?*[1]—is this reservedness of affirmation about God less worthy of him, than the astounding particularity and licence of affirmation of our dogmatists, as if he were a man in the next street! Nay, and nearly all the difficulties which torment theology,— as the reconciling God's justice with his mercy, and so on,—come from this licence and particularity; theologians having precisely, as it would often seem, built up a wall first, in order afterwards to run their own heads against it.

This, we say, is what comes of too much talent for abstract reasoning. One cannot help

[1] Job xi. 7.

seeing the theory of causation and such things, when one should only see a far simpler matter: the power, the grandeur, the necessity of righteousness. To be sure, a perception of these is at the bottom of popular religion, underneath all the extravagances theologians have taught people to utter, and makes the whole value of it. For the sake of this true practical perception one might be quite content to leave at rest a matter where practice, after all, is everything, and theory nothing. Only, when religion is called in question because of the extravagances of theology being passed off as religion, one disengages and helps religion by showing their utter delusiveness. They arose out of the talents of able men for reasoning, and their want (not through lack of talent, for the thing needs none; it needs only time, trouble, good fortune, and a fair mind; but through their being taken up with their reasoning power),—their want of literary experience. By a sad mishap the sphere where they show their talents is one for literary experience rather than for reasoning. This mishap has at the very outset,—in the dealings of theologians with that starting-point in our religion, the experience of Israel as set forth in the Old Testament,—been the cause, we have seen, of great confusion. Naturally, as we shall hereafter see, the confusion becomes worse confounded as they proceed.

CHAPTER II

ABERGLAUBE INVADING

WHEN people ask for our attention because of what has passed, they say, 'in the Council of the Trinity,' and been promulgated, for our direction, by 'a Personal First Cause, the moral and intelligent Governor of the universe,' it is certainly open to any man to refuse to hear them, on the plea that the very thing they start with they have no means of proving. And we see that many do so refuse their attention; and that the breach there is, for instance, between popular religion and what is called *science*, comes from this cause. But it is altogether different when people ask for our attention on the strength of this other first principle: 'To righteousness belongs happiness'; or this: 'There is an enduring power, not ourselves, which makes for righteousness.' The more we meditate on the starting-ground of theirs, the more we shall find that there is solidity in it, and the more we shall be inclined to go along with them and to see what will come of it.

And herein is the advantage of giving this plain, though restricted, sense to the Bible-phrases: 'Blessed is the man that feareth the Eternal!' and: 'Whoso trusteth in the Eternal, happy is he!'[1] By tradition, emotion, imagination, the Hebrews, no doubt, came to attach more than this plain sense to these phrases. But this plain, solid, and experimental sense they attached to them at bottom, they attached originally; and in attaching it they were on sure ground of fact, where we can all go with them. Their words, we shall find, taken in this sense have quite a new force for us, and an indisputable one. It is worth while accustoming ourselves to use them thus, in order to bring out this force and to see how real it is, limited though it be, and insignificant as it may appear. The very substitution of the word *Eternal* for the word *Lord* is something gained in this direction. The word *Eternal* has less of particularity and palpability for the imagination, but what it does affirm is real and verifiable.

Let us fix firmly in our minds, with this limited but real sense to the words we employ, the connection of ideas which was ever present to the spirit of the Hebrew people. *In the way of righteousness is life, and in the pathway thereof is no death; as righteousness tendeth to life, so he that pursueth evil, pursueth it to his own death; as the whirlwind passeth, so is the wicked no more, but the*

---

[1] Ps. cxii. 1; Prov. xvi. 20.

righteous is an everlasting foundation;—here is the ground idea.¹ Yet there are continual momentary suggestions which make for gratifying our apparent self, for unrighteousness; nevertheless, what makes for our real self, for righteousness, is lasting, and holds good in the end. Therefore: *Trust in the Eternal with all thine heart, and lean not unto thine own understanding; there is no wisdom, nor understanding, nor counsel against the Eternal; there is a way that seemeth right unto a man, but the end thereof are the ways of death; there are many devices in a man's heart, nevertheless, the counsel of the Eternal, that shall stand.*² To follow this counsel of the Eternal is the only true wisdom and understanding: *The fear of the Eternal, that is wisdom, and to depart from evil, that is understanding.*³ It is also happiness: *Blessed is every one that feareth the Eternal, that walketh in his ways; happy shall he be, and it shall be well with him!*⁴ *O taste and see how gracious the Eternal is! blessed is the man that trusteth in him.*⁵ *Blessed is the man whose delight is in the law of the Eternal; his leaf shall not wither, and whatsoever he doeth, it shall prosper.*⁶ And the more a man walks in this way of righteousness, the more he feels himself borne by a power not his own: *Not by might and not by power, but by my spirit, saith the Eternal.*⁷ *O Eternal, I know that*

---

[1] Prov. xii. 28; xi. 19; x. 25.
[2] Prov. iii. 5; xxi. 30; xiv. 12; xix. 21.
[3] Job xxviii. 28.   [4] Ps. cxxviii. 1.   [5] Ps. xxxiv. 8.
[6] Ps. i. 1, 2, 3.   [7] Zechariah iv. 6.

the way of man is not in himself! all things come of thee; in thy light do we see light; man's goings are of the Eternal; The Eternal ordereth a good man's going, and maketh his way acceptable to himself.[1] But man feels, too, how far he always is from fulfilling or even from fully perceiving this true law of his being, these indications of the Eternal, the way of righteousness. He says and must say: *I am a stranger upon earth, Oh, hide not thy commandments from me! Enter not into judgment with thy servant, O Eternal, for in thy sight shall no man living be justified!*[2] Nevertheless, as a man holds on to practice as well as he can, and avoids, at any rate, 'presumptuous sins,' courses he can clearly see to be wrong, films fall away from his eyes, the indications of the Eternal come out more and more fully, we are cleansed from faults which were hitherto secret to us: *Examine me, O God, and prove me, try out my reins and my heart; look well if there be any way of wickedness in me, and lead me in the way everlasting!*[3] *O cleanse thou me from my secret faults! thou hast proved my heart, thou hast visited me in the night, thou hast tried me and shalt find nothing.*[4] And the more we thus get to keep innocency, the more we wonderfully find joy and peace: *O how plentiful is thy goodness which thou hast laid up for them that fear thee! thou shalt hide them in*

---

[1] Jeremiah x. 23; 1 Chronicles xxix. 14; Ps. xxxvi. 9; Prov. xx. 24; Ps. xxxvii. 23.   [2] Ps. cxix. 19; cxliii. 2.
[3] Ps. xix. 13; cxxxix. 23, 24.   [4] Ps. xix. 12; xvii. 3.

the secret of thy presence from the provoking of men.¹ *Thou wilt show me the path of life, in thy presence is the fulness of joy, at thy right hand there are pleasures for evermore.*² More and more this dwelling on the joy and peace from righteousness, and on the power which makes for righteousness, becomes a man's consolation and refuge: *Thou art my hiding-place, thou shalt preserve me from trouble; if my delight had not been in thy law, I should have perished in my trouble.*³ *In the day of my trouble I sought the Eternal; a refuge from the storm, a shadow from the heat!*⁴ *O lead me to the rock that is higher than I!*⁵ *The name of the Eternal is as a strong tower, the righteous runneth into it and is safe.*⁶ And the more we experience this shelter, the more we come to feel that it is protecting even to tenderness: *Like as a father pitieth his own children, even so is the Eternal merciful unto them that fear him.*⁷ Nay, every other support, we at last find, every other attachment may fail us, this alone fails not: *Can a woman forget her sucking child, that she should not have compassion on the son of her womb? Yea, they may forget, yet will I not forget thee.*⁸

All this, we say, rests originally upon the simple but solid experience: 'Conduct brings happiness,' or, 'Righteousness tendeth to *life*.'⁹ And, by making it again rest there, we bring

---
[1] Ps. xxxi. 19, 20. [2] Ps. xvi. 11.
[3] Ps. xxxii. 7; cxix. 92. [4] Ps. lxxvii. 2; Isaiah xxv. 4.
[5] Ps. lxi. 2. [6] Prov. xviii. 10.
[7] Ps. ciii. 13. [8] Isaiah xlix. 15. [9] Prov. xi. 19.

out in a new but most real and sure way its truth and its power.

For it has not always continued to rest there, and in popular religion now, as we manifestly see, it rests there no longer. It is important to follow the way in which this change gradually happened, and the thing ceased to rest there. Israel's original perception was true: *Righteousness tendeth to life!*[1] It was true, that the workers of righteousness have *a covenant with the Eternal*, that their work shall be blessed and blessing, and shall endure for ever. But what apparent contradictions was this true original perception destined to meet with! what vast delays, at any rate, were to be interposed before its truth could become manifest! And how instructively the successive documents of the Bible, which popular religion treats as if it were all of one piece, one time, and one mind, bring out the effect on Israel of these delays and contradictions! What a distance between the eighteenth Psalm and the eighty-ninth! between the Book of Proverbs and the Book of Ecclesiastes! A time some thousand years before Christ, the golden age of Israel, is the date to which the eighteenth Psalm and the chief part of the Book of Proverbs belong. This is the time in which the sense of the necessary connection between righteousness and happiness appears with its full simplicity and force. *The*

[1] Prov. xi. 19.

righteous shall be recompensed in the earth, *much more the wicked and the sinner!* is the constant burden of the Book of Proverbs ; *the evil bow before the good, and the wicked at the gates of the righteous!*[1] And David, in the eighteenth Psalm, expresses his conviction of the intimate dependence of happiness upon conduct, in terms which, though they are not without a certain crudity, are yet far more edifying in their truth and naturalness than those morbid sentimentalities of Protestantism about man's natural vileness and Christ's imputed righteousness, to which they are diametrically opposed. 'I have kept the ways of the Eternal,' he says ; 'I was also upright before him, and I kept myself from mine iniquity ; *therefore* hath the Eternal rewarded me according to my righteousness, according to the cleanness of my hands hath he recompensed me ; great prosperity showeth he unto his king, and showeth loving-kindness unto David his anointed, and unto his seed for evermore.' That may be called a classic passage for the *covenant* Israel always thinks and speaks of as made by God with his servant David, Israel's second founder. And this covenant was but a renewal of the covenant made with Israel's first founder, God's servant Abraham, that '*righteousness shall inherit a blessing*,' and that '*in thy seed all nations of the earth shall be blessed.*'[2]

---

[1] Prov. xi. 31 ; xiv. 19.
[2] 1 Peter iii. 9 ; Genesis xxvi. 4.

But what a change in the eighty-ninth Psalm, a few hundred years later! 'Eternal, where are thy former loving-kindnesses which thou swarest unto David? thou hast abhorred and forsaken thine anointed, thou hast made void the covenant; O remember how short my time is!'[1] '*The righteous shall be recompensed in the earth!*' the speaker means; 'my death is near, and death ends all; where, Eternal, is thy promise?'

Most remarkable, indeed, is the inward travail to which, in the six hundred years that followed the age of David and Solomon, the many and rude shocks befalling Israel's fundamental idea, *Righteousness tendeth to life, and he that pursueth evil pursueth it to his own death*, gave occasion. 'Wherefore do the wicked live,' asks Job, 'become old, yea, are mighty in power? their houses are safe from fear, neither is the rod of God upon them?'[2] Job himself is righteous, and yet: 'On mine eyelids is the shadow of death, not for any injustice in mine hands.'[3] All through the Book of Job the question, how this can be, is over and over again asked and never answered; inadequate solutions are offered and repelled, but an adequate solution is never reached. The only solution reached is that of silence before the insoluble: 'I will lay mine hand upon my

---

[1] Psalm lxxxix. 49, 38, 39, 74.
[2] Job xxi. 7, 9. [3] Job xvi. 16, 17.

mouth.'¹ The two perceptions, *Righteousness tendeth to life*, and, *The ungodly prosper in the world*, are left confronting one another like Kantian antinomies.² ' *The earth is given unto the hand of the wicked!*' and yet: ' *The counsel of the wicked is far from me; God rewardeth him, and he shall know it!* '³ And this last, the original perception, remains indestructible. The Book of Ecclesiastes has been called sceptical, epicurean; it is certainly without the glow and hope which animate the Bible in general. It belongs, probably, to the fourth century before Christ, to the latter and worse days of the Persian power; with difficulties pressing the Jewish community on all sides, with a Persian governor lording it in Jerusalem, with resources light and taxes heavy, with the cancer of poverty eating into the mass of the people, with the rich estranged from the poor and from the national traditions, with the priesthood slack, insincere, and worthless. Composed under such circumstances, the book has been said, and with justice, to breathe *resignation at the grave of Israel*. Its author sees ' the tears of the oppressed, and they had no comforter, and on the side of their oppressors there was power; wherefore I praised the dead which are already dead more than the living which are yet alive.'⁴ He sees ' all things come alike to all, there is one event to the righteous

[1] Job xl. 4. [2] Prov. xi. 19; Ps. lxxiii. 12.
[3] Job ix. 24; xxi. 16, 19. [4] Eccles. iv. 1, 2.

and to the wicked.'[1] Attempts at a philosophic indifference appear, at a sceptical suspension of judgment, at an easy *ne quid nimis:* 'Be not righteous overmuch, neither make thyself overwise! why shouldst thou destroy thyself?'[2] Vain attempts, even at a moment which favoured them! shows of scepticism, vanishing as soon as uttered before the intractable conscientiousness of Israel! For the Preacher makes answer against himself: 'Though a sinner do evil a hundred times and his days be prolonged, yet surely I know that it shall be well with them that fear God; but it shall not be well with the wicked, because he feareth not before God.'[3]

Malachi, probably almost contemporary with the Preacher, felt the pressure of the same circumstances, had the same occasions of despondency. All around him people were saying: 'Every one that doeth evil is good in the sight of the Eternal, and he delighteth in them; where is the God of judgment? it is vain to serve God, and what profit is it that we have kept his ordinance?'[4] What a change from the clear certitude of the golden age: 'As the whirlwind passeth, so is the wicked no more; but the righteous is an everlasting foundation!'[5] But yet, with all the certitude of this happier past, Malachi answers on behalf of the Eternal:

[1] Eccles. ix. 2. [2] Eccles. vii. 16.
[3] Eccles. viii. 12, 13. [4] Malachi ii. 17; iii. 14.
[5] Prov. x. 25.

'Unto you that fear my name shall the sun of righteousness arise with healing in his wings!'[1]

Many there were, no doubt, who had lost all living sense that the promises were made to *righteousness;* who took them mechanically, as made to them and assured to them because they were the seed of Abraham, because they were, in St. Paul's words: 'Israelites, to whom pertain the adoption and the glory and the covenants and the giving of the law and the service of God, and whose are the fathers.'[2] These people were perplexed and indignant when the privileged seed became unprosperous; and they looked for some great change to be wrought in the fallen fortunes of Israel, wrought miraculously and materially. And they were, no doubt, the great majority, and of the mass of Jewish expectation concerning the future they stamped the character. With them, however, our interest does not for the present lie; it lies with the prophets and those whom the prophets represent. It lies with the continued depositaries of the original revelation to Israel, *Righteousness tendeth to life;* who saw clearly enough that the promises were to *righteousness,* and that what *tendeth to life* was not the seed of Abraham taken in itself, but *righteousness.* With this minority, and with its noble representatives the prophets, our present interest lies; the further development of their conviction about

---

[1] Malachi iv. 2.   [2] Rom. ix. 4, 5.

righteousness is what it here imports us to trace. An indestructible faith that *the righteous is an everlasting foundation* they had; yet they too, as we have seen, could not but notice, as time went on, many things which seemed apparently to contradict this their belief. In private life, there was the frequent prosperity of the sinner. In the life of nations, there was the rise and power of the great unrighteous kingdoms of the heathen, the unsuccessfulness of Israel: although Israel was undoubtedly, as compared with the heathen, the depositary and upholder of the idea of righteousness. Therefore prophets and righteous men also, like the unspiritual crowd, could not but look ardently and expectantly to the future, to some great change and redress in store.

At the same time, although their experience that the righteous were often afflicted, and the wicked often prosperous, could not but perplex pious Hebrews; although their conscience felt, and could not but feel, that, compared with the other nations with whom they came in contact, they themselves and their fathers had a concern for righteousness, and an unremitting sense of its necessity, which put them in covenant with the Eternal who makes for righteousness, and which rendered the triumph of other nations over them a triumph of people who cared little for righteousness over people who cared for it much, and a cause of perplexity, therefore, to men's trust in the Eternal,—though their conscience told them this, yet of their own shortcomings and perversities it told them louder still, and that their sins had in truth been enough to break their covenant with the Eternal a thousand times over, and to bring justly upon them all the miseries they suffered. To enable them to meet the terrible day, when the Eternal would avenge him of his enemies and make up his jewels, they themselves needed, they knew, the voice of a second Elijah, a change of the inner man, *repentance*.[1]

II

And then, with Malachi's testimony on its lips to the truth of Israel's ruling idea, *Righteousness tendeth to life!* died prophecy. Through some four hundred years the mind of Israel revolved those wonderful utterances, which, even now, on the ear of even those who only half understand them and who do not at all believe them, strike with such strange, incomparable power,—the promises of prophecy. Through four hundred years, amid distress and humiliation, the Hebrew race pondered those magnificent assurances that '*the Eternal's arm is not shortened*,' that '*righteousness shall be for ever*,'[2] and that the future would prove this, even if the present did not. 'The Eternal

---

[1] Malachi iii. 17; iv. 5.   [2] Isaiah lix. 1; li. 8.

fainteth not, neither is weary ; he giveth power to the faint.[1] They that wait on the Eternal shall renew their strength ; the redeemed of the Eternal shall return and come with singing to Zion, and everlasting joy shall be upon their head ; they shall repair the old wastes, the desolations of many generations ; and I, the Eternal, will make an everlasting covenant with them.[2] The Eternal shall be thine everlasting light, and the days of thy mourning shall be ended : the Gentiles shall come to thy light, and kings to the brightness of thy rising, and my salvation shall be for ever, and my righteousness shall not be abolished.'[3]

The prophets themselves, speaking when the ruin of their country was impending, or soon after it had happened, had for the most part had in prospect the actual restoration of Jerusalem, the submission of the nations around, and the empire of David and Solomon renewed. But as time went on, and Israel's return from captivity and resettlement of Jerusalem by no means answered his glowing anticipations from them, these anticipations had more and more a construction put upon them which set at defiance the unworthiness and infelicities of the actual present, which filled up what prophecy left in outline, and which embraced the world. The

---

[1] Isaiah xl. 28, 29.
[2] Isaiah xl. 31 ; xxxv. 10 ; lxi. 4, 8.
[3] Isaiah lx. 20, 3 ; li. 6.

Hebrew Amos, of the eighth century before Christ, promises to his hearers a recovery from their ruin in which they *shall possess the remnant of Edom;* the Greek or Aramaic Amos of the Christian era, whose words St. James produces in the conference at Jerusalem, promises a recovery for Israel in which *the residue of men shall seek the Eternal.*[1] This is but a specimen of what went forward on a large scale. The redeemer, whom the unknown prophet of the captivity foretold to Zion,[2] has, a few hundred years later, for the writer whom we call Daniel and for his contemporaries, become the miraculous agent of Israel's new restoration, the heaven-sent executor of the Eternal's judgment, and the bringer-in of the kingdom of righteousness— the Messiah, in short, of our popular religion. 'One like the Son of Man came with the clouds of heaven, and came to the Ancient of Days, and there was given him dominion and glory, and a kingdom, that all people, nations, and languages should serve him; and the kingdom and dominion shall be given to the people of the saints of the Most High.'[3] An impartial criticism will hardly find in the Old Testament writers before the times of the Maccabees (and certainly not in the passages usually quoted to prove it) the set doctrine of the immortality of the soul or of the resurrection

---

[1] Amos ix. 12; Acts xv. 17.   [2] Isaiah lix. 20.
[3] Daniel vii. 13, 14, 27.

of the dead. But by the time of the Maccabees, when this passage of the Book of Daniel was written, in the second century before Christ, the Jews have undoubtedly become familiar, not indeed with the idea of the immortality of the soul as philosophers like Plato conceived it, but with the notion of a resurrection of the dead to take their trial for acceptance or rejection in the Most High's judgment and kingdom.

To this, then, has swelled Israel's original and fruitful thesis:—*Righteousness tendeth to life! as the whirlwind passeth, so is the wicked no more, but the righteous is an everlasting foundation!*[1] The phantasmagories of more prodigal and wild imaginations have mingled with the product of Israel's own austere spirit; Babylon, Persia, Egypt, even Greece, have left their trace there; but the unchangeable substructure remains, and on that substructure is everything built which comes after.

In one sense, the lofty Messianic ideas of 'the great and notable day of the Eternal,' 'the consolation of Israel,' 'the restitution of all things,'[2] are even more important than the solid but humbler idea, *righteousness tendeth to life*, out of which they arose. In another sense they are much less important. They are more important, because they are the development of this idea and prove its strength. It might have

[1] Prov. xi. 19; x. 25.
[2] Acts ii. 20; Luke ii. 25; Acts iii. 21.

been crushed and baffled by the falsification events seemed to delight in giving it; that, instead of being crushed and baffled, it took this magnificent flight, shows its innate power. And they also in a wonderful manner attract emotion to the ideas of conduct and morality, attract it to them and combine it with them. On the other hand, the idea that *righteousness tendeth to life* has a firm, experimental ground, which the Messianic ideas have not. And the day comes when the possession of such a ground is invaluable.

That the spirit of man should entertain hopes and anticipations, beyond what it actually knows and can verify, is quite natural. Human life could not have the scope, and depth, and progress it has, were this otherwise. It is natural, too, to make these hopes and anticipations give in their turn support to the simple and humble experience which was their original ground. Israel, therefore, who originally followed righteousness because he felt that it tended to life, might and did naturally come at last to follow it because it would enable him to stand before the Son of Man at his coming, and to share in the triumph of the saints of the Most High.

But this latter belief has not the same character as the belief which it is thus set to confirm. It is a kind of fairy-tale, which a man tells himself, which no one, we grant, can prove impossible to turn out true, but which no one, also, can prove certain to turn out true. It is exactly what is expressed by the German word 'Aberglaube,' *extra-belief*, belief beyond what is certain and verifiable. Our word 'superstition' had by its derivation this same meaning, but it has come to be used in a merely bad sense, and to mean a childish and craven religiosity. With the German word it is not so; therefore Goethe can say with propriety and truth: '*Aberglaube* is the poetry of life,—*der Aberglaube ist die Poesie des Lebens.*' It is so. *Extra-belief*, that which we hope, augur, imagine, is the poetry of life, and has the rights of poetry. But it is not science; and yet it tends always to imagine itself science, to substitute itself for science, to make itself the ground of the very science out of which it has grown. The Messianic ideas, which were the poetry of life to Israel in the age when Jesus Christ came, did this; and it is the more important to mark that they did it, because similar ideas have so signally done the same thing with popular Christianity.

CHAPTER III

RELIGION NEW-GIVEN

JESUS CHRIST was undoubtedly the very last sort of Messiah whom the Jews expected. Christian theologians say confidently that the characters of humility, obscureness, and depression, were commonly attributed to the Jewish Messiah; and even Bishop Butler, in general the most severely exact of writers, gives countenance to this error. What is true is, that we find these characters attributed to *some one* by the prophets; that *we* attribute them to Jesus Christ; that Jesus is for us the Messiah, and that Jesus they suit. But for the prophets themselves, and for the Jews who heard and read them, these characters of lowliness and depression belonged to God's chastened servant, the idealised Israel. When Israel had been purged and renewed by these, the Messiah was to appear; but with glory and power for his attributes, not humility and weakness. It is impossible to resist acknowledging this, if we read the Bible to find from it what those who wrote it really intended to think and say, and not to put into it what we wish them to have thought and said. To find in Jesus the genuine Jewish Messiah, or to find in him the Son of Man of Daniel, one coming with the clouds of heaven and having universal dominion given him, must certainly, to a Jew, have been extremely difficult.

Nevertheless, there is undoubtedly in the Old Testament the germ of Christianity. In developing this germ lay the future of righteousness itself, of Israel's primary and immortal concern ; and the incomparable greatness of the religion founded by Jesus Christ comes from his having developed it. Jesus Christ is not the Messiah to whom the hopes of his nation pointed ; and yet Christendom with perfect justice has made him the Messiah, because he alone took, when his nation was on another and a false tack, a way obscurely indicated in the Old Testament, and the one only possible and successful way, for the accomplishment of the Messiah's function : —*to bring in everlasting righteousness.*[1] Let us see how this was so.

Religion in the Old Testament is a matter of national and social conduct mainly. First, it consists in devotion to Israel's God, the Eternal who loveth righteousness, and of separation from other nations whose concern for righteousness was less fervent,—of abhorrence of their idolatries which were sure to bewilder and diminish this

[1] Daniel ix. 24.

fervent concern. Secondly, it consists in doing justice, hating all wrong, robbery, and oppression, abstaining from insolence, lying, and slandering. The Jews' polity, their theocracy, was of such immense importance, because religion, when conceived as having its existence in these national and social duties mainly, requires a polity to put itself forth in; and the Jews' polity was adapted to religion so conceived. But this religion, as it developed itself, was by no means fully worthy of the intuition out of which it had grown. We have seen how, in its intuition of God,—of that 'not ourselves' of which all mankind form some conception or other,—as *the Eternal that makes for righteousness*, the Hebrew race found the revelation needed to breathe emotion into the laws of morality, and to make morality religion. This revelation is the capital fact of the Old Testament, and the source of its grandeur and power. But it is evident that this revelation lost, as time went on, its nearness and clearness; and that for the mass of the Hebrews their God came to be a mere magnified and non-natural man, like the God of our popular religion now, who has commanded certain courses of conduct and attached certain sanctions to them.

And though prophets and righteous men, among the Hebrews, might preserve always the immediate and truer apprehension of their God as *the Eternal who makes for righteousness*, they in vain tried to communicate this apprehension to the mass of their countrymen. They had, indeed, special difficulty to contend with in communicating it; and the difficulty was this. Those courses of conduct, which Israel's intuition of the Eternal had originally touched with emotion and made religion, lay chiefly, we have seen, in the line of national and social duties. By reason of the stage of their own growth and the world's, at which this revelation found the Hebrews, the thing could not well be otherwise. And national and social duties are peculiarly capable of a mechanical, exterior performance, in which the heart has no share. One may observe rites and ceremonies, hate idolatry, abstain from murder and theft and false witness, and yet have one's inward thoughts bad, callous, and disordered. Then even the admitted duties themselves come to be ill-discharged or set at nought, because the emotion which was the only certain security for their good discharge is wanting. The very power of religion, as we have seen, lies in its bringing *emotion* to bear on our rules of conduct, and thus making us care for them so much, consider them so deeply and reverentially, that we surmount the great practical difficulty of acting in obedience to them, and follow them heartily and easily. Therefore the Israelites, when they lost their primary intuition and the deep feeling which went with it, were perpetually idolatrous, perpetually slack or niggardly in the service of Jehovah, perpetually violators of judgment and justice.

The prophets earnestly reminded their nation of the superiority of judgment and justice to any exterior ceremony like sacrifice. But judgment and justice themselves, as Israel in general conceived them, have something exterior in them; now, what was wanted was more *inwardness*, more *feeling*. This was given by adding *mercy* and *humbleness* to judgment and justice. Mercy and humbleness are something inward, they are affections of the heart. And even in the Proverbs these appear: 'The *merciful* man doeth good to his own soul'; 'He that hath *mercy* on the poor, happy is he'; 'Honour shall uphold the *humble* in spirit'; 'When pride cometh, shame cometh, but with the *lowly* is wisdom.'[1] And the prophet Micah asked his nation: 'What doth the Eternal require of thee, but to do justly, and to love *mercy*, and to walk *humbly* with thy God?' adding mercy and humility to the old judgment and justice.[2] But a further development is given to humbleness, when the second Isaiah adds contrition to it: 'I' (the Eternal) 'dwell with him that is of a *contrite* and humble spirit';[3] or when the Psalmist says, 'The sacrifices of God are a *broken spirit*; a *broken* and a *contrite heart*, O God, thou wilt not despise!'[4]

This is *personal religion*; religion consisting

---

[1] Prov. xi. 17; xiv. 21; xxix. 23; xi. 2.   [2] Micah vi. 8.
[3] Isaiah lvii. 15.   [4] Psalm li. 17.

in the inward feeling and disposition of the individual himself, rather than in the performance of outward acts towards religion or society. It is the essence of Christianity, it is what the Jews needed, it is the line in which their religion was ripe for development. And it *appears* in the Old Testament. Still, in the Old Testament it by no means comes out fully. The leaning, there, is to make religion social rather than personal, an affair of outward duties rather than of inward dispositions. Soon after the very words we have just quoted from him, the second Isaiah adds: 'If thou take away from the midst of thee the yoke, the putting forth of the finger and speaking vanity, and if thou draw out thy soul to the hungry, and satisfy the afflicted soul, then shall thy light rise in obscurity and thy darkness be as the noon-day, and the Eternal shall guide thee continually and make fat thy bones.'[1] This stands, or at least appears to stand, as a full description of righteousness; and, as such, it is unsatisfying.

II

What was wanted, then, was a fuller description of righteousness. Now, it is clear that righteousness, the central object of Israel's concern, was the central object of Jesus Christ's concern also. Of the development and of the

[1] Isaiah lviii. 9-11.

cardinal points of his teaching we shall have to speak more at length by and by ; all we have to do here is to pass them in a rapid preliminary review. Israel had said : 'To him that ordereth his conversation right shall be shown the salvation of God.'[1] And Jesus said : 'Except your righteousness exceed the righteousness of the Scribes and Pharisees,'—that is, of the very people who then passed for caring most about righteousness and practising it most rigidly,— 'ye shall in no wise enter into the kingdom of heaven.'[2] But righteousness had by Jesus Christ's time lost, in great measure, the mighty impulse which emotion gives ; and in losing this, had lost also the mighty sanction which happiness gives. 'The whole head was sick and the whole heart faint' ;[3] the glad and immediate sense of being in the right way, in the way of peace, was gone ; the sense of being wrong and astray, of sin, and of helplessness under sin, was oppressive. The thing was, by giving a fuller idea of righteousness, to reapply *emotion* to it, and by thus reapplying emotion, to disperse the feeling of being amiss and helpless, to give the sense of being right and effective ; to restore, in short, to righteousness the sanction of *happiness*.

But this could only be done by attending to that inward world of feelings and dispositions which Judaism had too much neglected. The

[1] Psalm l. 23.   [2] Matthew v. 20.   [3] Isaiah i. 5.

first need, therefore, for Israel at that time, was to make religion cease to be mainly a national and social matter, and become mainly a personal matter. 'Thou blind Pharisee, cleanse first the *inside* of the cup, that the outside may be clean also!'[1] — this was the very ground-principle in Jesus Christ's teaching. Instead of attending so much to your outward acts, attend, he said, first of all to your inward thoughts, to the state of your heart and feelings. This doctrine has perhaps been overstrained and misapplied by certain people since; but it was the lesson which at that time was above all needed. It is a great progress beyond even that advanced maxim of pious Jews: 'To do justice and judgment is more acceptable than sacrifice.'[2] For to do justice and judgment is still, as we have remarked, something external, and may leave the feelings untouched, uncleared, and dead. What was wanted was to plough up, clear, and quicken the feelings themselves. And this is what Jesus Christ did.

'My son, *give me thy heart!*' says the teacher of righteousness in the golden age of Israel.[3] And when Israel had the Eternal revealed to him, and founded our religion, he *gave his heart*. But the time came when this direct vision ceased, and Israel's religion was a mere affair of tradition, and of doctrines and rules received

---

[1] Matthew xxiii. 26.   [2] Prov. xxi. 3.
[3] Prov. xxiii. 26.

from without. Then it might be truly said of this professed servant of the Eternal: 'This people honour me with their lips, but have removed *their heart* far from me, and their fear toward me is taught by the precept of men.'[1] With little or no power of distinguishing between what was rule of ceremonial and what was rule of conduct, they followed the prescriptions of their religion with a servile and sullen mind, 'precept upon precept, line upon line, here a little and there a little,' and no end to it all.[2] What a change since the days when it was *joy to the just to do judgment!*[3] The prophets saw clearly enough the evil, nay, they even could point to the springs which must be touched in order to work a cure. But they could not press these springs steadily enough or skilfully enough to work the cure themselves.

Jesus Christ's new and different way of putting things was the secret of his succeeding where the prophets failed. And this new way he had of putting things is what is indicated by the expression *epieikeia*,—an expression best rendered, as we have elsewhere said,[4] by these two words: 'sweet reasonableness.' For that which is *epieikes* is that which has an air of truth and likelihood; and that which has an air of truth and likelihood is prepossessing. Now, never were there utterances concerning conduct

---

[1] Isaiah xxix. 13.   [2] Isaiah xxviii. 13.   [3] Prov. xxi. 15.
[4] *St. Paul and Protestantism*, Preface, p. xx.

and righteousness,—Israel's master-concern, and the master-topic of the New Testament as well as of the Old, which so carried with them an air of consummate truth and likelihood as Jesus Christ's did; and never, therefore, were any utterances so irresistibly prepossessing. He put things in such a way that his hearer was led to take each rule or fact of conduct by its inward side, its effect on the heart and character; then the reason of the thing, the meaning of what had been mere matter of blind rule, flashed upon him. The hearer could distinguish between what was only ceremony, and what was *conduct;* and the hardest rule of conduct came to appear to him infinitely reasonable and natural, and therefore infinitely prepossessing. A return upon themselves, and a consequent intuition of the truth and reason of the matter of conduct in question, gave men for right action the clearness, spirit, energy, happiness, they had lost.

This power of returning upon themselves, and seeing by a flash the truth and reason of things, his disciples learnt of Jesus. They learnt too, from observing him and his example, much which, without perhaps any conscious process of being apprehended in its reason, was discerned instinctively to be true and life-giving as soon as it was recommended in Christ's words and illustrated by Christ's example. Two lessons in particular they learnt in this way, and added them to the great lesson of self-examination and an appeal to the inner man, with which they started. '*Whoever will come after me, let him renounce himself and take up his cross daily and follow me!*'[1] was one of the two. '*Learn of me that I am mild and lowly in heart, and ye shall find rest unto your souls!*'[2] was the other. Jesus made his followers first look within and examine themselves; he made them feel that they had a best and real self as opposed to their ordinary and apparent one, and that their happiness depended on saving this best self from being overborne. *To find his own soul,*[3] his true and permanent self, became set up in man's view as his chief concern, as the secret of happiness; and so it really is. 'How is a man advantaged if he gain the whole world and suffer the loss of *himself?*'[4] — was the searching question which Jesus made men ask themselves. And then, by recommending, and still more by himself exemplifying in his own practice, by the exhibition in himself with the most prepossessing pureness, clearness, and beauty, of the two qualities by which our ordinary self is indeed most essentially counteracted, *self-renouncement* and *mildness*, he made his followers feel that in these qualities lay the secret of their best self; that to attain them was in the highest degree requisite and natural, and that a man's whole happiness depended upon it.

[1] Luke ix. 23.
[2] Matthew xi. 29.
[3] Matthew xvi. 25.
[4] Luke ix. 25.

Self-examination, self-renouncement, and mildness, were, therefore, the great means by which Jesus Christ renewed righteousness and religion. All these means are indicated in the Old Testament: *God requireth truth in the inward parts! Not doing thine own ways, nor finding thine own pleasure! Seek meekness!*[1] But how far more strongly are they forced upon the attention in the New Testament, and set up clearly as the central mark for our endeavours! *Thou blind Pharisee, cleanse first the inside of the cup that the outside may be clean also!*[2] *Whoever will come after me, let him renounce himself and take up his cross daily and follow me!*[3] *Learn of me that I am mild and lowly in heart, and ye shall find rest unto your souls!*[4] So that, although personal religion is clearly recommended in the Old Testament, nevertheless these injunctions of the New Testament effect so much more for the extrication and establishment of personal religion than the general exhortations in the Old to *offer the sacrifice of righteousness*, to *do judgment*,[5] that, comparatively with the Old, the New Testament may be said to have really founded inward and personal religion. While the Old Testament says: *Attend to conduct!* the New Testament says: *Attend to the feelings and dispositions whence conduct proceeds!* And as attending to conduct

---

[1] Psalm li. 6; Isaiah lviii. 13; Zephaniah ii. 3.
[2] Matthew xxiii. 26.   [3] Luke ix. 23.
[4] Matthew xi. 29.   [5] Ps. iv. 5; Is. lvi. 1.

had very much degenerated into deadness and formality, attending to the *springs* of conduct was a revelation, a revival of intuitive and fresh perceptions, a touching of morals with emotion, a discovering of religion, similar to that which had been effected when Israel, struck with the abiding power not of man's causing which makes for righteousness, and filled with joy and awe by it, had in the old days named God *the Eternal*. Man came under a new dispensation, and made with God a second covenant.

III

To rivet the attention on the indications of personal religion furnished by the Old Testament; to take the humble, inward, and suffering 'servant of God' of the prophets, and to elevate *this* as the Messiah, the seed of Abraham and of David, in whom all nations should be blessed, whose throne should be as the days of heaven, who should redeem his people and restore the kingdom to Israel,—was a work of the highest originality. It cannot, as we have seen, be said, that by the suffering servant of God, and by the triumphant Messiah, the prophets themselves meant one and the same person. But language of hope and aspiration, such as theirs, is in its very nature malleable. Criticism may and must determine what the original speakers seem to have directly meant. But the very nature of their language justifies *any* powerful and fruitful application of it ; and every such application may be said, in the words of popular religion, to have been lodged there from the first by the spirit of God. Certainly it was a somewhat violent exegetical proceeding, to fuse together into one personage Daniel's Son of Man coming with the clouds of heaven, the first Isaiah's 'Branch out of the root of Jesse,' who should smite the earth with the rod of his mouth and reign in glory and peace and righteousness, and the second Isaiah's meek and afflicted Servant of God charged with the precious message of a golden future ; — to fuse together in one these three by no means identical personages ; to add to them the sacrificial lamb of the passover and of the temple-service, which was constantly before a Jew's eyes ; to add, besides, the Prophet like to himself whom Moses promised to the children of Israel ; to add, further, the Holy One of Israel and Redeemer, who for the prophets was the Eternal himself ; and then to say, that the combination thence resulting was the Messiah or Christ whom all the prophets had meant and predicted, and that Jesus was this Messiah. To us, who have been formed and fashioned by a theology whose set purpose is to efface all the difficulties in such a combination, and to make it received easily and unhesitatingly, it may appear natural. In itself and with the elements of which it is composed viewed singly and impartially, it cannot but be pronounced violent.

But the elements in question have their chief use and value, we repeat, not as objects of criticism; they belong of right to whoever can best possess himself of them for practice and edification. Simply of the Son of Man coming in the clouds, of the Branch of Jesse smiting the earth with the rod of his mouth, slaying the wicked with his breath, and re-establishing in unexampled splendour David's kingdom, nothing could be made. With such a Messiah filling men's thoughts and hopes, the real defects of Israel still remained, because these chiefly proceeded from Israel's making his religion too much a national and social affair, too little a personal affair. But a Messiah who did not strive nor cry, who was oppressed and afflicted without opening his mouth, who worked inwardly, obscurely, and patiently, yet failed not nor was discouraged until his doctrine made its way and transformed the world,—*this* was the Messiah whom Israel needed, and in whom the lost greatness of Israel could be restored and culminate. For the true greatness of Israel was *righteousness;* and only by an inward personal religion could the sense revive of what righteousness really was,—revive in Israel and bear fruit for the world.

Instead, then, of 'the Root of Jesse who should set up an ensign for the nations and assemble the outcasts of Israel,'[1] Jesus Christ took from prophecy and made pre-eminent 'the Servant whom man despiseth and the people abhorreth,' but 'who bringeth good tidings, who publisheth peace, publisheth salvation.'[2] And instead of saying like the prophets: 'This *people* must mend, this *nation* must do so and so, *Israel* must follow such and such ways,' Jesus took the individual Israelite by himself apart, made him listen for the voice of his conscience, and said to him in effect: 'If every *one* would mend *one*, we should have a new world.' So vital for the Jews was this change of character in their religion, that the Old Testament abounds, as we have said, in pointings and approximations to it; and most truly might Jesus Christ say to his followers, that many prophets and righteous men had desired, though unavailingly, to see the things which they, the disciples, saw and heard.[3]

The desire felt by pious Israelites for some new aspect of religion such as Jesus Christ presented, is, undoubtedly, the best proof of its timeliness and salutariness. Perhaps New Testament witnesses to the workings of this desire may be received with suspicion, as having arisen after the event and when the new ideal of the Christ had become established. Otherwise, John the Baptist's characterisation of the

[1] Isaiah xi. 10, 12.   [2] Isaiah xlix. 7; lii. 7.
[3] Matthew xiii. 17.

Messiah as 'the lamb of God that taketh away the sins of the world,'[1] and the bold Messianic turn given in the twelfth chapter of St. Matthew to the prophecy there quoted from the forty-second chapter of Isaiah, would be evidence of the highest importance. 'A bruised reed breaketh he not,' says Isaiah of the meek servant and messenger of God, 'and a glimmering wick quencheth he not; he declareth judgment with truth; far lands wait for his doctrine.'[2] 'A bruised reed shall he not break,' runs the passage in St. Matthew, 'and smoking flax shall he not quench, *until he send forth judgment unto victory:* in his name shall the Gentiles trust.'[3] The words, *until he send forth judgment unto victory*, words giving a clear Messianic stamp to the personage described, are neither in the original Hebrew nor in the Greek of the Septuagint. Where did the Gospel-writer find them? If, as is possible, they were in some version then extant, they prove in a striking way the existence and strength of the aspiration which Jesus Christ satisfied by transforming the old popular ideal of the Messiah. But there are in any case signs of the existence of such an aspiration, since a Jewish commentator, contemporary, probably, with the Christian era but not himself a Christian, assigns to this very prophecy a Messianic intention. And, indeed, the rendering

---

[1] John i. 29.   [2] Isaiah xlii. 3, 4.
[3] Matthew xii. 20, 21.

of the final words, *in his name shall the Gentiles trust*,[1] which is in the Greek of the Septuagint as well as in that of St. Matthew, shows a similar leaning in the Jews of Alexandria some two centuries before Christ.

Signs there are then, without doubt, of others trying to identify the Messiah of popular hope, —the triumphant Root of David, the mystic Son of Man,— with an ideal of meekness, inwardness, patience, and self-denial. And well might reformers try to effect this identification, for the true line of Israel's progress lay through it! But not he who tries makes an epoch, but he who effects; and the identification which was needed Jesus Christ *effected*. Henceforth the true Israelite was, undoubtedly, he who allied himself with this identification; who perceived its incomparable fruitfulness, its continuance of the real tradition of Israel, its correspondence with the ruling idea of the Hebrew spirit: *Through righteousness to happiness!* or, in Bible-words: *To him that ordereth his conversation right shall be shown the salvation of God!*[2] That the Jewish nation at large, and its rulers, refused to accept the identification, shows simply that want of power to penetrate through wraps and appearances to the essence of things, which

---

[1] These words are imported from an undoubtedly Messianic passage, the famous prediction of the 'rod out of the stem of Jesse' in the eleventh chapter of Isaiah. Compare, in the Septuagint, Isaiah xi. 10 with Isaiah xlii. 4.

[2] Psalm l. 23.

the majority of mankind always display. The national and social character of their theocracy was everything to the Jews, and they could see no blessings in a revolution which annulled it.

It has often been remarked that the Puritans are like the Jews of the Old Testament; and Mr. Froude thinks he defends the Puritans by saying that they, like the Jews of the Old Testament, had their hearts set on a theocracy, on a fashioning of politics and society to suit the government of God. How strange that he does not perceive that he thus passes, and with justice, the gravest condemnation on the Puritans as followers of *Jesus Christ!* At the Christian era the time had passed, in religion, for outward adaptations of this kind, and for all care about establishing or abolishing them. The time had come for inwardness and self-reconstruction,— a time to last till the self-reconstruction is fully achieved. It was the error of the Jews that they did not perceive this; and the old error of the Jews the Puritans, without the Jews' excuse, faithfully repeated. And the blunder of both had the same cause,—a want of tact to perceive what is really most wanted for the attainment of their own professed ideal, *the reign of righteousness.*

When Jesus appeared, his disciples were those who did not make this blunder. They were, in general, simple souls, without pretensions which Jesus Christ's new religious ideal cut short, or self-consequence which it mortified. And any

Israelite who was, on the one hand, not warped by personal pretensions and self-consequence, and on the other, not dull of feeling and gross of life like the common multitude, might well be open to the spell which, after all, was the great confirmation of Christ's religion, as it was the great confirmation of the original religion of Israel,—the spell of its *happiness*. 'Be *glad*, O ye righteous, and *rejoice* in the Eternal,'—the old and lost prerogative of Israel,—Christianity offered to make again a living and true word to him.[1]

IV

For we have already remarked how it is the great achievement of the Israel of the Old Testament, happiness being mankind's confessed end and aim, to have more than any one else felt, and more than any one else succeeded in making others feel, that *to righteousness belongs happiness*. Now, it will be denied by no one that Jesus, in his turn, was eminently characterised by professing to bring, and by being felt to bring, happiness. All the words that belong to his mission,—*gospel, kingdom of God, saviour, grace, peace, living water, bread of life*,—are brimful of promise and of joy. 'I am come,' he said, 'that ye might *have life*, and that ye might have it *more abundantly*'; 'Come to me, and ye shall find *rest unto your souls*'; 'I speak, that my disciples may

[1] Psalm xxxii. 11; xcvii. 12.

have *my joy fulfilled in themselves.*'[1] That the operation, professed and actual, of this 'son of peace'[2] was to replace his followers in 'the way of peace,'[3] no one can question. The only matter of dispute can be, *how* he replaced them there.

Now, this we have indicated in what has been said already. But that we may show it more clearly, let us return for a moment to what we said of *conduct;*—of conduct, which we found to be three-fourths, at least, of human life, and the object with which religion is concerned. We said of conduct, that it is the simplest thing in the world as far as knowledge is concerned, but the hardest thing in the world as far as doing is concerned. It is an affair, we said, of conscience, which speaks plainly enough if we will only listen to it; but we have to listen to it, and then we have to follow it. If we follow it, we shall have the sense of going right, succeeding, in the management of our conduct. We added, that going right, succeeding, in the management of this vast concern, gave naturally the liveliest possible sense of satisfaction and happiness; that attending to it was naturally the secret of success; that attachment made us attend; and that whatever, therefore, made us love to attend to it must inspire us with gratitude. Let us take, to guide ourselves in the New Testament, the help of the clue furnished by all this.

[1] John x. 10; Matthew xi. 28, 29; John xvii. 13.
[2] Luke x. 6.   [3] Luke i. 79.

First, as to the extreme simplicity of the matter concerned; a matter sophisticated, overlaid, and hidden in a thousand ways. The artless, unschooled perception of a child is, Jesus says, the right organ for apprehending it: 'Whosoever does not receive the kingdom of God as *a little child*, cannot enter therein.'[1] And yet it is so difficult of attainment that it seems we cannot obtain it of ourselves: 'No man can come to me unless it *be given him* of my Father.'[2] The things to be done are so simple and necessary that the doctrine about them proves itself as soon as we do them: 'Whoever will do God's will, *shall know of the doctrine*, whether it be of God.'[3] Only it is indispensable to *do* them. Speculating and professing are absolutely useless here, without *doing*: 'Why call ye me, Lord, Lord, and *do* not the things that I say?'[4] The great and learned people, the masters in Israel, have their authoritative version of what righteousness and the will of God is, of what the ideal for the Jewish nation is, of the correct way to interpret the prophets. But: 'Judge not according to the appearance, but judge *righteous* judgment'; 'beware of *insincerity*'; 'God sees the *heart*'; 'what comes from *within, that* defiles us.'[5] The new covenant, the *New Testament*, consists in the reign of this very inwardness, in a

---

[1] Mark x. 15. [2] John vi. 44, 65.
[3] John vii. 17. [4] Luke vi. 46.
[5] John vii. 24; Luke xii. 1; 1 Samuel xvi. 7, and Luke xvi. 15; Mark vii. 15.

RELIGION NEW-GIVEN

state of things when God 'puts his law in the inward parts and writes it in the heart,'[1] in *conscience* being made the test. You can see, Jesus says, you can see the leading religionists of the Jewish nation, with the current notions about righteousness, God's will, and the meaning of prophecy, you can see them saying and not doing, full of fierce temper, pride, and sensuality; —this shows they can be but blind guides for you. The saviour of Israel is he who makes Israel use his conscience simply and sincerely, who makes him change and sweeten his temper, conquer and annul his sensuality. Such a saviour will make unhappy Israel happy again. The prophets all point to such a saviour, and he is the Messiah, and the promised happiness to Israel is in him and in his reign. He is, in the exalted language of prophecy, the holy one of God, the son of God, the beloved of God, the chosen of God, the anointed of God, the son of man in an eminent and unique sense, the Messiah and Christ. In plainer language, he is 'a man who tells you the truth which he has heard of God'; who came not of himself and speaks not of himself, but who 'came forth from God,'—from the original God of Israel's worship, the God of righteousness and of happiness joined to righteousness,—'and is come to you.'[2] Israel is perpetually talking of God and calling him his

---

[1] Jeremiah xxxi. 33, 34; Hebrews viii. 8-12.
[2] John viii. 40, 42; xvi. 27, 28.

Father; and 'every one,' says Jesus Christ, 'who hears the Father, comes to *me*, for I know Him, and know His will, and utter His word.'[1] God's will and word, in the Old Testament, was *righteousness*. In the New Testament, it is righteousness explained to have its essence in *inwardness, mildness*, and *self-renouncement*. This is, in substance, the word of Jesus which he who hears 'shall never see death'; of which he who follows it 'shall know by experience whether it be of God.'[2]

But as the Israel of the Old Testament did not say or feel that he followed righteousness by his own power, or out of self-interest and self-love, but said and felt that he followed it in thankful self-surrender to '*the Eternal* who loveth righteousness,' and that 'the Eternal *ordereth* a good man's going and *maketh his way acceptable to Himself*,'[3]—so, in the restoration effected by Jesus, the motive which is of force is not the moral motive that inwardness, mildness, and self-renouncement make for man's happiness, but a far stronger motive, full of ardent affection and gratitude, and which, though it really has its ground and confirmation in the fact that inwardness, mildness, and self-renouncement do make for man's happiness, yet keeps no consciousness of this as its ground. For it acquired a far surer ground in personal devotion to Jesus Christ,

---

[1] John vi. 45; viii. 29, 16.   [2] John viii. 51; vii. 17.
[3] Psalm xi. 7; xxxvii. 23.

who brought the doctrine to his disciples and made a passage for it into their hearts; in believing that he was indeed the Christ come from God; in following him, loving him. And in the happiness which thus believing in Jesus Christ, following him, and loving him, gives, it found the mightiest of sanctions.

V

And thus was the great doctrine of the Old Testament: *To righteousness belongs happiness!* made a true and potent word again. Jesus Christ was the Messiah to restore the *all things* of Israel,[1]—righteousness, and happiness with righteousness; to bring light and recovery after long days of darkness and ruin, and to make good the belief written on Israel's heart: *The righteous is an everlasting foundation!*[2] But we have seen how in the hopes of the nation and in the promises of prophecy this true and vital belief of Israel was mixed with a quantity of what we have called *Aberglaube* or extra-belief, adding all manner of shade and circumstance to the original thought. The kingdom of David and Solomon was to be restored on a grander scale, the enemies of Israel were to lick the dust, kings were to bring gifts; there was to be the Son of Man coming in the clouds, judgment

---

[1] Matthew xvii. 11; Acts iii. 21.   [2] Prov. x. 25.

given to the saints of the Most High, and an eternal reign of the saints afterwards.

Now, most of this has a poetical value, some of it has a moral value. All of it is, in truth, a testimony to the strength of Israel's idea of righteousness. For the order of its growth is, as we have seen, this: '*To righteousness belongs happiness;* but this sure rule is often broken in the state of things which now is; there must, therefore, be in store for us, in the future, a state of things where it will hold good.' But none of it has a scientific value, a certitude arising from proof and experience. And indeed it cannot have this, for it professes to be an anticipation of a state of things not yet actually experienced.

But human nature is such, that the mind easily dwells on an anticipation of this kind until we come to forget the order in which it arose, place it first when it is by rights second, and make it support that by which it is in truth supported. And so there had come to be many Israelites,—most likely they were the great majority of their nation,—who supposed that righteousness was to be followed, not out of thankful self-surrender to 'the Eternal who loveth righteousness,'[1] but because the Ancient of Days was to sit before long, and judgment was to be given to the saints, and they were to possess the kingdom, and from the kingdom those who did not follow righteousness were to

[1] Psalm xi. 7.

be excluded. From this way of conceiving religion came naturally the religious condition of the Jews as Jesus at his coming found it; and from which, by his new and living way of presenting the Messiah, he sought to extricate the whole nation, and *did* extricate his disciples. He did extricate these, in that he fixed their thoughts upon himself and upon an ideal of inwardness, mildness, and self-renouncement, instead of a phantasmagory of outward grandeur and self-assertion. But at the same time the whole train of an extra-belief, or *Aberglaube*, which had attached itself to Israel's old creed: *The righteous is an everlasting foundation!* transferred itself to the new creed brought by Jesus: *I am the door; by me, if any man enter in, he shall be saved!*[1] And there arose, accordingly, a new *Aberglaube* like the old. The mild, inward, self-renouncing and sacrificed Servant of the Eternal, the new and better Messiah, was yet, before the present generation passed, to come on the clouds of heaven in power and glory like the Messiah of Daniel, to gather by trumpet-call his elect from the four winds, and to set his apostles on twelve thrones judging the twelve tribes of Israel. The motive of Christianity,—which was, in truth, that pure souls 'knew the voice'[2] of Jesus as sheep know the voice of their shepherd, and felt, after seeing and hearing him, that his doctrine and ideal was what they

---

[1] Prov. x. 25; John x. 9.   [2] John x. 4.

wanted, that he was 'indeed the saviour of the world,'[1]—this simple motive became a mixed motive, adding to its first contents a vast *extra-belief* of a phantasmagorical advent of Jesus Christ, a resurrection and judgment, Christ's adherents glorified, his rejectors punished everlastingly.

And when the generation, for which this advent was first fixed, had passed away without it, Christians discovered by a process of criticism common enough in popular theology, but by which, as Bishop Butler says of a like kind of process, 'anything may be made out of anything,'—they discovered that the advent had never really been fixed for that first generation by the writers of the New Testament, but that it was foretold, and certainly in store, for a later time. So the *Aberglaube* was perpetuated, placed out of reach of all practical test, and made stronger than ever. With the multitude, this *Aberglaube*, or extra-belief, inevitably came soon to surpass the original conviction in attractiveness and seeming certitude. The future and the miraculous engaged the chief attention of Christians; and, in accordance with this strain of thought, they more and more rested the proof of Christianity, not on its internal evidence, but on prophecy and miracle.

[1] John iv. 42.

CHAPTER IV

THE PROOF FROM PROPHECY

'*ABERGLAUBE* is the poetry of life.' That men should, by help of their imagination, take short cuts to what they ardently desire, whether the triumph of Israel or the triumph of Christianity, should tell themselves fairy-tales about it, should make these fairy-tales the basis for what is far more sure and solid than the fairy-tales, the desire itself,—all this has in it, we repeat, nothing which is not natural, nothing blameable. Nay, the region of our hopes and presentiments extends, as we have also said, far beyond the region of what we can know with certainty. What we reach but by hope and presentiment may yet be true; and he would be a narrow reasoner who denied, for instance, all validity to the idea of immortality, because this idea rests on presentiment mainly, and does not admit of certain demonstration. In religion, above all, *extra-belief* is in itself no matter, assuredly, for blame. The object of religion is conduct; and if a man helps himself in his conduct by taking an object of hope and presentiment as if it were an object of certainty, he may even be said to gain thereby an advantage.

And yet there is always a drawback to a man's advantage in thus treating, when he deals with religion and conduct, what is extra-belief and not certain as if it were matter of certainty, and in making it his ground of action. *He pays for it.* The time comes when he dicovers that it is *not* certain; and then the whole certainty of religion seems discredited, and the basis of conduct gone. This danger attends the reliance on prediction and miracle as evidences of Christianity. They have been attacked as a part of the 'cheat' or 'imposture' of religion and of Christianity. For us, religion is the solidest of realities, and Christianity the greatest and happiest stroke ever yet made for human perfection. Prediction and miracle were attributed to it as its supports because of its grandeur, and because of the awe and admiration which it inspired. Generations of men have helped themselves to hold firmer to it, helped themselves in conduct, by the aid of these supports. 'Miracles *prove*,' men have said and thought, 'that the order of physical nature is not fate, nor a mere material constitution of things, but the subject of a free, omnipotent Master. Prophecy fulfilled *proves* that neither fate nor man are masters of the world.'[1]

[1] Davison's *Discourses on Prophecy;* Discourse ii. Part 2.

IV THE PROOF FROM PROPHECY

And to take prophecy first. 'The conditions,' it is said, 'which form the true conclusive standard of a prophetic inspiration are these: That the prediction be known to have been promulgated before the event; that the event be such as could not have been foreseen, when it was predicted, by an effort of human reason; and that the event and the prediction correspond together in a clear accomplishment. There are prophecies in Scripture answering to the standard of an absolute proof. Their publication, their fulfilment, their supernatural prescience, are all fully ascertained.'[1] On this sort of ground men came to rest the proof of Christianity.

II

Now, it may be said, indeed, that a prediction fulfilled, an exhibition of supernatural prescience, proves nothing for or against the truth and necessity of conduct and righteousness. But it must be allowed, notwithstanding, that while human nature is what it is, the mass of men are likely to listen more to a teacher of righteousness, if he accompanies his teaching by an exhibition of supernatural prescience. And what were called the 'signal predictions' concerning the Christ of popular theology, as they stand in our Bibles, had and have undoubtedly a look of

[1] Discourses ix. and xii.

supernatural prescience. The employment of capital letters, and other aids, such as the constant use of the future tense, naturally and innocently adopted by interpreters who were profoundly convinced that Christianity needed these express predictions and that they *must* be in the Bible, enhanced, certainly, this look; but the look, even without these aids, was sufficiently striking.

Yes, that Jacob on his death-bed should two thousand years before Christ have 'been enabled,' as the phrase is, to foretell to his son Judah that 'the sceptre shall not depart from Judah until *Shiloh* (or the Messiah) come, and unto him shall the gathering of the people be,'[1] *does* seem, when the explanation is put with it that the Jewish kingdom lasted till the Christian era and then perished, a miracle of prediction in favour of our current Christian theology. That Jeremiah should during the captivity have 'been enabled' to foretell, in Jehovah's name: 'The days come that I will raise unto David a righteous Branch; in his days Judah shall be saved, and Israel shall dwell safely; and this is his name whereby he shall be called, THE LORD OUR RIGHTEOUSNESS!'[2]—*does* seems a prodigy of prediction in favour of that tenet of the Godhead of the Eternal Son, for which the Bishops of Winchester and Gloucester are so anxious to do something. For unquestionably, in the prophecy

---

[1] Genesis xlix. 10. [2] Jeremiah xxiii. 5, 6.

IV THE PROOF FROM PROPHECY

here given, the Branch of David, the future Saviour of Israel, who was Jesus Christ, appears to be expressly identified with the Lord God, with Jehovah. Again, that David should say: 'The Lord said unto my Lord, Sit thou on my right hand until I make thy foes thy footstool,' —*does* seem a prodigy of prediction to the same effect. And so long as these prophecies stand as they are here given, they no doubt bring to Christianity all the support (and with the mass of mankind this is by no means inconsiderable) which it can derive from the display of supernatural prescience.

But who will dispute that it more and more becomes known that these prophecies[1] cannot stand as we have here given them? Manifestly, it more and more becomes known, that the passage from Genesis, with its mysterious *Shiloh* and the gathering of the people to him, is rightly to be rendered as follows: 'The pre-eminence shall not depart from Judah *so long as the people resort to Shiloh* (the national sanctuary before Jerusalem was won); *and the nations* (the heathen Canaanites) *shall obey him.*' We here purposely leave out of sight any such

[1] A real *prediction* of Jesus Christ's Godhead, of the kind that popular religion desires, is to be found in Benjamin's prophecy of the coming, in the last days, of the King of Heaven to judge Israel, 'because when God came to them in the flesh they did not believe in him as their deliverer.' But this *prediction* occurs in an apocryphal Christian writing of the end of the first century, the *Testaments of the Twelve Patriarchs.* See Fabricius, *Codex Pseudepigraphus Veteris Testamenti,* vol. ii. p. 745.

consideration as that our actual books of the Old Testament came first together through the piety of the house of Judah, and when the destiny of Judah was already traced; and that to say roundly and confidently: '*Jacob was enabled to foretell*, The sceptre shall not depart from Judah,' is wholly inadmissible. For this consideration is of force, indeed, but it is a consideration drawn from the rules of literary history and criticism, and not likely to have weight with the mass of mankind. Palpable error and mistranslation are what will have weight with *them*.

And what, then, will they say as they come to know (and do not and must not more and more of them come to know it every day?) that Jeremiah's supposed signal identification of Jesus Christ with the Lord God of Israel: 'I will raise to David a righteous Branch, and this is the name whereby he shall be called, THE LORD OUR RIGHTEOUSNESS,' runs really: 'I will raise to David a righteous branch; in his days Judah shall be saved and Israel shall dwell safely; and this is the name whereby they shall call themselves: *The Eternal is our righteousness!*' The prophecy thus becomes simply one of the many promises of a successor to David under whom the Hebrew people should trust in the Eternal and follow righteousness; just as the prophecy from Genesis is one of the many prophecies of the enduring continuance of the greatness of Judah. 'The Lord said unto my

IV THE PROOF FROM PROPHECY

Lord,' in like manner;—will not people be startled when they find that it ought instead to run as follows: 'The Eternal said unto my lord the king,'—a simple promise of victory to a royal leader of God's chosen people?

III

Leslie, in his once famous *Short and Easy Method with the Deists*, speaks of the impugners of the current evidences of Christianity as men who consider the Scripture histories and the Christian religion 'cheats and impositions of cunning and designing men upon the credulity of simple people.' Collins, and the whole array of writers at whom Leslie aims this, greatly need to be re-surveyed from the point of view of our own age. Nevertheless, we may grant that some of them, at any rate, conduct their attacks on the current evidences for Christianity in such a manner as to give the notion that in their opinion Christianity itself, and religion, is a cheat and an imposture. But how far more prone will the mass of mankind be to hearken to this opinion, if they have been kept intent on predictions such as those of which we have just given specimens; if they have been kept full of the great importance of this line of mechanical evidence, and then suddenly find that this line of evidence gives way at all points? It can hardly be gainsaid, that, to a delicate and penetrating criticism, it has long been manifest that the chief *literal* fulfilment by Jesus Christ of things said by the prophets was the fulfilment such as would naturally be given by one who nourished his spirit on the prophets, and on living and acting their words. The great prophecies of Isaiah and Jeremiah are, critics can easily see, not strictly *predictions* at all; and predictions which are strictly meant as such, like those in the Book of Daniel, are an embarrassment to the Bible rather than a main element of it. The 'Zeit-Geist,' and the mere spread of what is called *enlightenment*, superficial and barren as this often is, will inevitably, before long, make this conviction of criticism a popular opinion held far and wide. And then, what will be *their* case, who have been so long and sedulously taught to rely on supernatural predictions as a mainstay?

The same must be said of miracles. The substitution of some other proof of Christianity for this accustomed proof is now to be desired most by those who most think Christianity of importance. That old friend of ours on whom we have elsewhere commented,[1] who insists upon it that Christianity is and shall be nothing else but this, 'that Christ promised Paradise to the saint and threatened the worldly man with hell-fire, and proved his power to promise and to threaten by rising from the dead and ascending into heaven,' is certainly not the guide whom

---

[1] *St. Paul and Protestantism*, p. 145.

IV THE PROOF FROM PROPHECY

lovers of Christianity, if they could discern what it is that he really expects and aims at, and what it is which they themselves really desire, would think it wise to follow.

But the subject of miracles is a very great one; it includes within itself, indeed, the whole question about 'supernatural prescience,' which meets us when we deal with prophecy. And this great subject requires, in order that we may deal with it properly, some little recapitulation of our original design in this essay, and of the circumstances in which the cause of religion and of the Bible seems to be at this moment placed.

CHAPTER V

THE PROOF FROM MIRACLES

We have seen that some new treatment or other the religion of the Bible certainly seems to require, for it is attacked on all sides, and the theologians are not so successful as one might wish in defending it. One critic says, that if these islands had no religion at all, it would not enter into his mind to introduce the religious and ethical idea by the agency of the Bible. Another, that though certain commonplaces are common to all systems of morality, yet the Bible-way of enunciating these commonplaces no longer suits us. And we may rest assured, he adds, that by saying what we think in some other, more congenial, language, we shall really be taking the shortest road to discovering the new doctrines which will satisfy at once our reason and our imagination. Another critic goes farther still, and calls Bible-religion not only destitute of a modern and congenial way of stating its commonplaces of morality, but a defacer and disfigurer of moral treasures which

CH. V THE PROOF FROM MIRACLES

were once in better keeping. The more one studies, the more, says he, one is convinced that the religion which calls itself revealed contains, in the way of what is good, nothing which is not the incoherent and ill-digested residue of the wisdom of the ancients. To the same effect the Duke of Somerset,—who has been affording proof to the world that our aristocratic class are not, as has been said, inaccessible to ideas and merely polite, but that they are familiar, on the contrary, with modern criticism of the most advanced kind,—the Duke of Somerset finds very much to condemn in the Bible and its teaching; although the soul, he says, has (outside the Bible, apparently) one unassailable fortress to which she may retire,—faith in God.

All this seems to threaten to push Bible-religion from the place it has long held in our affections. And even what the most modern criticism of all sometimes does to save it and to set it up again, can hardly be called very flattering to it. For whereas the Hebrew race imagined that to them were committed the oracles of God, and that their God, 'the Eternal who loveth righteousness,'[1] was the God to whom 'every knee shall bow and every tongue shall swear,'[2] there now comes M. Emile Burnouf, the accomplished kinsman of the gifted orientalist Eugène Burnouf, and will prove to us in a thick

[1] Psalm xi. 7. [2] Isaiah xlv. 23.

volume[1] that the oracles of God were not committed to a Semitic race at all, but to the Aryan; that the true God is not Israel's God at all, but is 'the idea of the absolute' which Israel could never properly master. This 'sacred theory of the Aryas,' it seems, passed into Palestine from Persia and India, and got possession of the founder of Christianity and of his greatest apostles St. Paul and St. John ; becoming more perfect, and returning more and more to its true character of a 'transcendent metaphysic,' as the doctors of the Christian Church developed it. So that we Christians, who are Aryas, may have the satisfaction of thinking that 'the religion of Christ has not come to us from the Semites,' and that 'it is in the hymns of the Veda, and not in the Bible, that we are to look for the primordial source of our religion.' The theory of Christ is accordingly the theory of the Vedic Agni, or *fire*. The Incarnation represents the Vedic solemnity of the production of *fire*, symbol of force of every kind, of all movement, life, and thought. The Trinity of Father, Son, and Spirit is the Vedic Trinity of Sun, Fire, and Wind ; and God, finally, is 'a cosmic unity.'

Such speculations almost take away the breath of a mere man of letters. What one is inclined to say of them is this. Undoubtedly these exploits of the Aryan genius are gratifying to us members of the Aryan race. The original God

[1] *La Science des Religions:* Paris, 1872.

V THE PROOF FROM MIRACLES

of the Hebrews, M. Burnouf says expressly, 'was *not* a cosmic unity'; the religion of the Hebrews 'had *not* that transcendent metaphysic which the genius of the Aryas requires'; and, 'in passing from the Aryan race to the inferior races, religion underwent a deterioration due to the physical and moral constitution of these races.' For religion, it must be remembered, is, in M. Burnouf's view, fundamentally a *science*; 'a metaphysical conception, a theory, a synthetic explanation of the universe.' Now 'the perfect Arya is capable of a great deal of science; the Semite is inferior to him.' As Aryas or Aryans, then, we ought to be pleased at having vindicated the greatness of our race, and having not borrowed a Semitic religion as it stood, but transformed it by importing our own metaphysics into it.

And this seems to harmonise very well with what the Bishops of Winchester and Gloucester say about 'doing something for the honour of Our Lord's Godhead,' and about 'the infinite separation for time and for eternity which is involved in rejecting the Godhead of the Eternal Son, Very God of Very God, Light of Light'; and also with the Athanasian Creed generally, and with what the clergy write to the *Guardian* about 'eternal life being unquestionably annexed to a right knowledge of the Godhead.' For all these have in view high science and metaphysics, worthy of the Aryas. But to Bible-religion, in the plain sense of the word, it is not flattering;

for it throws overboard almost entirely the Old Testament, and makes the essence of the New to consist in an esoteric doctrine not very visible there, but more fully developed outside of it. The metaphysical element is made the fundamental element in religion. But, 'the Bible-books, especially the more ancient of them, are destitute of metaphysics, and consequently of method and classification in their ideas.' Israel, therefore, instead of being a light of the Gentiles and a salvation to the ends of the earth, falls to a place in the world's religious history behind the Arya. He is dismissed as ranking anthropologically between the Aryas and the yellow men; as having frizzled hair, thick lips, small calves, flat feet, and belonging, above all, to those 'occipital races' whose brain cannot grow after the age of sixteen; whereas the brain of a theological Arya, such as one of our bishops, may go on growing all his life.

But we, who think that the Old Testament leads surely up to the New, who believe that, indeed, 'salvation is of the Jews,'[1] and that, for what concerns conduct or righteousness (that is, for what concerns three-fourths of human life), they and their documents can no more be neglected by whoever would make proficiency in it, than Greece can be neglected by any one who would make proficiency in art, or Newton's discoveries by whoever would comprehend the

[1] John iv. 22.

V THE PROOF FROM MIRACLES

world's physical laws,—*we* are naturally not satisfied with this treatment of Israel and the Bible. And admitting that Israel shows no talent for metaphysics, we say that his religious greatness is just this, that he does *not* found religion on metaphysics, but on moral experience, which is a much simpler matter; and that, ever since the apparition of Israel and the Bible, religion is no longer what, according to M. Burnouf, to our Aryan forefathers in the valley of the Oxus it was,—and what perhaps it really was to *them*,—a metaphysical theory, but is what Israel has made it.

And what Israel made, and how he made it, we seek to show from the Bible itself. Thus we hope to win for the Bible and its religion, which seem to us so indispensable to the world, an access to many of those who now neglect them. For there is this to be said against M. Burnouf's metaphysics: no one can allege that the Bible has failed to win access for want of metaphysics being applied to it. Metaphysics are just what all our theology runs up into, and our bishops, as we know, are here particularly strong. But we see every day that the making religion into metaphysics is the weakening of religion; now, M. Burnouf makes religion into metaphysics more than ever. Yet evidently the metaphysical method lacks power for laying hold on people, and compelling them to receive the Bible from it; it is felt to be inconclusive as thus employed, and its inconclusiveness tells against the Bible. This is the case with the old metaphysics of our bishops, and it will be the case with M. Burnouf's new metaphysics also. They will be found, we fear, to have an inconclusiveness in their recommendation of Christianity. To very many persons, indeed to the great majority, such a method, in such a matter, *must* be inconclusive.

II

Therefore we would not allow ourselves to start with any metaphysical conception at all, not with the monotheistic idea, as it is styled, any more than with the pantheistic idea; and, indeed, we are quite sure that Israel himself began with nothing of the kind. The idea of *God*, as it is given us in the Bible, rests, we say, not on a metaphysical conception of the necessity of certain deductions from our ideas of cause, existence, identity, and the like; but on a moral perception of a rule of conduct not of our own making, into which we are born, and which exists whether we will or no; of awe at its grandeur and necessity, and of gratitude at its beneficence. This is the great original revelation made to Israel, this is his 'Eternal.'

Man, however, as Goethe says, *never knows how anthropomorphic he is*. Israel described his Eternal in the language of poetry and emotion, and could not thus describe him but with the

v THE PROOF FROM MIRACLES

characters of a man. Scientifically he never attempted to describe him at all. But still the Eternal was ever at last reducible, for Israel, to the reality of experience out of which the revelation sprang; he was 'the righteous Eternal who loveth righteousness.' They who 'seek the Eternal,' and they who 'follow after righteousness,' were identical; just as, conversely, they who 'fear the Eternal,' and they who 'depart from evil,' were identical.[1] Above all: '*Blessed is the man that feareth the Eternal*'; 'it is *joy* to the just to do judgment'; 'righteousness tendeth to *life*'; 'the righteous is *an everlasting foundation.*'[2]

But, as time went on, facts seemed, we saw, to contradict this fundamental belief, to refute this faith in the Eternal; material forces prevailed, and God appeared, as they say, to be on the side of the big battalions. The great unrighteous kingdoms of the world, kingdoms which cared far less than Israel for righteousness, and for the Eternal who makes for righteousness, overpowered Israel. Prophecy assured him that the triumph of the Eternal's cause and people was certain: *Behold, the Eternal's hand is not shortened, that it cannot save.*[3] The triumph was but adjourned through Israel's own sins: *Your iniquities have separated between you and your God.*[4]

---

[1] Isaiah li. 1; Prov. iii. 7.
[2] Psalm cxii. 1; Prov. xxi. 15; xi. 19; x. 25.
[3] Isaiah lix. 1.   [4] Isaiah lix. 2.

Prophecy directed its hearers to the future, and promised them a new, everlasting kingdom, under a heaven-sent leader. The characters of this kingdom and leader were more spiritualised by one prophet, more materialised by another. As time went on, in the last centuries before our era, they became increasingly turbid and phantasmagorical. In addition to his original experimental belief in the almighty Eternal who makes for righteousness, Israel had now a vast *Aberglaube*, an after or extra-belief, not experimental, in an approaching kingdom of the saints, to be established by an Anointed, a Messiah, or by 'one like the Son of Man,' commissioned from the Ancient of Days and coming in the clouds of heaven.

Jesus came, calling himself the Messiah, the Son of Man, the Son of God; and the question is, what is the true meaning of these assertions of his, and of all his teaching? It is the same question we had about the Old Testament. Is the language scientific, or is it, as we say, *literary?* —that is, the language of poetry and emotion, approximative language, thrown out, as it were, at certain great objects which the human mind augurs and feels after, but not language accurately defining them? Popular religion says, we know, that the language is scientific; that the God of the Old Testament is a great Personal First Cause, who thinks and loves (for this too, it seems, we ought to have added), the moral and

v THE PROOF FROM MIRACLES

intelligent Governor of the universe. Learned religion, the metaphysical theology of our bishops, proves or confirms this by abstruse reasoning from our ideas of cause, design, existence, identity, and so on. Popular religion rests it altogether on *miracle*.

The God of Israel, for popular religion, is a magnified and non-natural man who has really worked stupendous miracles, whereas the Gods of the heathen were vainly imagined to be able to work them, but could not, and had therefore no real existence. Of this God, Jesus for popular religion is the Son. He came to appease God's wrath against sinful men by the sacrifice of himself; and he proved his Sonship by a course of stupendous miracles, and by the wonderful accomplishment in him of the supernatural Messianic predictions of prophecy. Here, again, learned religion elucidates and develops the relation of the Son to the Father by a copious exhibition of metaphysics ; but for popular religion the relationship, and the authority of Jesus which derives from it, is altogether established by *miracle*.

Now, we have seen that our bishops and their metaphysics are so little convincing, that many people throw the Bible quite aside and will not attend to it, because they are given to understand that the metaphysics go necessarily along with it, and that one cannot be taken without the other. So far, then, the talents of the Bishops of Winchester and Gloucester, and their zeal to do something for the honour of the Eternal Son's Godhead, may be said to be actual obstacles to the receiving and studying of the Bible. But the same may now be also said of the popular theology which rests the Bible's authority and the Christian religion on miracle. To a great many persons this is tantamount to stopping their use of the Bible and of the Christian religion; for they have made up their minds that what is popularly called *miracle* never really happens nor can happen, and that the belief in it arises out of either ignorance or mistake. To these persons we restore the use of the Bible, if, while showing them that the Bible-language is not scientific, but the language of common speech or of poetry and eloquence, approximative language thrown out at certain great objects of consciousness which it does not pretend to define fully, we convince them at the same time that this language deals with facts of positive experience, most momentous and real.

We have sought to do this for the Old Testament first, and we now seek to do it for the New. But our attempt has in view those who are incredulous about the Bible and inclined to throw it aside, not those who at present receive it on the grounds supplied either by popular theology or by metaphysical theology. For persons of this kind, what we say neither will have, nor seeks to have, any constraining force

v THE PROOF FROM MIRACLES

at all; only it is rendered necessary by the want of constraining force, for others than themselves, in their own theology. How little constraining force metaphysical dogma has, we all see. And we have shown, too, how the proof from the fulfilment in Jesus Christ of a number of detailed predictions, supposed to have been made with supernatural prescience about him long beforehand, is losing, and seems likely more and more to lose, its constraining force. It is found that the predictions and their fulfilment are not what they are said to be.

Now we come to *miracles,* more specially so called. And we have to see whether the constraining force of this proof, too, must not be admitted to be far less than it used to be, and whether some other source of authority for the Bible is not much to be desired.

III

That miracles, when fully believed, are felt by men in general to be a source of authority, it is absurd to deny. One may say, indeed: Suppose I could change the pen with which I write this into a penwiper, I should not thus make what I write any the truer or more convincing. That may be so in reality, but the mass of mankind feel differently. In the judgment of the mass of mankind, could I visibly and undeniably change the pen with which I write this into a penwiper, not only would this which I write acquire a claim to be held perfectly true and convincing, but I should even be entitled to affirm, and to be believed in affirming, propositions the most palpably at war with common fact and experience. It is almost impossible to exaggerate the proneness of the human mind to take miracles as evidence, and to seek for miracles as evidence; or the extent to which religion, and religion of a true and admirable kind, has been, and is still, held in connection with a reliance upon miracles. This reliance will long outlast the reliance on the supernatural prescience of prophecy, for it is not exposed to the same tests. To pick Scripture-miracles one by one to pieces is an odious and repulsive task; it is also an unprofitable one, for whatever we may think of the affirmative demonstrations of them, a negative demonstration of them is, from the circumstances of the case, impossible. And yet the human mind is assuredly passing away, however slowly, from this hold of reliance also; and those who make it their stay will more and more find it fail them, will more and more feel themselves disturbed, shaken, distressed, and bewildered.

For it is what we call the *Time-Spirit* which is sapping the proof from miracles,—it is the 'Zeit-Geist' itself. Whether we attack them, or whether we defend them, does not much matter. The human mind, as its experience

V THE PROOF FROM MIRACLES

widens, is turning away from them. And for this reason: *it sees, as its experience widens, how they arise.* It sees that, under certain circumstances, they always do arise; and that they have not more solidity in one case than another. Under certain circumstances, wherever men are found, there is, as Shakspeare says:—

> No natural exhalation in the sky,
> No scape of nature, no distemper'd day,
> No common wind, no customed event,
> But they will pluck away his natural cause,
> And call them meteors, prodigies, and signs,
> Abortives, presages, and tongues of heaven.

Imposture is so far from being the general rule in these cases, that it is the rare exception. Signs and wonders men's minds will have, and they create them honestly and naturally; yet not so but that we can see *how* they create them.

Roman Catholics fancy that Bible-miracles and the miracles of their Church form a class by themselves; Protestants fancy that Bible-miracles, alone, form a class by themselves. This was eminently the posture of mind of the late Archbishop Whately:—to hold that all other miracles would turn out to be impostures, or capable of a natural explanation, but that Bible-miracles would stand sifting by a London special jury or by a committee of scientific men. No acuteness can save such notions, as our knowledge widens, from being seen to be mere extravagances, and the Protestant notion is doomed to an earlier ruin than the Catholic. For the Catholic notion admits miracles,—so far as Christianity, at least, is concerned,—in the mass; the Protestant notion invites to a criticism by which it must before long itself perish. When Stephen was martyred, he looked up into heaven, and saw the glory of God and Jesus standing on the right hand of God. That, says the Protestant, is solid fact. At the martyrdom of St. Fructuosus, Babylas and Mygdone, the Christian servants of the Roman governor, saw the heavens open, and the saint and his deacon Eulogius carried up on high with crowns on their heads. That is, says the Protestant, imposture or else illusion. St. Paul hears on his way to Damascus the voice of Jesus say to him: 'Saul, Saul, why persecutest thou me?' That is solid fact. The companion of St. Thomas Aquinas hears a voice from the crucifix say to the praying saint: 'Thou hast written well of me, Thomas; what recompense dost thou desire?' That is imposture or else illusion. Why? It is impossible to find any criterion by which one of these incidents may establish its claim to a solidity which we refuse to the others.

One of two things must be made out in order to place either the Bible-miracles alone, or the Bible-miracles and the miracles of the Catholic Church with them, in a class by themselves. Either they must be shown to have arisen in a time eminently unfavourable to such a process

v   THE PROOF FROM MIRACLES

as Shakspeare describes, to amplification and the production of legend ; or they must be shown to be recorded in documents of an eminently historical mode of birth and publication. But surely it is manifest that the Bible-miracles fulfil neither of these conditions. It was said that the waters of the Pamphylian Sea miraculously opened a passage for the army of Alexander the Great. Admiral Beaufort, however, tells us that, 'though there are no tides in this part of the Mediterranean, a considerable depression of the sea is caused by long-continued north winds, and Alexander, taking advantage of such a moment, may have dashed on without impediment.'[1] And we accept the explanation as a matter of course. But the waters of the Red Sea are said to have miraculously opened a passage for the children of Israel ; and we insist on the literal truth of *this* story, and reject natural explanations as impious. Yet the time and circumstances of the flight from Egypt were a thousand times more favourable to the rise of some natural incident into a miracle, than the age of Alexander. They were a time and circumstances of less broad daylight. It was said, again, that during the battle of Leuctra the gates of the Heracleum at Thebes suddenly opened, and the armour of Hercules vanished from the temple, to enable the god to take part with the Thebans in the battle. Probably there was some real

[1] Beaufort's *Karamania*, p. 116.

circumstance, however slight, which gave a foundation for the story. But this is the most we think of saying in its favour; the literal story it never even occurs to one of us to believe. But that the walls of Jericho literally fell down at the sound of the trumpets of Joshua, we are asked to believe, told that it is impious to disbelieve it. Yet which place and time were most likely to generate a miraculous story with ease,—Hellas and the days of Epaminondas, or Palestine and the days of Joshua? And of documentary records, which are the most historical in their way of being generated and propagated, which the most favourable for the admission of legend and miracle of all kinds, —the Old Testament narratives with their incubation of centuries, and the New Testament narratives with their incubation of a century (and tradition active all the while), or the narratives, say, of Herodotus or Plutarch?

None of them are what we call critical. Experience of the history of the human mind, and of men's habits of seeing, sifting, and relating, convinces us that the miraculous stories of Herodotus or Plutarch do grow out of the process described by Shakspeare. But we shall find ourselves inevitably led, sooner or later, to extend the same rule to all miraculous stories; nay, the considerations which apply in other cases, apply, we shall most surely discover, with even greater force in the case of Bible-miracles.

v   THE PROOF FROM MIRACLES

IV

This being so, there is nothing one would more desire for a person or document one greatly values, than to make them independent of miracles. And with regard to the Old Testament we have done this; for we have shown that the essential matter in the Old Testament is the revelation to Israel of the immeasurable grandeur, the eternal necessity, the priceless blessing of that with which not less than three-fourths of human life is indeed concerned,—*righteousness*. And it makes no difference to the preciousness of this revelation, whether we believe that the Red Sea miraculously opened a passage to the Israelites, and the walls of Jericho miraculously fell down at the blast of Joshua's trumpet, or that these stories arose in the same way as other stories of the kind. But in the New Testament the essential thing is the revelation of Jesus Christ. For this too, then, if one values it, one's great wish must in like manner be to make it independent of miracle, if miracle is a stay which one perceives, as more and more we are all coming to perceive it, to be not solid.

Now, it may look at first sight a strange thing to say, but it is a truth which we will make abundantly clear as we go on, that one of the very best helps to prepare the way for valuing the Bible and believing in Jesus Christ, is to convince oneself of the liability to mistake in the Bible-writers. Our popular theology supposes that the Old Testament writers were miraculously inspired, and could make no mistakes; that the New Testament writers were miraculously inspired, and could make no mistakes; and that there this miraculous inspiration stopped, and all writers on religion have been liable to make mistakes ever since. It is as if a hand had been put out of the sky presenting us with the Bible, and the rules of criticism which apply to other books did not apply to the Bible. Now, the fatal thing for this supposition is, that its owners stab it to the heart the moment they use any palliation or explaining away, however small, of the literal words of the Bible; and *some* they always use. For instance, it is said in the Eighteenth Psalm, that a consuming fire went out of the mouth of God, so that coals were kindled at it. The veriest literalist will cry out: Every one knows that this is not to be taken literally! The truth is, even *he* knows that *this* is not to be taken literally; but others know that a great deal more is not to be taken literally. *He* knows very little; but, as far as his little knowledge goes, he gives up his theory, which is, of course, palpably hollow. For indeed it is only by applying to the Bible a criticism, such as it is, that any man makes out that criticism does not apply to the Bible.

v THE PROOF FROM MIRACLES

But suppose that the Bible itself put forth (which it does not) this theory, and made its own value all depend on the truth of it, then the result would be, at the best, not firmer conviction, but utter puzzle and bewilderment. Contradictions would meet us, and we should have no means of escape from them. There would grow up an irresistible sense that the belief in miracles was due to man's want of experience, to his ignorance, agitation, and helplessness; and yet we should have a book, which if true was precious, staking all its truth and value upon its having been put out of the sky, upon its being guaranteed by miracles, and upon their being true. Then it is that the cry, *Imposture!* would more and more, in spite of all we could do, gather strength, and the book be thrown aside more and more.

But when we convince ourselves that, in the New Testament as in the Old, what is given us is words *thrown out* at an immense reality not fully or half fully grasped by the writers, but, even thus, able to affect us with indescribable force; when we convince ourselves that, as in the Old Testament, we have Israel's inadequate yet inexhaustibly fruitful testimony to *the Eternal that makes for righteousness,* so we have in the New Testament a report inadequate, indeed, but the only report we have, and therefore priceless, by men, some more able and clear, others less able and clear, but *all* full of the influences of their time and condition, partakers of some of its simple or its learned ignorance,—inevitably, in fine, expecting miracles and demanding them, —a report, I say, by these men of that immense reality not fully or half fully grasped by them, *the mind of Christ ;*—then we shall be drawn to the Gospels with a new zest and as by a fresh spell. We shall throw ourselves upon their narratives with an ardour answering to the value of the pearl of great price they hold, and to the difficulty of reaching it.

So, to profit fully by the New Testament, the first thing to be done is to make it perfectly clear to oneself that its reporters both could err and did err. For a plain person, an incident in the report of St. Paul's conversion,—which comes into our minds the more naturally as this incident has been turned against something we have ourselves said,[1]—would, one would think, be enough. We had spoken of the notion that St. Paul's miraculous vision at his conversion proved the truth of his doctrine. We related a vision which converted Sampson Staniforth, one of the early Methodists ; and we said that just so much proving force, and no more, as Sampson Staniforth's vision had to confirm the truth of anything he might afterwards teach, St. Paul's vision had to establish *his* subsequent doctrine. It was eagerly rejoined that Staniforth's vision was but a fancy of his own, whereas the reality

[1] *St. Paul and Protestantism*, p. 60.

v THE PROOF FROM MIRACLES

of Paul's was proved by his companions hearing the voice that spoke to him. And so in one place of the Acts we are told they did; but in another place of the Acts we are told by Paul himself just the contrary: that his companions did *not* hear the voice that spoke to him. Need we say that the two statements have been 'reconciled'? They have, over and over again; but by one of those processes which are the opprobrium of our Bible-criticism, and by which, as Bishop Butler says, anything can be made to mean anything. There is between the two statements a contradiction as clear as can be. The contradiction proves nothing against the good faith of the reporter, and St. Paul undoubtedly had his vision; he had it as Sampson Staniforth had his. What the contradiction proves is the incurable looseness with which the circumstances of what is called and thought *a miracle* are related; and that this looseness the Bible-relaters of a miracle exhibit, just like other people. And the moral is, what an unsure stay, then, must miracles be!

But, after all, that there is here any contradiction or mistake, some do deny; so let us choose a case where the mistake is quite undeniably clear. Such a case we find in the confident expectation and assertion, on the part of the New Testament writers, of the approaching end of the world. Even this mistake people try to explain away; but it is so palpable that no words can cloud our perception of it. The *time is short. The Lord is at hand. The end of all things is at hand. Little children, it is the final time. The Lord's coming is at hand; behold, the judge standeth before the door.*[1] Nothing can really obscure the evidence furnished by such sayings as these. When Paul told the Thessalonians that they and he, at the approaching coming of Christ, should have their turn after, not before, the faithful dead :—' For the Lord himself shall descend from heaven with a shout, with the voice of the archangel and with the trump of God, and the dead in Christ shall rise first, then we which are alive and remain shall be caught up together with them in the clouds, to meet the Lord in the air,'[2]— when he said this, St. Paul was purely simply mistaken in his notion of what was going to happen. This is as clear as anything can be.

And not only were the New Testament writers thus demonstrably liable to commit, like other men, mistakes in fact; they were also demonstrably liable to commit mistakes in argument. As before, let us take a case which will be manifest and palpable to every one. St. Paul, arguing to the Galatians that salvation was not by the Jewish law but by Jesus Christ, proves his point from the promise to Abraham

---

[1] 1 Cor. vii. 29; Phil. iv. 5; 1 Peter iv. 7; 1 John ii. 18; James v. 8, 9. We have here the express declarations of St. Paul, St. Peter, St. John, and St. James.
[2] 1 Thess. iv. 16, 17.

v THE PROOF FROM MIRACLES

having been made to him and his *seed*, not *seeds*. The words are not, he says, '*seeds*, as of many, but as of one; to thy *seed*, which is Christ.'[1] Now, as to the point to be proved, we all agree with St. Paul; but his argument is that of a Jewish Rabbi, and is clearly both fanciful and false. The writer in Genesis never intended to draw any distinction between *one* of Abraham's seed, and Abraham's seed *in general*. And even if he had expressly meant, what Paul says he did *not* mean, Abraham's seed in general, he would still have said *seed*, and not *seeds*. This is a good instance to take, because the Apostle's substantial doctrine is here not at all concerned. As to the root of the matter in question, we are all at one with St. Paul. But it is evident how he could, like the rest of us, bring a quite false argument in support of a quite true thesis.

And the use of prophecy by the writers of the New Testament furnishes really, almost at every turn, instances of false argument of the same kind. Habit makes us so lend ourselves to their way of speaking, that commonly nothing checks us; but, the moment we begin to attend, we perceive how much there is which ought to check us. Take the famous allegation of the parted clothes but lot-assigned coat of Christ as fulfilment of the supposed prophecy in the Psalms: 'They parted my garments among them, and for my vesture did they cast

[1] Gal. iii. 16.

lots.'[1] The words of the Psalm are taken to mean contrast, when they do in truth mean identity. According to the rules of Hebrew poetry, *for my vesture they did cast lots* is merely a repetition, in different words, of *they parted my garments among them*, not an antithesis to it. The alleged 'prophecy' is, therefore, due to a dealing with the Psalmist's words which is arbitrary and erroneous. So, again, to call the words, *a bone of him shall not be broken*,[2] a prophecy of Christ, fulfilled by his legs not being broken on the cross, is evidently, the moment one considers it, a playing with words which nowadays we should account childish. For what do the words, taken, as alone words can rationally be taken, along with their context, really prophesy? The entire *safety* of the righteous, not his death. *Many are the troubles of the righteous, but the Eternal delivereth him out of all; he keepeth all his bones, so that not one of them is broken.*[3] Worse words, therefore, could hardly have been chosen from the Old Testament to apply in that connection where they come; for they are really contradicted by the death of Christ, not fulfilled by it.

It is true, this verbal and unintelligent use of Scripture is just what was to be expected from the circumstances of the New Testament writers. It was inevitable for them; it was

---

[1] Psalm xxii. 18.   [2] See John xix. 36.
[3] Psalm xxxiv. 19, 20.

v THE PROOF FROM MIRACLES

the sort of trifling which then, in common Jewish theology, passed for grave argument and made a serious impression, as it has in common Christian theology ever since. But this does not make it the less really trifling; or hinder one nowadays from seeing it to be trifling, directly we examine it. The mistake made will strike some people more forcibly in one of the cases cited, some in another, but in one or other of the cases the mistake will be visible to everybody.

Now, this recognition of the liability of the New Testament writers to make mistakes, both of fact and of argument, will certainly, as we have said, more and more gain strength, and spread wider and wider. The futility of their mode of demonstration from prophecy, of which we have just given examples, will be more and more felt. The fallibility of that demonstration from miracles to which they and all about them attached such preponderating weight, which made the disciples of Jesus believe in him, which made the people believe in him, will be more and more recognised.

Reverence for all, who, in those first dubious days of Christianity, chose the better part, and resolutely cast in their lot with 'the despised and rejected of men'! Gratitude to all, who, while the tradition was yet fresh, helped by their writings to preserve and set clear the precious record of the words and life of Jesus!

And honour, eternal honour, to the great and profound qualities of soul and mind which some of these writers display! But the writers are admirable for what they are, not for what, by the nature of things, they could not be. It was superiority enough in them to attach themselves firmly to Jesus; to feel to the bottom of their hearts that power of his *words*, which alone held permanently,—held, when the miracles, in which the multitude believed as well as the disciples, failed to hold. The good faith of the Bible-writers is above all question, it speaks for itself; and the very same criticism, which shows us the defects of their exegesis and of their demonstrations from miracles, establishes their good faith. But this could not, and did not, prevent them from arguing in the methods by which every one around them argued, and from expecting miracles where everybody else expected them.

In one respect alone have the miracles recorded by them a more real ground than the mass of miracles of which we have the relation. Medical science has never gauged,—never, perhaps, enough set itself to gauge,—the intimate connection between moral fault and disease. To what extent, or in how many cases, what is called *illness* is due to moral springs having been used amiss, whether by being over-used or by not being used sufficiently, we hardly at all know, and we too little inquire.

v THE PROOF FROM MIRACLES

Certainly it is due to this very much more than we commonly think; and the more it is due to this, the more do moral therapeutics rise in possibility and importance.[1] The bringer of light and happiness, the calmer and pacifier, or invigorator and stimulator, is one of the chiefest of doctors. Such a doctor was Jesus; such an operator, by an efficacious and real, though little observed and little employed agency, upon what we, in the language of popular superstition, call the *unclean spirits,* but which are to be designated more literally and more correctly as the *uncleared, unpurified spirits,* which came raging and madding before him. This his own language shows, if we know how to read it. '*What does it matter whether I say, Thy sins are forgiven thee! or whether I say, Arise and walk!*'[2] And again: '*Thou art made whole; sin no more, lest a worse thing befall thee.*'[3] His reporters, we must remember, are men who saw thaumaturgy in all that Jesus did, and who saw in all sickness and disaster visitations from God, and they bend his language accordingly. But indications enough remain to show the line of the Master, his perception of the large part of moral cause in many kinds of disease, and his method of addressing to this part his cure.

It would never have done, indeed, to have

[1] Consult the *Charmides* of Plato (cap. v.) for a remarkable account of the theory of such a treatment, attributed by Socrates to Zamolxis, the god-king of the Thracians.
[2] Matthew ix. 5.   [3] John v. 14.

men pronouncing right and left that this and that was a judgment, and how, and for what, and on whom. And so, when the disciples, seeing an afflicted person, asked whether this man had done sin or his parents, Jesus checked them and said: 'Neither the one nor the other, but that the works of God might be made manifest in him.'[1] Not the less clear is his own belief in the moral root of much physical disease, and in moral therapeutics; and it is important to note well the instances of miracles where this belief comes in. For the action of Jesus in these instances, however it may be amplified in the reports, was real; but it is not, therefore, as popular religion fancies, thaumaturgy,—it is not what people are fond of calling the *supernatural*, but what is better called the *non-natural*. It is, on the contrary, like the grace of Raphael, or the grand style of Phidias, eminently natural; but it is above common, low-pitched nature; it is a line of nature not yet mastered or followed out.

Its significance as a guarantee of the authenticity of Christ's mission is trivial, however, compared with the guarantee furnished by his sayings. Its importance is in its necessary effect upon the beholders and reporters. This element of what was really wonderful, unprecedented, and unaccountable, they had actually before them; and we may estimate how it must have

[1] John ix. 3.

v THE PROOF FROM MIRACLES

helped and seemed to sanction that tendency which in any case would have carried them, circumstanced as they were, to find all the performances and career of Jesus miraculous.

But, except for this, the miracles related in the Gospels will appear to us more and more, the more our experience and knowledge increases, to have but the same ground which is common to all miracles, the ground indicated by Shakspeare; to have been generated under the same kind of conditions as other miracles, and to follow the same laws. When once the 'Zeit-Geist' has made us entertain the notion of this, a thousand things in the manner of relating will strike us which never struck us before, and will make us wonder how we could ever have thought differently. Discrepancies which we now labour with such honest pains and by such astonishing methods to explain away,—the voice at Paul's conversion, heard by the bystanders according to one account, not heard by them according to another; the Holy Dove at Christ's baptism, visible to John the Baptist in one narrative, in two others to Jesus himself, in another, finally, to all the people as well; the single blind man in one relation, growing into two blind men in another; the speaking with tongues, according to St. Paul a sound without meaning, according to the Acts an intelligent and intelligible utterance,—all this will be felt to require really no explanation at all, to explain itself, to be natural to the whole class of incidents to which these miracles belong, and the inevitable result of the looseness with which the stories of them arise and are propagated.

And the more the miraculousness of the story deepens, as after the death of Jesus, the more does the texture of the incidents become loose and floating, the more does the very air and aspect of things seem to tell us we are in wonderland. Jesus after his resurrection not known by Mary Magdalene, taken by her for the gardener ; appearing *in another form*, and not known by the two disciples going with him to Emmaus and at supper with him there ; not known by his most intimate apostles on the borders of the Sea of Galilee ;—and presently, out of these vague beginnings, the recognitions getting asserted, then the ocular demonstrations, the final commissions, the ascension ;—one hardly knows which of the two to call the most evident here, the perfect simplicity and good faith of the narrators, or the plainness with which they themselves really say to us : *Behold a legend growing under your eyes !*

And suggestions of this sort, with respect to the whole miraculous side of the New Testament, will meet us at every turn ; we here but give a sample of them. It is neither our wish nor our design to accumulate them, to marshal them, to insist upon them, to make their force felt. Let those who desire to keep them at

v   THE PROOF FROM MIRACLES

arm's length continue to do so, if they can, and go on placing the sanction of the Christian religion in its miracles. Our point is, that the objections to miracles do, and more and more will, without insistence, without attack, without controversy, make their own force felt ; and that the sanction of Christianity, if Christianity is not to be lost along with its miracles, must be found elsewhere.

CHAPTER VI

THE NEW TESTAMENT RECORD

Now, then, will be perceived the bearing and gravity of what we some little way back said, that the more we convince ourselves of the liability of the New Testament writers to mistake, the more we really bring out the greatness and worth of the New Testament. For the more the reporters were fallible and prone to delusion, the more does Jesus become independent of the mistakes they made, and unaffected by them. We have plain proof that here was a very great spirit; and the greater he was, the more certain were his disciples to misunderstand him. The depth of their misunderstanding of him is really a kind of measure of the height of his superiority. And this superiority is what interests us in the records of the New Testament; for the New Testament exists to reveal Jesus Christ, not to establish the immunity of its writers from error.

Jesus himself is not a New Testament writer; he is the object of description and comment

CH. VI THE NEW TESTAMENT RECORD

to the New Testament writers. As the Old Testament speaks about the Eternal and bears an invaluable witness to him, without yet ever adequately in words defining and expressing him; so, and even yet more, do the New Testament writers speak about Jesus and give a priceless record of him, without adequately and accurately comprehending him. They are altogether on another plane from Jesus, and their mistakes are not his. It is not Jesus himself who relates his own miracles to us; who tells us of his own apparitions after his death; who alleges his crucifixion and sufferings as a fulfilment of the prophecy: *The Eternal keepeth all the bones of the righteous so that not one of them is broken;*[1] who proves salvation to be by Christ alone, from the promise to Abraham being made to *seed* in the singular number, not the plural. If, therefore, the human mind is now drawing away from reliance on miracles, coming to perceive the community of character which pervades them all, to understand their natural laws, so to speak,—their loose mode of origination and their untrustworthiness,—and is inclined rather to distrust the dealer in them than to pin its faith upon him; then it is good for the authority of Jesus, that his reporters are evidently liable to ignorance and error. He is reported to deal in miracles, to be above all a thaumaturgist. But the more his reporters were

[1] Psalm xxxiv. 20.

intellectually men of their nation and time, and of its current beliefs,—the more, that is, they were open to mistakes,—the more certain they were to impute miracles to a wonderful and half-understood personage like Jesus, whether he would or no. He himself may, at the same time, have had quite other notions as to what he was doing and intending.

Again, the mistake of imagining that the world was to end, as St. Paul announces, within the lifetime of the first Christian generation, is palpable. But the reporters of Jesus make him announcing just the same thing: 'This generation shall not pass away till they shall see the Son of Man coming in the clouds with great power and glory, and then shall he send his angels and gather his elect from the four winds.'[1] Popular theology can put a plain satisfactory sense upon this, but, as usual, through that process described by Butler by which anything can be made to mean anything; and from this sort of process the human mind is beginning to shrink. A more plausible theology will say that the words are an accommodation; that the speaker lends himself to the fancies and expectations of his hearers. A good deal of such accommodation there is in this and other sayings of Jesus; but accommodation to the *full extent* here supposed would surely have been impossible. To suppose it, is most violent and

[1] Matthew xxiv. 30, 31, 34.

VI THE NEW TESTAMENT RECORD

unsatisfactory. Either, then, the words were, like St. Paul's announcement, a mistake, or they are not really the very words Jesus said, just as he said them. That is, the reporters have given them a turn, however slight, a tone and a colour, a connection, to make them comply with a fixed idea in their own minds, which they unfeignedly believed was a fixed idea with Jesus also. Now, the more we regard the reporters of Jesus as men liable to err, full of the turbid Jewish fancies about 'the grand consummation' which were then current, the easier we can understand these men inevitably putting their own eschatology into the mouth of Jesus, when they had to report his discourse about the kingdom of God and the troubles in store for the Jewish nation, and the less need have we to make Jesus a co-partner in their eschatology.

Again, the futility of such demonstrations from prophecy as those of which we have given examples, and generally of all that Jewish exegesis, based on a mere unintelligent catching at the letter of the Old Testament, isolated from its context and real meaning, of which the New Testament writers give us so much, begins to disconcert attentive readers of the Bible more and more, and to be felt by them as an embarrassment to the cause of Jesus, not a support. Well, then, it is good for the authority of Jesus, that those who establish it by arguments of this sort should be clearly men of their race and time, not above its futile methods of reasoning and demonstration. The more they were this, and the more they were sure to mix up much futile logic and exegesis with their presentation of Jesus, the less is Jesus himself responsible for such logic and exegesis, or at all dependent upon it. He may himself have rated such argumentation at precisely its true value, and have based his mission and authority upon no grounds but solid ones. Whether he did so or not, his hearers and reporters were sure to base it on their own fantastic grounds also, and to credit Jesus with doing the same.

In short, the more we conceive Jesus as almost as much over the heads of his disciples and reporters then, as he is over the heads of the mass of so-called Christians now, the more we see his disciples to have been, as they were, men raised by a truer moral susceptiveness above their countrymen, but in intellectual conceptions and habits much on a par with them, all the more do we make room, so to speak, for Jesus to be a personage immensely great and wonderful; as wonderful as anything his reporters imagined him to be, though in a different manner.

II

We make room for him to be this, and through the inadequate reporting of his followers

vi THE NEW TESTAMENT RECORD

there breaks and shines, and will more and more break and shine the more the matter is examined, abundant evidence that he *was* this. It is most remarkable, and the best proof of the simplicity, seriousness, and good faith which intercourse with Jesus Christ inspired, that witnesses with a fixed prepossession, and having no doubt at all as to the interpretation to be put on Christ's acts and career, should yet admit so much of what makes against themselves and their own power of interpreting. For them, it was a thing beyond all doubt, that by miracles Jesus manifested forth his glory, and induced the faithful to believe in him. Yet what checks to this paramount and all-governing belief of theirs do they report from Jesus himself! Everybody will be able to recall such checks, although he may never yet have been accustomed to consider their full significance. *Except ye see signs and wonders, ye will not believe!*[1]—as much as to say: 'Believe on right grounds you cannot, and you must needs believe on wrong!' And again: 'Believe me that I am in the Father and the Father in me; *or else believe for the very works' sake!*'[2] — as much as to say: 'Acknowledge me on the ground of my healing and restoring acts being miraculous, if you must; but it is not the right ground.' No, not the right ground; and when Nicodemus came and would put conversion on this ground ('We

[1] John iv. 48.   [2] John xiv. 11.

know that thou art a teacher come from God, *for no one can do the miracles that thou doest except God be with him*'), Jesus rejoined : 'Verily, verily, I say unto thee, *except a man be born from above*, he cannot see the kingdom of God!' thus tacitly changing his disciple's ground and correcting him.[1] Even distress and impatience at this false ground being taken is visible sometimes : 'Jesus *groaned in his spirit* and said, Why doth this generation ask for a sign? Verily I say unto you, there shall no sign be given to this generation!'[2] Who does not see what double and treble importance these checks from Jesus to the reliance on miracles gain, through their being reported by those who relied on miracles devoutly? Who does not see what a clue they offer as to the real mind of Jesus? To convey at all to such hearers of him that there was any objection to miracles, his own sense of the objection must have been profound; and to get them, who neither shared nor understood it, to repeat it a few times, he must have repeated it many times.

Take, again, the eschatology of the disciples, their notion of the final things, and of the approaching great judgment and end of the world. This consisted mainly in a literal appropriation of the apocalyptic pictures of the book of Daniel and the book of Enoch, and a transference of them to Jesus Christ

---

[1] John iii. 2, 3. [2] Mark viii. 12.

VI THE NEW TESTAMENT RECORD

and his kingdom. It is not surprising, certainly, that men with the mental range of their time, and with so little flexibility of thought that when Jesus told them to beware of 'the leaven of the Pharisees,'[1] or when he called himself 'the bread of life' and said, *He that eateth me shall live by me*,[2] they stuck hopelessly fast in the literal meaning of the words, and were accordingly puzzled or else offended by them, —it is not surprising that these men should have been incapable of dealing in a large spirit with prophecies like those of Daniel, that they should have applied them to Jesus narrowly and literally, and should therefore have conceived his kingdom unintelligently. This is not remarkable; what *is* remarkable is, that they should themselves supply us with their Master's blame of their too literal criticism, his famous sentence: 'The kingdom of God is *within* you!'[3] Such an account of the kingdom of God has more right, even if recorded only once, to pass with us for Jesus Christ's own account, than the common materialising accounts, if repeated twenty times; for it was manifestly quite foreign to the disciples' own notions, and they could never have invented it. Evidence of the same kind, again, evidence borne by the reporters themselves against their own power of rightly

---

[1] Matthew xvi. 6-12.   [2] John vi. 48, 57.
[3] Luke xvii. 21.

understanding what their Master, on this topic of the kingdom of God and its coming, meant to say, is Christ's warning to his apostles, that the subject of final things was one where they were all out of their depth: '*It is not for you to know* the times and seasons which the Father hath put in his own power.'[1]

So, too, with the use of prophecy and of the Old Testament generally. A very small experience of Jewish exegesis will convince us that, in the disciples, their catching at the letter of the Scriptures, and mistaking this play with words for serious argument, was nothing extraordinary. The extraordinary thing is that Jesus, even in the report of these critics, uses Scripture in a totally different manner; he wields it as an instrument of which he truly possesses the use. Either he puts prophecy into act, and by the startling point thus made he engages the popular imagination on his side, makes the popular familiarity with prophecy serve him; as when he rides into Jerusalem on an ass, or clears the Temple of buyers and sellers. Or else he applies Scripture in what is called 'a superior spirit,' to make it yield to narrow-minded hearers a lesson of wisdom; as, for instance, to rebuke a superstitious observance of the Sabbath he employs the incident of David's taking the shewbread. His reporters,

[1] Acts i. 7.

VI THE NEW TESTAMENT RECORD

in short, are the servants of the Scripture-letter, Jesus is its master; and it is from the very men who were servants to it themselves, that we learn that he was master of it. How signal, therefore, must this mastery have been! how eminently and strikingly different from the treatment known and practised by the disciples themselves!

Finally, for the reporters of Jesus the rule was, undoubtedly, that men 'believed on Jesus when they saw the miracles which he did.'[1] Miracles were in these reporters' eyes, beyond question, the evidence of the Christian religion. And yet these same reporters indicate another and a totally different evidence offered for the Christian religion by Christ himself. *Every one that heareth and learneth from the Father cometh unto me.*[2] *As the Father hath taught me, so I speak;*[3] *he that is of God heareth the words of God;*[4] *if God was your Father, ye would have loved me!*[5] This is inward evidence, direct evidence. From that previous knowledge of God, as 'the Eternal that loveth righteousness,' which Israel possessed, the hearers of Jesus could and should have concluded irresistibly, when they heard his words, that he came from God. Now, miracles are outward evidence, indirect evidence, not conclusive in this fashion. To walk on the sea cannot

[1] John ii. 23.   [2] John vi. 45.
[3] John viii. 28.   [4] John viii. 47.   [5] John viii. 42.

really prove a man to proceed from the Eternal that loveth righteousness; although undoubtedly, as we have said, a man who walks on the sea will be able to make the mass of mankind believe about him almost anything he chooses to say. But there is, after all, no necessary connection between walking on the sea and proceeding from the Eternal that loveth righteousness. Jesus propounds, on the other hand, an evidence of which the whole force lies in the necessary connection between the proving matter and the power that makes for righteousness. This is *his* evidence for the Christian religion.

His disciples felt the force of the evidence, indeed. Peter's answer to the question 'Will ye also go away?'—'*To whom should we go? thou hast the words of eternal life!*'[1]—proves it. But feeling the force of a thing is very different from understanding and possessing it. The evidence, which the disciples were *conscious* of understanding and possessing, was the evidence from miracles. And yet, in their report, Jesus is plainly shown to us insisting on a different evidence, an internal one. The character of the reporters gives to this indication a paramount importance. That they should indicate this internal evidence once, as the evidence on which Jesus insisted, is more significant, we say, than their indicating, twenty times, the evidence from

[1] John vi. 68.

VI THE NEW TESTAMENT RECORD

miracles as the evidence naturally convincing to mankind, and recommended, as they thought, by Jesus. The notion of the one evidence they would have of themselves; the notion of the other they could only get from a superior mind. This mind must have been full of it to induce them to feel it at all; and their exhibition of it, even then, must of necessity be inadequate and broken.

But is it possible to overrate the value of the ground thus gained for showing the riches of the New Testament to those who, sick of the popular arguments from prophecy, sick of the popular arguments from miracles, are for casting the New Testament aside altogether! The book contains all that we know of a wonderful spirit, far above the heads of his reporters, still farther above the head of our popular theology, which has added its own misunderstanding of the reporters to the reporters' misunderstanding of Jesus. And it was quite inevitable that anything so superior and so profound should be imperfectly understood by those amongst whom it first appeared, and for a very long time afterwards; and that it should come at last gradually to stand out clearer only by time,—*Time*, as the Greek maxim says, *the wisest of all things, for he is the unfailing discoverer.*

Yet, however much is discovered, the object of our scrutiny must still be beyond us, must still transcend our adequate knowledge, if for no other reason, because of the character of the first and only records of him. But in the view now taken we have,—even at the point to which we have already come,—at least a wonderful figure transcending his time, transcending his disciples, attaching them, but transcending them; in very much that he uttered going far above their heads, treating Scripture and prophecy like a master while they treated it like children, resting his doctrine on internal evidence while they rested it on miracles; and yet, by his incomparable lucidity and penetrativeness, planting his profound veins of thought in their memory along with their own notions and prepossessions, to come out all mixed up together, but still distinguishable one day and separable;—and leaving his word thus to bear fruit for the future.

III

Surely to follow and extract these veins of true ore is a wise man's business; not to let them lie neglected and unused, because the beds where they are found are not all of the same quality with them. The beds are invaluable because they contain the ore; and though the search for it in them is undoubtedly a grave and difficult quest, yet it is not a quest of the elaborate and endless kind that it will at first, perhaps, be fancied to be. It is a quest with this for its governing idea: *Jesus was over the*

VI THE NEW TESTAMENT RECORD

heads of his reporters ; what, therefore, in their report of him, is Jesus, and what is the reporters ?

Now, this excludes as unessential much of the criticism which is bestowed on the New Testament, and gives a sure point of view for the remainder. And what it excludes are those questions as to the exact date, the real authorship, the first publication, the rank of priority, of the Gospels ;—questions which have a great attraction for critics, which are perhaps in themselves good to be entertained, which lead to much close and fruitful observation of the texts, and in which very high ingenuity may be shown and very great plausibility reached, but not more ;—they cannot be really settled, the data are insufficient. And for our purpose they are not essential. Neither is it essential for our purpose to get at the very primitive text of the New Testament writers, deeply interesting and deeply important as this is. The changes that have befallen the text show, no doubt, the constant tendency of popular Christianity to add to the element of theurgy and thaumaturgy, to increase and develop it. To clear the text of these changes, will show the New Testament writers to have been less preoccupied with this tendency, and is, so far, very instructive. But it will not, by re-establishing the real words of the writers, necessarily give the real truth as to Jesus Christ's religion ; because to the writers themselves this religion was, in a considerable degree certainly, a theurgy and a thaumaturgy, although not quite in the mechanical and extravagant way that it is in our present popular theology.

For instance, the famous text of the three heavenly witnesses[1] is an imposture, and an extravagant one. It shows us, no doubt, theologians like our bishops already at work,—men with more metaphysics than literary tact, full of the Aryan genius, of the notion that religion is a metaphysical conception; anxious to do something for the thesis of 'the Godhead of the Eternal Son,' or of 'the blessed truth that the God of the universe is a person,'—or, as the Bishop of Gloucester writes it, ' PERSON,'—and so on. But *something* of the same intention is unquestionably visible,—never, indeed, in Jesus, but in the author of the Fourth Gospel. Much of the conversation with Nicodemus is a proof of it; the forty-sixth verse of the sixth chapter is a signal proof of it. One can there almost see the author, after recording Christ's words: *Every one that heareth and learneth of the father cometh unto me*, take alarm at the notion that this looks too downright and natural, and, sincerely persuaded that he 'did something' for the honour of Jesus by making him more abstract, bring in and put into the mouth of Jesus the 46th verse: *Not that any one hath seen the father, except he that is from*

[1] 1 John v. 7.

VI THE NEW TESTAMENT RECORD

God, he hath seen the father. This verse has neither rhyme nor reason where it stands in Christ's discourse, it jars with the words which precede and follow, and is in quite another vein from them. Yet it is the author's own, it is no interpolation.

Again, Unitarians lay much stress on the probability that in the first words of St. Mark's Gospel: 'The beginning of the gospel of Jesus Christ, the Son of God,' *the Son of God* is an interpolation. And, no doubt, if the words are an interpolation, this shows that the desire to prove the dogma of Christ's Godhead was not so painfully ever-present to the writer of the Second Gospel as it became to later theologians. But it shows no more; it does not show that he had the least doubt about Jesus being the Son of God. Ten verses later, in an undisputed passage, he calls him so.

Again, in the last chapter of the same Gospel, all which follows the eighth verse,—all the account of Christ's resurrection and ascension,— is probably an addition by a later hand. But the resurrection is plainly indicated in the first eight verses; and that the writer of the Second Gospel stops after the eighth verse, proves rather that he was writing briefly than that he did not believe in the resurrection and ascension as much as, for instance, the writer of the Third Gospel; unless, indeed, there are other signs (for example, in his way of relating such an incident as the Transfiguration) to show that he was suspicious of the preternatural. But there are none; and he plainly was not, and could not have been.

Again; it seems impossible that the very primitive original of the First Gospel should have made Jesus say, that 'the sign of Jonas' consisted in his being three days and three nights in the whale's belly as the Son of Man was to be a like time in the heart of the earth.[1] It spoils the argument, and in the next verse the argument is given simply and rightly. Jonas was a sign to the Jews, because the Ninevites repented at his preaching and a greater than Jonas stood now preaching to the Jews. But whether the words are genuine (and there seems no evidence to the contrary) in that particular place or not, to get rid of them brings us really but a very little way, when it is plain that their argument is exactly one which the Evangelists would be disposed to use, and to think that Jesus meant to use. For so they make him to have said, for instance: *Destroy this temple, and in three days I will raise it up!*[2] in prediction of his own death and resurrection.

In short, to know accurately the history of our documents is impossible, and even if it were possible, we should yet not know accurately what Jesus said and did; *for his reporters were incapable of rendering it, he was so much above*

[1] Matthew xii. 40.   [2] John ii. 19.

VI THE NEW TESTAMENT RECORD

them. This is the important thing to get firmly fixed in our minds. And the more it becomes established to us, the more we shall see the futility of what is called *rationalism, rationalism* proper, and the *rationalistic* treatment of the New Testament;—of the endeavour, that is, to reduce all the supernatural in it to real events, much resembling what is related, which have got a little magnified and coloured by being seen through the eyes of men having certain prepossessions, but may easily be brought back to their true proportions and made historical and reasonable. A famous specimen of this kind of treatment is Schleiermacher's fancy of the death on the cross having been a swoon, and the resurrection of Jesus a recovery from this swoon. Victorious indeed, whatever may be in other ways his own shortcomings, is Strauss's demolition of this fancy of Schleiermacher's! Like the rationalistic treatment of Scripture throughout, it makes far more difficulties than it solves, and rests on too narrow a conception of the history of the human mind, and of its diversities of operation and production. It puts us ourselves in the original disciples' place, imagines the original disciples to have been men rational in our sense and way, and then explains their record as it might be made explicable if it were ours. And it may safely be said that in this fashion it is *not* explicable. Imaginations so little creative, and with so substantial a framework of fact for each of their wonderful stories as this theory assumes, would never have created so much as they did; at least, they could not have done so and retained their manifest simplicity and good faith. They must have fallen, we in like case should fall, into arrangement and artifice.

But the original disciples were *not* men rational in our sense and way. The real wonderfulness of Jesus, and their belief in him, being given, they needed no such full and parallel body of fact for each miracle as we suppose. Some hint and help of fact, undoubtedly, there almost always was, and we naturally seek to explore it. Sometimes our guesses may be right, sometimes wrong, but we can never be *sure*, the range of possibility is so wide; and we may easily make them too elaborate. Shakspeare's explanation is far the soundest :—

> No natural exhalation in the sky,
> No scape of nature, no distemper'd day,
> No common wind, no customed event,
> But they will pluck away his natural cause,
> And call them meteors, prodigies, and signs,
> Abortives, presages, and tongues of heaven.

And it must be remembered, moreover, that of none of these recorders have we, probably, the very original record. The whole record, when we first get it, has passed through at least half a century, or more, of oral tradition,

VI THE NEW TESTAMENT RECORD

and through more than one written account. Miraculous incidents swell and grow apace; they are just the elements of a tradition that swell and grow most. These incidents, therefore, in the history of Jesus, the preternatural things he did, the preternatural things that befell him, are just the parts of the record which are least solid. Beyond the historic outlines of the life of Jesus,—his Galilean origin, his preaching in Galilee, his preaching in Jerusalem, his crucifixion,—much the firmest element in the record is his *words*. Happily it is of these that he himself said : 'The *words* that I speak unto you, they are spirit and they are life.'[1] But in reading them, we have still to bear in mind our governing idea, that they are words of one *inadequately comprehended by his hearers*, men though these be of pureness of heart, discernment to know and love the good, perfect uprightness of intention, faithful simplicity.

What they will have reported best, probably, is discourse where there was the framework of a story and its application to guide them,—discourse such as the parables. Instructive and beautiful as the parables are, however, they have not the importance of the direct teaching of Jesus. But in his direct teaching we are on the surest ground in single sentences, which have their ineffaceable and unforgettable stamp : *My yoke is kindly and my burden light ;—Many are*

[1] John vi. 63.

called, few chosen;—*They that are whole need not a physician, but they that are sick;*—*No man having put his hand to the plough, and looking back, is fit for the kingdom of God.*[1] The longer trains of discourse, and many sayings in immediate connection with miracles, present much more difficulty. Probably there are very few sayings attributed to Jesus which do not contain what he on some occasion actually said, or much of what he actually said. But the connection, the juncture, is plainly often missed; things are put out of their true place and order. Failure of memory would occasionally cause this with any reporters; failure of comprehension would with the reporters of Jesus frequently cause it. The surrounding tradition insensibly biases them, their love of miracles biases them, their eschatology biases them. All these three exercise an attraction on words of Jesus, and draw them into occasions, placings, and turns, which are not exactly theirs. The one safe guide to the extrication and right reception of what comes from Jesus is the internal evidence. And wherever we find what enforces this evidence or builds upon it, there we may be especially sure that we are on the trace of Jesus; because turn or bias in this direction the disciples were more likely to omit from his discourse than to import into it, they were themselves so wholly preoccupied with the evidence from miracles.

[1] Matthew xi. 30; xxii. 14; ix. 12; Luke ix. 62.

VI THE NEW TESTAMENT RECORD

IV

This is what gives such eminency and value to the Fourth Gospel.[1] The confident certainty with which Ewald settles the authorship of this gospel, and assigns it to St. John, is an exhibition of that learned man's weakness. To settle the authorship is impossible, the data are insufficient; but from what data we have, to believe that the Gospel is St. John's is extremely difficult. But, on the other hand, the stress which Ewald, following Luther, lays on this Gospel, the value which he attributes to it, is an exhibition of his power,—of his deep, sure feeling, and true insight, in the essential matters of religious history; and of his superiority, here, to the best of his rivals, Baur, Strauss, and even M. Renan. 'The true evangelical bread,' says Strauss, 'Christians have always gone to the three first Gospels for!' But what, then, means this sentence of Luther,

[1] Some critics object that the Fourth Gospel has been proved by Baur to be entirely unhistorical, and to give for sayings of Jesus, wherever it does not follow the synoptics, the free inventions of some Christian dogmatist of late date. So little do I think Baur to have *proved* this, that I hold adherence to his thesis to be a conclusive sign of the adherent's want of real critical insight. To discuss controversially in the text the date, mode of composition, and character of the Fourth Gospel would be quite unsuitable to the design of the present work. But I have noticed objections, and amongst them this as to my use of the Fourth Gospel, elsewhere. See *God and the Bible: A Review of Objections to Literature and Dogma.*

who stands as such a good, though favourable, representative of ordinary Christianity: 'John's Gospel is the one proper Head-Gospel, and far to be preferred to the three others'? Again, M. Renan, often so ingenious as well as eloquent, says that the narrative and incidents in the Fourth Gospel are probably in the main historical, the discourses invented. Reverse the proposition, and it would be more plausible! The narrative, so meagre, and skipping so unaccountably backwards and forwards between Galilee and Jerusalem, might well be thought, not indeed invented, but a matter of infinitely little care and attention to the writer of the Gospel, a mere slight framework in which to set the doctrine and discourses of Jesus. The doctrine and discourses of Jesus, on the other hand, *cannot* in the main be the writer's, because in the main they are clearly out of his reach.

The Fourth Gospel delights the heart of M. Burnouf. For its writer shows, M. Burnouf thinks, signal traces of the Aryan genius, has much to favour the notion that religion is a metaphysical conception, and was perhaps even capable, with time, of reaching the grand truth that God is a cosmic unity! And undoubtedly the writer of the Fourth Gospel seems to have come in contact, in Asia or Egypt, with Aryan metaphysics whether from India or Greece; and to have had this advantage, whatever it amounts to, in writing his Gospel. But who,

VI THE NEW TESTAMENT RECORD

that has eyes to read, cannot see the difference between the places in his Gospel, such as the introduction, where the writer speaks in his own person, and the places where Jesus himself speaks? The moment Jesus speaks, the metaphysical apparatus falls away, the simple intuition takes its place; and wherever in the discourse of Jesus the metaphysical apparatus is intruded, it jars with the context, breaks the unity of the discourse, impairs the thought, and comes evidently from the writer, not Jesus. It may seem strange and incredible to M. Burnouf that metaphysics should not always confer the superiority upon their possessor; but such is the case.

Who, again, cannot understand that the philosophical acquirements of the author of the Fourth Gospel, like the rabbinical training and intellectual activity of Paul, though they may have sometimes led each of them astray, must yet have given each of them a range of thought, and an enlarged mental horizon, enabling them to perceive and follow ideas of Jesus which escaped the ken of the more scantily endowed authors of the synoptical Gospels? Plato sophisticates somewhat the genuine Socrates; but it is very doubtful whether the culture and mental energy of Plato did not give him a more adequate vision of this true Socrates than Xenophon had. It proves nothing for the superiority of the first three

Gospels that their authors are without the logic of Paul and the metaphysics of John (by this commonly received name let us for shortness' sake call the author of the Fourth Gospel), and that Jesus also was without them. Jesus was without them because he was above them; the authors of the synoptical Gospels because they were (we say it without any disrespect) below them. Therefore, the author of the Fourth Gospel, by the very characters which make him inferior to Jesus, was made superior to the three synoptics, and better able than they to seize and reproduce the higher teaching of Jesus.

Does it follow, then, that his picture of Christ's teaching can have been his own invention? By no means; since Christ's teaching is as plainly over his head (at that time of day it could not have been otherwise) as it is over theirs. He deals in miracles as confidingly as they do, while unconsciously indicating, far more than they do, that the evidence of miracles is superseded. In those two great chapters, the fifth and sixth, where Jesus deals with the topics of life, death, and judgment, and with his thesis: *He that eateth me shall live by me!*[1] invaluable and full of light as is what is given, the eschatology and the materialising conceptions of the writer do yet evidently intervene, as they did with all the disciples, as they did with the

[1] John vi. 57.

VI THE NEW TESTAMENT RECORD

Jews in general, to hinder a perfectly faithful mirroring of the thought of Jesus. We have already remarked how his metaphysical acquirements intervene in like manner. In the discourse with Nicodemus in the third chapter, from the thirteenth verse to the end, phrases and expressions of Jesus of the highest worth are scattered; but they are manifestly set in a short theological lecture interposed by the writer himself, a lecture which is, as a whole, without vital connection with the genuine discourse of Jesus, and needing only to be carefully studied side by side with this for its disparateness to become apparent.

But a failure of right understanding, which will be visible to every one, occurs with this writer in his seventh chapter. Jesus, with a reference to words of the second Isaiah,[1] says here: 'He that believeth on me, as the Scripture saith, out of his belly shall flow rivers of living water.'[2] The thought is plain; it belongs to the same order as the thought of the saying: 'If any thirst, let him come unto me and drink'; or of the words to the woman of Samaria: 'If thou hadst known the gift of God, and who it is that talketh with thee, thou wouldst have asked of him and he would have given thee living water.' It means that a man, receiving

---

[1] Chap. lviii. 10; where it is promised to the righteous: 'Thou shalt be like a watered garden, and like a spring of water, whose waters fail not.'   [2] John vii. 38.

Jesus, obtains a source of refreshment for himself and becomes a source of refreshment for others; and it means this generally, without any limitation to a special time. But the reporter explains: 'Now this he said concerning the Spirit (*Pneuma*) which they who believed on him should receive; for *Pneuma* was not yet, because Jesus was not yet glorified.'[1] A clearer instance of a narrow and mechanical interpretation of a great and free thought can hardly be imagined; and the words of Jesus himself enable us here to control the inadequacy of the interpretation, and to make it palpable.

So that the superior point of view in the Fourth Gospel, the more spiritual treatment of things, the insistence on internal evidence, not external, cannot, we say, be the writer's, for they are above him; and while his gifts and acquirements are such as to make him report them, they are not such as to enable him to originate them. The great evidential line of this Gospel: 'You are always talking about God, and about your founder Abraham, the father of God's faithful people; here is a man who says nothing of his own head, who tells you the truth, as he has learnt it of God; if you were really of God you would hear the words of God! if you were really Abraham's children you would follow the truth like Abraham!'—this simple but profound line,

---

[1] John vii. 39.

VI THE NEW TESTAMENT RECORD

sending Israel back to amend its conventional, barren notions of God, of righteousness, and of the founders of its religion, sending it to explore them afresh, to sound them deeper, to gather from them a new revelation and a new life, was, we say, at once too simple and too profound for the author of the Fourth Gospel to have invented. Our endless gratitude is due to him, however, for having caught and preserved so much of it. And our business is to keep hold of the clue he has thus given to us, and to use it as profitably as possible.

V

Truly then, some one will exclaim, we may say with the 'Imitation': *Magna ars est scire conversari cum Jesu!* And so it is. To extract from his reporters the true Jesus entire, is even impossible; to extract him in considerable part is one of the highest conceivable tasks of criticism. And it is vain to use that favourite argument of popular theology that man could never have been left by Providence in difficulty and obscurity about a matter of so much importance to him. For the cardinal rule of our present inquiry is that rule of Newton's: *Hypotheses non fingo;* and this argument of popular theology rests on the eternal hypothesis, of a magnified and non-natural man at the head of mankind's and the world's affairs. And a further answer is, that, as to the argument itself, even if we allowed the hypothesis, yet the course of things, so far as we can see, is *not* so; they do *not* proceed in this fashion. Because a man has frequently to make sea-passages, he is *not* gifted with an immunity from sea-sickness; because a thing is of the highest interest and importance to know, it is *not*, therefore, easy to know; on the contrary, in general, in proportion to its magnitude it is difficult, and requires time.

But the right commentary on the sentence of the 'Imitation' is given by the 'Imitation' itself in the sentence following: *Esto humilis et pacificus, et erit tecum Jesus!* What men could take at the hands of Jesus, what they could use, what could save them, he made as clear as light; and Christians have never been able, even if they would, to miss seeing it. No, never; but still they have superadded to it a vast *Aberglaube*, an after or extra-belief of their own; and the *Aberglaube* has pushed on one side, for very many, the saving doctrine of Jesus, has hindered attention from being riveted on this and on its line of growth and working, has nearly effaced it, has developed all sorts of faults contrary to it. This *Aberglaube* has sprung out of a false criticism of the literary records in which the doctrine is conveyed; what is called 'orthodox divinity' is, in fact, an immense literary misapprehension. Having caused the saving doctrines enshrined in these records to be neglected, and having

VI THE NEW TESTAMENT RECORD

credited the records with existing for the sake of its own *Aberglaube*, this blunder now threatens to cause the records themselves to be neglected by all those (and their numbers are fast increasing) whom its own *Aberglaube* fills with impatience and aversion. Therefore it is needful to show the line of growth of this *Aberglaube*, and its delusiveness; to show anew, and with more detail than we have admitted hitherto, the line of growth of Jesus Christ's doctrine, and the far-reaching sanctions, the inexhaustible attractiveness, the grace and truth, with which he invested it. But the doctrine itself is essentially simple; and what *is* difficult,—the literary criticism of the documents containing the doctrine,—is not the doctrine.

This literary criticism, however, *is* extremely difficult. It calls into play the highest requisites for the study of letters;—great and wide acquaintance with the history of the human mind, knowledge of the manner in which men have thought, of their way of using words and of what they mean by them, delicacy of perception and quick tact, and, besides all these, a favourable moment and the 'Zeit-Geist.' And yet every one among us criticises the Bible, and thinks it is of the essence of the Bible that it can be thus criticised with success! And the Four Gospels, the part of the Bible to which this sort of criticism is most applied and most confidently, are just the part which for literary criticism is infinitely the hardest, however simple they may look, and however simple the saving doctrine they contain really is. For Prophets and Epistlers speak for themselves; but in the Four Gospels reporters are speaking for Jesus, who is far above them.

Now, we all know what the literary criticism of the mass of mankind is. To be worth anything, literary and scientific criticism require, both of them, the finest heads and the most sure tact; and they require, besides, that the world and the world's experience shall have come some considerable way. But, ever since this last condition has been fulfilled, the finest heads for letters and science, the surest tact for these, have turned themselves in general to other departments of work than criticism of the Bible, this department being occupied already in such force of numbers and hands, if not of heads, and there being so many annoyances and even dangers in freely approaching it. As our Reformers were to Shakspeare and Bacon in tact for letters and science, or as Luther, even, was to Goethe in this respect, such almost has on the whole been, since the Renascence, the general proportion in rate of power for criticism between those who have given themselves to secular letters and science, and those who have given themselves to interpreting the Bible, and who, in conjunction with the popular interpretation of it both traditional and contemporary, have made what is

VI THE NEW TESTAMENT RECORD

called 'orthodox theology.' It is as if some simple and saving doctrines, essential for men to know, were enshrined in Shakspeare's *Hamlet* or in Newton's *Principia* (though the Gospels are really a far more complex and difficult object of criticism than either); and a host of second-rate critics, and official critics, and what is called 'the popular mind' as well, threw themselves upon *Hamlet* and the *Principia*, with the notion that they could and should extract from these documents, and impose on us for our belief, not only the saving doctrines enshrined there, but also the right literary and scientific criticism of the entire documents. A pretty mess they would make of it! and just this sort of mess is our so-called orthodox theology. And its professors are nevertheless bold, overweening, and even abusive, in maintaining their criticism against all questioners; although really, if one thinks seriously of it, it was a kind of impertinence in such professors to attempt any such criticism at all.

Happily, the faith that saves is attached to the saving doctrines in the Bible, which are very simple; not to its literary and scientific criticism, which is very hard. And no man is to be called 'infidel' for his bad literary and scientific criticism of the Bible; but if he were, how dreadful would the state of our orthodox theologians be! They themselves freely fling about this word *infidel* at all those who reject their literary and scientific criticism, which turns out to be quite false. It would be but just to mete to them with their own measure, and to condemn them by their own rule; and, when they air their unsound criticism in public, to cry indignantly: *The Bishop of So-and-So, the Dean of So-and-So, and other infidel lecturers of the present day!* or: *That rampant infidel, the Archdeacon of So-and-So, in his recent letter on the Athanasian Creed!* or: '*The Rock*,' '*The Church Times*,' *and the rest of the infidel press!* or: *The torrent of infidelity which pours every Sunday from our pulpits!* Just would this be, and by no means inurbane; but hardly, perhaps, Christian. Therefore we will not permit ourselves to say it; but it is only kind to point out, in passing, to these loud and rash people to what they expose themselves, at the hands of adversaries less scrupulous than we are.

CHAPTER VII

THE TESTIMONY OF JESUS TO HIMSELF

WE have said,—and it cannot be repeated too often,—that what is called orthodox theology is, in fact, an immense misunderstanding of the Bible, due to the junction of a talent for abstruse reasoning with much literary inexperience. It cannot be repeated too often; because our dogmatic friends seem to imagine that the truth of their dogma is conceded on all hands, and that the only objection is to the harsh or over-rigid way in which it is put. Dr. Pusey and the *Church Review* assume that what the Athanasian Creed, for instance, does, is ' to take up *the admitted facts of Christian faith*, and arrange them sentence after sentence'; and then they ask us why we should be so squeamish about ' letting the Prayer Book contain once, at least, the statement that Christian faith is necessary to salvation.' Others, we know, talk of the contest going on between ' definite religion,' ' religion with the sinew and bone of doctrine,' and ' indefinite religion,' ' nerveless religion,' ' vague, negative, and cloudy religion'; and Lord Salisbury, as we have seen, declares that 'religion is no more to be severed from dogma than light from the sun.'

To be sure, to make this maxim of Lord Salisbury's indisputable, it ought to run: 'Religion is no more to be severed from *the true doctrine of religion* than light from the sun.' And *dogma* and *the true doctrine of religion* are not exactly synonyms. Dogma means, not necessarily a *true* doctrine, but merely a doctrine or system of doctrine *determined, decreed, received*. Lord Salisbury, however, takes it as in this case another word for *truth*, and so do the other speakers. And they accordingly represent their opponents as either secret enemies of the truth of religion, men who are, as the *Rock* says in a Biblical figure addressed to the Dean of Westminster, 'the degenerate plant of a strange vine bringing forth the grapes of Sodom and the clusters of Gomorrah'; or, at best, as amiable, soft-headed people, afraid of clear thought and plain speech, and requiring with their light a very unnecessary dose of sweetness.

We, however, try to keep our love of sweetness within reasonable bounds; and the *Rock* will hardly call *us* a Gomorrah vine, when we agree to say heartily after it, as we do, that 'Christian faith is necessary to salvation.' But what *is* Christian faith? Is it 'the admitted facts taken up and arranged, sentence after sentence, in the Athanasian Creed'? Are these facts *admitted?*—the whole question is here. So far from these facts being *admitted*, or from the enumeration of them being the enumeration of *the facts of the Christian faith*, we say that they are deductions from the Bible of matters which are not the real matters of Christian faith at all; and that, moreover, they are false deductions from the Bible, blunders arising from a want of skill and experience in dealing with a very complex literary problem.

Therefore we can honestly tell our dogmatic friends that we agree with them in disliking an indefinite religion, in preferring a definite one. Our quarrel with them is, not that they define religion, but that they define it so abominably. And to the eloquent and impetuous Chancellor of Oxford, who cannot away with a hazy amiability in religious matters, and brandishes before us his dogma, not vague, he says, but *precise:*— 'Precise enough,' we answer, 'precisely wrong!' And having thus, we hope, put ourselves right with our adversaries as to the real question between us and them, we will proceed with our endeavour to free the Bible,—by showing that it is not science but literature, by following it continuously and by interpreting it naturally,—to free the Bible from the serious dangers with which their advocacy threatens it. Because, when the bishops talk of 'doing something for the Godhead of the Eternal Son,' they are doing nothing, we say, for the Bible, they are endangering it. For their notions about the Godhead of the Eternal Son, and what it is, cannot possibly stand; and yet these notions they have drawn, they tell us, from the Bible, they impute them to the Bible. But they have drawn them wrongly, and the Bible is to be made answerable for no such doctrine. And we have now come to that point where we may see, clearer than we were in a position to see before, what is rightly to be drawn from the Bible on this matter, and what the doctrine of Jesus himself about his own Godhead really is.

II

Following the Bible continuously and interpreting it naturally, we saw the people of 'the Eternal that loveth righteousness,' and that 'blesseth the man that putteth his trust in Him,'[1] we saw Israel—confounded and perplexed by the misfortunes of God's people and the success of the unrighteous world—construct a vast *Aberglaube*, an after or extra-belief, according to which there should come about, in no distant future, a grand and wonderful change. God should send his Messiah, judge the world, punish the wicked, and restore the kingdom to Israel. For Israel's original revelation and intuition had been: *The Eternal loveth righteousness: to him that ordereth his conversation right shall be shown the*

[1] Psalm xi. 7; xxxiv. 8.

salvation of God.[1] And the natural corollary from this was: *As the whirlwind passeth, so is the wicked no more; but the righteous is an everlasting foundation.*[2]

Both the revelation and the corollary from it were true; but the virtue of both, for Israel, turned upon knowing what *righteousness* and *righteous* meant. And this indispensable intuition Israel is always represented as having once had, and with time in great measure lost. 'Stand ye in the ways and see,' says Jeremiah, 'and ask for *the old paths*, where is *the good way*, and walk therein, and ye shall find rest for your souls.'[3] The prophets may be seen trying to reawaken in Israel this intuition, by inculcating inwardness, humbleness, sincerity. But the mass of people naturally inclined to place righteousness rather in something mechanically to be given or done,—in being endowed with the character of God's chosen people, or in punctually observing a law full of minute observances. And the promises to righteousness they in like manner construed as promises of things material: a mighty Jewish kingdom, God's people 'shepherding the nations with a rod of iron,'[4] the heathen licking the dust.

This material conception of the promises to righteousness fell in with the mechanical conception of righteousness itself, and each

---

[1] Psalm xi. 7; l. 23. [2] Proverbs x. 25.
[3] Jeremiah vi. 16. [4] Rev. xix. 15 and Psalm ii. 9.

heightened the hurtfulness of the other. Between them both, a type of soul more and more hard, impervious, and impracticable, was formed in the Jewish people; and the intuition, in which their greatness began, died out more and more. There still remained of it so much as this: that of all the nations of the world they were the only one that felt the all-importance of righteousness, and the eternity of the promises made to it. But what righteousness really was they knew not; and their situation, when Jesus Christ came, is admirably summed up in these two verses of prophecy, which every one who wishes for a clear sense of the Jews' relations with Jesus would do well to write as a reminder on the blank page of his Bible between the Old Testament and the New:—

'*Forasmuch as this people draw near me with their mouth, and with their lips do honour me, but have removed their heart from me, and their fear towards me is taught by the precept of men;*

'*Therefore, behold, I will proceed to do a marvellous work among this people, even a marvellous work and a wonder; for the wisdom of the wise man shall perish, and the understanding of their prudent men shall be hid.*'[1]

Meanwhile, the Jews were full of their *Aberglaube,* their added or extra-belief in a Messianic advent, a great judgment, a world-wide reign of the saints; and it is well to have distinctly before

---

[1] Isaiah xxix. 13, 14.

VII THE TESTIMONY OF JESUS

us the main texts which they had gathered from the Old Testament in support of this belief, and which were in everybody's mind and mouth. They are all indicated to us by the New Testament. Moses had said: 'The Eternal thy God will raise up unto thee a Prophet from the midst of thee, of thy brethren, like unto me; unto him shall ye hearken.'[1] In the Psalms it was written: 'The Eternal hath sworn a faithful oath unto David: *Of the fruit of thy body will I set upon thy seat; thy seed will I stablish for ever, and set up thy throne from one generation to another.*'[2] Isaiah had said: 'There shall come forth a Rod out of the stem of Jesse and a Branch shall grow out of his roots; and the Spirit of the Eternal shall rest upon him, and he shall smite the earth with the breath of his mouth, and with the breath of his lips shall he slay the wicked.'[3] Finally, Malachi, the last prophet, had announced from God: 'Behold, I will send you Elijah the prophet before the coming of the great and dreadful day of the Eternal.'[4]

These may stand, perhaps, as four fundamental texts forming the ground for popular Jewish *Aberglaube* as it developed itself; and it will be seen of what large and loose construction they admit. But the ground-plan thus given was filled out from later and inferior scriptures, full of the spirit of the time, grandiose, but turbid

[1] Deut. xviii. 15. [2] Psalm cxxxii. 11; lxxxix. 4.
[3] Isaiah xi. 1, 2, 4. [4] Malachi vi. 5.

and phantasmagoric, such as the Book of Enoch and the Book of Daniel. The Book of Daniel is in our Bibles; we can all verify there the elements which constituted, when Jesus Christ came, the popular religious belief and expectation of the Jews. It may be hoped that we ourselves, most of us, read other parts of the Bible far more than the Book of Daniel; but we know how, in general, those who use the Bible most unintelligently have a peculiar fondness for the apocalyptic and phantasmagoric parts of it. The Book of Daniel gave form and body to the *Prophet* of Moses, the *seed of David* of the Psalms, *the great and dreadful day* of Malachi; it enabled the popular imagination to see and figure them. 'A time of trouble such as never was since there was a nation to that time! The Ancient of days did sit, whose garment was white as snow and the hair of his head like the pure wool; his throne was like the fiery flame; the judgment was set and the books were opened. And behold, one like the Son of Man came with the clouds of heaven, and came to the Ancient of days, and there was given him dominion and glory, that all people, nations, and languages should serve him; his dominion is an everlasting dominion which shall not pass away. And judgment was given to the saints of the Most High, and the time came that the saints possessed the kingdom. At that time the people of God shall be delivered, every one that shall be found written

VII   THE TESTIMONY OF JESUS

in the book; and many of them that sleep in dust shall awake, some to everlasting life, and some to shame and everlasting contempt.'[1]

Other figures which laid hold on men's imaginations the Book of Enoch supplied. It told how, in the great visitation: 'They shall rise up to destroy one another, neither shall a man acknowledge his friend and his brother, nor the son his father and his mother.' It told how: 'Ye shall enter into the holes of the earth and into the cliffs of the rocks'; and how, finally, the proud rulers of the world 'shall see the Son of Man sitting on the throne of his glory.' The Book of Enoch described this Son of Man, also, as 'The Son of Man, living with the Lord of Spirits'; 'The Elect One, whom the Lord of Spirits hath gifted and glorified.' Both books gave him the name of 'Son of God' and of 'Messiah.'

It was of all this that the heart of the Jews was full when Jesus Christ came; it was on this that their thoughts fed and their hopes brooded. The old words, God, the Eternal, the Father, the Redeemer, were perpetually in their mouths; but in this connection. The goal of their lives was still, as of old, 'the salvation of God'; but this was what they understood the salvation of God to be. They had lost the intuition, and they had thrown themselves, heart and soul, upon a great extra-belief, or *Aberglaube*.

[1] Daniel xii. 1; vii. 9, 13, 14, 22; xii. 1, 2.

III

Now, if we describe the work of Jesus Christ by a short expression which may give the clearest view of it, we shall describe it thus:—that he came *to restore the intuition*. He came, it is true, to *save*, and to *give eternal life*; but the way in which he did this was by *restoring the intuition*.

This we have already touched upon in our third chapter. We there passed in brief review the teaching of Jesus. But there the objection met us, that what attested Jesus Christ was miracles, and the preternatural fulfilment in him of certain detailed predictions made about him long before; and that such is the teaching of Jesus Christ himself and of the Bible. We had to pause and deal with this objection. And now, as it disperses, we come in full view of our old point again:—that what *did* attest Christ was his *restoration of the intuition*. Jesus Christ found Israel all astray, with an endless talk about God, the law, righteousness, the kingdom, everlasting life,—and no real hold upon any one of them. Israel's old, sure proof of being in the right way, —the sanction of joy and peace,—was plainly wanting; and this was a test which anybody could at once apply. 'O Eternal, *blessed* is the man that putteth his trust in thee,'[1] was a corner-stone of Israel's religion. Now, the Jewish

[1] Psalm lxxxiv. 13.

people, however they might talk about putting their trust in the Eternal, were evidently, as they stood there before Jesus, not blessed at all; and they knew it themselves as well as he did. 'Great *peace* have they who love thy law,'[1] was another corner-stone. But the Jewish people had at that time in its soul as little peace as it had joy and blessedness; it was seething with inward unrest, irritation, and trouble. Yet the way of the Eternal was most indubitably a way of peace and joy; so, if Israel felt no peace and no joy, Israel could not be walking in the way of the Eternal. Here we have the firm unchanging ground on which the operations of Jesus both began, and always proceeded.

And it is to be observed that Jesus by no means gave a new, more precise, scientific definition of God, but took up this term just as Israel used it, to stand for *the Eternal that loveth righteousness.* If therefore this term was, in Israel's use of it, not a term of science, but, as we say, a term of common speech, of poetry and eloquence, *thrown out* at a vast object of consciousness not fully covered by it, so it was in Jesus Christ's use of it also. And if the substratum of real affirmation in the term was, with Israel, not the affirmation of 'a great Personal First Cause, the moral and intelligent Governor of the universe,' but the affirmation of 'an enduring Power, not ourselves, that makes for

[1] Psalm cxix. 165.

righteousness,' so it remained with Jesus Christ likewise. He set going a great process of searching and sifting; but this process had for its direct object the idea of *righteousness*, and only touched the idea of God through this, and not independently of this and immediately. If the idea of righteousness was changed, this implied, undoubtedly, a corresponding change in the idea of the Power that makes for righteousness; but in this manner only, and to this extent, does the teaching of Jesus re-define the idea of God.

But search and sift and renew the idea of righteousness Jesus did. And though the work of Jesus, like the name of God, calls up in the believer a multitude of emotions and associations far more than any brief definition can cover, yet, remembering Jeremy Taylor's advice to avoid exhortations *to get Christ, to be in Christ*, and to seek some more distinct and practical way of speaking of him, we shall not do ill, perhaps, if we summarise to our own minds his work by saying, that he restored the intuition of God through transforming the idea of righteousness; and that, to do this, he brought a *method*, and he brought a *secret*. And of those two great words which fill such a place in his gospel, *repentance* and *peace*,—as we see that his Apostles, when they preached his gospel, preached ' *Repentance* unto life ' [1] and ' *Peace* through Jesus Christ,' [2] — of these two great words, one, *repentance*,

---

[1] Acts xi. 18.   [2] Acts x. 36.

VII THE TESTIMONY OF JESUS

attaches itself, we shall find, to his *method*, and the other, *peace*, to his *secret*.

There was no question between Jesus Christ and the Jews as to the object to aim at. 'If thou wouldst enter into life, keep the commandments,' said Jesus.[1] And Israel, too, on his part, said: 'He that keepeth the commandments keepeth his own soul.'[2] But *what* commandments? The commandments of God; about this, too, there was no question. But: 'Leaving the commandment of God, ye hold the *tradition of men*; ye make the commandment of God of none effect by your *tradition*,' said Jesus.[3] Therefore the commandments which Israel followed were *not* those commandments of God by which a man keeps his own soul, enters into life. And the practical proof of this was, that Israel stood before the eyes of the world manifestly neither blessed nor at peace; yet these characters of bliss and peace the following of the real commandments of God was confessed to give. So a rule, or method, was wanted, by which to determine on what the keeping of the real commandments of God depended.

And Jesus gave one: 'The things that come from *within a man's heart*, they it is which defile him!'[4]

We have seen what an immense matter

[1] Matt. xix. 17.   [2] Prov. xix. 16.
[3] Mark vii. 9, 13.   [4] Matt. xv. 18; Mark vii. 20, 21.

conduct is;—that it is three-fourths of life. We have seen how plain and simple a matter it is, so far as knowledge is concerned. We have seen how, moreover, philosophers are for referring all conduct to one or other of man's two elementary instincts,—the instinct of self-preservation and the reproductive instinct. It is the suggestions of one or other of these instincts, philosophers say, which call forth all cases in which there is scope for exercising morality, or conduct. And this does, we saw, cover the facts well enough. For we can run up nearly all faults of conduct into two classes — faults of temper and faults of sensuality; to be referred, all of them, to one or other of these two instincts. Now, Jesus not only says that things coming from within a man's heart defile him, he adds expressly what these things that, coming from within a man, defile him, are. And what he enumerates are the following: 'Evil thoughts, adulteries, fornications, murders, stealings, greeds, viciousnesses, fraud, dissoluteness, envy, evil-speaking, pride, folly.'[1] These fall into two groups: one, of faults of self-assertion, graspingness, and violence, all of which we may call faults of *temper;* and the other, of faults of *sensuality*. And the two groups, between them, do for practical purposes cover all the range of faults proceeding from these two sources, and therefore all the range of

[1] Mark vii. 21, 22.

VII THE TESTIMONY OF JESUS

conduct. So the motions or impulses to faults of *conduct* were what Jesus said the real commandments of God are concerned with. And it was plain what such faults are; but, to make assurance more sure, he went farther and said what they are. But no outward observances were *conduct*, were that keeping of the commandments of God which was the keeping of a man's own soul and made him enter into life. To have the *heart* and *thoughts* in order as to certain matters, was conduct.

This was the 'method' of Jesus: the setting up a great unceasing inward movement of attention and verification in matters which are three-fourths of human life, where to see true and to verify is not difficult, the difficult thing is to care and to attend. And the inducement to attend was because joy and peace, missed on every other line, were to be reached on this.

'Keep judgment and do righteousness!'[1] had not been guidance enough. The Jews found themselves taking 'meats and drinks and divers washings' for judgment; taking for righteousness 'gifts and sacrifices which cannot perfect the worshipper as to his *conscience*'[2] (here is the word of Jesus!); tithing mint, anise and cummin;[3] saying to a father or mother, when filial succour was claimed, *It is Corban!*[4] —evil disposed, and not at all blessed. But:

[1] Isaiah lvi. 1.
[2] Hebrews ix. 9, 10.
[3] Matthew xxiii. 23.
[4] Mark vii. 11.

'As to all wherein what men commonly call *conduct* is exercised,—eating, drinking, ease, pleasure, money, the intercourse of the sexes, the giving full swing to one's tempers and instincts, —as to all this, watch attentively what passes *within* you, that you may obey the voice of conscience! so you will keep God's commandment and be blessed';—this is the new and much more exact guidance. 'The things that come from *within* a man's *heart*, *they* defile him! cleanse the *inside* of the cup! beware of the leaven of the Pharisees, which is *insincerity!* judge not after the *appearance*, but judge *righteous* judgment!'[1]—this, we say, is the 'method' of Jesus. To it belongs his use of that important word which in the Greek is 'metanoia.' We translate it *repentance*, a groaning and lamenting over one's sins; and we translate it wrong. Of 'metanoia,' according to the meaning of Jesus, the bewailing one's sins was a small part. The main part was something far more active and fruitful—the setting up an immense *new inward movement* for obtaining one's rule of life. And 'metanoia,' accordingly, is: *A change of the inner man.*

Mention and recommendation of this inwardness there often was, we know, in prophet or psalmist. But to make mention of it was one thing, to erect it into a positive method was another. Christianity has made it so familiar,

[1] Matthew xv. 18; xxiii. 16; Luke xii. 1; John vii. 24.

VII   THE TESTIMONY OF JESUS

that to give any freshness to one's words about it is now not easy; but to its first recipients it was abundantly fresh and novel. It was the introduction, in morals and religion, of the famous *know thyself* of the Greeks; and this among a people deeply serious, but also wedded to moral and religious routine, and singularly devoid of flexibility and play of mind. For them it was a revolution. Of course the hard thing is, not to *say*, 'Cleanse the inside of the cup,' but to make people *do* it. In morals and religion, the man who is 'founded upon rock' is always, as Jesus said, the man who *does*, never the man who only *hears*.[1] To say, 'Look within,' was therefore not everything; yet we none of us, probably, enough feel the power which at first resided in the mere saying of it as Jesus said it. And this is because his words have become so trite to us, that we fail to see how powerfully they were all adapted to call forth the new habit of inwardness; and if we want to see this, we must for a time either re-translate his words for ourselves, or paraphrase them. And not only the words he employed, but also the words he occasioned; the words which the effect produced by him made men use about him. Just as it is well to substitute *Eternal* for *Lord*, and *the good news* for *the gospel*, so we must put new words in the place of the now hackneyed *repentance*, *truth*, *grace*, *spirit*, if we wish at all to know how these

[1] Matthew vii. 24.

words worked originally. 'Metanoia,' we have seen, is a change of the inner man. *Repentance unto life* was *a life-giving change of the inner man.* 'Aletheia' is not so well rendered *truth*, which is often speculative only, as it is *reality*. 'Charis' is the boon of *happiness*.[1] Instead, then, of: 'Grace and truth came through Jesus Christ,' let us say: '*Happiness and reality* came through Jesus Christ.' Instead of: 'To know the grace of God in truth,' let us say: 'To know the *happiness* of God in *reality*.' Even though the new rendering be not so literally correct as the old, not permanently to be adopted, it will prove of use to us for a while to show us how the words worked.

Above all is this true in regard to the word *spirit*, made so mechanical by popular religion, that it has come to mean *a person without a body*, which is the child's definition of a ghost. This word, specially designed by Jesus to serve in restoring the intuition, and in bringing Israel's religion face to face with Israel's inward consciousness, is rather *influence*. 'Except a man be born of *cleansing* and of *a new influence*, he cannot enter into the kingdom of God.[2] Instead of proclaiming what the Bishop of Gloucester calls 'the blessed truth that the God of the

[1] Professor F. Newman has truly remarked that this rendering is not closely accurate. But see what I have said in the next sentence but one. The most literal rendering of a word such as *charis* is not, in the present case, what we want.

[2] John iii. 5.

VII THE TESTIMONY OF JESUS

universe is a PERSON,' Jesus uttered a warning for all time against this unprofitable jargon, when he said: 'God is an *influence*, and those who would serve him must serve him not by any form of words or rites, but by inward motion and in reality!' No rendering can too strongly bring out the original bent to inwardness and intuition in language of this kind, which has now become almost formal to us.

Just the same bent appears in Jesus taking, as the rule for a man's action in regard to another's conduct, simply and solely the effect on the actor's own character. This is what is so striking in the story of the woman taken in adultery. '*Let him that is without fault cast the first stone! and they were all convicted by their conscience.*' And who is without fault, and where is the judge whom the conviction of conscience might not thus paralyse? Punishment, then, is impossible; and, with punishment, government and society! But punishment, government, and society, are all of them after-inventions; creations of assemblages of men, and not matter of the individual's intuition. Jesus regarded simply what was primary,—the individual and the intuition. And in truth, if the individual and the intuition are once reached, the after-inventions may be left to take care of themselves. And if conscience ever became enough of a power, there would be no offenders to punish. This is the true line of religion; it was the line of Jesus. To work the renovation needed, he concentrated his efforts upon a method of *inwardness,* of taking counsel of *conscience.*

IV

But for this world of busy inward movement created by the *method* of Jesus, a rule of action was wanted; and this rule was found in his *secret.* It was this of which the Apostle Paul afterwards possessed himself with such energy, and called it 'the word of the cross,'[1] or, *necrosis,* 'dying.' The rule of action St. Paul gave was: 'Always bearing about in the body the *dying* of Jesus, that the *life* also of Jesus may be made manifest in our body!'[2] In the popular theurgy, these words are commonly referred to what is called 'pleading the blood of the covenant,'—relying on the death and merits of Christ, in pursuance of the contract originally passed in the Council of the Trinity, to satisfy God's wrath against sinners and to redeem us. But they do really refer to words of Jesus, often and often repeated, and of which the following may very well stand as pre-eminently representative: '*He that loveth his life shall lose it, and he that hateth his life in this world shall keep it unto life eternal. Whosoever*

---

[1] ὁ λόγος ὁ τοῦ σταυροῦ.—1 Cor. i. 18.
[2] 2 Cor. iv. 10 (according to the Vatican manuscript).

VII THE TESTIMONY OF JESUS

will come after me, let him renounce himself, and take up his cross daily, and follow me.'[1]

These words, or words like them, were repeated again and again, so that no reporter could miss them. No reporter did miss them. We find them, as we find the 'method' of conscience, in all the four Gospels. Perhaps there is no other maxim of Jesus which has such a combined stress of evidence for it, and may be taken as so eminently his. And no wonder. For the maxim contains his *secret*, the secret by which, emphatically, his gospel 'brought life and immortality to light.'[2] Christ's 'method' directed the disciple's eye inward, and set his consciousness to work; and the first thing his consciousness told him was, that he had two selves pulling him different ways. Till we attend, till the *method* is set at work, it seems as if 'the wishes of the flesh and of the current thoughts'[3] were to be followed as a matter of course; as if an impulse to do a thing must mean that we should do it. But when we attend, we find that an impulse to do a thing is really in itself no reason at all why we should do it; because impulses proceed from two sources, quite different, and of quite different degrees of authority. St. Paul contrasts them as the inward man, and the man in our members; the mind of the flesh, and the

---

[1] John xii. 25; Luke ix. 23.   [2] 2 Tim. i. 10.
[3] τὰ θελήματα τῆς σαρκὸς καὶ τῶν διανοιῶν.—Ephesians ii. 3.

spiritual mind.[1] Jesus contrasts them as *life*, properly so named, and *life in this world*.[2] And the moment we seriously attend to conscience, to the suggestions which concern practice and conduct, we can see plainly enough from which source a suggestion comes, and that the suggestions from one source are to overrule those from the other.

But this is a negative state of things, a reign of check and constraint, a reign, merely, of morality. Jesus changed it into what was positive and attractive, lighted it up, made it religion, by the idea of *two lives*. One of them *life* properly so called, full of light, endurance, felicity, in connection with the higher and permanent self; and the other of them life improperly so called, in connection with the lower and transient self. The first kind of life was already a cherished ideal with Israel ('Thou wilt show me the path of *life!*');[3] and a man might be placed in it, Jesus said, by dying to the second. For it is to be noted that our common expression, '*deny* himself,' is an inadequate and misleading version of the words used by Jesus. To deny one's self is commonly understood to mean that one refuses one's self something. But what Jesus says is: 'Let a

---

[1] Romans chap. viii.
[2] John xii. 25. The strict grammatical and logical connection of the words ἐν τῷ κόσμῳ τούτῳ is with ὁ μισῶν, but the sense and effect is as given above. [3] Ps. xvi. 11.

man *disown* himself, *renounce* himself, die as regards his old self, and so live.' *Himself*, the *old man*, the *life in this world*, meant following those 'wishes of the flesh and of the current thoughts' which Jesus had, by his method, already put his disciples in the way of sifting and scrutinising, and of trying by the standard of conformity to conscience.

Thus, after putting him by his method in the way to find *what* doing righteousness was, by his secret Jesus put the disciple in the way of *doing* it. For the breaking the sway of what is commonly called *one's self*, ceasing our concern with it and leaving it to perish, is not, Jesus said, being thwarted or crossed, but *living*. And the proof of this is that it has the characters of life in the highest degree,—the sense of going right, hitting the mark, succeeding. That is, it has the characters of *happiness*; and happiness is, for Israel, the same thing as having the Eternal with us, seeing the salvation of God. 'The tree,' as Jesus said, and as men's common sense and proverbial speech say with him, ' is known by its *fruits* ';[1] and Jesus, then, was to be received by Israel as sent from God, because the secret of Jesus leads to the salvation of God, which is what Israel most desired. *The word of the cross*, in short, turned out to be at the same time *the word of the kingdom*.[2] And to this experimental sanction of

---

[1] Matt. xii. 33. [2] ὁ λόγος τῆς Βασιλείας.—Matt. xiii. 19.

his secret, this sense it gives of having the Eternal on our side and approving us, Jesus appealed when he said of himself: '*Therefore doth my Father love me, because I lay down my life, that I may take it again.*'[1] This, again, in our popular theurgy, is materialised into the First Person of the Trinity approving the Second, because he stands to the contract already in the Council of the Trinity passed. But what it really means is, that the joy of Jesus, of this 'Son of peace,'[2] the 'joy' he was so desirous that his disciples should find 'fulfilled in themselves,'[3] was due to his having himself followed his own secret. And the great counterpart to: *A life-giving change of the inner man*,—the promise: *Peace through Jesus Christ!*[4]—is peace through this secret of his.

Now, the value of this rule that one should die to one's apparent self, live to one's real self, depends upon whether it is true. And true it certainly is;—a profound truth of what our scientific friends, who have a systematic philosophy and a nomenclature to match, and who talk of *Egoism* and *Altruism*, would call, perhaps, psycho-physiology. And we may trace men's experience affirming and confirming it, from a very plain and level account of it to an account almost as high and solemn as that of Jesus. That an opposition there is, in all matter of

---

[1] John x. 17. [2] Luke x. 6.
[3] John xvii. 13. [4] Acts xi. 18; x. 36.

VII THE TESTIMONY OF JESUS

what we call *conduct*, between a man's first impulses and what he ultimately finds to be the real law of his being; that a man accomplishes his right function as a man, fulfils his end, hits the mark, in giving effect to the real law of his being; and that happiness attends his thus hitting the mark,—all good observers report. No statement of this general experience can be simpler or more faithful than one given us by that great naturalist, Aristotle.[1] 'In all wholes made up of parts,' says he, 'there is a ruler and a ruled; throughout nature this is so; we see it even in things without life, they have their *harmony* or *law*. The living being is composed of soul and body, whereof the one is naturally ruler and the other ruled. Now what is natural we are to learn from what fulfils the law of its nature most, and not from what is depraved. So we ought to take the man who has the best disposition of body and soul; and in him we shall find that this is so; for in people that are grievous both to others and to themselves the body may often appear ruling the soul, because such people are poor creatures and false to nature.' And Aristotle goes on to distinguish between the *body*, over which, he says, the rule of the soul is absolute, and the *movement of thought and desire*, over which reason has, says he, 'a constitutional rule,' in words which exactly recall St. Paul's phrase for our double enemy: 'the *flesh* and the *current*

[1] *Politics*, i. 5.

thoughts.' So entirely are we here on ground of general experience. And if we go on and take this maxim from Stobæus : 'All fine acquirement implies a foregoing *effort* of *self-control*' ;[1] or this from Horace : '*Rule* your current self or it will rule *you*! bridle it in and chain it down!'[2] or this from Goethe's autobiography : 'Everything cries out to us that we must *renounce*' ;[3] or still more this from his *Faust:* 'Thou must *go without, go without!* that is the everlasting song which every hour, all our life through, hoarsely sings to us!'[4]—then we have testimony not only to the necessity of this natural law of rule and suppression, but also to the strain and labour and suffering which attend it. But when we come a little further and take a sentence like this of Plato : 'Of sufferings and pains cometh *help*, for it is not possible by any other way to be ridded of our iniquity';[5] then we get a higher strain, a strain like St. Peter's : 'He that hath suffered in the flesh hath ceased from sin';[6] and we are brought to see, not only the *necessity*

---

[1] παντὸς καλοῦ κτήματος πόνος προηγεῖται ὁ κατ' ἐγκράτειαν.
[2] 'Animum rege, qui nisi paret
  Imperat ; hunc frænis, hunc tu compesce catenis.'
[3] 'Alles ruft uns zu, dass wir entsagen sollen.'
[4] 'Entbehren sollst du! sollst entbehren!
  Das ist der ewige Gesang,
  Den unser ganzes Leben lang
  Uns heiser jede Stunde singt.'
[5] δι' ἀλγηδόνων καὶ ὀδυνῶν γίγνεται ἡ ὠφέλεια · οὐ γὰρ οἷόν τε ἄλλως ἀδικίας ἀπαλλάττεσθαι.
[6] 1 Peter iv. 1.

VII   THE TESTIMONY OF JESUS

of the law of rule and suppression, not only the *pain* and *suffering* in it, but also its beneficence. And this positive sense of beneficence, salutariness, and hope, come out yet more strongly when Wordsworth says to Duty: 'Nor know we anything so fair as is the smile upon thy face'; or when Bishop Wilson says: 'They that deny themselves will be sure to find their strength increased, their affections raised, and their inward peace continually augmented'; and most of all, perhaps, when we hear from Goethe: 'Die and come to life! for so long as this is not accomplished thou art but a troubled guest upon an earth of gloom!'[1] But this is evidently borrowed from Jesus, and by one whose testimony is of all the more weight, because he certainly would not have become thus a borrower from Jesus, unless the truth had compelled him.

And never certainly was the joy, which in self-renouncement underlies the pain, so brought out as when Jesus boldly called the suppression of our first impulses and current thoughts: *life, real life, eternal life.* So that Jesus not only *saw* this great necessary truth of there being, as Aristotle says, in human nature a part to rule and a part to be ruled; he saw it so *thoroughly*, that he saw through the suffering at its surface

---

[1] 'Stirb und werde!
   Denn, so lang du das nicht hast,
   Bist du nur ein trüber Gast
   Auf der dunkeln Erde!'

to the joy at its centre, filled it with promise and hope, and made it infinitely attractive. As Israel, therefore, is 'the people of righteousness,' because, though others have perceived the importance of righteousness, Israel, above every one, perceived the *happiness* of it; so self-renouncement, the main factor in conduct or righteousness, is 'the secret of Jesus,' because, although others have seen that it was necessary, Jesus, above every one, saw that it was *peace, joy, life*.

Now, we may observe, that even Aristotle (and it is a mark of his greatness) does not, in the passage we have quoted from him, begin with a complete system of psycho-physiology, and show us where and how and why in this system the rule of renouncement comes in, and draw out for us definitively the law of our being towards which this rule leads up. He says that the rule exists, that it is ancillary to the law of our being, and that we are to study the best men, in whom it most exists, to make us see that it is thus ancillary. He here appeals throughout to a verifying sense, such as we have said that every one in this great but plain matter of conduct really has; he does not appeal to a speculative theory of the system of things, and deduce conclusions from it. And he shows his greatness in this, because the law of our being is *not* something which is already definitively known and can be exhibited as part of a speculative theory of

VII THE TESTIMONY OF JESUS

the system of things; it is something which discovers itself and *becomes*, as we follow (among other things) the rule of renouncement. What we can say with most certainty about the law of our being is, that we find the rule of renouncement practically lead up to it. In matters of practice and conduct, therefore, an experience like this is really a far safer ground to insist on than any speculative theory of the system of things. And to a theory of such sort Jesus never appeals. Here is what characterises his teaching, and distinguishes him, for instance, from the author of the Fourth Gospel. This author handles what we may call theosophical speculation in a beautiful and impressive manner; the introduction to his Gospel is undoubtedly in a very noble and profound strain. But it is *theory;* an intellectual theory of the divine nature and the system of things, which was then, and is still at present, utterly irreducible to experience. And therefore it is impossible even to conceive Jesus himself uttering the introduction to the Fourth Gospel; because *theory* Jesus never touches, but bases himself invariably on experience. True, the experience must, for philosophy, have its place in a theory of the system of human nature, when the theory is perfect; but the point is, that the experience is ripe and solid, and to be used safely, long before the theory. And it was the *experience* which Jesus always used.

Undoubtedly, however, attempts may not improperly be made, even now,—by those, at least, who have a talent for these matters,—to exhibit the experience, with what leads to it and what derives from it, in a system of psycho-physiology. And then, perhaps, it will be found to be connected with other truths of psycho-physiology, such as the unity of life, as it is called, and the impersonality of reason. Only, thus exhibited, it will be philosophy, mental exercitation, and will concern us as a matter of science, not of conduct. And, as the discipline of *conduct* is three-fourths of life, for our æsthetic and intellectual disciplines, real as these are, there is but one-fourth of life left; and if we let art and science divide this one-fourth fairly between them, they will have just one-eighth of life each.

So the exhibition of the truth: '*He that loveth his life shall lose it, and he that hateth his life in this world shall keep it unto life eternal,*' in its order and place as a truth of psycho-physiology, concerns one-eighth of our life and no more. But Jesus, we say, exhibited nothing for the benefit of this one-eighth of us; this is what distinguishes him from all moralists and philosophers, and even from the greatest of his own disciples. How he reached a doctrine we cannot say; but he always exhibited it as an intuition and practical rule, and a practical rule which, if adopted, would have the force of an intuition

VII THE TESTIMONY OF JESUS

for its adopter also. This is why none of his doctrines are of the character of that favourite doctrine of our theologians, 'the blessed truth that the God of the universe is a Person'; because this doctrine is incapable of application as a practical rule, and can never come to have the force of an intuition. But what we call the secret of Jesus: '*He that loveth his life shall lose it, and he that hateth his life in this world shall keep it unto life eternal,*' was a truth of which he could say: 'It is so; try it yourself and you will see it is so, by the sense of going right, hitting the mark, succeeding, *living*, which you will get.'

And the same with the commandment, '*Love one another*,'[1] which is the positive side of the commandment, '*Renounce thyself*,'[2] and, like this, can be drawn out as a truth of psycho-physiology. Jesus exhibited it as an intuition and a practical rule; and as what, by being practised, would, through giving *happiness*, prove its own truth as a rule of life. This, we say, is of the very essence of his secret of self-renouncement, as of his method of inwardness;—that its truth will be found to commend itself by *happiness*, to prove itself by *happiness*. And of the secret more especially is this true. And as we have said, that though there gathers round the word 'God' very much besides, yet we shall in

---

[1] John xiii. 34.
[2] 'We *know* that we have passed from death to life,'—how? '*because we love the brethren.*' See 1 John iii. 14.

general, in reading the Bible, get the surest hold on the word 'God' by giving it the sense of *the Eternal Power, not ourselves, which makes for righteousness*, so we shall get the best hold on many expressions of Jesus by referring them, though they include more, yet primarily and pointedly to his 'secret,' and to the happiness which this contained. *Bread of life, living water*, these are, in general, Jesus, Jesus in his whole being and in his total effect; but in especial they are Jesus as offering his *secret*. And when Jesus says: 'He that eateth me shall live by me!'[1] we shall understand the words best if we think of his *secret*.

And so again with the famous words to the woman by the well in Samaria: 'Whosoever drinketh of *this* water shall thirst again, but whosoever drinketh of the water that I shall give him shall never thirst, but the water that I shall give him shall be in him a fount of water springing up unto everlasting life.'[2] These words, how are we to take them, so as to reach their meaning best? What distinctly *is* this 'water that I shall give him'? Jesus himself and his word, no doubt; yet so we come but to that very notion, which Jeremy Taylor warns us against as vague, of *getting Christ*. The Bishop of Gloucester will tell us, perhaps, that it is 'the blessed truth that the Creator of the universe is a Person,' or the doctrine of the consubstantiality

[1] John vi. 57.   [2] John iv. 13, 14.

VII THE TESTIMONY OF JESUS

of the Eternal Son. But surely it would be a strong figure of speech to say of these doctrines, that a man, after receiving them, could never again feel thirsty! See, on the contrary, how the words suit *the secret:* 'He that loveth his life shall lose it, and he that hateth his life in this world shall keep it unto life eternal.' This 'secret of Jesus,' as we call it, will be found applicable to all the thousand problems which the exercise of conduct daily offers; it alone can solve them all happily, and may indeed be called 'a fount of water springing up unto everlasting life.' And, in general, wherever the words *life* and *death* are used by Jesus, we shall do well to have his 'secret' at hand; for in his thoughts, on these occasions, it is never far off.

And now, too, we can see why it is a mistake, and may lead to much error, to exhibit any series of maxims, like those of the Sermon on the Mount, as the ultimate sum and formula into which Christianity may be run up. Maxims of this kind are but *applications* of the method and the secret of Jesus; and the method and secret are capable of yet an infinite number more of such applications. Christianity is a *source;* no one supply of water and refreshment that comes from it can be called the sum of Christianity.

V

·A method of *inwardness*, a secret of *self-renouncement*;—but can any statement of what Jesus brought be complete, which does not include that element of *mildness* and *sweetness* in which both these worked? To the representative texts already given there is certainly to be added this other: '*Learn of me that I am mild and lowly in heart, and ye shall find rest unto your souls!*'[1] Shall we attach mildness to the *method*, because, without it, a clear and limpid view inwards is impossible? Or shall we attach it to the *secret?* —the dying to faults of temper is a part, certainly, of dying to one's ordinary self, one's *life in this world*. *Mildness*, however, is rather an element in which, in Jesus, both method and secret worked; the medium through which both the method and the secret were exhibited. We may think of it as perfectly illustrated and exemplified in his answer to the foolish question, *Who is the greatest in the kingdom of heaven?*— when, taking a little child and setting him in the midst, he said: 'Whosoever receives the kingdom of God as a little child, the same is the greatest in it.'[2] Here are both inward appraisal and self-renouncement; but what is most admirable is the sweet reasonableness, the

---

[1] Matt. xi. 29.
[2] Matt. xviii. 1-4; Mark ix. 15.

VII THE TESTIMONY OF JESUS

exquisite, mild, winning felicity, with which the renouncement and the inward appraisal are applied and conveyed. And the conjunction of the three in Jesus—the method of inwardness, and the secret of self-renouncement, working in and through this element of mildness—produced the total impression of his 'epieikeia,' or sweet reasonableness; a total impression ineffable and indescribable for the disciples, as also it was irresistible for them, but at which their descriptive words, words like this '*sweet reasonableness*,' and like '*full of grace and truth*,' are thrown out and aimed.[1]

And this total stamp of 'grace and truth,' this exquisite conjunction and balance, in an element of mildness, of a method of inwardness perfectly handled and a self-renouncement perfectly kept, was found in Jesus alone. What are the method of inwardness and the secret of self-renouncement without the sure balance of Jesus, without his *epieikeia*? Much, but very far indeed from what he showed or what he meant; they come to be used blindly, used mechanically, used amiss, and lead to the strangest aberrations. St. Simeon Stylites on his column, Pascal girdled with spikes, Lacordaire flogging himself on his death-bed, are what the *secret* by itself produces. The *method* by itself

---

[1] Bossuet calls him *le débonnaire Jésus;* Cowper speaks of his questioning the disciples going to Emmaus 'with a *kind, engaging* air.'

gives us our political Dissenter, pluming himself on some irrational 'conscientious objections,' and not knowing that with conscience he has done nothing until he has got to the bottom of conscience, and made it tell him *right*. Therefore the disciples of Jesus were not told to believe in his method, or to believe in his secret, but to believe in *him*; they were not told to follow the method or to follow the secret, but they were told: 'Follow *me!*' For it was only by fixing their heart and mind on Jesus that they could learn to use the method and secret right; by '*feeding* on him,' by, as he often said, '*remaining* in him.'

But this is just what Israel had been told to do as regards the Eternal himself. 'I have set the Eternal *always before me*'; 'Mine eyes are *ever toward* the Eternal'; 'The Eternal is the *strength of my life*'; '*Wait*, I say, *on* the Eternal!'[1] Now, then, let us go back again for a little to Israel, and to Israel's belief.

VI

We have seen how the Jews, at the coming of Jesus Christ, had their thoughts full of a grand and turbid phantasmagory;—a vision of God judging the world, sending the Son of Man on the clouds of heaven, taking vengeance on the wicked, restoring the kingdom to Israel.

[1] Psalm xvi. 8; xxv. 15; xxvii. 1, 14.

VII THE TESTIMONY OF JESUS

And we marked the line of texts which this expectation followed: from the 'Prophet' of Moses to the victorious 'Rod out of the stem of Jesse' of Isaiah, and thence to the 'Son of Man,' the 'Son of God,' of the Book of Daniel, and to the 'Messiah.'

But there was *another* line of texts pointing to a servant and emissary of God, besides the line pointing to the Lion of the tribe of Judah, the princely and conquering Root of David. It stood written: 'Behold my servant whom I uphold, mine elect in whom my soul delighteth! I have put my spirit upon him; he shall declare judgment to the Gentiles. He shall not strive nor cry, nor cause his voice to be heard in the street; he shall declare judgment with truth. He shall not fail nor be discouraged, until he set judgment in the earth; far lands wait for his law.'[1] Who is this?

And again: 'He was despised, and we esteemed him not; but he was wounded for our transgressions, he was bruised for our iniquities. All we like sheep were gone astray, we were turned every one to his own way; and the Eternal hath laid on him the iniquity of us all. And he made his grave with the wicked, although he had done no violence; yet it pleased the Eternal to bruise him. When he hath made his life an offering for sin, he shall see his seed, he shall prolong his days, and

[1] Isaiah xlii. 1-4.

the pleasure of the Eternal shall prosper in his hand; he shall see of the travail of his soul and shall be satisfied!'[1] Who, again, is this?

Is it the 'Prophet' like great Moses? Is it the brilliant 'Branch' out of the root of Jesse, smiting the earth with the rod of his mouth, and with the breath of his lips slaying the wicked; with his dominion stretching from the one sea to the other, all things falling down before him, all nations serving him; with his seed to endure for ever, and his throne as the days of heaven? This 'Branch' it was, whom Israel identified with the Messiah coming in the clouds of heaven to give the kingdom to the saints of the Most High, with the Son of Man sitting on the throne of his glory. Was the *afflicted and lowly servant* at the same time the Branch, and therefore the Messiah, the Son of God, and the bringer of the kingdom? Israel never identified them. Here and there he made guesses and snatches at the truth. Momentary elevations of it there were, faint approaches towards connecting the two ideals, isolated tentatives; but the Jewish people at large had never grasped the idea of the identification, and it had never been so presented to them that they *could* grasp it.

And, as we have already said, it was an extraordinary novelty, although the profound

[1] Isaiah liii. 3, 5, 6, 9-11.

VII THE TESTIMONY OF JESUS

and the only true solution of Israel's wonderful history, when this identification was by Jesus boldly made. 'A little while,' the Jews were saying, 'and *the God of heaven shall set up a kingdom which shall never be destroyed.*'[1]—'Nay,' answered Jesus, '*the time is fulfilled and the kingdom of God is close here! change the inner man, and believe the good news!*'[2]—'But,' said the Jews, '*Elias must first come.*'[3] Jesus replied: '*Elias has come already;*[4] John the Baptist, my precursor, who preached a change of the inner man as I do!'—'But *there shall be a time of trouble,*' the Jews urged, '*such as never was since there was a nation to that time; abomination and desolation; a fiery stream issuing from before the throne of the Ancient of days; one like the Son of Man coming with the clouds of heaven!*'[5] Jesus surveyed the fierce and impracticable people before him, with their inevitable future: 'Fear not,' he answered mournfully, '*where the carcase is, there will the eagles be gathered together!*[6] soon enough you will have the affliction such as was not from the beginning of the world to this time, the Son of Man coming, Jerusalem encompassed with armies, abomination and desolation, not one stone of the Temple left on another.'—'*But the judgment shall sit!*' said the Jews, 'and at that time the people shall be delivered, every

---

[1] Dan. ii. 44.   [2] Mark i. 15.   [3] Mark ix. 11.
[4] Matt. xvii. 12.   [5] Dan. xii. 1, 11; vii. 10, 13.
[6] Matt. xxiv. 28.   See the whole chapter, and Luke xxi. 20.

one that shall be found written in the book!'[1] —'And the judgment is coming,' Jesus answered, 'the world-judgment of Jerusalem's ruin![2] but, moreover, to this outward *crisis* shall correspond an inward judgment, the new *crisis* of conscience. The hour is coming, *and now is*, when the dead shall *hear the voice of the Son of God;* and he who heareth shall live!'[3] Every one that is of the truth heareth my voice;[4] the word that I speak, the same shall *judge* him.'[5]—'But the righteous,' the Jews said, '*shall awake to everlasting life!*'[6] —'If a man keep my word,' answered Jesus, '*he shall never see death;*[7] but it shall be in him a fount of water, springing up unto *everlasting life*.'[8]—'But God's Messiah,' finally rejoined the Jews, '*shall shepherd the nations with a rod of iron,*[9] *shall slay the wicked with the breath of his lips!*[10] *his throne shall endure for ever, and his dominion shall be from the one sea to the other! the Gentiles shall be given to him!*'[11]—'Ye know not what spirit ye are of!' said Jesus: 'He is *mild, and lowly in heart;*[12] he *breaks not the bruised reed and quenches not the smoking flax;*[13] he must *suffer many things and be rejected of his generation.*[14] Except a corn of wheat fall to the ground and *die, it abideth alone, but if it die it bringeth forth much*

---

[1] Dan. vii. 10; xii. 1.
[2] Matt. xxiii. 36-39.   [3] John v. 25.   [4] John xviii. 37.
[5] John xii. 48.   [6] Dan. xii. 2.   [7] John viii. 51.
[8] John iv. 14.   [9] Ps. ii. 9.   [10] Isaiah xi. 4.
[11] Ps. lxxxix. 4; lxxii. 8; ii. 8; and Isaiah liv. 3.
[12] Matt. xi. 29.   [13] Matt. xii. 20.   [14] Luke xvii. 25.

VII THE TESTIMONY OF JESUS

fruit ;[1] and *I, if I be lifted up from the earth, will draw all men unto me !*'[2] Then, turning to the disciples : 'Fear not, little flock, for it is your Father's good pleasure *to give you the kingdom !*[3] And other sheep I have, not of this fold ; *they also shall be brought !* and there shall be one flock, one shepherd !'[4]

By a line like this did Jesus identify the two ideals,—the ideal of popular *Aberglaube* and his own. And this is why the phrases of the popular *Aberglaube* come so often from his lips. He was for ever translating it into the sense of the higher ideal, the only sense in which it had truth and grandeur. It was hopeless that the Jews should go along with him. The best of his disciples went along with him but imperfectly, and popular Christianity has fallen far behind the best of his disciples. *The hour is coming, and now is, when the dead shall hear the voice of the Son of God, and they who hear shall live !*[5]—this saying could not lift the Jews out of their Aberglaube into the ideal of Jesus, with its new meaning for the words *life* and *death*. But neither has it lifted popular Christianity ; which out of this and other like sayings has fashioned for itself an Aberglaube precisely corresponding to that of the Jews.

Yet Jesus could not but use the dominant phrases of the Jewish religion, if he was to talk

---

[1] John xii. 24. [2] John xii. 32. [3] Luke xii. 32.
[4] John x. 16. [5] John v. 25.

to the Jewish people about religion at all. And we have now seen that he did use them, and how. And this leads us further, and explains his way of using such words as the *Christ* or *Messiah*, the *Son of Man*, the *Son of God*. For, as the Jews were always talking about the Messiah, so they were always talking, we know, about God. And they believed in God's Messiah after their notion of him, because they believed in God after their notion of *him*;—but both notions were wrong. All their aspirations were now turned towards the Messiah; whoever would do them good, must first change their ideal of the Messiah. But their ideal of God's Messiah depended upon their notion of God. This notion was now false, like their ideal of the Messiah; but once it had been true, or, at least, true comparatively;—once Israel had had the intuition of God as *the Eternal that loveth righteousness*. And the intuition had never been so lost but that it was capable of being revived. To change their dangerous and misleading ideal of God's Messiah, therefore, and to make the Jews believe in the true Messiah, could only be accomplished by bringing them back to a truer notion of God and his righteousness. By this it could, perhaps, be accomplished, but by this only.

And this is what Jesus sought to do. He sought to do it in the way we have seen, by his 'method' and his 'secret.' First, by his 'method'

VII THE TESTIMONY OF JESUS

of a change of the inner man. 'Do not be all abroad, *do not be in the air*,'[1] he said to his nation. 'You look for the kingdom of God. The kingdom of God is the reign of righteousness, God's will done by all mankind. Well, then, seek the kingdom of God! *the kingdom of God is within you!*'[2] And, next, by his 'secret' of peace. '*Renounce thyself, and take up thy cross daily and follow me!*'[3] '*He that loveth his life shall lose it, and he that hateth his life in this world shall keep it unto life eternal.*'[4] And the revolution thus made was so immense, that the least in this new kingdom of heaven, this realm of the 'method' and the 'secret,' was greater, Jesus said, than one who, like John the Baptist, was even greatest in the old realm of Jewish religion.[5] And those who obeyed the gospel of this new kingdom came to the *light*;[6] they had *joy*;[7] they entered into *peace*;[8] they ceased to *thirst*; the word became in them a fount of water springing up unto *everlasting life*.[9] But these were the admitted tests of righteousness, of obeying the voice of the Eternal who loveth righteousness. 'There ariseth *light* for the righteous, and *gladness* for the upright in heart;[10] he that feareth the Eternal, *blessed* is he!'[11]

Now, the special value of the Fourth Gospel

---

[1] μὴ μετεωρίζεσθε.—Luke xii. 29. [2] Luke xvii. 21.
[3] Luke ix. 23. [4] John xii. 25. [5] Matt. xi. 11.
[6] John iii. 21. [7] John xvii. 13. [8] John xvi. 33.
[9] John iv. 14. [10] Ps. xcvii. 11. [11] Ps. cxii. 1.

is, not that it exhibits the method and secret of Jesus,—for all the Gospels exhibit them,—but that it exhibits the establishment of them by means of Israel's own idea of God, cleared and re-awakened. The argument is: 'You are always talking about God, God's word, righteousness; always saying that God is your Father, and will send his Messiah for your salvation. Well, he who receives me shows that he talks about God with a knowledge of what he is saying; he *sets to his seal* that God is true.¹ *He who is of God heareth the words of God;* ² *every one that heareth and learneth of the Father cometh unto me,*³ *and ye have not his word abiding in you, because, whom he hath sent, him ye believe not;* ⁴ *if any one will do God's will he shall know of the doctrine, whether it be of God.*' ⁵ This, therefore, is what Jesus said:—'I, whose message of salvation is: *If a man keep my word he shall never see death!* ⁶ am sent of God; because he who obeys my saying: *Renounce thyself and follow me!* ⁷ shall feel that he truly lives, and that he is following, therefore, Israel's God, of whom it is said: *Thou wilt show me the path of life.*' ⁸

The doctrine therefore is double:—*Renounce thyself*, the secret of Jesus, involving a foregoing exercise of his method; and, *Follow me, who am sent from God!* That is the favourite expression:

¹ John iii. 33. ² John viii. 47. ³ John vi. 45.
⁴ John v. 38. ⁵ John vii. 17. ⁶ John viii. 51.
⁷ Matt. xvi. 24. ⁸ Ps. xvi. 11.

VII THE TESTIMONY OF JESUS

—*Sent from God.* 'I come forth from the Father; the Father hath sent me; God hath sent me.'[1] Now this identified Jesus and his salvation with the Messiah whom, with his salvation, the Jews were expecting. For his disciples therefore, and for Christendom after them, Jesus was and is the *Messiah* or *Christ*. This, we say, his disciples, and Christendom after them, have comprehended and accepted: his identification of himself with the Messiah. On the other hand, his fruitful and profound harmonisation of the two ideals,— the mild and suffering Servant of God, and the Anointed Prince conquering the earth in the cause of righteousness and giving the kingdom to the saints,—was not understood and accepted. At least, only so far as this was it accepted: that the turbid *Aberglaube*, with which the Jews had surrounded this latter ideal, was by the disciples of Jesus borrowed and transferred wholesale to their Master and his future advent.

Meanwhile, as with the word *God*, so with the word *Christ*. Jesus did not give any scientific definition of it,—such as, for instance, that Christ was the Logos. He took the word Christ as the Jews used it, as he took the word *God* as the Jews used it. And as he amended their notion of God, *the Eternal who loveth righteousness*, by showing what *righteousness* really was, so he amended their notion of the Messiah, *the chosen bringer of God's salvation*, by showing what *salvation*

[1] John xvi. 27, 28, 30; vi. 57; vii. 29; viii. 42; xvii. 8.

really was. And though his own application of terms to designate himself is not a matter where we can perfectly trust his reporters (as it is clear, for instance, that the writer of the Fourth Gospel was more metaphysical than Jesus himself),[1] yet there is no difficulty in supposing him to have applied to himself each and all of the terms which the Jews in any way used to describe the Messiah,—*Messiah* or *Christ*, God's *Chosen* or *Beloved* or *Consecrated* or *Glorified One*, the *Son of God*, the *Son of Man;* because his concern, as we have said, was with his countrymen's idea of salvation, not with their terms for designating the bringer of it. But the simplest term, the term which gives least opening into theosophy,—*Son of Man*,—he certainly preferred. So, too, he loved the simple expressions, 'God *sent* me,' 'The Father *hath sent* me'; and he chose so often to say, in a general manner, 'I am *He*,'[2] rather than to say positively, 'I am *Christ*.'

And evidently this mode of speaking struck his hearers. We find the Jews saying: 'How long dost thou *make us to doubt?* if thou be Christ, tell us *plainly!*'[3] And even then Jesus

---

[1] It is to be remembered, too, that whereas Jesus spoke in Aramaic, the most concrete and unmetaphysical of languages, he is reported in Greek, the most metaphysical. What, in the mouth of Jesus, was the word which comes to us as μονογενής (*only begotten*)? Probably the simple Aramaic word for *unique, only*. And yet, in the Greek record, even the word μονογενής is not, like *only begotten* in our translation, reserved for Christ. See Luke vii. 12; viii. 42; ix. 38.

[2] John iv. 26; viii. 24, 28.   [3] John x. 24.

does not answer point-blank, but prefers to say: 'I have told you, and ye believe not.' Yet this does not imply that he had the least doubt or hesitation in naming himself the Messiah, the Son of God; but only that his concern was, as we have said, with God's *righteousness* and Christ's *salvation*, and that he avoided all use of the names *God*, and *Christ*, which might give an opening into mere theosophical speculation. And this is shown, moreover, by the largeness and freedom,—almost, one may say, indifference, —of his treatment of both names; as names, in using which, his hearers were always in danger of going off into a theosophy that did them no good and had better occupy them as little as possible. '*I and my Father are one!*'[1] he would say at one time; and '*My Father is greater than I!*'[2] at another. When the Jews were offended at his calling himself the Son of God, he quotes Scripture to show that even mere men were in Scripture called *Gods;* and for you, he says, who go by the letter of Scripture, surely this is sanction enough for calling any one, whom God sends, *the Son of God!*[3] He did not at all mean, that the Messiah was a son of God merely in the sense in which any great man might be so called; but he meant that these questions of theosophy were useless for his hearers, and that they puzzled themselves with them in vain. All they were concerned with

[1] John x. 30. [2] John xiv. 28. [3] John x. 34-36.

was, that *he* was the Messiah they expected, sent to them with salvation from God.

It is the same when Jesus says: 'Before Abraham was, I am!'¹ He was baffling his countrymen's theosophy, showing them how little his doctrine was meant to offer a field for it. 'Life,' he means, 'the life of him who *lays down his life that he may take it again,*² is not what you suppose. Your notions of life and death are all false, and with your present notions you cannot discuss theology with me; *follow me!*' So, again, to the Jews in the rut of their traditional theology, and haggling about the Son of David;—Jesus, they insisted, could not be the Christ, because the Christ was the Son of David. Jesus answers them by the objection that in the Psalms (and the Scripture cannot be broken!) David calls the Christ his Lord; and 'if he call him Lord, how is he then his son?'³ The argument as a serious argument is perfectly futile. The king of God's chosen people is going out to war, and what the Psalmist really sings is: 'The Eternal saith unto the king's majesty, *Thou shalt conquer!*' St. Peter in the Acts gravely uses the same verse to prove Jesus to be Christ: 'God,' says he, 'tells my Lord, *Sit thou upon my right hand!* Yet David never went up into heaven.'⁴ Now, this is exactly of a piece with St. Paul's proving

---

[1] John viii. 58. [2] John x. 17.
[3] Matt. xxii. 42-45. [4] Acts ii. 34.

THE TESTIMONY OF JESUS

salvation to be by Christ alone, from *seed*, in the promise to Abraham, being in the singular, not the plural.[1] It is merely false criticism of the Old Testament, such as the Jews were full of, and of which the Apostles retained far too much. But the Jews *were* full of it, and therefore the objection of Jesus was just such an objection as the Jews would think weighty. He used it as he might have used a *crux* about personality or consubstantiality with the Bishops of Winchester or Gloucester; to baffle and put to rout their false dogmatic theology, to disenchant them with it and make them cast it aside and come simply to *him*. 'See,' he says to the Jewish doctors, 'what a mess you make of it with your learning, and evidences, and orthodox theology; with *the wisdom of your wise men and the understanding of your prudent men!* You can do nothing with them, your arms break in your hands. Fling the rubbish away, *cease from your own wisdom*,[2] and throw yourselves upon my method and secret,—upon *me!* Believe that the Father hath sent me; he that receiveth me receiveth Him that sent me. If any man will do His will, he shall know of the doctrine whether it be of God, or whether I have invented it!'[3]

And no grand performance or discovery of a man's own to bring him thus to joy and peace, but an attachment! the influence of *One*

---

[1] Gal. iii. 16. [2] Prov. xxiii. 4.
[3] John xii. 44; xiii. 20; vii. 17.

full of grace and truth! An influence, which we feel we know not how, and which subdues us we know not when; which, like the wind, breathes where it lists, passes here, and does not pass there! Once more, then, we come to that root and ground of religion, that element of awe and gratitude which fills religion with emotion, and makes it other and greater than morality, —the *not ourselves.* We did not make the order of conduct, or provide that happiness should belong to it, or dispose our hearts to it. *Man's goings are of the Eternal,* as Israel said; *Eternal, I know that the way of man is not in himself!*[1] Neither did we invent Jesus, or make the 'grace and truth' of Jesus, or provide that happiness should belong to feeling them, or dispose our hearts to feel them. *No man can come to me,* as Jesus said, *except the father, which sent me, draw him!*[2] So the revelation of Jesus Christ in the New Testament is like the revelation of the God of Israel in the Old, in being the revelation of 'the Eternal *not ourselves* which makes for righteousness.' It is like it, and has the same power of religion in it.

VII

Now, then, we see what the doctrine, *I came forth from God,*[3] really means. We see how far

---

[1] Prov. xx. 24; Jer. x. 23.　　[2] John vi. 44.
[3] John xvi. 27, 28, 30.

it has any kinship with that doctrine of the Godhead of the Eternal Son, for which our two bishops are so anxious to 'do something.' We see how far the pseudo-scientific language of our creeds, about *persons*, and *substance*, and *godhead*, and *co-equal*, and *co-eternal*, and *created*, and *begotten*, and *proceeding*, has anything at all to do with what Jesus said or meant. We see how impossible it is that one should concede to our clerical friends what they assume to be beyond dispute:—that the so-called Athanasian Creed 'takes the facts of Christian doctrine, and just arranges them sentence after sentence.' We see how wide of the mark is that metaphysical clergyman, who writes to the *Guardian* that 'Our Lord unquestionably annexes eternal life to a right knowledge of the Godhead,' in imagining that when Jesus said, 'This is life eternal, to know Thee the only true God, and Jesus Christ whom thou hast sent,'[1] Jesus had in view anything at all like the 'facts' which the Athanasian Creed 'arranges, sentence after sentence.' But we see more than this. We see how much a very common use of the word *faith*, which gives rise to false notions like that of this clergyman, needs amending.

For it is constantly assumed that there is an opposition between faith and reason; and that those, whom Jesus Christ calls to *believe in him*, he calls to receive a doctrine puzzling to the

[1] John xvii. 3.

reason, but which, if adopted, will gradually become clear. It is obvious how well this notion of faith suits the recommenders of such doctrine as that which the Athanasian Creed 'arranges, sentence after sentence,' which is certainly very puzzling to the reason. But this is of the essence of faith, it is said :—to take on trust what perplexes the reason. Only adopt the doctrine which perplexes the reason, be a Christian, and afterwards 'you shall know of the doctrine whether it be of God.' And with this is connected what is so often said in the Bible about 'receiving the kingdom of God as a little child,' about 'babes seeing what is hidden from the wise and prudent.'[1] The unlettered believer is, in fact,—according to this version of what the Bible means to say,—represented in the Bible as a better judge about a thing which perplexes the reason than the philosopher. And this explains the disdain with which the possessors of *gospel-truth*, as it is called, are apt to treat art, and literature, and science. These happy men are supposed to have, by faith, a certainty in matters perplexing in the highest degree to the reason, which the vaunted exercise of the reason can never attain to. And as with faith in Christ, so with faith in God : it is taking on trust something perplexing to the reason. Texts like : *They that seek the Eternal understand all things*,[2]

---

[1] Mark x. 15 ; Matt. xi. 25.
[2] Prov. xxviii. 5.

and : *I have more understanding than my teachers, for Thy testimonies are my study ; I am wiser than the aged because I keep Thy commandments,*[1] mean, that we are better off and see clearer than men of study and experience, if, in spite of its puzzling the reason, we accept in faith, and they do not, some truth like the 'blessed truth that the God of the universe is a PERSON.'

No one has more insisted on this opposition between faith and reason than a writer whom we can never name but with respect,—Dr. Newman. 'The moral trial involved in faith,' he says, 'lies in the *submission of the reason* to external realities partially disclosed.' And again : 'Faith is, in its very nature, the acceptance of what our *reason* cannot reach, simply and absolutely upon testimony.' But surely faith is in its very nature (with all deference be it spoken !) nothing of the kind ; else how could Jesus Christ say to the Jews : 'If I tell you the truth, why do ye not believe me ?'[2] Surely this implies that faith, instead of being a submission of the reason to what puzzles it, is rather a recognition of what is perfectly clear, if we will *attend* to it.[3] We cannot always attend, all of us ; and here is the *not ourselves* in the matter, 'the grace of God.' But *attention, cleaving, attaching oneself fast* to what is undeniably true,—this is what the faith of Scripture, 'in its very nature,' is ; and not the

---

[1] Psalm cxix. 99, 100. [2] John viii. 46.
[3] πάντα τὰ ἀναγκαῖα δῆλα, says Chrysostom.

submission of the reason to what puzzles it, or the acceptance, simply and absolutely upon testimony, of what our reason cannot reach. And all that the Bible says of bringing to nought the wisdom of the wise, and of receiving the kingdom of God as a little child, has nothing whatever to do with the believer's acceptance of some dogma that perplexes the reason; it is aimed at those who sophisticate a very simple thing, religion, by importing into it a so-called science with which it has nothing to do. Jewish theological learning, the system of divinity of the Jewish hierarchy, who did not know how simple a thing righteousness really was, and who, when simple souls saw it in Jesus Christ and were drawn to it, cried out: '*This people that knoweth not the law are cursed!*'[1] it was at these, and at whatever resembles these, that Jesus Christ aimed the words about receiving the kingdom of God as a little child.

And the 'marvellous work and wonder' about the saving truth which the simple receive is, not that, being difficult to the reason, it is yet got hold of by the unlettered and not by the wise; but that, being so simple, it should yet be so immense, important, indispensable; and that, being so immense, important, indispensable, it should yet so often be followed by quite unlettered people, and neglected by such very clever ones. The clever are attending to other

[1] John vii. 49.

VII THE TESTIMONY OF JESUS

things,—things which *do* task the reason and intelligence, and in which the unlettered have no skill and no voice; these things however are, at most, only one-fourth of life. And this absurdity, for such it really is, we see every day;—people attending to the difficult *science* of matters where the plain *practice* they quite let slip. How many people will be now[1] busy with Mr. Darwin's new book, so admirably ingenious, on the natural history of the emotions, who yet are always using their own emotions in the worst possible manner! They are eager to know how their emotions arose, how these came to express themselves as they do; yet there the emotions now are, and have for a long time been, and the first thing for any sane man to do is to make a proper use of them, and to know how to make a proper use is not difficult;—but all this we never think of, but investigate zealously how they arose! Such persons are just like those learned inquirers the Cynic laughed at, who were so busy about the strayings of Ulysses, so inattentive to their own.

And Israel's greatness was that he was so impatient of trifling of this kind, of being busy with one-fourth of life while the three-fourths, conduct, was forgotten. And Israel boldly said: 'They that seek the Eternal understand *all things*';[2] that is, they are occupied with conduct, righteousness, which truly is, as we have seen,

[1] Written in 1872.   [2] Proverbs xxviii. 5.

at least three-fourths of life, and which Israel thought the whole of it. They have a hold on three-fourths of life, while it may be that their great, clever, and accomplished neighbours have a hold on only one-fourth, or part of one-fourth, of life. Which is the solid and sensible man, which understands most, which *lives* most? Compare a Methodist day-labourer with some dissolute, gifted, brilliant grandee, who thinks nothing of him!—but the first deals successfully with nearly the whole of life, while the second is all abroad in it. Compare some simple and pious monk, at Rome, with one of those frivolous men of taste whom we have all seen there!—each knows nothing of what interests the other; but which is the more vital concern for a man: conduct, or arts and antiquities?

Nay, and however false his science and Biblical criticism, the believer who applies the method and secret of Jesus has a width of range and sureness of foothold in life, which even the best scientific and literary critic of the Bible, who applies them not, is without; because the first is right in what affects three-fourths of life, and the second in what affects but one-fourth, or even but one-eighth. Each has a secret of which the other, who has no experience of it, does not know the value; but the value of the learned man's secret is ridiculously least. This, I say, is the very glory and marvel of the religion of the true Israel, and what makes this religion, as Jesus

VII THE TESTIMONY OF JESUS

called it, 'the good news to the *poor*';[1] that it covers nearly the whole of life, and yet is so simple.

The only right contrast, therefore, to set up between faith and reason is, not that faith grasps what is too hard for reason, but that reason does not, like faith, attend to what is at once so great and so simple. The *difficulty* about faith is, to attend to what is very simple and very important, but liable to be pushed by more showy or tempting matters out of sight. The *marvel* about faith is, that what is so simple should be so all-sufficing, so necessary, and so often neglected. And faith is neither the submission of the reason, nor is it the acceptance simply and absolutely upon testimony of what reason cannot reach. Faith is : *the being able to cleave to a power of goodness appealing to our higher and real self, not to our lower and apparent self.*

VIII

So we see how unlike is Jesus Christ's own doctrine of his being the Son of God to the difficult doctrine of the Godhead of the Eternal Son, as the Athanasian Creed 'arranges it, sentence after sentence,' and in the form in which our bishops want to 'do something' for it ; as unlike as the original revelation to Israel of *the*

[1] Luke iv. 18.

Eternal that loveth righteousness is to ' the blessed doctrine that the God of the universe is a PERSON.' And we see how the clergymen who write to the *Guardian* deceive themselves, when they imagine that it is to these doctrines of our bishops that Jesus Christ ' unquestionably attaches eternal life,' and how they are led into this error by having more of turn for abstruse reasoning than of literary experience. They are not conversant enough with the many different ways in which men think and speak, so as to be able to distinguish rightly between them, and to perceive that the Bible is *literature;* and that its words are used, like the words of common life and of poetry and eloquence, approximately, and not like the terms of science, adequately.

And if they fall into mistakes about words applied to the Father and the Son, by thus making them scientific, how much more do they fall into mistakes when they extend this treatment to words applied to the Holy Ghost. We have seen how the word *Pneuma*, just by reason of its inward and infinite character, was much employed by Jesus for his method of inwardness and of deliverance from binding traditions and formulas; and how, since *Holy Ghost* has become to us a formula, just as *God* and *righteousness* were to the Jews, to get the force of Christ's use of the word 'Pneuma,' we ought to retranslate the word for ourselves, and to call it, for a time at any rate, rather *influence, intuition,* or some such name.

VII THE TESTIMONY OF JESUS

For it was thus that Jesus himself used it. When Jesus was going away, above all, and his disciples were to be thrown on themselves and left to use his method of inwardness more deeply and thoroughly, not having him to go to,—then they would find, he said, a new power come to their help ; a power of insight such as they had never had before, and which was none of their making, but came from God as Jesus did, and said nothing of itself, but only what God said or Jesus said ; a ' Paraclete,' or reinforcement working in aid of God and Jesus : *even the Spirit of Truth.*[1] While Jesus was with them, the disciples had lived in contact with *aletheia*, or reality ; and they were promised now an *intuition of reality* within themselves.

Now, will it be believed, that the Athanasian Creed, and our bishops, and the clergymen who write to the *Guardian*, and dogmatic theology in general, should have imagined that Jesus Christ here meant to convey to us the ' blessed doctrine ' that this Spirit of truth, too, ' is a PERSON ' ? The force of metaphysical talent outrunning literary experience could really, we say, no farther go ! The Muse, who visited Hesiod when he was tending his sheep on the side of Helicon, and ' breathed into him a divine voice, and taught him the things to come and the former things,' might every bit as well be made, with much display of metaphysical apparatus, ' a PERSON.' The

[1] John xiv. 16, 17, 26 ; xvi. 7-14.

influence which visited Hesiod was a *real* one,—that is as much metaphysics as we can without error, in a case of this sort, apply. Whoever applies more, falls into absurdity.

The spiritual visitant, indeed, which rejoiced the wise poet of Ascra, was not the Paraclete of Jesus. No, it was the Muse of art and science, the Muse of the gifted few, the Muse who brings to the ingenious and learned among mankind 'a forgetfulness,' as Hesiod sings, 'of evils and a truce from cares.' The Paraclete that Jesus promised, on the other hand, was the Muse of *righteousness*; the Muse of the work-day, care-crossed, toil-stained millions of men,—the Muse of humanity. To all who live, for all that concerns three-fourths of life, this divine Muse offers 'a forgetfulness of evils and a truce from cares.' That is why it is far more real, and far greater, than the Muse of Hesiod; not from any metaphysical personality.

IX

But the whole centre of gravity of the Christian religion, in the popular as well as in the so-called orthodox notion of it, is placed in Christ's having, by his death in satisfaction for man's sins, performed the contract originally passed in the Council of the Trinity, and having thus enabled the magnified and non-natural Man in heaven, who is the God of theology and of

VII THE TESTIMONY OF JESUS

the multitude alike, to consider his justice satisfied, and to allow his mercy to go forth on all who heartily believe that Jesus Christ has paid their debt for them. Now we have seen how that whole structure of materialising mythology, which the Bible is supposed to deliver, and in which this conception of the *Atonement*, as it is called, holds the central place, drops away and disappears as the Bible comes to be better known. The true centre of gravity of the Christian religion is in the *method* and the *secret* of Jesus, approximating, in their application, ever closer to the *epieikeia*, the sweet reasonableness and unerring sureness of Jesus himself. But, as the method of Jesus led up to his secret, and his secret was dying to 'the life in this world' and living to 'the eternal life,' both his method and his secret culminated in his 'perfecting' on the cross, which he himself foresaw and foretold.

The miracle of the corporeal resurrection ruled the minds of those who have reported Christ's sayings for us; and their report, *how* he foretold his death, cannot always be entirely accepted. One of them alleges him to have foretold it by pointing to his body and saying: *Destroy this temple, and in three days I will raise it up!*[1] Now, here is certainly an instance of the retrospective pressure exercised on words of Jesus by the established belief in the resurrection.

[1] John ii. 19.

He had said of the Temple at Jerusalem: *There shall not be left of it one stone upon another.*[1] He had said of himself and this much-reverenced Temple: *There standeth here One greater than the Temple.*[2] He had said he should be put to death, and the death of the worst malefactors, crucifixion.[3] This death he had also called his glorification, his perfection.[4] He had said, using a Hebrew form of expression, that this his perfection or glorification should come *in three days* (that is, very shortly): *I do cures to-day and to-morrow, and the third day I shall be perfected.*[5] Nothing more was needed. All the elements for a simply miraculous prediction by Jesus of his own death and bodily resurrection were ready to the miracle-maker's hand! Jesus had not only said: *They shall crucify me, and the third day I will rise again.*[6] He had also said, pointing to his own body: *Destroy this temple and in three days I will raise it up!*

In sayings of this kind, the internal evidence is all-important. Now, the sure clue of internal evidence to follow, in tracing any words of Jesus about his death and rising again, is the clue given by the ideal of the stricken Servant of God in the fifty-third chapter of Isaiah. This ideal, as we have seen, Jesus had adopted and

---

[1] Matt. xxiv. 2. [2] Matt. xii. 6.
[3] Matt. xx. 18, 19. [4] John xii. 23.
[5] Luke xiii. 32; Hosea vi. 3. See also *God and the Bible*, pp. 292-296.
[6] Matt. xvi. 21; xx. 19; Mark x. 34; Luke xviii. 33.

VII THE TESTIMONY OF JESUS

elevated as the true ideal of Israel's Saviour; he had corrected by it the favourite popular ideals he found regnant. And in this ideal of the stricken Servant of God, the notion of *sacrifice* is, that this lover of righteousness falls because of a state of iniquity and wickedness which he has had no share in making, and as the only remedy for it. The notion of *redemption* is, that by endurance to the end, and by his death crowning his life, he establishes all seekers after good in their allegiance to good, enables them to follow it and to reach true life through it. Finally, the notion of *resurrection* is, that his death makes an epoch of victory for him and his cause, which thenceforward live and reign indestructibly. *He had done no violence, neither was any deceit in his mouth; he was bruised for our iniquities, the Eternal hath laid on him the iniquity of us all;* [1]—there is the sacrifice. *With his stripes we are healed;* [2]—there is the redemption. But: *When he hath made his life an offering for sin, he shall see his seed, he shall prolong his days, and the pleasure of the Eternal shall prosper in his hand;* [3]— there, to crown all, is the resurrection.

And just these stages we find again in Jesus, *Which of you convicteth me of sin?* [4] he asked the Jews; nevertheless: *The Son of Man must suffer many things and be rejected of this generation,* [5] *the Son of Man must be lifted up;* [6]—there is the

---

[1] Is. liii. 9, 5, 6.   [2] Is. liii. 5.   [3] Is. liii. 10.
[4] John viii. 46.   [5] Luke xvii. 25.   [6] John iii. 14.

sacrifice. *Except a grain of corn fall to the ground and die, it abideth alone;*[1] *the Son of Man came to give his life a ransom for many;*[2]—there is the redemption. But: *If the grain of corn die, it bringeth forth much fruit; I, if I be lifted up from the earth, will draw all men unto me;*[3] *If I go not away the Spirit of truth will not come unto you, but if I depart I will send him unto you, and when he is come he will convince the world of sin, of righteousness, and of judgment;*[4]—there, there is the resurrection and triumph!

The use by Jesus of the words *life* and *death* must on no account, however, be limited to this his crucifixion and after-triumph, though in these, no doubt, his dying and living culminated. Yet both here, and always in his use of them, they are properly to be referred to his secret: '*He that loveth his life shall lose it, and he that hateth his life in this world shall keep it unto life eternal;*[5] *renounce thyself, and take up thy cross daily, and follow Me!*'[6] Long before his signal Crucifixion Jesus had died, by taking up daily that cross which his disciples, after his daily example, were to take up also. 'Therefore doth my Father love me,' he says, '*because I lay down my life that I may take it again.*'[7] He had risen to life long before his crowning Resurrection, risen to life in what he calls '*my joy,*'[8]

[1] John xii. 24.   [2] Matthew xx. 28.   [3] John xii. 24, 32.
[4] John xvi. 7, 8.   [5] John xii. 25.   [6] Luke ix. 23.
[7] John x. 17.   [8] John xvii. 13.

VII THE TESTIMONY OF JESUS

which he desired to see fulfilled in his disciples also;—'*my joy*, to have kept my Father's commandment and abide in his love.'[1]

Nay, and there is no more powerful testimony to Jesus Christ's real use of the words *life* and *death*, than a famous text, borrowed from Jewish *Aberglaube*, which popular Christianity has wrested in support of its tenet of a physical resurrection at the Messiah's second advent. Whatever we may think of the narrative of the raising of Lazarus, we need have no difficulty in believing that Jesus really did say to the brother or sister of a dead disciple: 'Thy brother shall rise again!' and that the mourner replied: 'I know that he shall rise again in the resurrection at the last day.'[2] For the answer which follows has the certain stamp of Jesus: '*I am the resurrection and the life; he that believeth on me, though he die, shall live, and whosoever liveth and believeth on me shall never die.*'[3] Now, Martha believed already in the resurrection of Jewish and Christian *Aberglaube*,—the resurrection according to the Book of Daniel and the Book of Enoch, the resurrection of the last day, when 'they that sleep in the dust of the earth shall awake, some to everlasting life, and some to shame and everlasting contempt.'[4] But Jesus corrects her *Aberglaube*, by telling her that her brother is not dead at all; and his words, out of

[1] John xv. 10, 11.   [2] John xi. 23, 24.
[3] John xi. 25, 26.   [4] Daniel xii. 2.

which the story of the miracle very likely grew, do really make the miracle quite unnecessary. 'He that has believed on me and had my secret,' says Jesus, 'though his body die to the life of this world, still lives; for such an one had died to the life of this world already, and found true life, life out of himself, life in the Eternal that loveth righteousness, by doing so.'[1]

Just in the same way, moreover, in his promise to see his disciples again after his crucifixion and to take up his abode with them, Jesus corrects, for those who have eyes to read, he corrects in the clearest and most decisive way those very errors, with which our common material conceptions of life and death have made us invest his death and resurrection. 'Yet a little while,' he says, 'and the world seeth me no more; but ye see me, because I live, and ye shall live too. He that hath my commandments and keepeth them, he it is that loveth me; and him that loveth me I will love, *and will manifest myself to him.*' Jude naturally objects: '*How* is it that thou wilt manifest thyself to us and not to the world?' And Jesus answers: 'If a man love me, he will keep my word, and my Father will love him, and *we will come unto him and make our abode with him.*'[2] Therefore the manifestation of himself he speaks of is nothing external and

---

[1] For additional remarks on this miracle of the raising of Lazarus, see *God and the Bible*, pp. 342-343.

[2] John xiv. 19-23. See also *God and the Bible*, pp. 284-297.

material. It is,—like the manifestation of God to him that ordereth his conversation right,—the internal life and joy in keeping the commandments. It is the life for the disciples of Christ, in and with Christ, in keeping the commandments of God; those commandments, which had at last in their true scope been made known to men, but solely through Jesus Christ's method and through his secret.

X

Thus, then, did Jesus seek to transform the immense materialising *Aberglaube* into which the religion of Israel had fallen, and to spiritualise it at all points; while in his method and secret he supplied a sure basis for practice. But to follow him entirely there was needed an *epieikeia*, an unfailing sweetness and unerring perception, like his own. It was much if his disciples got firm hold on his method and his secret; and if they transmitted fragments enough of his lofty spiritualism to make it in the fulness of time discernible, and to make it at once and from the first in a large degree serviceable. Who can read in the Gospels the comments preserved to us, both of disciples and of others, on what he said, and not feel that Jesus must have known, while he nevertheless persevered in saying them, how things like: '*Before Abraham was, I am,*'[1]

[1] John viii. 58.

or: '*I will not leave you comfortless, I will come unto you,*'[1] would be misapprehended by those who heard them?

But, indeed, Jesus himself tells us that he knew and foresaw this. With the promise of the Spirit of truth which should, after his departure, work in his disciples first, then in the world, and which should convince the world of sin, of righteousness, and of judgment, and finally transform it, we are all familiar. But we do not enough remark the impressive words, uttered to the crowd around him only a little while before, and of far wider application than the reporter imagined. '*Yet a little while is the light with you; walk while ye have the light, lest the darkness overtake you unawares!*'[2] The real application cannot have been to the unconverted only;—a call to the unconverted to make haste because their chance of conversion would soon, with Christ's departure, be gone. No, converts came in far thicker after Christ's departure than in his life. The words are for the converted also. It is as if Jesus foresaw the want of his sweet reasonableness, which he could not leave, to help his method and his secret, which he could leave;—as if he foresaw his words misconstrued, his rising to eternal life turned into a physical miracle, the advent of the Spirit of truth turned into a scene of thaumaturgy, Peter proving his Master's Messiahship from a Psalm

---

[1] John xiv. 18. [2] John xii. 35.

VII THE TESTIMONY OF JESUS

that does not prove it, the great Apostle of the Gentiles word-splitting like a pedantic Rabbi, the most beautiful soul among his own reporters saddling him with metaphysics;—foresaw the growth of creeds, the growth of dogma, and so through all the confusion worse confounded of councils, schoolmen, and confessions of faith, down to our own two bishops bent on 'doing something' for the honour of the Godhead of the Eternal Son!

CHAPTER VIII

THE EARLY WITNESSES

Our object in this essay has never been to argue against miracles. Even with Lourdes and La Salette before our eyes, we may yet say that miracles are doomed; they will drop out, like fairies or witchcraft, from among the matters which serious people believe. Our one object is to save the revelation in the Bible from being made *solidary*, as our Comtist friends say, with miracles; from being attended to or held cheap just in proportion as miracles are attended to or are held cheap.

In like manner, nay far more, our object is not, and never can be, to pick holes in the apostles and reporters of Jesus. But much which they say cannot stand; our one object is to hinder people from making Jesus solidary with this, and with his reporters' and apostles' character for infallibility. To this extent, and to this only, we are brought at moments into collision with miracles, into collision with the disciples of Jesus and with the writers of the

CH. VIII   THE EARLY WITNESSES

New Testament. We have to show that, the men being what and when and whence they were, the miracles would certainly grow up for them around and in the wake of Jesus.

How did Jesus Christ's words: '*I will see you again, I go to prepare a place for you!*'[1] grow into the legend,—so beautiful, and round which have for centuries gathered such sacred feelings and aspirations, yet a legend,—of his corporeal resurrection and ascension? How? Why, Herod's first words, when after the execution of John the Baptist he heard of Jesus, were: 'It is John the Baptist; *he is risen from the dead!*'[2] In such an atmosphere of belief were the disciples living, when their loss of Jesus, the greatest loss that ever befel men, happened. All his discourse, when he was with them, had run on life and death,—apparent death, enduring life; and how many are the stories of the survivors, in an atmosphere of belief like that of those Palestine times, refusing to believe in the death of a leader even far less precious to them, full of reports of his reappearance in this place and that place, feeding themselves on the promise of his triumphant return! How many thousands at this moment, in Persia, refuse to credit the death of the Bâb, their *Gate of life*, executed some years ago; assert that he will return, that he has been seen, that they have seen him!

But the reporters of Jesus were not as others;

---

[1] John xvi. 22; xiv. 2, 3.   [2] Matt. xiv. 2.

they were infallible! So infallible, that they report themselves, when Jesus reappeared, after all his labours to transform and spiritualise for them the old Jewish ideal,—they report themselves to have met him with the inquiry: *Lord, wilt thou at this time restore the kingdom to Israel?*[1] But the Holy Ghost had not then been given? And after the Holy Ghost *was* given, we find them with one voice asserting that in the lifetime of that generation should come Christ's second advent and the end of the world; Peter falling back into Judaism, so that Paul had to withstand him to the face because he was to be blamed, and Paul himself proving salvation to be by Jesus, from *seed,* in the promise to Abraham, being used in the singular! That it is impossible the disciples of Jesus should have been, alone of all the disciples in the world, infallible, that it is begging the question to say they were infallible, need not be made out. It is conspicuous, on the face of their own showing of themselves, that they were *not* infallible. And well it is that it should be so. For this favourite Protestant Doctrine of the infallibility of the Bible-writers, inherited, indeed, from the Fathers along with that of the infallibility of the Church, but kept and extolled by Protestants as the true single anchor to ride at, whereas the other was rotten, — this doctrine involves Christianity in dangers quite as serious as its discarded rival does.

[1] Acts i. 6.

VIII   THE EARLY WITNESSES

But it was not for nothing that the Apostles had lived with Jesus ; or even, in the case of a great religious spirit like Paul, lived in his time, lived in his country, had his presence and words near and fresh to them. And, untrue and dangerous as is the popular Protestant doctrine of the plenary inspiration of the Apostles, an inspiration making them infallible, but vouchsafed no more to any one after the Apostles were gone, yet it rests on a true perception of the vast distance which separates them from after-writers on Christianity, from the Fathers as from Luther and Calvin, all alike. This they owe to their contact with Jesus ; or, in Paul's case, to their nearness to him. The impression of him was too fresh and vivid, his method and secret still had too firmly the prominence he had given them, the atmosphere of his sweet reasonableness still hung round his disciples too much, to permit of the deep confusions and misunderstandings of after-times. There is no pleasure in proving that the Apostles sometimes made mistakes ; but to trace in the Apostles the reproduction of the method and secret of Jesus, is one of the most delightful of tasks. And since to show such reproduction of Jesus in his followers throws light on what we have said of Jesus himself, and confirms it, we will permit ourselves to do this very briefly. And we will show it, first and above all, in the case of the three great witnesses to him in the New

Testament,—St. Peter, St. Paul, and the writer who is called, properly or improperly, St. John.

II

To begin with St. Peter. The First Epistle of St. Peter commends itself as much, one may say, as the genuine work of the author whose name it bears, as the Second Epistle bespeaks itself the contrary. And, except for the one strange passage about the spirits in prison and Noah's flood, at the end of the third chapter,—where the meaning which was in the writer's mind is probably now irrecoverable for us,—there is shed over this whole production more, perhaps, of the *epieikeia*, or what we call the sweet reasonableness, of Christ, than over any other epistle we possess. Very much this is due to its simplicity, to the unambitious nature of its topics and of its treatment of them; because, clearly, the application of prophecy, the adjustment of the old ideal of Israel to the new, the management of the ideas of life and death, of justification and the like,—in all of which the *epieikeia* of Jesus himself shone forth so matchlessly,—are much harder to treat with the winning simplicity and limpid intuitiveness which make the charm of *epieikeia*, than conduct itself is.

And conduct is what this epistle is concerned with, almost from the first line to the last.

'Your *good conversation* in Christ';[1] 'As He who called you is *holy*, be ye also *holy* in all your *conversation*';[2]—this is the head and front of the matter with the writer. Holiness is but, as we have said, a deep and finished righteousness. And the method for it is the method of Jesus:—the inward man awakened, conscience. '*Born again* through the word of God that liveth and abideth';[3] 'The *hidden man of the heart*';[4] 'Having *a good conscience*';[5]—again and again this word 'conscience,' so strange to the Old Testament, appears. And the two great groups of faults which, in a rough way, do sufficiently comprehend all conduct, are again, as they were by Jesus, marked as the matter to be dealt with: — faults of temper and faults of sensuality. 'Not conformed to the former *lusts* of your time of ignorance';[6] 'The time past may suffice us to have wrought the will of the Gentiles, having walked in *dissoluteness, lusts, excess of wine, revellings*';[7] 'Abstain from *fleshly lusts*, which war against the soul';[8] 'Be *temperate*, be *sober*';[9]—this is for faults of sensuality. 'Putting away all *malice*, and all *deceit*, and *insincerities*, and *envies*, and all *evil-speakings*';[10] 'Be *of one mind, feel with one another, love as brethren*'; 'Be *tender-hearted, humble-minded*';[11]

[1] 1 Peter iii. 16.   [2] *Ibid.* i. 15.   [3] *Ibid.* i. 23.
[4] *Ibid.* iii. 4.   [5] *Ibid.* iii. 16.   [6] *Ibid.* i. 14.
[7] *Ibid.* iv. 3.   [8] *Ibid.* iv. 11.   [9] *Ibid.* iv. 7.
[10] *Ibid.* ii. 1.   [11] *Ibid.* iii. 8.

'The incorruptible of that *mild and quiet spirit* which is, in the sight of God, of great price';[1] —this is for the faults of temper.

So far the 'method' of Jesus; and next for his 'secret' of self-renouncement, of dying to our apparent self, to our 'life in this world.' 'Even though ye *suffer* for righteousness, happy are ye!'[2] 'For *to suffering ye are called*, because Christ also suffered for our sakes, leaving us an ensample that we should follow his steps';[3] 'As Christ suffered in the flesh, arm yourselves likewise with the same mind, for *he that suffers in the flesh is freed from sin*';[4] 'Elected of God unto *obedience and sprinkling with the blood of Christ.*'[5] And nowhere does the *joy*, which with Jesus is the great test and sanction of his method and secret, come out fuller and stronger than in this epistle. 'But ye are a chosen race, a royal priesthood, a holy nation, a peculiar people, to tell forth the excellences of Him *who called you out of darkness into his marvellous light!*'[6]

The belief in the bodily resurrection of Jesus, and the expectation of his second advent in the lifetime of the generation then living, are signal supports to the writer's mind. But our popular notion of the *Atonement*,—Christ's death represented as a satisfaction of God's offended justice, —does not yet appear. The governing idea of

---

[1] 1 Peter iii. 4. [2] *Ibid.* iii. 14. [3] *Ibid.* ii. 21.
[4] *Ibid.* iv. 1. [5] *Ibid.* i. 2.   [6] *Ibid.* ii. 9.

the fifty-third chapter of Isaiah, adopted by Jesus himself, is still faithfully preserved. Jesus Christ died for his people 'to redeem them from their vain conversation delivered by tradition'; Jesus Christ suffered, 'in order that we, dying to sins, might live to righteousness.'[1]

III

Next we come to St. Paul; but elsewhere[2] we have spoken so fully of St. Paul's theology that we shall be very brief here. Need we say that righteousness is its ground-thought, — *real righteousness discerned to be such by means of a change of the inner man?* 'Circumcision is nothing, and uncircumcision is nothing, but *the keeping of the commandments of God.*'[3] Righteousness is the end and aim. This to begin with; then, in the words: 'I exercise myself to have *a conscience void of offence* towards God and men continually,'[4] we find ourselves in the method of Jesus. 'Let every man *prove by experience* his own work, and then shall he have rejoicing *in himself alone* and not in another';[5] '*Prove* all things *by experience*, keep what is good';[6] '*Prove by experience* what things are excellent';[7] 'Able to *prove by experience* what is that good and perfect and acceptable will of God.'[8] All

---

[1] 1 Peter i. 18; ii. 24. [2] See *St. Paul and Protestantism.*
[3] 1 Cor. vii. 19. [4] Acts xxiv. 16. [5] Gal. vi. 4.
[6] 1 Thess. v. 21. [7] Philipp. i. 10. [8] Romans xii. 2.

this points to inward appraisal, the method of inwardness, the individual conscience. Jesus has given a new faculty of judging things, *light:* ' All things that are convicted as wrong are shown to be what they really are by the *light;* for whatever shows things to be what they really are, is *light.* Wherefore he saith : Awake thou that sleepest, and arise from the dead, and Christ shall give thee *light!* '[1] This is the new power of the method of Jesus, of conscience. And no one has so well described as St. Paul the working of conscience as first set going by Christianity. 'Commending ourselves, by the manifesting of *the reality*, to *every human conscience!* '[2] '*The hidden things of a man's heart are made manifest*,' he says ; ' all that he hears *convicts* him, *sifts him to the bottom:* he falls on his face and worships, declaring that God is indeed here!'[3] Nor does St. Paul fail to specify again and again the matter wherewith conscience deals : — ' *the works of the flesh*,' as he calls them ; ' fornication, uncleanness, dissoluteness, idol-worship, witchcraft, hatreds, strife, jealousy, angers, contentions, divisions, sects, envies, drunkennesses, revellings, and such like.'[4] *They are manifest*, says he, and so they are ; for they roughly cover what all the Galatians, to whom

---

[1] Eph. v. 13, 14. The Epistle to the Ephesians cannot well be altogether Paul's, but it is full of Pauline things, and this is certainly among them. [2] 2 Cor. iv. 2.
[3] 1 Cor. xiv. 24, 25.   [4] Gal. v. 19, 20.

he wrote, understood by *conduct*,—the whole body of faults connected with our two great primary instincts, faults of temper and faults of sensuality. Elsewhere, to the Colossians, he even seems to follow,—but still in an informal, approximative manner, such as one uses when one speaks of matters so familiar that to be precise is pedantic,—he even seems to actually follow this division, and to throw faults of conduct into two groups which nearly correspond to it.[1] Finally, to the works of the flesh, which are thus evidently conduct *wrong*, he opposes the fruits of the Spirit, which are as evidently conduct *right:* 'Love, joy, peace, patience, kindness, goodness, faith, mildness, self-control.'[2] By following the inward method of Jesus, he tells us, we perceive that here is the subject-matter of righteousness, that this is what *keeping the commandments of God* really is.

And that the 'secret' of Jesus was applied to this subject-matter by Paul, who can doubt when that secret is the very heart of Paul's theology, and he came to view the crucifixion and resurrection of Christ altogether in connection with it? In elevating as his sum of knowledge 'Jesus Christ *crucified*,'[3] his first thought was to insist on 'the scandal of the cross'[4] as the strength, not the weakness, of Christianity; to enthrone resolutely Jesus

---

[1] Colossians iii. 5, 8. [2] Gal. v. 22, 23.
[3] 1 Cor. i. 23. [4] Gal. v. 11.

Christ's new Messias-ideal of the suffering servant, in opposition to the Jews' old Messias-ideal of a triumphing conqueror. His second thought was the 'secret.' It is to be noted that the secret of Jesus takes a twofold form in Paul's writings, a simple and a mystic one. The simple form is given in such a passage as this: 'If ye live after the flesh ye shall die, but if through the spirit ye mortify the doings of the body, ye shall live.'[1] Here is the same easily intelligible play on the ideas of life and death which Jesus himself used. But Paul's favourite form for the secret was a more mystic one, in which Christ's death upon the cross stood for death in general, and his resurrection for life in general. 'If we correspond to his death,' says Paul, 'into which our baptism buries us with him, we shall correspond also to his resurrection';[2] that is, in his other and simpler phrase, 'we shall *live*.' But of all this we have spoken elsewhere; let us at present content ourselves with quoting, as Paul's general witness to the secret of Jesus, these three texts, so strong and plain that they may well stand as the great signal-marks pointing to it:—'I am *crucified* with Christ';[3] 'If ye *die* with him, ye shall also *live* with him';[4] 'Always bearing about in the body the *dying* of Jesus, that the life also of Jesus

---

[1] Rom. viii. 13.   [2] Rom. vi. 4, 5.
[3] Gal. ii. 19.   [4] 2 Tim. ii. 11.

may be manifested in our body.'[1] *The word of the cross*,[2] as he calls it, is his pole-star. By the method and example of Jesus he has become aware of a new principle of choosing and refusing, of going after things and retiring from them. This principle acts always in view of *a new creature*,[3] the higher or real self, agreeing with the 'will of God,' conflicting with the lower or apparent self, or the 'wishes of the flesh and of the current thoughts.' With this new principle, a man's great aim is now 'to put off, as regards our former way of life, *the old man that perishes by compliance with the misleading lusts ;*[4] and to put on *the new man that after God is created in righteousness.*' And the secret for this is, says Paul, *being crucified with Christ*, or, *being conformed to Christ's death*, or, *always bearing about in the body the dying of Jesus.*[5] Paul told his converts he was 'in travail of them till Christ be fashioned in them,'[6]—the entire Christ, with his method, secret, and sweet reasonableness ; but the great stress is laid on the 'secret,' on *dying*, because this *was* Christ's secret, because the heart of the matter is indeed here. And as we shall do well to have always the 'secret' in our minds when Jesus talks of 'the living water,' 'the bread of life,' so it is of

[1] 2 Cor. iv. 10. [2] 1 Cor. i. 18. [3] 2 Cor. v. 17.
[4] τὸν παλαιὸν ἄνθρωπον, τὸν φθειρόμενον κατὰ τὰς ἐπιθυμίας τῆς ἀπάτης.—Eph. iv. 22.
[5] Gal. ii. 19 ; Philipp. iii. 10 ; 2 Cor. iv. 10.
[6] Gal. iv. 19.

the possession of this same secret that Paul is specially thinking when he talks of 'counting all things but loss *for the excellency of the knowledge of Christ Jesus my Lord*';[1] or when he says: 'God forbid that I should glory, *save in the cross of our Lord Jesus Christ, whereby the world is crucified unto me, and I unto the world!*'[2]

And the evidence of *joy* which testifies to the salvation there is in Jesus and in his secret, and the sense of 'not ourselves' which fills this joy with awe and gratitude, and makes it *religious* to the core, who has rendered them like Paul? '*Rejoice* evermore!' '*Rejoice* in the Lord alway; again I say, *rejoice!*' 'Sorrowful, yet alway *rejoicing!*' 'As the sufferings of Christ abound with us, so through Christ abounds also the *consolation*.' 'The *unsearchable riches* of Christ!' '*Who shall separate us from the love of* Christ?' '*O the depth of the riches* both of the wisdom and knowledge of God!' '*It is God that worketh in you*, both to will and to do, of his good pleasure.' 'He that glorieth, *let him glory in the Eternal!*'[3]

All this is in Paul. And there is, besides, the *Aberglaube*, or extra-belief, of the bodily resurrection, of Christ's second advent during the lifetime of men then living;[4] there is

---

[1] Philipp. iii. 8. [2] Gal. vi. 14.
[3] 1 Thess. v. 16; Philipp. iv. 4; 2 Cor. vi. 10; i. 5; Eph. iii. 8; Rom. viii. 35; xi. 33; Philipp. ii. 13; 1 Cor. i. 31.
[4] 1 Thess. iv. 15.

the Calvinistical God 'willing to show his wrath and to make his power known by vessels of wrath fitted to destruction';[1] there is the Rabbinical logic, and the unsound use of prophecy and of the Old Testament. For popular theology the writings of Paul are a fatal rock; because they are the products of a mind that was constantly growing, and because they affect the forms of logic and science which a complete notional system adopts, while their true character and force is that of an approximative experience. So the mechanical theory of inspiration makes strange work indeed with Paul's writings. They are, however, to those who can use them aright, inexhaustible, not only in their power of animation and edification, but also in their illustration of the genuine doctrine of Jesus.

IV

The author of the Fourth Gospel passes for the author of the epistle which we call the First Epistle of St. John; at any rate, the Epistle is written by one who had the ideas of this Gospel moving his mind. We of course, therefore, might expect that the Epistle should tally with the Gospel. And so it does; only it upholds, one may say, in a certain very

---

[1] Rom. ix. 22.

important respect, the doctrine of Jesus against the Fourth Gospel itself.

We have seen how the author of this Gospel had a leaning to metaphysics; so that he delights M. Burnouf by showing a quite Indo-European turn for making God into a metaphysical source of things, such as is not unworthy, perhaps, of being called a cosmic unity; and Jesus into the Logos, necessarily related, by some lofty metaphysical law or other, to this cosmic unity. But presently came the Gnostics, still more full of the Aryan genius, and still more admired by M. Burnouf; full of religion's being a *knowing* rather than a *doing*, a metaphysical conception rather than *righteousness*. And, in fact, as we have said already, it may well seem wonderful that so great a thing as religion should be taken up with so simple a thing as conduct; or that Jesus Christ should say, that he who receives the kingdom of God *as a little child,*—that is, who simply receives it as concerned with this simple matter,—the same is the greatest in that kingdom.[1] Jesus Christ *does* say so, however; and no one who had lived with him, and felt his influence, could doubt that so it was. But the Gnostics, who had not lived with him, did not think thus; and they naturally imagined that a man who was right about such grand things as the cosmic unity, and the *pleroma*, and emanation, and

[1] Matthew xviii. 3, 4.

personality, and consubstantiality, and the like, must have true religion and be the perfect man. And they naturally imagined, too, that the Christ, the Saviour of the world, could not have been anything so unmetaphysical, so unworthy of the cosmic unity, as a mere man with flesh and blood; and the *Docetæ*, or Apparitionists, taught accordingly that Jesus had been an apparition or phantom, not a man at all. The writings of the Apostles can hardly be understood unless we know that very often they are alluding to these Gnostics and their productions, which had even at that early time their successful beginnings.

Now, the author of the Fourth Gospel had a turn, as we have seen, for metaphysics, and the author of the First Epistle of St. John shows a conversance with the ideas of the Fourth Gospel. But a man in vital contact with Jesus and *aletheia*, knew what reality was, the reality of Jesus, too well, to carry his play of metaphysics into the domain of that reality. And by a sort of compensation, glorious indeed to the writer, still more glorious to the power of Jesus Christ's word, the two great points of that close cousin of the Fourth Gospel, that document which we call the First Epistle of St. John, are these: *Jesus Christ come in the flesh!* and: *He that doeth righteousness is righteous!*[1] Jesus is no metaphysical phantom, but a living

---

[1] 1 John iv. 2; iii. 7.

man having to do with conduct. Religion is no intellectualism, but righteousness. Here we have the substratum as Jesus laid it: *righteousness*.

And we have also the 'method' of conscience, which tells us *what* righteousness is, and how great it is, and that it is indeed the substratum. 'Ye have an unction from the Holy One, and ye know all things; the unction which ye received from him abideth in you, and ye need not that any one should teach you, but his unction teacheth you of all things, and is true and is no lie, and as he taught you, abide ye in him!'[1]

It is characteristic of this beautiful soul, the source of our Epistle, that he does not go into detail and give lists of faults. He has fixed the method, *conscience*, and the subject-matter of the method, *righteousness;* and that is enough. It is characteristic, in like manner, that he states and restates the 'secret' of Jesus by its positive and loveliest side. The 'method' gives us *light*, and the 'secret' gives us the power of '*walking* in the light'; and, 'If we walk in the light, we *have fellowship one with another*.'[2] For to live by dying to our life in this world is to transfer the natural love of life from the personal self to the impersonal self,—the self that we share with all other men; so that to die to oneself is *to love the brethren*, and by this side is the secret of Jesus always in our Epistle

[1] 1 John ii. 20, 27.   [2] 1 John i. 7.

presented. 'Let us *love one another!*' 'We know that we have passed from death to life because *we love the brethren.*'[1]

And it agrees with what we have seen in the Fourth Gospel of the author's ear for Christ's profounder teaching, that in the Epistle, too, we find the proof of God, of Christ, and of eternal life, made *experimental*, rested on internal evidence. 'No man hath ever yet seen God; if we love one another, God dwelleth in us.'[2] Therefore we must not attempt to define God adequately, or in a way that goes beyond our experience,— to say, like our theologians: *God is a person!* —but we define God approximately, according to our actual experience of him. And as Jesus had said of this infinite *not ourselves*, 'God is an *influence*,' so our Epistler says, 'God is *love*.'[3] And he says indifferently, 'He that loveth is born of God,' and, 'He that believeth that Jesus is the Christ is born of God,'[4] because believing that Jesus is the Christ means, mainly, admitting the authority of his message or secret, and his secret is: *Love one another!* And God's *evidence* for his Son is this: 'The eternal life which God gives us, this life is in his Son.'[5] That is: in righteousness we have the sense of being truly alive, and through the method, secret, and sweet reasonableness of Jesus, and only through these, we get at righteousness.

[1] 1 John iv. 7; iii. 14. [2] *Ibid.* iv. 12.
[3] *Ibid.* iv. 16.   [4] *Ibid.* iv. 7; v. 1.   [5] *Ibid.* v. 11.

As in the Fourth Gospel, and indeed in all the Gospels, the *joy*, which is the signal accompaniment of life, is in our Epistle strongly marked: 'These things write I unto you, that your *joy may be full*.'[1] And the *not ourselves*, that element wherein religion has its being:— 'Herein is love, not that we loved God, but that he loved us; we love, because he first loved us!'[2] As we did not make the law of righteousness, so we did not, the writer means, make 'the fulfilling of the law,' which is love. It arises in us from the way the *not ourselves* affects us.

In our Epistle, the *Aberglaube* of the approaching second advent appears, of course, prominently; not so that of Christ's physical resurrection. On the other hand, there are here launched phrases destined to rank one day as foremost texts for the doctrine of the Atonement: 'The *blood* of Jesus Christ *cleanses us from all sin*'; 'He is the *propitiation* for our sins.'[3] No development is given to them. How much in them is figure, how much is tenet or the commencements of tenet, we cannot say; but there they are, they are launched, and the hint is given to popular religion to materialise and blunder with.

[1] 1 John i. 4.   [2] 1 John iv. 10, 19.   [3] 1 John i. 7; ii. 2.

V

The Epistle attributed to St. James, and the Epistle to the Hebrews, though not of equal importance with the documents we have been reviewing, suggest, nevertheless, two or three remarks. The zeal of St. James for works carries us back to Jesus Christ's sentence: 'If thou wouldst enter into life, *keep the commandments!*'[1] It is the voice of the indestructible sense in the writer that with Jesus *righteousness* was always the end and aim. The opposition to St. Paul, of which so much has been said, does not really exist; with both Apostles the aim is identical, *righteousness*. Only Paul observed righteousness to be in danger from men using the Jewish law as a kind of spell which they could conjure mechanically with, and therefore he elevated the *faith* by which we get hold of the 'secret' of Jesus, of the 'doctrine of the cross.' James, in his turn, observed righteousness being in danger from men using faith, as it may easily be used, as a spell or charm to conjure mechanically with; and therefore he elevated *works*, the being a *doer*, not an idle hearer and talker. But his noble expression, 'If a man offend *in one point*, he is guilty of all!' and his calling the law which he had in view, 'the law of *liberty*,'[2] proves sufficiently

---

[1] Matt. xix. 17. [2] James ii. 10; i. 25.

that in no unsound sense did he elevate works, as Paul in no unsound sense elevated faith.

The matter whereon the 'secret' of Jesus finds exercise, 'the wishes of the flesh and of the current thoughts,' is well called by St. James: 'Our *pleasures* which war in our members.'[1] And when he goes on and says: 'Being *in* with the world is being *out* with God!'[2] he has on his lips, and in his thoughts too, the very words of the 'secret': 'He that *hateth his life in this world* shall keep it unto life eternal.' For he means, not as many readers suppose: 'He that stands well with the world stands ill with God'; he means: 'He that is *in* with the pleasures which war in our members, is *out* with God.'

But we must not dwell at length on this writer, instructive as he is, and ill as he has been often judged. In fineness or richness of spiritual perception his Epistle may be inferior to other Epistles; without undue disparagement of him we can own this. All the more remarkable, as a testimony to what was chiefly striking in Jesus Christ, is his signalling and extolling that character in Christianity into which fineness of perception enters most: *epieikeia*. 'The wisdom from above,' says St. James, 'is *sweetly reasonable*.'[3]

---

[1] James iv. 1.
[2] ἡ φιλία τοῦ κόσμου ἔχθρα τοῦ Θεοῦ ἐστίν.—James iv. 4.
[3] James iii. 17.

VIII THE EARLY WITNESSES

It is more difficult to limit ourselves in speaking of the Epistle to the Hebrews. Almost alone in the Bible, it is, like later theology, a *notional* work as distinguished from an *experimental* work. That is, instead of being found to run up, at last, into an *experience* of the Eternal that makes for righteousness, it will be found to run up into a *notion* of Jesus being the Logos, with the characters of the Logos as they are stated, for instance, in Philo ; and of this being provable from Scripture and putting an end to the old Jewish dispensation. And because of this notional character, later theology has so much used the Epistle to the Hebrews, and is really in great part built on it. For later theology is notional, too ; 'the blessed truth that the God of the Universe is a PERSON,' is just such a notion as the ground-thesis of the Epistle to the Hebrews, that Jesus is the Logos of Jewish-Alexandrian philosophy. Religion has nothing really to do with either thesis, and that is fortunate ; for neither thesis is demonstrable, and the demonstrations attempted are often palpably hollow. For instance, the whole of the first chapter of the Epistle to the Hebrews is an allegation of text after text as meaning Jesus, and as therefore establishing the writer's thesis, not one of which texts does really mean Jesus. The seventh chapter, again, is one tissue of clever, learned trifling, all based on the false assumption that 'Thou art a priest for ever after the order of Melchisedek!' was really said to *Jesus*, whereas it was not.

Now, just because of this notional character, the Epistle to the Hebrews could not have been St. Paul's; for St. Paul goes upon experience, not notion. And such a work can never have the value and interest of Paul's writings, for it is, in truth, all in the air. But a man who puts a hollow notion as the basis of his theology, may yet in treating it give us all kinds of real and valuable experience; of this we have abundant examples in the writings of theologians. And so the Epistle to the Hebrews is full of beautiful things, and things of real religious experience; but they are independent of the ground-thesis of the Epistle, their value has another source than the value of the writer's main design, and indeed is often marred by it. Their value is as reminiscences of Jesus, and their witness to Jesus is the more striking because of the medium where they appear. To have survived and appear in such a medium, they must have been originally very strong.

The sense that in righteousness religion begins and ends, the writer of the Epistle to the Hebrews has not. He talks of 'not laying again the foundations,' by which he means righteousness, but 'going on unto perfection';[1] by which he means such things as the doctrine that Jesus Christ is, like the Logos of theosophy,

[1] Hebrews vi. 1.

High Priest, and as the demonstration about Melchisedek. All this is of the same order with the 'blessed truth that the God of the universe is a PERSON,' which our bishops imagine to be the marrow of religion, whereas in truth it is not religion at all. But it is remarkable how frequently the writer of our Epistle has the word of the 'method,' *conscience*. Again and again it recurs with him; nowhere in the Bible does it appear, within equal limits of space, so often. The word has evidently established itself and become a power.

But most remarkable is the testimony of this writer to the 'secret.' His view of the sacrifice of Christ as replacing the sacrifices of the Jewish law is all notional, and is really quite independent of Christ's sacrifice as the 'secret.' Yet the 'secret' appears; and in phrases so striking and so much profounder than the strain of this writer's argument, that one is tempted to see in them a tradition of words, not otherwise preserved, of Jesus himself. 'It behoved God, in bringing many sons to glory, to make the leader of their salvation *perfect through suffering*.'[1] Christ '*learned obedience from the things that he suffered*, and, being perfected, became *the author of eternal salvation to all who obey him*.'[2] Christ, like mankind, partook of flesh and blood, 'in order that *by death he might deliver them who through fear of death were all their life subject to*

[1] Heb. ii. 10.   [2] Heb. iv. 8, 9.

bondage.[1] This is precisely the 'secret.' The pain and fear and gloom of dying to our apparent self, to 'the wishes of the flesh and the current thoughts' are so great, that only Jesus and his 'secret,' lighting the process up with joy by showing it to be really life not death, could overcome them, and could enable mankind to overcome them. In like manner the noble phrase, '*without shedding of blood is no remission,*'[2] notional and unfruitful as is its use in the connection where our author employs it, is in itself, perhaps, a reminiscence of actual words of Jesus; certainly it is a reminiscence of his 'secret.' In itself it ranks with the beautiful and profound phrase of St. Peter: '*He that suffers in the flesh hath ceased from sin.*'

VI

Finally, in the ardour for martyrdom which followed in the Christian Church a little later, in the passion for seeking out this kind of death, courting it, provoking it by every means discoverable, we shall not err if we believe that there is again visible the trace of the 'secret.' Assuredly many martyrs, in the temper with which they provoked their death, were false to the *epieikeia*, the 'sweet reasonableness,' of Jesus, and laid themselves open to that sentence of Paul, the sentence which will be the final

---

[1] Heb. ii. 14, 15.   [2] Heb. ix. 22.

verdict of religious history on Puritanism also, Puritanism glorying in its resistances : 'Though I give my body to be burned, *and have not charity*, it profiteth me nothing.'[1] And there was nothing to command or advise the repetition, upon every disciple, of the actual bodily execution of Jesus. But Jesus had enjoined *dying, taking up the cross*, the 'secret';—a long inward travail, other, and often much harder, than being once for all executed. Paul still understood what Jesus meant by *dying*. But the apostolic age passed; and now the Christian community took the word literally, and Christians vied with each other which should run fastest to the place of execution. The wonderful spectacle accelerated Christianity's conquest of the world; but it was already an evidence of failure, in some sort, to follow the mind of Jesus and the teaching of his greatest apostles. *Yet a little while is the light with you! walk while ye have the light, lest the darkness overtake you unawares!*[2]

[1] 1 Cor. xiii. 3. [2] John xii. 35.

CHAPTER IX

ABERGLAUBE RE-INVADING

So spoke the men who had had the Light with them or near them. Mistakes they made and could not but make. But they still knew, that to believe Jesus to be the Son of God, meant to receive and apply the method and secret of Jesus; and therefore their word is the Christian's greatest source of instruction and inspiration after the word of Jesus Christ himself.

But miracles, and the crowning miracles of the Resurrection and Ascension to be followed by the second Advent, were from the first firmly fixed as parts of the disciples' belief. '*Behold, he cometh with clouds; and every eye shall see him, and they also which pierced him; and all kindreds of the earth shall wail because of him!*'[1] As time went on, and Christianity spread wider and wider among the multitudes, and with less and less of control from the personal influence of Jesus, Christianity developed more and more its side of miracle and legend; until to believe Jesus to be

[1] Revelation i. 7.

CH. IX ABERGLAUBE RE-INVADING

the Son of God meant to believe the points of the legend, — his preternatural conception and birth, his miracles, his descent into hell, his bodily resurrection, his ascent into heaven, and his future triumphant return to judgment. And these and like matters are what popular religion drew forth from the records of Jesus as the essentials of belief. These essentials got embodied in a short formulary; and so the creed which is called the Apostles' Creed came together.

It is not the apostles' creed, for it took more than five hundred years to grow to maturity. It was not the creed of any single doctor or body of doctors, but it was a sort of summary of Christianity which the people, the church at large, would naturally develop; it is the *popular science* of Christianity. Given the alleged charge: 'Go ye and teach all nations, baptizing them in the name of the Father, the Son, and the Holy Spirit,'[1] and the candidate for baptism would naturally come to have a profession of faith to make respecting that whereinto he was baptized; this profession of faith would naturally become just such a summary as the Apostles' Creed. It contains no mention of either the 'method' or the 'secret,' it is occupied entirely with external facts; and it may be safely said, not only that such a summary of religious faith could never have been delivered by Jesus, but it could never

[1] Matthew xxviii. 19.

have been adopted as adequate by any of his principal apostles, by Peter, or Paul, or John. But it is, as we have said, the *popular science* of Christianity.

Years proceeded. The world came in to Christianity; the world, and the world's educated people, and the educated people's Aryan genius with its turn for making religion a metaphysical conception; and all this in a time of declining criticism, a time when the possibility of true scientific criticism, in any direction whatever, was lessening rather than increasing. The popular science was found not elaborate enough to satisfy. Ingenious men took its terms and its data, and applied to them, not an historical criticism showing how they arose, but abstruse metaphysical conceptions. And so we have the so-called Nicene Creed, which is the *learned science* of Christianity, as the Apostles' Creed is the popular science.

Now, how this learned science is related to the Bible we shall feel, if we compare the religious utterances of its doctors with the religious utterances of the Bible. Suppose, for instance, we compare with the Psalms the *Soliloquies* of St. Augustine, a truly great and religious man; and of St. Augustine, not in school and controversy, but in religious soliloquy. St. Augustine prays: 'Come to my help, thou one God, one eternal true substance, where is no discrepancy, no confusion, no transience, no indigency, no death; where is supreme concord, supreme evidence, supreme constancy, supreme plenitude, supreme life; where nothing is lacking, nothing is over and above; where he who begets and he who is begotten of him are one; God, above whom is nothing, outside whom is nothing, without whom is nothing; God, beneath whom is the whole, in whom is the whole, with whom is the whole . . . hearken, hearken, hearken unto me, my God, my Lord; open thy door unto me that knock!' And a further *Book of Soliloquies*, popularly ascribed to St. Augustine and printed with his works, but probably of a later date and author, shows the full-blown development of all this, shows the inevitable results of bringing to the idea of God this play of the intellectual fancy so alien to the Bible. The passages we will quote take evidently their inspiration from the words of St. Augustine just given, and retain even in some degree his very forms of expression: 'Holy Trinity, superadmirable Trinity, and superinenarrable, and superinscrutable, and superinaccessible, superincomprehensible, superintelligible, superessential, superessentially surpassing all sense, all reason, all intellect, all intelligence, all essence of supercelestial minds; which can neither be said, nor thought, nor understood, nor known, even by the eyes of angels!' And again, more practically, but still in the same style: 'O three co-equal and co-eternal Persons, one and true God, Father and Son and Holy Ghost, who by thyself inhabitest eternity and light inaccessible, who hast founded the earth in thy power, and rulest the world by thy prudence, Holy, Holy, Holy, Lord God of Sabaoth, terrible and strong, just and merciful, admirable, laudable, amiable, one God, three persons, one essence, power, wisdom, goodness, one and undivided Trinity, open unto me that cry unto Thee the gates of righteousness!'

And now compare this with the Bible:— '*Teach me to do the thing that pleaseth thee, for thou art my God! let thy loving spirit lead me forth into the land of righteousness!*'[1] That is Israel's way of praying! that is how a poor ill-endowed Semite, belonging to the occipital races, unhelped by the Aryan genius and ignorant that religion is a metaphysical conception, talks religion! and we see what a different thing he makes of it.

But, finally, the original Semite fell more and more into the shade. The Aryans came to the front, the notion of religion being a metaphysical conception prevailed. But the doctors differed in their metaphysics; and the doctors who conquered enshrined their victorious form of metaphysics in a creed, the so-called Creed of St. Athanasius, which is learned science like the Nicene Creed, but learned science which has fought and got ruffled by fighting, and is fiercely dictatorial now that it has won;—learned science

[1] Psalm cxliii. 10.

IX ABERGLAUBE RE-INVADING

with a strong dash of violent and vindictive temper.
Thus we have the three creeds: the so-called
Apostles' Creed, popular science; the Nicene
Creed, learned science; the Athanasian Creed,
learned science with a strong dash of temper.
And the two latter are founded on the first,
taking its data just as they stand, but dressing
them metaphysically.

Now this first Creed is founded on a supposed
final charge from Jesus to his apostles: 'Go ye
and teach all nations, baptizing them in the
name of the Father, the Son, and the Holy
Ghost!'[1] It explains and expands what Jesus
here told his apostles to baptize the world into.
But we have already remarked the difference in
character between the narrative in the Gospels,
of what happened before Christ's death and the
narrative of what happened after it. For all
words of Jesus placed *after* his death, the internal
evidence becomes pre-eminently important. He
may well have said words attributed to him, but
not then. So the speech to Thomas: 'Because
thou hast seen me thou hast believed; blessed
are they who have not seen and yet have
believed!'[2] may quite well have been a speech
of Jesus uttered on some occasion during his
life, and then transferred to the story of the
days after his resurrection and made the centre
of this incident of the doubt of Thomas. On
the other hand, again, the prophecy of the

[1] Matthew xxviii. 19.   [2] John xx. 29.

details of Peter's death[1] is almost certainly an addition after the event, because it is not at all in the manner of Jesus. What *is* in his manner, and what he had probably said, are the words given elsewhere: 'Whither I go thou canst not follow me now, but thou shalt follow me afterwards.'[2] So, too, it is extremely improbable that Jesus should have ever charged his apostles to 'baptize all nations in the name of the Father, the Son, and the Holy Ghost.' There is no improbability in his investing them with a very high commission. He may perfectly well have said: 'Whosoever sins ye remit, they are remitted; whosoever sins ye retain, they are retained.'[3] But it is almost impossible he can have given this charge to baptize in the name of the Father, the Son, and the Holy Ghost; it is by far too systematic, and what people are fond of calling an *anachronism*. It is not the least like what Jesus was in the habit of saying, and it is just like what would be attributed to him as baptism and its formula grew in importance. The genuine charge of Jesus to his apostles was, almost certainly: 'As my Father sent me, even so send I you,'[4] and not this. So that our three creeds, and with them the whole of our so-called orthodox theology, are founded upon words which Jesus in all probability never uttered.

[1] John xxi. 18. [2] John xiii. 36.
[3] John xx. 23. [4] John xx. 22.

ABERGLAUBE RE-INVADING

II

We may leave all questions about the Church, its rise, and its organisation, out of sight altogether. Much as is made of them, they are comparatively unimportant. Jesus never troubled himself with what are called Church matters at all; his attention was fixed solely upon the individual. His apostles did what was necessary, as such matters came to require a practical notice and arrangement; but to the apostles, too, they were still quite secondary. The Church grew into something quite different from what they or Jesus had, or could have had, any thought of. But this was of no importance in itself; and how believers should organise their society as circumstances changed, circumstances themselves might very well decide.

The one important question was and is, how believers laid and kept hold on the revelations contained in the Bible; because for the sake of these it confessedly is that every church exists. Even the apostles, we have seen, did not lay hold on them perfectly. In their attachment to miracles, in the prominence they gave to the crowning miracles of Christ's bodily resurrection and second advent, they went aside from the saving doctrine of Jesus themselves, and were sure,—which was worse,—to make others go aside from it ten thousand times more.

But they were too near to Jesus not to have been able to preserve the main lines of his teaching, to preserve his way of using words; and they did, as we have shown, preserve them.

But at their death the immediate remembrance of Jesus faded away, and whatever *Aberglaube* the apostles themselves had had and sanctioned was left to work without check. And, at the same time, the world and society presented conditions constantly less and less favourable to sane criticism. And it was then, and under these conditions, that the dogma which is now called orthodox, and which our dogmatic friends imagine to be purely a methodical arrangement of the admitted facts of Christianity, grew up. We have shown from the thing itself, by putting the dogma in comparison with the genuine teaching of Jesus, how little it is this; but it is well to make clear to oneself also (for one can) from the circumstances of the case, that it *could* not be this.

For dogmatic theology is, in fact, an attempt at both literary and scientific criticism of the highest order; and the age which developed dogma had neither the resources nor the faculty for such a criticism. It is idle to talk of the theological instinct, the analogy of faith, as if by the mere occupation with a limited subject-matter one could reach the truth about it. It is as if one imagined that by the mere

IX ABERGLAUBE RE-INVADING

study of Greek we could reach the truth about the origin of Greek words, and dogmatise about them; and could appeal to our supposed possession, through our labours, of the philological instinct, the analogy of language, to make our dogmatism go down. In general such an instinct, whether theological or philological, will mean merely, that, having accustomed ourselves to look at things through a glass of a certain colour, we see them always of that colour. What the science of Bible-criticism, like all other science, needs, is a very wide experience from comparative observation in many directions, and a very slowly acquired habit of mind. All studies have the benefit of these guides, when they exist, and one isolated study can never have the benefit of them by itself. There is a common order, a general level, an uniform possibility, for these things. As were the geography, history, physiology, cosmology, of the men who developed dogma, so was also their faculty for a scientific Bible-criticism, such as dogma pretends to be. Now we know what their geography, history, physiology, cosmology, were. Cosmas Indicopleustes, a Christian navigator of Justinian's time, denies that the earth is spherical, and asserts it to be a flat surface with the sky put over it like a dish-cover. The Christian metaphysics of the same age, applying the ideas of substance and identity to what the Bible says about God, Jesus, and the Holy Spirit, are on a par with this natural philosophy.

And again, as one part of their scientific Bible-criticism, so the rest. We have seen in the Bible-writers themselves a quite uncritical use of the Old Testament and of prophecy. Now, does this become less in the authors of our dogmatic theology,—a far more pretentious effort of criticism than the Bible-writers ever made,—or does it become greater? It becomes a thousand times greater. Not only are definite predictions found where they do not exist,—as, for example, in Isaiah's *I will restore thy judges as at the first*,[1] is found a definite foretelling of the Apostles,—but in the whole Bible a secret allegorical sense is supposed, higher than the natural sense; so that Jerome calls tracing the natural sense an eating dust like the serpent, *in modum serpentis terram comedere*. Therefore, for one expounder, Isaiah's prophecy against Egypt: *The Eternal rideth upon a light cloud, and shall come into Egypt*,[2] is the flight into Egypt of the Holy Family, and the *light cloud* is the virgin-born body of Jesus; for another, *The government shall be upon his shoulder*,[3] is Christ's carrying upon his shoulder the cross; for another, *The lion shall eat straw like the ox*,[4] is the faithful and the wicked alike receiving the body of Christ in the Eucharist.

---

[1] Isaiah i. 26.   [2] Isaiah xix. 1.
[3] Isaiah ix. 6.   [4] Isaiah lxv. 25.

IX ABERGLAUBE RE-INVADING

These are the men, this is the critical faculty, from which our so-called orthodox dogma proceeded. The worth of all the productions of such a critical faculty is easy to estimate, for the worth is nearly uniform. When the Rabbinical expounders interpret: *Woe unto them that lay field to field!*[1] as a prophetic curse on the accumulation of Church property, or: *Woe unto them that rise up early in the morning that they may follow strong drink!*[2] as a prediction of the profligacy of the Church clergy, or: *Woe unto them that draw iniquity with cords of vanity!*[3] as God's malediction on Church bells, we say at once that such critics thus give their measure as interpreters of the true sense of the Bible. The moment we think seriously and fairly, we must see that the Patristic interpretations of prophecy give, in like manner, their authors' measure as interpreters of the true sense of the Bible. Yet this is what the dogma of the Nicene and Athanasian Creeds professes to be, and must be if it is to be worth anything,—*the true sense extracted from the Bible;* for, 'the Bible is the record of the whole revealed faith,' says Dr. Newman. But we see how impossible it is that this true sense the dogma of these creeds should be.

Therefore it is, that it is useful to give signal instances of the futility of patristic and mediæval criticism; not to raise an idle laugh, but because

[1] Isaiah v. 8.   [2] Isaiah v. 11.   [3] Isaiah v. 18.

our whole dogmatic theology has a patristic and mediæval source, and from the nullity of the deliverances of this criticism, where it can be brought manifestly to book, may be inferred the nullity of its deliverances, where, from the impalpable and incognisable character of the subjects treated, to bring it manifestly to book is impossible. In the account of the Creation, in the first chapter of Genesis, 'the greater light to rule the day' is the priesthood; 'the lesser light to rule the night,'[1] borrowing its beams from the greater, is the Holy Roman Empire. When the disciples of Jesus produced two swords, and Jesus said: 'It is enough,'[2] he meant, we are told, the temporal and the spiritual power, and that both were necessary and both at the disposal of the Church; but by saying afterwards to Peter, after he had cut off the ear of Malchus: 'Put up thy sword into the sheath,'[3] he meant that the Church was not to wield the temporal power itself, but to employ the secular government to wield it. Now, this is the very same force of criticism which in the Athanasian Creed 'arranged sentence after sentence,' that doctrine of the Godhead of the Eternal Son for which the Bishops of Winchester and Gloucester are so anxious to 'do something.'

The Schoolmen themselves are but the same false criticism developed, and clad in an apparatus

---

[1] Genesis i. 16.   [2] Luke xxii. 38.
[3] John xviii. 11.

of logic and system. In that grand and instructive repertory founded by the Benedictines, the *Histoire Littéraire de la France*, we read that in the theological faculty of the University of Paris, the leading mediæval university, it was seriously discussed whether Jesus at his ascension had his clothes on or not. If he had not, did he appear before his apostles naked? if he had, what became of the clothes? *Monstrous!* every one will say.[1] Yes, but the very same criticism, only full-blown, which produced: 'Neither confounding the Persons nor dividing the Substance.' The very same criticism, which originally treated terms as scientific which were not scientific; which, instead of applying literary and historical criticism to the data of popular *Aberglaube*, took these data just as they stood and merely dressed them scientifically.

Catholic dogma itself is true, urges, however, Dr. Newman, because intelligent Catholics have dropped errors and absurdities like the False Decretals or the works of the pretended Dionysius the Areopagite, but have not dropped dogma. This is only saying that men drop the more palpable blunder before the less palpable. The adequate criticism of the Bible is extremely difficult, and slowly does the 'Zeit-Geist' unveil

[1] Be it observed, however, that there is an honest scientific effort in the Schoolmen, and that to this sort of thing one really *does* come, when one fairly sets oneself to treat miracles literally and exactly; but most of us are content to leave them in a half light.

it. Meanwhile, of the premature and false criticism to which we are accustomed, we drop the evidently weak parts first; we retain the rest, to drop it gradually and piece by piece as it loosens and breaks up. But it is all of one order, and in time it will all go. Not the Athanasian Creed's damnatory clauses only, but the whole Creed; not this one Creed only, but the three Creeds,—our whole received application of *science*, popular or learned, to the Bible. For it was an inadequate and false science, and could not, from the nature of the case, be otherwise.

III

And now we see how much that clergyman deceives himself, who writes to the *Guardian*: 'The objectors to the Athanasian Creed at any rate admit, that its doctrinal portions are truly the carefully distilled essence of the scattered intimations of Holy Scripture on the deep mysteries in question,— priceless discoveries made in that field.' When one has travelled to the Athanasian Creed along the gradual line of the historical development of Christianity, instead of living stationary all one's life with this Creed blocking up the view, one is really tempted to say, when one reads a deliverance like that of this clergyman: *Sancta simplicitas!* It is just because the Athanasian Creed pretends to be, in its doctrine, 'the carefully distilled essence of the scattered intimations of Holy Scripture,' and *is so very far from it*, that it is worthless. It is 'the carefully distilled essence of the scattered intimations of Holy Scripture' just as that allegory of the two swords was. It is really a mixture,—for true criticism, as it ripens, it is even a grotesque mixture,—of learned pseudo-science with popular *Aberglaube*.

But it cannot be too carefully borne in mind that the real 'essence of Holy Scripture,' its saving truth, is no such criticism at all as the so-called orthodox dogma attempts, and attempts unsuccessfully. No, the real essence of Scripture is a much simpler matter. It is, for the Old Testament: *To him that ordereth his conversation right shall be shown the salvation of God!*—and, for the New Testament: *Follow Jesus!* This is Bible-dogma, as opposed to the dogma of our formularies. On this Bible-dogma if Churches were founded, and to preach this Bible-dogma if ministers were ordained, Churches and ministers would have all the dogma to which the Bible attaches eternal life. Plain and precise enough it is, in all conscience; with the advantage of being precisely *right*, whereas the dogma of our formularies is precisely *wrong*. And if any one finds it too simple, let him remember that its hardness is practical, not speculative. It is a rule of *conduct;* let him act it, and he will find it hard enough. *Utinam per unum diem bene essemus conversati in hoc mundo!* But as a matter of mere knowledge it is very simple, it lies on the surface of the Bible and cannot be missed.

And the holders of ecclesiastical dogma have always, we must repeat and remember, held and professed this Bible-dogma too. Their ecclesiastical dogma may have prevented their attending closely enough to the Bible-dogma, may have led them often to act false to it; but they have always held it. The method and the secret of Jesus have been always prized. The Catholic Church from the first held aloft the secret of Jesus; the monastic orders were founded, we may say, in homage to it. And from time to time, through the course of ages, there have arisen men who threw themselves on the method and secret of Jesus with extraordinary force, with intuitive sense that here was salvation; and who really cared for nothing else, though ecclesiastical dogma, too, they professed to believe, and sincerely thought they did believe,—but their heart was elsewhere. These are they who 'received the kingdom of God as a little child,' who perceived how simple a thing Christianity was, though so inexhaustible, and who are therefore 'the greatest in the kingdom of God.' And they, not the theological doctors, are the true lights of the Christian Church; not Augustine, Luther, Bossuet, Butler, but the nameless author of the *Imitation*, but Tauler, but St. Francis of Sales, Wilson of Sodor and Man. Yet not only these men, but the whole body of Christian churches and sects always, have all at least *professed* the method and secret of Jesus, and to some extent used them. And whenever these were used, they have borne their natural fruits of joy and life; and this joy and this life have been taken to flow from the ecclesiastical dogma held along with them, and to sanction and prove it. And people, eager to praise the bridge which carried them over from death to life, have taken this dogma for the bridge, or part of the bridge, that carried them over, and have eagerly praised it. Thus religion has been made to stand on its apex instead of its base. Righteousness is supported on ecclesiastical dogma, instead of ecclesiastical dogma being supported on righteousness.

But in the beginning it was not so. Because righteousness is eternal, necessary, life-giving, *therefore* the mighty 'not ourselves which makes for righteousness' was the Eternal, Israel's God; was all-powerful, all-merciful; sends his Messiah, elects his people, establishes his kingdom, receives into everlasting habitations. But gradually this petrifies, gradually it is more and more added to; until at last, because righteousness was originally perceived to be eternal, necessary, life-giving, we find ourselves 'worshipping One God in Trinity and Trinity in Unity, neither confounding the Persons nor dividing the Substance.' And then the original order is reversed. Because there is One God in

Trinity and Trinity in Unity, who receives into everlasting habitations, establishes his kingdom, elects his people, sends his Messiah, is all-merciful, all-powerful, Israel's God, the Eternal, —*therefore* righteousness is eternal, necessary, life-giving. And shake the belief in the One God in Trinity and Trinity in Unity, the belief in righteousness is shaken, it is thought, also. Whereas righteousness and the God of righteousness, the God of the Bible, are in truth quite independent of the God of ecclesiastical dogma, the work of critics of the Bible,—critics understanding neither what they say nor whereof they affirm.

IV

Nor did the Reformation and Protestantism much mend the work of these critics; the time was not yet ripe for it. Protestantism, nevertheless, was a strenuous and noble effort at improvement; for it was an effort of return to the 'method' of Jesus,—that leaven which never, since he set it in the world, has ceased or can cease to work. Catholicism, we have said, laid hold on the 'secret' of Jesus, and strenuously, however blindly, employed it; this is the grandeur and the glory of Catholicism. In like manner Protestantism laid hold on his 'method,' and strenuously, however blindly, employed it; and herein is the greatness of Protestantism. The preliminary labour of in-

IX ABERGLAUBE RE-INVADING

wardness and sincerity in the conscience of each individual man, which was the method of Jesus and his indispensable discipline for learning to employ his secret aright, had fallen too much out of view; *obedience* had in a manner superseded it. Protestantism drew it into light and prominence again; was even, one may say, over-absorbed by it, so as to leave too much out of view the 'secret.' This, if one would be just both to Catholicism and to Protestantism, is the thing to bear in mind:—Protestantism had hold of Jesus Christ's 'method' of inwardness and sincerity, Catholicism had hold of his 'secret' of self-renouncement. The chief word with Protestantism is the word of the method: *repentance, conversion;* the chief word with Catholicism is the word of the secret: *peace, joy*.

And since, though the method and the secret are equally indispensable, the secret may be said to have in it more of practice and conduct, Catholicism may claim perhaps to have more of religion. On the other hand, Protestantism has more light; and, as the method of inwardness and sincerity, once gained, is of general application, and a power for all the purposes of life, Protestantism, we can see, has been accompanied by most prosperity. And here is the answer to Mr. Buckle's famous parallel between Spain and Scotland, that parallel which every one feels to be a sophism. Scotland has had, to make her different from Spain, the 'method' of Jesus;

and though, in theology, Scotland may have turned it to no great account, she has found her account in it in almost everything else. Catholicism, again, has had, perhaps, most happiness. When one thinks of the bitter and contentious temper of Puritanism,— temper being, nevertheless, such a vast part of *conduct*, —and then thinks of St. Theresa and her sweetness, her never-sleeping hatred of 'detraction,' one is tempted almost to say, that there was more of Jesus in St. Theresa's little finger than in John Knox's whole body. Protestantism has the method of Jesus with his secret too much left out of mind; Catholicism has his secret with his method too much left out of mind. Neither has his unerring balance, his intuition, his *sweet reasonableness*. But both have hold of a great truth, and get from it a great power.

And many of the reproaches cast by one on the other are idle. If Catholicism is reproached with being indifferent to much that is called *civilisation*, it must be answered: So was Jesus. If Protestantism, with its private judgment, is accused of opening a wide field for individual fancies and mistakes, it must be answered: So did Jesus when he introduced his method. Private judgment, '*the fundamental and insensate doctrine of Protestantism*,' as Joseph de Maistre calls it, is in truth but the necessary 'method,' the eternally incumbent *duty*, imposed by Jesus himself, when he said: 'Judge not according to the appearance, but judge righteous judgment.'[1] 'Judge *righteous* judgment' is, however, the duty imposed; and the duty is not, whatever many Protestants may seem to think, fulfilled if the judgment be *wrong*. But the duty of inwardly judging is the very entrance into the way and walk of Jesus.

Luther, then, made an inward verifying movement, the individual conscience, once more the base of operations; and he was right. But he did so to the following extent only. When he found the priest coming between the individual believer and his conscience, standing to him in the stead of conscience, he pushed the priest aside and brought the believer face to face with his conscience again. This explains, of course, his battle against the sale of indulgences and other abuses of the like kind; but it explains also his treatment of that cardinal point in the Catholic religious system, the mass. He substituted for it, as the cardinal point in the Protestant system, justification by faith. The miracle of Jesus Christ's atoning sacrifice, satisfying God's wrath, and taking off the curse from mankind, is the foundation both of the mass and of the famous Lutheran tenet. But, in the mass, the priest makes the miracle over again and applies its benefits to the believer. In the tenet of justification, the believer is himself in contact with the miracle of Christ's atonement,

[1] John vii. 24.

and applies Christ's merits to himself. The conscience is thus brought into direct communication with Christ's saving act; but this saving act is still taken,—just as popular religion conceived it, and as formal theology adopted it from popular religion,—as a miracle, the miracle of the Atonement. This popular and imperfect conception of the sense of Christ's death, and in general the whole inadequate criticism of the Bible involved in the Creeds, underwent at the Reformation no scrutiny and no change. Luther's actual application, therefore, of the 'method' of Jesus to the inner body of dogma, developed as we have seen, which he found regnant, proceeded no farther than this.

And *justification by faith*, our being saved by 'giving our hearty consent to Christ's atoning work on our behalf,' by 'pleading simply the blood of the covenant,' Luther made the essential matter not only of his own religious system but of the entire New Testament. We must be enabled, he said, and we *are* enabled, to distinguish among the books of the Bible those which are the best; now, those are the best which *show Christ*, and teach what would be enough for us to know even if no other parts of the Bible existed. And this *evangelical element*, as it has been called, this *fundamental thought of the Gospel*, is, for Luther, our 'being justified by the alone merits of Christ.' This is the doctrine of 'passive or Christian righteousness,' as Luther

IX ABERGLAUBE RE-INVADING

is fond of naming it, which consists in 'doing nothing, but simply knowing and believing that Christ is gone to the Father and we see him no more; that he sits in Heaven at the right hand of the Father, not as our judge, but made unto us by God wisdom, righteousness, sanctification, and redemption;[1] in sum, that he is our high-priest making intercession for us.' Every one will recognise the consecrated watchwords of Protestant theology.

Such is Luther's criticism of the New Testament, of its fundamental thought. And he picks out, as the kernel and marrow of the New Testament, the Fourth Gospel and the First Epistle by the author of this Gospel, St. Paul's Epistles,—in especial those to the Romans, Galatians, and Ephesians,—and the First Epistle of St. Peter. Now, the common complaint against Luther is on the score of his audacity in thus venturing to make a table of precedence for the equally inspired books of the New Testament. Yet in this he was quite right, and was but following the method of Jesus, if the *good news* conveyed in the whole New Testament is, as it is, something definite, and all parts do not convey it equally. Where he was wrong, was in his *delineation* of this fundamental thought of the New Testament, in his *description* of the good news; and few, probably, who have followed us thus far, will have difficulty in

[1] I Corinthians i. 30.

admitting that he *was* wrong here, and quite wrong. And this has been the fault of Protestantism generally: not its presumption in interpreting Scripture for itself,—for the Church interpreted it no better, and Jesus has thrown on each individual the duty of interpreting it for himself,—but that it has interpreted it *wrong*, and no better than the Church. 'Calvinism has borne ever an inflexible front to illusion and mendacity,' says Mr. Froude. Surely this is but a flourish of rhetoric; for the Calvinistic doctrine is in itself, like the Lutheran doctrine, and like Catholic dogma, a false criticism of the Bible, an *illusion*. And the Calvinistic and Lutheran doctrines both of them sin in the same way; not by using a method which, after all, is the method of Jesus, but by not using the method enough, by not applying it to the Bible thoroughly, by keeping too much of what the traditions of men chose to tell them.

V

The time was not then ripe for doing more; and we, if we can do more, have the fulness of time to thank for it, not ourselves. Yet it needs all one's sense of the *not ourselves* in these things, to make us understand how doctrines, supposed to be the essence of the Bible by great Catholics and by great Protestants, should ever have been supposed to be so, and by such men.

IX ABERGLAUBE RE-INVADING

To take that chief stronghold of ecclesiasticism and sacerdotalism, the institution of the Eucharist. As Catholics present it, it makes the Church indispensable, with all her apparatus of an apostolical succession, an authorised priesthood, a power of absolution. Yet, as Jesus founded it, it is the most anti-ecclesiastical of institutions, pulverising alike the historic churches in their beauty and the dissenting sects in their unloveliness;—it is the consecration of absolute individualism. 'This cup is *the new covenant* in my blood which is shed for you.'[1] When Jesus so spoke, what did he mean, what was in his mind? Undoubtedly these words of the prophet Jeremiah: 'Behold the days come, saith the Eternal, that I will make *a new covenant* with the house of Israel, not according to the covenant that I made with their fathers, which covenant they brake; but this shall be the covenant that I will make with the house of Israel: After those days, saith the Eternal, I will put my law in their *inward parts*, and write it in their *hearts*, and *they shall teach no more every man his neighbour and every man his brother*, saying: Know the Eternal! for *they shall all know me*, from the least to the greatest.'[2] No more scribes, no more doctors, no more priests! the crowning act in the 'secret' of Jesus seals at the same time his 'method,'— his method of pure

[1] Luke xxii. 20. [2] Jeremiah xxxi. 31.

inwardness, individual responsibility, personal religion.

Take, again, the Protestant doctrine of Justification; of trusting in the alone merits of Christ, pleading the Blood of the Covenant, imputed righteousness. In our railway stations are hung up, as every one knows, sheets of Bible-texts to catch the passer's eye; and very profitable admonitions to him they in general are. It is said that the thought of thus exhibiting them occurred to Dr. Marsh, a venerable leader of the so-called Evangelical party in our Church, the party which specially clings to the special Protestant doctrine of justification; and that he arranged the texts we daily see. And there is one which we may all remember to have often seen. Dr. Marsh asks the prophet Micah's question: 'Wherewith shall I come before the Lord, and bow myself before the high God?'[1] and he answers it with one short sentence from the New Testament: 'With the precious blood of Christ.' This is precisely the popular Protestant notion of *the Gospel;* and we are all so used to it that Dr. Marsh's application of the text has probably surprised no one. And yet, if one thinks of it, how astonishing an application it is! For even the Hebrew Micah, some seven or eight centuries before Christ, had seen that this sort of *gospel*, or good news,

[1] Micah vi. 6.

was none at all; for even he suggests this always popular notion of *atoning blood* only to reject it, and ends: 'He hath showed thee, O man, what is good; and what doth the Eternal require of thee, but to do justly, and to love mercy, and to walk humbly with thy God?' So that the Hebrew Micah, nearly three thousand years ago, under the old dispensation, was far in advance of this venerable and amiable coryphæus of our Evangelical party now, under the Christian dispensation!

Dr. Marsh and his school go wrong, it will be said, through their false criticism of the New Testament, and we have ourselves admitted that the perfect criticism of the New Testament is extremely difficult. True, the *perfect* criticism; but not such an elementary criticism of it as shows the gospel of Dr. Marsh and of our so-called Evangelical Protestants to be a false one. For great as their literary inexperience is, and unpractised as is their tact for perceiving the manner in which men use words and what they mean by them, one would think they could understand such a plain caution against mistaking Christ's death for a miraculous atonement as St. Paul has actually given them. For St. Paul, who so admirably seized the secret of Jesus, who preached *Christ crucified*,[1] but who placed salvation in being able to say, *I am crucified with Christ!*[2]—St. Paul warns us clearly,

[1] 1 Cor. i. 23.   [2] Gal. ii. 20.

that this *word of the cross*, as he calls it, is so simple, being neither miracle nor metaphysics, that it would be thought foolishness. The Jews want miracle, he says, and the Greeks want metaphysics, but I preach *Christ crucified!*[1]— that is, the 'secret' of Jesus, as we call it. *The Jews want miracle!*—that is a warning against Dr. Marsh's or Mr. Spurgeon's doctrine, against Evangelical Protestantism's phantasmagories of the 'Contract in the Council of the Trinity,' the 'Atoning Blood,' and 'Imputed Righteousness.' *The Greeks want metaphysics!*—that is a warning against the Bishops of Winchester and Gloucester, with their Aryan genius (if so ill-sounding a word as Aryan, spell it how one may, can ever be properly applied to our bishops, and one ought not rather to say Indo-European), dressing the popular doctrine out with fine speculations about the Godhead of the Eternal Son, his Consubstantiality with the Father, and so on. But *we* preach, says St. Paul, *Christ crucified!*— to Mr. Spurgeon and to popular religion a stumbling-block, to the bishops and to learned religion foolishness ; but to them that are called, Christ the power of God and the wisdom of God. That is, we preach a doctrine, not thaumaturgical and not speculative, but practical and experimental ; a doctrine which has no meaning except in positive application to conduct, but in this application is inexhaustible.

[1] 1 Corinthians i. 23.

IX ABERGLAUBE RE-INVADING

VI

So false, so astoundingly false (thus one is inclined to say by the light which the 'Zeit-Geist' is beginning to hold out over them) are both popular and learned science in their criticism of the Bible. And for the learned science one feels no tenderness, because it has gone wrong with a great parade of exactitude and philosophy; whereas all it really did was to take the magnified and non-natural Man of popular religion as God, and to take Jesus as his son, and then to state the relations between them metaphysically. No difficulties suggested by the popular science of religion has this learned science ever removed, and it has created plenty of its own.

But for the popular science of religion one has, or ought to have, an infinite tenderness. It is the spontaneous work of nature. It is the travail of the human mind to adapt to its grasp and employment great ideas of which it feels the attraction, but for which, except as given to it by this travail, it would have been immature. The imperfect science of the Bible, formulated in the so-called Apostles' Creed, was the only vehicle by which, to generation after generation of men, the method and secret of Jesus could gain any access; and in this sense we may even call it, taking the point of view of popular theology, *Providential*. And this rude criticism is full of poetry, and in this poetry we have been all nursed. To call it, as many of our philosophical Liberal friends are fond of calling it, 'a degrading superstition,' is as untrue as it is a poor compliment to human nature, which produced this criticism and used it. It is an *Aberglaube*, or extra-belief and fairy-tale, produced by taking certain great names and great promises too literally and materially; but it is *not* a degrading superstition.

Protestants, on their part, have no difficulty in calling the Catholic doctrine of the mass 'a degrading superstition.' It is indeed a rude and blind criticism of Jesus Christ's words: *He that eateth me shall live by me*. But once admit the miracle of the 'atoning sacrifice,' once move in this order of ideas, and what can be more natural and beautiful than to imagine this miracle every day repeated, Christ offered in thousands of places, everywhere the believer enabled to enact the work of redemption and unite himself with the Body whose sacrifice saves him? And the effect of this belief has been no more degrading than the belief itself. The fourth book of the *Imitation*, which treats of *The Sacrament of the Altar*, is of later date and lesser merit than the three books which precede it; but it is worth while to quote from it a few words for the sake of the testimony they bear to the practical operation, in many cases at any rate, of this belief. 'To us in our weakness thou hast given, for the refreshment of mind and body, thy sacred Body. The devout communicant thou, my God, raisest from the depth of his own dejection to the hope of thy protection, and with a hitherto unknown grace renewest him and enlightenest him within; so that they who at first, before this Communion, had felt themselves distressed and affectionless, after the refreshment of this meat and drink from heaven find themselves changed to a new and better man. For this most high and worthy Sacrament is the saving health of soul and body, the medicine of all spiritual languor; *by it my vices are cured, my passions bridled, temptations are conquered or diminished, a larger grace is infused, the beginnings of virtue are made to grow, faith is confirmed, hope strengthened, and charity takes fire and dilates into flame.*' So little is the doctrine of the mass to be hastily called 'a degrading superstition,' either in its character or in its working.

But it is *false!* sternly breaks in the Evangelical Protestant. O Evangelical Protestant, is thine own doctrine, then, so true? As the Romish doctrine of the mass, the Real Presence, is a rude and blind criticism of: *He that eateth me shall live by me;*[1] so the Protestant tenet of justification, 'pleading the blood of the Covenant,' is a rude and blind criticism of: *The Son of Man*

[1] John vi. 57.

came to give his life a ransom for many.[1] It is a taking of the words of Scripture literally and unintelligently. And our friends, the philosophical Liberals, are not slow to call this, too, a degrading superstition, just as Protestants call the doctrine of the mass a degrading superstition. We say, on the contrary, that a degrading superstition neither the one nor the other is. In imagining a sort of infinitely magnified and improved Lord Shaftesbury, with a race of vile offenders to deal with, whom his natural goodness would incline him to let off, only his sense of justice will not allow it ; then a younger Lord Shaftesbury, on the scale of his father and very dear to him, who might live in grandeur and splendour if he liked, but who prefers to leave his home, to go and live among the race of offenders, and to be put to an ignominious death, on condition that his merits shall be counted against their demerits, and that his father's goodness shall be restrained no longer from taking effect, but any offender shall be admitted to the benefit of it on simply pleading the satisfaction made by the son ; — and then, finally, a third Lord Shaftesbury, still on the same high scale, who keeps very much in the background, and works in a very occult manner, but very efficaciously nevertheless, and who is busy in applying everywhere the benefits of the son's satisfaction, and the father's goodness ;—in an imagination,

[1] Matthew xx. 28.

IX   ABERGLAUBE RE-INVADING

I say, such as this, there is nothing degrading, and this is precisely the Protestant story of *Justification*. And how awe of the first Lord Shaftesbury, gratitude and love towards the second, and earnest co-operation with the third, may fill and rule men's hearts so as to transform their conduct, we need not go about to show, for we have all seen it with our eyes. Therefore in the practical working of this tenet there is nothing degrading; any more than there is anything degrading in the tenet as an imaginative conception. And looking to the infinite importance of getting right conduct,—three-fourths of human life,—established, and to the inevitable anthropomorphism and *extra-belief* of men in dealing with ideas, one might well hesitate to attack an anthropomorphism or an extra-belief by which men helped themselves in conduct, merely because an anthropomorphism or an extra-belief it is, so long as it served its purpose, so long as it was firmly and undoubtingly held, and almost universally prevailing.

But, after all, the question sooner or later arises in respect to a matter taken for granted, like the Catholic doctrine of the Mass or the Protestant doctrine of Justification: Is it *sure?* can what is here assumed be *verified?* And this is the real objection both to the Catholic and to the Protestant doctrine as a basis for conduct;—not that it is a degrading superstition, but that it is *not sure;* that it assumes what cannot be *verified*.

For a long time this objection occurred to scarcely anybody. And there are still, and for a long time yet there will be, many to whom it does not occur. In particular, on those 'devout women' who in the history of religion have at all times played a part in many respects so beautiful but in some respects so mischievous, —on them, and on a certain number of men like them, it has and can as yet have, so far as one can see, no effect at all. Who that watches the energumens during the celebration of the Communion in some Ritualistic church, their gestures and behaviour, the floor of the Church strewn with what seem to be the dying and the dead, progress to the altar almost barred by forms suddenly dropping as if they were shot in battle,—who that observes this delighted adoption of vehement rites, till yesterday unknown, adopted and practised now with all that absence of tact, measure, and correct perception in things of form and manner, all that slowness to see when they are making themselves ridiculous, which belongs to the people of our English race,—who, I say, that marks this can doubt, that for a not small portion of the religious community, a difficulty to the intelligence will for a long time yet be no difficulty at all? With their mental condition and habits, given a story to which their religious emotions can attach themselves, and the famous *Credo quia ineptum* will hold good with them still. To think they know what passed in the Council of the Trinity is not hard to them; they could easily think they even knew what were the hangings of the Trinity's council-chamber.

Arbitrary and unsupported, however, as the story they have taken up with may be, yet it puts them in connection with the Bible and the religion of the Bible,—that is, with righteousness and with the method and secret of Jesus. These are so clear in the Bible that no one who uses it can help seeing them there; and of these they do take for their use something, though on a wrong ground. But these, so far as they are taken into use, are saving.

CHAPTER X

OUR 'MASSES' AND THE BIBLE

MANY, however, and of a much stronger and more important sort, there now are, who will not thus take on trust the story which is made the reason for putting ourselves in connection with the Bible and learning to use its religion; be it the story of the divine authority of the Church, as in Catholic countries, or,—as generally with us,—the story of the three Lord Shaftesburys standing on its own merits. Is what this story asserts *true*, they are beginning to ask; can it be verified?—since experience proves, they add, that whatever for man is true, man can verify. And certainly the fairy-tale of the three Lord Shaftesburys no man can verify. They find this to be so, and then they say: The Bible takes for granted this story and depends on the truth of it; what, then, can rational people have to do with the Bible? So they get rid, to be sure, of a false ground for using the Bible, but they at the same time lose the Bible itself, and the true

CH. X OUR 'MASSES' AND THE BIBLE

religion of the Bible: righteousness, and the method and secret of Jesus. And those who lose this are *the masses*, as they are called; or rather they are what is most strenuous, intelligent, and alive among the masses, and what will give the signal for the rest to follow.

This is what every one sees to constitute the special moral feature of our times: *the masses* are losing the Bible and its religion. At the Renascence, many cultivated wits lost it; but the great solid mass of the common people kept it, and brought the world back to it after a start had seemed to be made in quite another direction. But now it is *the people* which is getting detached from the Bible. The masses can no longer be relied on to counteract what the cultivated wits are doing, and stubbornly to make clever men's extravagances and aberrations, if about the Bible they commit them, of no avail. When our philosophical Liberal friends say, that by universal suffrage, public meetings, Church-disestablishment, marrying one's deceased wife's sister, secular schools, industrial development, man can very well live; and that if he studies the writings, say, of Mr. Herbert Spencer into the bargain, he will be perfect, he will have 'in modern and congenial language the truisms common to all systems of morality,' and the Bible is become quite old-fashioned and superfluous for him;—when our philosophical friends now say this, the masses, far from checking them, are disposed to applaud them to the echo. Yet assuredly, of conduct, which is more than three-fourths of human life, the Bible, whatever people may thus think and say, is the great inspirer; so that from the great inspirer of more than three-fourths of human life the masses of our society seem now to be cutting themselves off. This promises, certainly, if it does not already constitute, a very unsettled condition of things. And the cause of it lies in the Bible being made to depend on a story, or set of asserted facts, which it is impossible to verify; and which hard-headed people, therefore, treat as either an imposture, or a fairy-tale that discredits all which is found in connection with it.

II

Now if we look attentively at the story, or set of asserted but unverified and unverifiable facts, which we have summarised in popular language above, and which is alleged as the basis of the Bible, we shall find that the difficulty really lies all in one point. The whole difficulty is with the elder Lord Shaftesbury. If *he* could be verified, the data we have are, possibly, enough to warrant our admitting the truth of the rest of the story. It is singular how few people seem to see this, though it is really quite clear. The Bible is supposed to assume a Great Personal First Cause, who thinks and loves, the moral and intelligent Governor of the Universe; a sort of elder Lord Shaftesbury, as we call him, infinitely magnified. This is the God, also, of *natural religion*, as people call it; and this supposed certainty learned reasoners take, and render it more certain still by considerations of causality, identity, existence, and so on. These, however, are not found to help the certainty much; but a certainty in itself the Great Personal First Cause, the God of both natural and revealed religion, is supposed to be.

Then, to this given beginning, all that the Bible delivers has to fit itself on. And so arises the account of the God of the Old Testament, and of Christ and of the Holy Ghost, and of the incarnation and atonement, and of the sacraments, and of inspiration, and of the church, and of eternal punishment and eternal bliss, as theology presents them. But difficulties strike people in this or that of these doctrines. The incarnation seems incredible to one, the vicarious atonement to another, the real presence to a third, inspiration to a fourth, eternal punishment to a fifth, and so on. And they set to work to make religion more pure and rational, as they suppose, by pointing out that this or that of these doctrines is false, that it must be a mistake of theologians; and by interpreting the Bible so as to show that the doctrine is not really there. The Unitarians are, perhaps, the great people for this sort of partial and local rationalising of religion ; for taking what here and there on the surface seems to conflict most with common sense, arguing that it cannot be in the Bible and getting rid of it, and professing to have thus relieved religion of its difficulties. And now, when there is much loosening of authority and tradition, much impatience of what conflicts with common sense, the Unitarians are beginning confidently to give themselves out as the Church of the Future.

But in all this there is in reality a good deal of what we must call intellectual shallowness. For, granted that there are things in a system which are puzzling, yet they belong to a *system ;* and it is childish to pick them out by themselves and reproach them with error, when you leave untouched the basis of the system where they occur, and indeed admit it for sound yourself. The Unitarians are very loud about the unreasonableness and unscripturalness of the common doctrine of the Atonement. But in the Socinian Catechism it stands written : ' It is necessary for salvation to know that God *is ;* and to know that God is, is to be firmly persuaded that there exists in reality some One, who has supreme dominion over all things.' Presently afterwards it stands written, that among the testimonies to Christ are ' miracles very great and immense,' *miracula admodum magna et immensa.* Now, with the One Supreme

x OUR 'MASSES' AND THE BIBLE

Governor, and miracles, given to start with, it may fairly be urged that that construction put by common theology on the Bible-data, which we call the story of the three Lord Shaftesburys, and in which the Atonement fills a prominent place, is the natural and legitimate construction to put on them, and not unscriptural at all. Neither is it unreasonable; in a system of things, that is, where the Supreme Governor and miracles, or even where the Supreme Governor without miracles, are already given.

And this is Butler's great argument in the *Analogy*. You all concede, he says to his deistical adversaries, a Supreme Personal First Cause, the moral and intelligent Governor of the universe; this, you and I both agree, is the order of nature. But you are offended at certain things in revelation; that is, at things, Butler means, like the story of the three Lord Shaftesburys as theology collects it from the Bible. Well, I will show you, he says, that in your and my admitted system of nature there are just as great difficulties as in the system of revelation. And he does show it; and by adversaries such as his, who grant what the Deist or Socinian grants, he never has been answered, he never can be answered. The spear of Butler's reasoning will even follow and transfix the Duke of Somerset, who finds so much to condemn in the Bible, but 'retires into one unassailable fortress,—faith in God.'

The only question, perhaps, is, whether Butler, as an Anglican bishop, puts an adequate construction upon what Bible-revelation, this basis of the Supreme Governor being supposed, may be allowed to be; whether Catholic dogma is not the truer construction to put upon it. Dr. Newman urges, fairly enough: Butler admits, analogy is in some sort violated by the fact of revelation; only, with the precedent of natural religion given, we have to own that the difficulties against revelation are not greater than against this precedent, and therefore the admission of this precedent of natural religion may well be taken to clear them. And must we not go farther in the same way, says Dr. Newman, and own that the precedent of revelation, too, may be taken to cover more than itself; and that as, the Supreme Governor being given, it is credible that the Incarnation is true, so, the Incarnation being true, it is credible that God should not have left the world to itself after Christ and his Apostles disappeared, but should have lodged divine insight in the Church and its visible head? So pleads Dr. Newman; and if it be said that facts are against the infallibility of the Church, or that Scripture is against it, yet to wide, immense things like facts and Scripture, a turn may easily be given which makes them favour it; and so an endless field for discussion is opened, and no certain conclusion is possible. For, once launched on this line of hypothesis and inference, with a Supreme Governor assumed, and the task thrown upon us of making out what he means us to infer and what we may suppose him to do and to intend, one of us may infer one thing and another of us another, and neither can possibly prove himself to be right or his adversary to be wrong.

Only, there may come some one, who says that the basis of all our inference, the Supreme Governor, is *not* the order of nature, is an assumption, and not a fact; and then, if this is so, our whole superstructure falls to pieces like a house of cards. And this is just what is happening at present. The masses, with their rude practical instinct, go straight to the heart of the matter. They are told there is a Great Personal First Cause, who thinks and loves, the moral and intelligent Author and Governor of the Universe; and that the Bible and Bible-righteousness come to us from him. Now, they do not begin by asking, with the intelligent Unitarian, whether the doctrine of the Atonement is worthy of this moral and intelligent Ruler; they begin by asking what proof we have of him at all. Moreover, they require plain experimental proof, such as that fire burns them if they touch it. If they are to study and obey the Bible because it comes from the Personal First Cause who is Governor of the Universe, they require to be able to ascertain that there *is* this Governor, just as they are able to ascertain that fire burns. And if they cannot ascertain it, they will let the intelligent Unitarian perorate for ever about the Atonement if he likes, but they themselves pitch the whole Bible to the winds.

Now, it is remarkable what a resting on mere probabilities, or even on less than probabilities, the proof for religion comes, in the hands of its great apologist, Butler, to be, even after he has started with the assumption of his moral and intelligent Governor. And no wonder: for in the primary assumption itself there is and can be nothing experimental and clearly known. So that of Christianity, as Butler grounds it, the natural criticism would really be in these words of his own : 'Suppositions are not to be looked upon as true, because not incredible.' However, Butler maintains that in matters of practice, such as religion, this is not so. In them it is prudent, he says, to act on even a supposition, if it is not incredible. Even the doubting about religion implies, he argues, that it *may* be true. Now, in matters of practice, we are bound in prudence, he says, to act upon what may be a low degree of evidence ; yes, '*even though it be so low as to leave the mind in very great doubt what is the truth.*'

Was there ever such a way of establishing righteousness heard of? And suppose we tried this with rude, hard, downright people, with the masses, who for what is told them want a plain experimental proof, such as that fire will burn you if you touch it. Whether in prudence they *ought* to take the Bible and religion on a low degree of evidence or not, it is quite certain that on this ground they never *will* take them. And it is quite certain, moreover, that never on this ground did Israel, from whom we derive our religion, take it himself or recommend it. He did not take it in prudence, because he found at any rate a low degree of evidence for it; he took it in rapture, because he found for it an evidence irresistible. But his own words are the best: 'Thou, O Eternal, art the thing that I long for, thou art my hope even from my youth; through thee have I been *holden up* ever since I was born.[1] The statutes of the Eternal rejoice the heart; more *desirable* they are than *gold, sweeter* than *honey;* in keeping of them there is *great reward*.[2] The Eternal is my *strength*, my heart hath trusted in him and I am *helped*; therefore my heart danceth for joy, and in my song will I praise him.'[3] That is why Israel took his religion.

III

But if Israel spoke of the Eternal thus, it was, we say, because he had a plain experimental proof of him. God was to Israel neither an assumption nor a metaphysical idea; he was a

[1] Ps. lxxi. 5, 6.   [2] Ps. xix. 8, 10, 11.   [3] Ps. xxviii. 7.

power that can be verified as much as the power of fire to burn or of bread to nourish : *the power, not ourselves, that makes for righteousness.* And the greatness of Israel in religion, the reason why he is said to have had religion revealed to him, to have been entrusted with the oracles of God, is because he had in such extraordinary force and vividness the perception of this power. And he communicates it irresistibly because he feels it irresistibly ; that is why the Bible is not as other books that inculcate righteousness. Israel speaks of his intuition as still feeling it to be an intuition, an experience ; not as something which others have delivered to him, nor yet as a piece of metaphysical notion-building. Anthropomorphic he is, for all men are, and especially men not endowed with the Aryan genius for abstraction ; but he does not make arbitrary assertions which can never be verified, like our popular religion, nor is he ever pseudo-scientific, like our learned religion.

He is credited with the metaphysical ideas of the personality of God, of the unity of God, and of creation as opposed to evolution : ideas depending, the first two of them, on notions of essence, existence, and identity, the last of them on the notion of cause and design. But he is credited with them falsely. All the countenance he gives to the metaphysical idea of the personality of God is given by his anthropomorphic language, in which, being a man himself, he naturally speaks of the Power with which he is concerned, as a man also. So he says that Moses saw God's hinder parts;[1] and he gives just as much countenance to the scientific assertion that God has hinder parts, as to the scientific assertion of God's personality. That is, he gives no countenance at all to either. As to his asserting the unity of God the case is the same. He would give, indeed, his heart and his worship to no manifestation of power, except of the power which makes for *righteousness;* but he affords to the metaphysical idea of the unity of God no more countenance than this, and this is none at all. Then, lastly, as to the idea of creation. He viewed, indeed, all order as depending on the supreme order of righteousness, and all the fulness and beauty of the world as a boon added to that holder of the greatest of all boons already, the righteous. This, however, is as much countenance as he gives to the famous argument from design, or to the doctrine of creation as opposed to evolution. And it is none at all.

Free as is his use of anthropomorphic language, Israel had far too keen a sense of reality not to shrink, when he comes anywhere near to the notion of exact speaking about God, from affirmation, from professing to know a whit more than he does know. 'Lo, these are parts of his ways,' he says of what he has

[1] Exodus xxxiii. 23.

experienced, '*but how little a portion is known of him!*'[1] And again: '*The secret things belong unto the Eternal our God; but the revealed things belong unto us and to our children for ever: that we may do all the words of this law.*'[2] How different from our licence of full and particular statement: 'A Personal First Cause, who thinks and loves, the moral and intelligent Governor of the Universe!' Israel knew, concerning the eternal *not ourselves*, that it was ' a power that made for righteousness.' This was revealed to Israel and his children, and through them to the world; all the rest about the eternal *not ourselves* was this power's own secret. And all Israel's language about this power, except that *it makes for righteousness*, is approximate language,—the language of poetry and eloquence, thrown out at a vast object of our consciousness not fully apprehended by it, but extending infinitely beyond it.

This, however, was ' a revealed thing,' Israel said, to him and to his children: 'the Eternal *not ourselves* that makes for righteousness. ' And now, then, let us go to the masses with what Israel really did say, instead of what our popular and our learned religion may choose to make him say. Let us announce, not : ' There rules a Great Personal First Cause, who thinks and loves, the moral and intelligent Governor of the Universe, and *therefore* study your Bible and

[1] Job xxvi. 14.   [2] Deut. xxix. 29.

learn to obey this!' No; but let us announce: 'There rules an enduring Power, not ourselves, which makes for righteousness, and *therefore* study your Bible and learn to obey this.' For if we announce the other instead, and they reply: 'First let us *verify* that there rules a Great Personal First Cause, who thinks and loves, the moral and intelligent Governor of the Universe,' —what are we to answer? We *cannot* answer.

But if, on the other hand, they ask: 'How are we to *verify* that there rules an enduring Power, not ourselves, which makes for righteousness?'—we may answer at once: 'How? why, as you verify that fire burns,—*by experience!* It *is* so; try it! you *can* try it; every case of *conduct*, of that which is more than three-fourths of your own life and of the life of all mankind, will prove it to you! Disbelieve it, and you will find out your mistake, as sure as, if you disbelieve that fire burns and put your hand into the fire, you will find out your mistake! Believe it, and you will find the benefit of it!' This is the first experience.

But then they may go on, and say: 'Why, however, even if there *is* an enduring Power, not ourselves, that makes for righteousness, should we study the *Bible* that we may learn to obey him?—will not other teachers or books do as well?' And here again the answer is: 'Why?—why, because this Power is *revealed* in Israel and the Bible, and not by other teachers and books! that is, there is infinitely more of him there, he is plainer and easier to come at, and incomparably more impressive. If you want to know plastic art, you go to the Greeks; if you want to know science, you go to the Aryan genius. And why? Because they have the specialty for these things; for making us feel what they are and giving us an enthusiasm for them. Well, and so have Israel and the Bible a specialty for righteousness, for making us feel what it is and giving us an enthusiasm for it. And here again it is experience that we invoke: *try it!* Having convinced yourself that there is an enduring Power, not ourselves, that makes for righteousness, set yourself next to try to learn more about this Power, and to feel an enthusiasm for it. And to this end, take a course of the Bible first, and then a course of Benjamin Franklin, Horace Greeley, Jeremy Bentham, and Mr. Herbert Spencer; see which has most effect, which satisfies you most, which gives you most moral force. Why, the Bible is of such avail for teaching righteousness, that even to those who come to it with all sorts of false notions about the God of the Bible, it yet does teach righteousness, and fills them with the love of it; how much more those who come to it with a *true* notion about the God of the Bible!' And this is the second experience.

IV

Now here, at the beginning of things, is the point, we say, where to apply correction to our current theology, if we are to bring the religion of the Bible home to the masses. It is of no use beginning lower down, and amending this or that ramification, such as the Atonement, or the Real Presence, or Eternal Punishment, when the root from which all springs is unsound. Those whom it most concerns us to teach will never interest themselves at all in our amended religion, so long as the whole thing appears to them unsupported and in the air.

Yet that original conception of God, on which all our religion is and must be grounded, has been very little examined, and very few of the controversies which arise in religion go near it. Religious people say solemnly, as if we doubted it, that 'he that cometh to God must believe that He *is*, and that He is a rewarder of them that seek Him';[1] and that 'a man who preaches that Jesus Christ is not God is virtually out of the pale of Christian communion.' We entirely agree with them; but we want to know what they mean by *God*. Now on this matter the state of their thoughts is, to say the truth, extremely vague; but what they really do at bottom mean by God is, in general: *the best one knows*. And this is the

[1] Hebrews xi. 6.

soundest definition they will ever attain; yet scientifically it is not a satisfying definition, for clearly *the best one knows* differs for everybody. So they have to be more precise; and when they collect themselves a little, they find that they mean by God *a magnified and non-natural man.* But this, again, they can hardly say in so many words; therefore at last, when they are pressed, they collect themselves all they can, and make a great effort, and out they come with their piece of science: God is *a Great Personal First Cause, who thinks and loves, the moral and intelligent Governor of the Universe.* But this piece of science of theirs we will have nothing to say to, for we account it quite hollow; and we say, and have shown (we think), that the Bible, rightly read, will have nothing to say to it either. Yet the whole pinch of the matter is here; and till we are agreed as to what we mean by *God*, we can never, in discussing religious questions, understand one another or discuss seriously. Yet, as we have said, hardly any of the discussions which arise in religion turn upon this cardinal point. This is what cannot but strike one in that torrent of *petitiones principii* (for so one really must call them) in the shape of theological letters from clergymen, which pours itself every week through the columns of the *Guardian.* They all employ the word *God* with such extraordinary confidence! as if 'a Great

x OUR 'MASSES' AND THE BIBLE

Personal First Cause, who thinks and loves, the moral and intelligent Governor of the Universe,' were a verifiable fact given beyond all question; and we had now only to discuss what such a Being would naturally think about Church vestments and the use of the Athanasian Creed. But everything people say, under these conditions, is in truth quite in the air.

Even those who have treated Israel and his religion the most philosophically, seem not to have enough considered that so wonderful an effect must have had some cause to account for it, other than any which they assign. Professor Kuenen, whose excellent History of the Religion of Israel[1] ought to find an English translator, suggests that the Hebrew religion was so unlike that of any other Semitic people because of the simple and austere life led by the Beni-Israel as nomads of the desert; or because they did not, like other Semitic people, put a feminine divinity alongside of their masculine divinity, and thus open the way to all sorts of immorality. But many other tribes have had the simple and austere life of nomads of the desert, without its bringing them to the religion of Israel. And, if the Hebrews did not put a feminine divinity alongside of their masculine divinity, while other Semitic people did, surely there must have been

[1] *De Godsdienst van Israel tot den Ondergang van den Joodschen Staat* (The Religion of Israel till the Downfall of the Jewish State); Haarlem. An English translation has now appeared.

something to cause this difference! and what we want to know is this *something*.

And to this *something*, we say, the 'Zeit-Geist' and a prolonged and large experience of men's expressions, and how they employ them, leads us. It was because, while other people, in the operation of that mighty *not ourselves* which is in us and around us, saw this thing and that thing and many things, Israel saw in it one thing only:—that it made for *conduct*, for *righteousness*. And it does; and conduct is nearly the whole of human life. And hence, therefore, the extraordinary reality and power of Israel's God and of Israel's religion. And the more we strictly limit ourselves, in attempting to give a scientific account of God, to Israel's authentic intuition of him, and say that he is 'the Eternal Power, not ourselves, that makes for righteousness,' the more real and profound will Israel's words about God become to us, for we can then verify his words as we use them.

Eternal, thou hast been our refuge from one generation to another![1] If we define the *Eternal* to ourselves, 'a Great Personal First Cause, who thinks and loves, the moral and intelligent Governor of the Universe,' we can never verify that *this* has from age to age been a refuge to men. But if we define the *Eternal*, 'the enduring power, not ourselves, that makes for

[1] Psalm xc. 1.

righteousness,' then we can know and feel the truth of what we say when we declare: *Eternal, thou hast been our refuge from one generation to another!* For in all the history of man we can verify it. Righteousness has been salvation; and to verify the God of Israel in man's long history is the most animating, the most exalting, and the most pure of delights. *Blessed is the nation whose God is the Eternal!*[1] is a text, indeed, of which the world offers to us the most inexhaustible and the most marvellous illustration.

Nor is the change here proposed, in itself, any difficult or startling change in our habits of religious thought, but a very simple one. However, simple as may be this change which is to be made high up and at the outset, it undeniably governs everything farther down. Jesus is the Son of *God*; the Holy Spirit is the Spirit of truth that proceeds from *God*. What God? 'A Great Personal First Cause, who thinks and loves, the moral and intelligent Governor of the Universe'?—to whom Jesus and the Holy Spirit are related in the way described in the Athanasian Creed, so that the operations of the three together produce what the Westminster divines call 'the Contract passed in the Council of the Trinity,' and what we, for plainness, describe as the fairy-tale of the three Lord Shaftesburys? This is all in the air, but in the air it all hangs together. There stand

[1] Psalm xxxiii. 12.

the Bible words! how you construe them depends entirely on what definition of God you start with. If Jesus is the Son of 'a Great Personal First Cause,' then the words of the Bible, literally taken, may well enough lend themselves to a story like that of the three Lord Shaftesburys. The story can never be verified; but it may nevertheless be what the Bible means to say, if the Bible have started, as theology starts, with the 'Great Personal First Cause.' And the story may, when it comes to be examined, have many minor difficulties, have things to baffle us, things to shock us; but still it may be what the Bible means to say. However, the masses will get rid of all minor difficulties in the simplest manner, by rejecting the Bible altogether on account of the major difficulty,—its starting with an assumption which cannot possibly be verified.

But suppose the Bible is discovered, when its expressions are rightly understood, to start with an assertion which *can* be verified: the assertion, namely, not of 'a Great Personal First Cause,' but of 'an enduring Power, not ourselves, that makes for righteousness.' Then by the light of this discovery we read and understand all the expressions that follow. Jesus comes forth from this enduring Power that makes for righteousness, is sent by this Power, is this Power's son; the Holy Spirit proceeds from this same Power, and so on.

x OUR 'MASSES' AND THE BIBLE

Now, from the innumerable minor difficulties which attend the story of the three Lord Shaftesburys, this right construction, put on what the Bible says of Jesus, of the Father, and of the Holy Spirit, is free. But it is free from the major difficulty also; for it neither depends upon what is unverifiable, nor is it unverifiable itself. That Jesus *is* the Son of a Great Personal First Cause is itself unverifiable; and that there *is* a Great Personal First Cause is unverifiable too. But that there *is* an enduring power, not ourselves, which makes for righteousness, is verifiable, as we have seen, by experience; and that Jesus *is* the offspring of this power is verifiable from experience also. For God is the author of righteousness; now, Jesus is the son of God because he gives the method and secret by which alone is righteousness possible. And that he *does* give this, we can verify, again, from experience. It *is* so! try, and you will find it to be so! Try all the ways to righteousness you can think of, and you will find that no way brings you to it except the way of Jesus, but that this way does bring you to it! And, therefore, as we found we could say to the masses: 'Attempt to do without Israel's God that makes for righteousness, and you will find out your mistake!' so we find we can now proceed farther, and say: 'Attempt to reach righteousness *by any way except that of Jesus*, and you will find out your mistake!' This is a thing that *can* prove itself, if it is so; and it *will* prove itself, because it is so.

Thus we have the authority of both Old and New Testament placed on just the same solid basis as the authority of the injunction to take food and rest: namely, that experience proves we cannot do without them. And we have neglect of the Bible punished just as putting one's hand into the fire is punished: namely, by finding we are the worse for it. Only, to *attend* to this experience about the Bible, needs more steadiness than to attend to the momentary impressions of hunger, fatigue, and pain; therefore it is called *faith*, and counted a virtue. But the appeal is to experience in this case just as much as in the other; only to experience of a far deeper and greater kind.

V

So there is no doubt that we get a much firmer, nay an impregnable, ground for the Bible, and for recommending it to the world, if we put the construction on it we propose. The only question is: Is this the *right* construction to put on it? is it the construction which properly belongs to the Bible? And here, again, our appeal is to the same test which we have employed throughout, the only possible test for man to employ,—the test of reason and experience. Given the Bible-documents, what, it is inquired, is the right construction to put upon them? Is it the construction we propose? or is it the construction of the theologians, according to which the dogmas of the Trinity, the Incarnation, the Atonement, and so on, are presupposed all through the Bible, are sometimes latent, sometimes come more visibly to the surface, but are always there; and to them every word in the Bible has reference, plain or figured?

Now, the Bible does not and cannot tell us itself, in black and white, what is the right construction to put upon it; we have to make this out. And the only possible way to make it out,—for the dogmatists to make out their construction, or for us to make out ours,—is by reason and experience. 'Even such as are readiest,' says Hooker very well, 'to cite for one thing five hundred sentences of Scripture, what warrant have they that any one of them doth mean the thing for which it is alleged?' They can have none, he replies, but reasoning and collection; and to the same effect Butler says of reason, that 'it is indeed the only faculty we have wherewith to judge concerning *anything*, even revelation itself.' Now it is simply from experience of the human spirit and its productions, from observing as widely as we can the manner in which men have thought, their way of using words and what they mean by them, and from reasoning upon this observation and experience, that we conclude the construction theologians put upon the Bible to be false, and ours to be the truer one.

In the first place, from Israel's master-feeling, the feeling for *righteousness*, the predominant sense that men are, as St. Paul says, 'created unto good works which God hath prepared beforehand that we should walk in them,'[1] we collect the origin of Israel's conception of God, —of that mighty 'not ourselves' which more or less engages all men's attention,—as the Eternal Power that makes for *righteousness*. This we do, because the more we come to know how ideas and terms arise, and what is their character, the more this explanation of Israel's use of the word 'God' seems the true and natural one. Again, the construction we put upon the doctrine and work of Jesus is collected in the same way. From the data we have, and from comparison of these data with what we have besides of the history of ideas and expressions, this construction seems to us the true and natural one. The Gospel-narratives are just that sort of account of such a work and teaching as the work and teaching of Jesus Christ, according to our construction of it, was, which would naturally have been given by devoted followers who did not fully understand it. And understand it fully they then could not, it was so very new, great, and profound;

[1] Ephesians ii. 10.

only time gradually brings its lines out more clear.

On the other hand, the theologians' notion of dogmas presupposed in the Bible, and of a constant latent reference to them, we reject, because experience is against it. The more we know of the history of ideas and expressions, the more we are convinced that this account is not and cannot be the true one; that the theologians have credited the Bible with this presupposition of dogmas and this constant latent reference to them, but that they are not really there. 'The Fathers *recognised*,' says Dr. Newman, 'a certain truth lying hid under the tenor of the sacred text as a whole, and showing itself more or less in this verse or that, as it might be. The Fathers *might have traditionary information* of the general drift of the inspired text which we have not.' Born into the world twenty years later, and touched with the breath of the 'Zeit-Geist,' how would this exquisite and delicate genius have been himself the first to feel the unsoundness of all this! that we have heard the like about other books before, and that it always turns out to be not so, that the right interpretation of a document, such as the Bible, is *not* in this fashion. Homer's poetry was the Bible of the Greeks, however strange a one; and just in the same way there grew up the notion of a mystical and inner sense in the poetry of Homer, underlying the apparent sense, but brought to light by the commentators; perhaps, even, they might have traditionary information of the drift of the Homeric poetry which we have not;—who knows? But, once for all, as our literary experience widens, this notion of a secret sense in Homer proves to be a mere dream. So, too, is the notion of a secret sense in the Bible, and of the Fathers' disengagement of it.

Demonstration in these matters is impossible. It is a maintainable thesis that the allegorising of the Fathers is right, and that this is the true sense of the Bible. It is a maintainable thesis that the theological dogmas of the Trinity, the Incarnation, and the Atonement, underlie the whole Bible. It is a maintainable thesis, on the other hand, that Jesus was himself immersed in the *Aberglaube* of his nation and time, and that his disciples have reported him with absolute fidelity; in this case we should have, in our estimate of Jesus, to make deductions for his *Aberglaube*, and to admire him for the insight he displayed in spite of it. This thesis, we repeat, or that thesis, or another thesis, is *maintainable* as to the construction to be put on such a document as the Bible. Absolute demonstration is impossible, and the only question is: Does experience, as it widens and deepens, make for this or that thesis, or make against it? And the great thing against any such thesis as either of the two we have just mentioned is,

x OUR 'MASSES' AND THE BIBLE

that the more we know of the history of the human spirit and its deliverances, the more we have reason to think such a thesis improbable, and it loses hold on our assent more and more. On the other hand, the great thing, as we believe, in favour of such a construction as we put upon the Bible is, that experience, as it increases, constantly confirms it; and that, though it cannot *command* assent, it will be found to *win* assent more and more.

CHAPTER XI

THE TRUE GREATNESS OF THE OLD TESTAMENT

WIN assent in the end the new construction will, but not at once; and there will be a passage-time of confusion first. It is not for nothing, as we have said, that people take short cuts and tell themselves fairy-tales, because the immense scale of the history of 'bringing in everlasting righteousness' is too much for their narrow minds. It is not for nothing; they *pay for it*. It is not for nothing that they found religion on prediction and miracle, guarantee it by preternatural interventions and the coming of the Son of Man in the clouds, consummate it by a banquet with Abraham, Isaac, and Jacob, in a city shining with gold and precious stones. They are like people who have fed their minds on novels or their stomachs on opium; the reality of things is flat and insipid to them, although it is in truth far grander than the phantasmagorical world of novels and of opium. But it is long before the novel-reader or the opium-eater can rid himself of his bad habits,

XI GREATNESS OF OLD TESTAMENT

and brace his nerves, and recover the tone of his mind enough to perceive it. Distress and despair at the loss of his accustomed stimulant are his first sensations.

Miracles, the mainstay of popular religion, are touched by Ithuriel's spear. They are beginning to dissolve; but what are we to expect during the process? Probably, amongst many religious people, vehement efforts at reaction, a recrudescence of superstition; the passionate resolve to keep hold on what is slipping away from them by giving up more and more the use of reason in religion, and by resting more and more on authority. The Church of Rome is the great upholder of authority as against reason in religion; and it will be strange if in the coming time of transition the Church of Rome does not gain.

But for many more than those whom Rome attracts, there will be an interval, between the time when men take the religion of the Bible to be a thaumaturgy and the time when they perceive it to be something different, in which they will be prone to throw aside the religion of the Bible altogether as a delusion. And this, again, will be mainly the fault,—if fault that can be called which was an inevitable error,—of the religious people themselves, who, from the time of the Apostles downwards, have insisted upon it that religion shall be a thaumaturgy or nothing. For very many, therefore, when it cannot be a thaumaturgy, it will be nothing. And very likely there will come a day when there will be less religion than even now. For the religion of the Bible is so simple and powerful that even those who make the Bible a thaumaturgy get hold of the religion, because they read the Bible; but, if men do not read the Bible, they cannot get hold of it. And then will be fulfilled the saying of the prophet Amos: 'Behold, the days come, saith the Eternal, that I will send a famine in the land, not a famine of bread, nor a thirst for water, but of hearing the words of the Eternal; and they shall wander from sea to sea, and from the north even to the east they shall run to and fro to seek the word of the Eternal, and shall not find it.'[1]

Nevertheless, as after this mournful prophecy the herdsman of Tekoah goes on to say: '*There shall yet not the least grain of Israel fall to the earth!*'[2] To the Bible men will return; and why? Because they cannot do without it. Because happiness is our being's end and aim, and happiness belongs to righteousness, and righteousness is revealed in the Bible. For this simple reason men will return to the Bible, just as a man who tried to give up food, thinking it was a vain thing and he could do without it, would return to food; or a man who tried to give up sleep, thinking it was a vain thing and

[1] Amos viii. 11, 12. [2] Amos ix. 9.

XI GREATNESS OF OLD TESTAMENT

he could do without it, would return to sleep. Then there will come a time of reconstruction; and then, perhaps, will be the moment for labours, like this attempt of ours, to be found useful. For though every one must read the Bible for himself, and the perfect criticism of it is an immense matter, and it may be possible to go much beyond what we here achieve or can achieve, yet the *method* for reading the Bible we, as we hope and believe, here give. And although, in this or that detail, the construction we put upon the Bible may be wrong, yet the main lines of the construction will be found, we hope and believe, right; and the reader who has the main lines may easily amend the details for himself.

II

Meanwhile to popular Christianity, from those who can see its errors, is due an indulgence inexhaustible, except where limits are required to it for the good of religion itself. Two considerations make this indulgence right. One is, that the language of the Bible being,—which is the great point a sound criticism establishes against dogmatic theology,—*approximate*, not scientific, in all expressions of religious feeling approximate language is lawful, and indeed is all we can attain to. It cannot be adequate, more or less proper it can be; but, in general, approximate language consecrated by use and religious feeling acquires therefrom a propriety of its own. This is the first consideration. The second is, that on both the 'method' and the 'secret' of Jesus popular Christianity in no contemptible measure both can and does, as we have said, lay hold, in spite of its inadequate criticism of the Bible. Now, to lay hold on the method and secret of Jesus is a very great thing; an inadequate criticism of the Bible is a comparatively small one.

Certainly this consideration should govern our way of regarding many things in popular Christianity;—its missions, for instance. The non-Christian religions are not to the wise man mere monsters; he knows they have much good and truth in them. He knows that Mahometanism, and Brahminism, and Buddhism, are not what the missionaries call them; and he knows, too, how really unfit the missionaries are to cope with them. For any one who weighs the matter well, the missionary in clerical coat and gaiters whom one sees in wood-cuts preaching to a group of picturesque Orientals, is, from the inadequacy of his criticism both of his hearers' religion and of his own, and his signal misunderstanding of the very Volume he holds in his hand, a hardly less grotesque object in his intellectual equipment for his task than in his outward attire. Yet every one allows that this

xi GREATNESS OF OLD TESTAMENT

strange figure carries something of what is called European civilisation with him, and a good part of this is due to Christianity. But even the Christianity itself that he preaches, imbedded in a false theology though it be, cannot but contain, in a greater or lesser measure as it may happen, these three things: the all-importance of *righteousness*, the *method* of Jesus, the *secret* of Jesus. No Christianity that is ever preached but manages to carry something of these along with it.

And if it carries them to Mahometanism, they are carried where of the all-importance of righteousness there is a knowledge, but of the method and secret of Jesus, by which alone is righteousness possible, hardly any sense at all. If it carries them to Brahminism, they are carried where of the all-importance of righteousness, the foundation of the whole matter, there is a wholly insufficient sense; and where religion is, above all, that metaphysical conception, or metaphysical play, so dear to the Aryan genius and to M. Emile Burnouf. If it carries them to Buddhism, they are carried to a religion to be saluted with respect, indeed; for it has not only the sense for righteousness, it has, even, it has the secret of Jesus. But it employs the secret ill, because greatly wanting in the method, because utterly wanting in the sweet reasonableness, the unerring balance, the *epieikeia*. Therefore to all whom it visits, the Christianity of our missions, inadequate as may be its criticism of the Bible, brings what may do them good. And if it brings the Bible itself, it brings what may not only help the good preached, but may also with time dissipate the erroneous criticism which accompanies this and impairs it. All this is to be said for popular religion ; and it all makes in favour of treating popular religion tenderly, of sparing it as much as possible, of trusting to time and indirect means to transform it, rather than to sudden, violent changes.

III

Learned religion, however, the pseudo-science of dogmatic theology, merits no such indulgence. It is a separable accretion, which never had any business to be attached to Christianity, never did it any good, and now does it great harm, and thickens an hundredfold the religious confusion in which we live. Attempts to adopt it, to put a new sense into it, to make it plausible, are the most misspent labour in the world. Certainly no religious reformer who tries it, or has tried it, will find his work live.

Nothing is more common, indeed, than for religious writers, who have a strong sense of the genuine and moral side of Christianity, and who much enlarge on the pre-eminence of this,

xi GREATNESS OF OLD TESTAMENT

to put themselves right, as it were, with dogmatic theology, by a passing sentence expressing profound belief in its dogmas, though in discussing them, it is implied, there is little profit. So Mr. Erskine of Linlathen, that unwearying and much-revered exponent of the moral side of the Bible: 'It seems difficult,' he says, 'to conceive that any man should read through the New Testament candidly and attentively, without being convinced that the doctrine of the Trinity is essential to and implied in every part of the system.' Even already many readers of Mr. Erskine feel, when they come across such a sentence as that, as if they had suddenly taken gravel or sand into their mouth. Twenty years hence this feeling will be far stronger; the reader will drop the book, saying that certainly it can avail him nothing. So, also, Bunsen was fond of maintaining, putting some peculiar meaning of his own into the words, that the whole of Christianity was in the Lutheran doctrine of justification by faith. Thus, too, the Bishop of Exeter chooses to say that his main objection to keeping the Athanasian Creed is, that it endangers the doctrine of the Trinity, which is so important. Mr. Maurice, again, that pure and devout spirit,—of whom, however, the truth must at last be told, that in theology he passed his life beating the bush with deep emotion and never starting the hare,—Mr. Maurice declared that by reading between the lines he saw in the Thirty-nine Articles and the Athanasian Creed the altogether perfect expression of the Christian faith.

But all this is mischievous as well as vain. It is vain, because it is meant to conciliate the so-called orthodox, and it does not conciliate them. Of his attachment to the doctrine of the Trinity the Bishop of Exeter may make what protestations he will, Archdeacon Denison will still smell a rat in them; and the time has passed when Bunsen's Evangelical phrases could fascinate the Evangelicals. Such language, however, does also actual harm, because it proceeds from a misunderstanding and prolongs it. For it may be well to read between the lines of a man labouring with an experience he cannot utter; but to read between the lines of a notion-work is absurd, for it is of the essence of a notion-work not to need it. And the Athanasian Creed is a notion-work, of which the fault is that its basis is a chimæra. It is an application of the forms of Greek logic to a chimæra, its own notion of the Trinity, a notion unestablished, not resting on observation and experience, but assumed to be given in Scripture, yet not really given there. Indeed the very expression, *the Trinity*, jars with the whole idea and character of Bible-religion. But, lest the Unitarian should be unduly elated at hearing this, let us hasten to add that so too, and just

XI GREATNESS OF OLD TESTAMENT

as much, does the expression, *a Great Personal First Cause.*

Learned pseudo-science applied to the data of the Bible is best called plainly what it is,—utter blunder; criticism of the same order, and of which the futility will one day be just as visible, as that criticism about the two swords which some way back we quoted. To try to tinker such criticism only makes matters worse. The best way is to throw it aside altogether, and forget it as fast as possible. This is what the good of religion demands, and what all the enemies of religion would most deprecate. The hour for softening down, and explaining away, is passed; the whole false notion-work has to go. Mild defences of it leave on the mind a sense of the defender's hopeless inability to perceive our actual situation; violent defences read, alas! only like '*a tale told by an idiot, full of sound and fury, signifying nothing.*'

IV

But the great work to be done for the better time which will arrive, and for the time of transition which will precede it, is not a work of destruction, but to show that the truth is really, as it is, incomparably higher, grander, more wide and deep-reaching, than the *Aberglaube* and false science which it displaces.

The propounders of 'The Great Personal First Cause, who thinks and loves,' are too modest when they sometimes say, taking their lesson from the Bible, that, after all, man can know next to nothing of the Divine nature. They do themselves signal injustice; they themselves know a great deal, far too much. They know so much, that they make of God a magnified and non-natural man, a sort, as we have said, of infinitely extended Lord Shaftesbury; and when this leads them into difficulties, and they think to escape from these by saying that God's ways are not man's ways, they do not succeed in making their God cease to resemble a man, they only make him resemble a man puzzled. But the truth is, that one may have a great respect for Lord Shaftesbury, and yet be permitted, even however much he be magnified, to imagine something far beyond him. And this is the good of such an unpretending definition of God as ours: *the Eternal Power, not ourselves, that makes for righteousness;*—it leaves the infinite to the imagination, and to the gradual efforts of countless ages of men, slowly feeling after more of it and finding it. Ages and ages hence, no such adequate definition of the infinite *not ourselves* will yet be possible, as any sciolist of a theologian will now pretend to rattle you off in a moment. But on one point of the operation of this *not ourselves* we are clear: that it makes for conduct, righteousness. So far

xi GREATNESS OF OLD TESTAMENT

we know God, that he is 'the Eternal that *loveth righteousness*'; and the farther we go in righteousness, the more we shall know him.

And as this true and authentic God of Israel is far grander than the God of popular religion, so is his real affirmation of himself in human affairs far grander than that poor machinery of prediction and miracle, by which popular religion imagines that he affirms himself. The greatness of the scale on which he operates makes it hard for men to follow him; but the greatness of the scale, too, makes the grandeur of the operation. Take the Scripture-promises and their accomplishment. *As the whirlwind passeth, so is the wicked no more; but the righteous is an everlasting foundation.*[1] And again: *They shall call Jerusalem the throne of the Eternal, and all the nations shall be gathered unto it.*[2] It is objected that this is not fulfilled. It is not fulfilled yet, because the whole career of the human race has to bring out its fulfilment, and this career is still going forward. 'Men are impatient, and for precipitating things,' says Butler; and Davison, whom on a former occasion we quoted to differ from him,—Davison, not the least memorable of that Oriel group, whose reputation I, above most people, am bound to cherish,—says with a weighty and noble simplicity worthy of Butler: 'Conscience and the present constitution of things are not

[1] Prov. x. 25.   [2] Jer. iii. 17.

corresponding terms ; it is conscience and *the issue of things* which go together.' It is so ; and this is what makes the spectacle of human affairs so edifying and so sublime. Give time enough for the experience, and experimentally and demonstrably it is true, that 'the path of the just is as the shining light which shineth more and more unto the perfect day.'[1] Only the limits for the experience are wider than people think. 'Yet a little while, and the ungodly *shall* be clean gone!'[2] but 'a little while' according to the scope and working of that mighty Power to which a thousand years are as one day. The world goes on, nations and men arrive and depart, with varying fortune, as it appears, with time and chance happening unto all. Look a little deeper, and you will see that one strain runs through it all : nations and men, whoever is shipwrecked, is shipwrecked on *conduct*. It is the God of Israel steadily and irresistibly asserting himself ; *the Eternal that loveth righteousness.*

In this sense we should read the Hebrew prophets. They did not foresee and foretell curious coincidences, but they foresaw and foretold this inevitable triumph of righteousness. First, they foretold it for all the men and nations of their own day, and especially for those colossal unrighteous kingdoms of the heathen world, which looked everlasting ; then,

[1] Prov. iv. 18.   [2] Ps. xxxvii. 10.

XI GREATNESS OF OLD TESTAMENT

for all time. 'As the whirlwind passeth, so is the wicked no more';—sooner or later it is, it must be, so. Hebrew prophecy is never read aright until it is read in this sense, which indeed of itself it cries out for; it is, as Davison, again, finely says, *impatient for the larger scope.* How often, throughout the ages, how often, even, by the Hebrew prophets themselves, has some immediate visible interposition been looked for! 'I looked,' they make God say, 'and there was no man to help, and I wondered that there was none to uphold; therefore mine own arm brought salvation unto me. The day of vengeance is in mine heart, the year of my redeemed is come.'[1] O long-delaying arm of might, will the Eternal never put thee forth, to smite these sinners who go on as if righteousness mattered nothing? There is no need; they *are* smitten. Down they come, one after another; Assyria falls, Babylon, Greece, Rome; they all fall for want of *conduct,* righteousness. 'The heathen make much ado, and the kingdoms are moved; but God hath showed his voice, and the earth doth melt away.'[2] Nay, but Judæa itself, the Holy Land, the land of God's Israel, perishes too,—and perishes for want of *righteousness.*

Yes, Israel's visible Jerusalem is in ruins; and how, then, shall men 'call Jerusalem the throne of the Eternal, and all the nations shall

[1] Isaiah lxiii. 4, 5.   [2] Psalm xlvi. 6.

be gathered unto it?' But the true Israel was Israel the bringer-in and defender of the idea of *conduct*, Israel the lifter-up to the nations of the banner of *righteousness*. The true Jerusalem was the city of this ideal Israel. And this ideal Israel could not and cannot perish, so long as its idea, righteousness and its necessity, does not perish, but prevails. Now, that it does prevail, the whole course of the world proves, and the fall of the actual Israel is of itself witness. Thus, therefore, the ideal Israel for ever lives and prospers; and its city is the city whereto all nations and languages, after endless trials of everything else except conduct, after incessantly attempting to do without righteousness and failing, are slowly but surely gathered.

To this Israel are the promises, and to this Israel they are fulfilled. 'The nation and kingdom that will not serve thee shall perish, yea, those nations shall be utterly wasted.'[1] It is so; since all history is an accumulation of experiences that what men and nations fall by is want of *conduct*. To call it by this plain name is often not amiss, for the thing is never more great than when it is looked at in its simplicity and reality. Yet the true name to touch the soul is the name Israel gave: *Righteousness*. And to Israel, as the representative of this imperishable and saving idea of righteousness, all the promises come true, and the

[1] Isaiah lx. 12.

XI GREATNESS OF OLD TESTAMENT

language of none of them is pitched too high. *The Eternal*, Israel says truly, *is on my side*.[1] 'Fear not, thou worm Jacob, and thou handful Israel! I will help thee, saith the Eternal. Behold, I have graven thee upon the palms of my hands, thy walls are continually before me. The Eternal hath chosen Zion; O pray for the peace of Jerusalem! they shall prosper that love thee. Men shall call Jerusalem *the throne of the Eternal*, and all the nations shall be gathered unto it. And he will destroy in this mountain the face of the covering cast over all people, and the veil that is spread over all nations; he will swallow up death in victory. And it shall be said in that day: Lo, this is our God! this is the Eternal, we have waited for him, we will be glad and rejoice in his salvation.'[2]

V

And if Assyria and Babylon seem too remote, let us look nearer home for testimonies to the inexhaustible grandeur and significance of the Old Testament revelation, according to that construction which we here put upon it. Every educated man loves Greece, owes gratitude to Greece. Greece was the lifter-up to the nations of the banner of art and science, as Israel was

[1] Psalm cxviii. 6.
[2] Is. xli. 14; xlix. 16; Ps. cxxxii. 13; cxxii. 6; Jer. iii. 17; Is. xxv. 7, 8, 9.

the lifter-up of the banner of righteousness. Now, the world cannot do without art and science. And the lifter-up of the banner of art and science was naturally much occupied with them, and conduct was a homely plain matter. Not enough heed, therefore, was given by him to conduct. But conduct, plain matter as it is, is six-eighths of life, while art and science are only two-eighths. And this brilliant Greece perished for lack of attention enough to *conduct;* for want of conduct, steadiness, character. And there is this difference between Greece and Judæa: both were custodians of a revelation, and both perished; but Greece perished of *over*-fidelity to her revelation, and Judæa perished of *under*-fidelity to hers. Nay, and the victorious revelation now, even now,—in this age when more of beauty and more of knowledge are so much needed, and knowledge, at any rate, is so highly esteemed,—the revelation which rules the world even now, is not Greece's revelation, but Judæa's; not the pre-eminence of art and science, but the pre-eminence of righteousness.

It reminds one of what is recorded of Abraham, before the true inheritor of the promises, the humble and homely Isaac, was born. Abraham looked upon the vigorous, bold, brilliant young Ishmael, and said appealingly to God: 'Oh that *Ishmael* might live before thee!'[1] But it cannot be; the promises are to *conduct*,

[1] Genesis xvii. 18.

XI GREATNESS OF OLD TESTAMENT

conduct only. And so, again, we in like manner behold, long after Greece has perished, a brilliant successor of Greece, the Renascence, present herself with high hopes. The preachers of righteousness, blunderers as they often were, had for centuries had it all their own way. Art and science had been forgotten, men's minds had been enslaved, their bodies macerated. But the gloomy, oppressive dream is now over. '*Let us return to Nature!*' And all the world salutes with pride and joy the Renascence, and prays to Heaven: 'Oh that *Ishmael* might live before thee!' Surely the future belongs to this brilliant new-comer, with his animating maxim: *Let us return to Nature!* Ah, what pitfalls are in that word *Nature!* Let us return to art and science, which are a part of Nature; yes. Let us return to a proper conception of righteousness, to a true use of the method and secret of Jesus, which have been all denaturalised; yes. But, 'Let us return to *Nature*';—do you mean that we are to give full swing to our inclinations, to throw the reins on the neck of our senses, of those sirens whom Paul the Israelite called 'the deceitful lusts,'[1] and of following whom he said 'Let no man beguile you with vain words, for because of these things cometh the wrath of God upon the children of disobedience'?[2] Do you mean that *conduct* is not three-fourths of life, and that the secret of Jesus has no use?

[1] Eph. iv. 22.   [2] Eph. v. 6.

And the Renascence did mean this, or half-meant this; so disgusted was it with the cowled and tonsured Middle Age. And it died of it, this brilliant Ishmael died of it! it died of provoking a collision with the homely Isaac, righteousness. On the Continent came the Catholic reaction; in England, as we have said elsewhere, 'the great middle class, the kernel of the nation, entered the prison of Puritanism, and had the key turned upon its spirit there for two hundred years.' After too much glorification of art, science, and culture, too little; after Rabelais, George Fox.

France, again, how often and how impetuously for France has the prayer gone up to Heaven: 'Oh that *Ishmael* might live before thee!' It is not enough perceived what it is which gives to France her attractiveness for everybody, and her success, and her repeated disasters. France is *l'homme sensuel moyen*, the average sensual man; Paris is the city of *l'homme sensuel moyen*. This has an attraction for all of us. We all have in us this *homme sensuel*, the man of the 'wishes of the flesh and of the current thoughts'; but we develop him under checks and doubts, and unsystematically and often grossly. France, on the other hand, develops him confidently and harmoniously. She makes the most of him, because she knows what she is about and keeps in a mean, as her climate is in a mean, and her situation. She does not develop him with

XI GREATNESS OF OLD TESTAMENT

madness, into a monstrosity, as the Italy of the Renascence did; she develops him equably and systematically. And hence she does not shock people with him but attracts them, she names herself the France of tact and measure, good sense, logic. In a way, this is true. As she develops the senses, the apparent self, all round, in good faith, without misgivings, without violence, she has much reasonableness and clearness in all her notions and arrangements; a sort of balance even in conduct; as much art and science, and it is not a little, as goes with the ideal of *l'homme sensuel moyen*. And from her ideal of the average sensual man France has deduced her famous gospel of the Rights of Man, which she preaches with such an infinite crowing and self-admiration. France takes 'the wishes of the flesh and of the current thoughts' for a man's *rights*; and human happiness, and the perfection of society, she places in everybody's being enabled to gratify these wishes, to get these rights, as equally as possible and as much as possible. In Italy, as in ancient Greece, the satisfying development of this ideal of the average sensual man is broken by the imperious ideal of art and science disparaging it; in the Germanic nations, by the ideal of morality disparaging it. Still, whenever, as often happens, the pursuers of these higher ideals are a little weary of them or unsuccessful with them, they turn with a sort of envy and admiration to the ideal set up by France,—so positive, intelligible, and up to a certain point satisfying. They are inclined to try it instead of their own, although they can never bring themselves to try it thoroughly, and therefore well. But this explains the great attraction France exercises upon the world. All of us feel, at some time or other in our lives, a hankering after the French ideal, a disposition to try it. More particularly is this true of the Latin nations; and therefore everywhere, among these nations, you see the old indigenous type of city disappearing, and the type of modern Paris, the city of *l'homme sensuel moyen*, replacing it. *La Bohême*, the ideal, free, pleasurable life of Paris, is a kind of Paradise of Ishmaels. And all this assent from every quarter, and the clearness and apparent reasonableness of their ideal besides, fill the French with a kind of ecstatic faith in it, a zeal almost fanatical for propagating what they call French civilisation everywhere, for establishing its predominance, and their own predominance along with it, as of the people entrusted with an oracle so showy and taking. *Oh that Ishmael might live before thee!* Since everybody has something which conspires with this Ishmael, his success, again and again, seems to be certain. Again and again he seems drawing near to a worldwide success, nay, to have succeeded;—but always, at this point, disaster overtakes him, he signally breaks down. At this crowning moment, when all seems triumphant

xi GREATNESS OF OLD TESTAMENT

with him, comes what the Bible calls a *crisis*, or judgment. *Now is the judgment of this world! now shall the prince of this world be cast out!*[1] Cast out he is, and always must be, because his ideal, which is also that of France in general, however she may have noble spirits who contend against it and seek a better, is after all a false one. Plausible and attractive as it may be, the constitution of things turns out to be somehow or other against it. And why? Because the free development of our senses all round, of our *apparent* self, has to undergo a profound modification from the law of our higher *real* self, the law of righteousness; because he, whose ideal is the free development of the senses all round, *serves* the senses, is a *servant*. But: *The servant abideth not in the house for ever; the son abideth for ever.*[2]

Is it possible to imagine a grander testimony to the truth of the revelation committed to Israel? What miracle of making an iron axehead float on water, what successful prediction that a thing should happen just so many years and months and days hence, could be really half so impressive?

VI

So that the whole history of the world to this day is in truth one continual establishing of

[1] John xii. 31. [2] John viii. 35.

the Old Testament revelation: '*O ye that love the Eternal, see that ye hate the thing that is evil! to him that ordereth his conversation right, shall be shown the salvation of God.*'[1] And whether we consider this revelation in respect to human affairs at large, or in respect to individual happiness, in either case its importance is so immense, that the people to whom it was given, and whose record is in the Bible, deserve fully to be singled out as the Bible singles them. '*Behold, darkness doth cover the earth, and gross darkness the nations; but the Eternal shall arise upon thee, and his glory shall be seen upon thee!*'[2] For, while other nations had the misleading idea that this or that, other than righteousness, is saving, and it is not; that this or that, other than conduct, brings happiness, and it does not; Israel had the true idea that *righteousness* is saving, that to *conduct* belongs happiness.

Nor let it be said that other nations, too, had at least something of this idea. They had, but they were not *possessed* with it; and to feel it enough to make the world feel it, it was necessary to be possessed with it. It is not sufficient to have been visited by such an idea at times, to have had it forced occasionally on one's mind by the teaching of experience. No: *he that hath the bride is the bridegroom;*[3] the idea belongs to him who has most *loved* it. Common

---

[1] Ps. xcvii. 10; l. 23.   [2] Is. lx. 2.   [3] John iii. 29.

XI GREATNESS OF OLD TESTAMENT

prudence can say : Honesty is the best policy ; morality can say : To conduct belongs happiness. But Israel and the Bible are filled with religious joy, and rise higher and say : '*Righteousness is salvation!*'—and this is what is inspiring. 'I have *stuck* unto thy testimonies! Eternal, what *love* have I unto thy law! *all the day long* is my study in it. Thy testimonies have I claimed as *mine heritage for ever*, and why? *they are the very joy of my heart!*'[1] This is why the testimonies of righteousness are Israel's heritage for ever, because they were *the very joy of his heart.* Herein Israel stood alone, the friend and elect of the Eternal. 'He showeth his word unto *Jacob*, his statutes and ordinances unto *Israel.* He hath not dealt so with any nation, neither have the heathen knowledge of his laws.'[2]

Poor Israel! poor *ancient people!*[3] It was revealed to thee that righteousness is salvation ; the question, *what* righteousness is, was thy stumbling-stone. Seer of the vision of peace, that yet couldst not see the things which belong unto thy peace! with that blindness thy solitary pre-eminence ended, and the new Israel, made up out of all nations and languages, took thy room. But, thy visitation complete, thy temple in ruins, thy reign over, thine office done, thy children dispersed, thy teeth drawn, thy shekels of silver and gold plundered, did there yet stay

[1] Ps. cxix. 31, 97, 111.
[2] Ps. cxlvii. 19, 20.
[3] Is. xliv. 7.

with thee any remembrance of thy primitive intuition, simple and sublime, of *the Eternal that loveth righteousness*? Perhaps not; the Talmudists were fully as well able to efface it as the Fathers. But if there did, what punishment can have been to thee like the punishment of watching the performances of the Aryan genius upon the foundation which thou hadst given to it?—to behold this terrible and triumphant philosopher, with his monotheistic idea and his metaphysical Trinity, 'neither confounding the Persons nor dividing the Substance'? Like the torture for a poet to hear people laying down the law about poetry who have not the sense what poetry is,—a sense with which *he* was born! like the affliction to a man of science to hear people talk of things as *proved* who do not even know what constitutes a fact! From the Council of Nicæa down to Convocation and our two bishops 'doing something' for the Godhead of the Eternal Son, what must thou have had to suffer!

CHAPTER XII

THE TRUE GREATNESS OF CHRISTIANITY

No; the *mystery* hidden from ages and generations,[1] which none of the rulers of this world knew,[2] the mystery revealed finally by Jesus Christ and rejected by the Jews, was not the doctrine of the Trinity, nor anything speculative. It was the method and the secret of Jesus. Jesus did not change the object for men,—righteousness. He made clear what it was, and that it was this:—his *method* and his *secret*.

This was the *mystery*, and the Apostles had still the consciousness that it was. To 'learn Christ,' to 'be taught the truth as it is in Jesus,' was not, with them, to acquire certain tenets about One God in Trinity and Trinity in Unity. It was, '*to be renewed in the spirit of your mind, and to put on the new man which after God is created in righteousness and true holiness.*'[3] And this exactly amounts to the method and secret of Jesus.

For Catholic and for Protestant theology

[1] Col. i. 26.   [2] 1 Cor. ii. 8.   [3] Eph. iv. 23, 24.

alike, this consciousness, which the Apostles had still preserved, was lost. For Catholic and Protestant theology alike, the truth as it is in Jesus, the mystery revealed in Christ, meant something totally different from his method and secret. But they recognised, and indeed the thing was so plain that they could not well miss it, they recognised that on all Christians the method and secret of Jesus were enjoined. So to this extent the method and secret of Jesus were preached and had their effect. To this extent true Christianity has been known, and to the extent before stated it has been neglected. Now, as we say that the truth and grandeur of the Old Testament most comes out *experimentally*, —that is, by the whole course of the world establishing it, and confuting what is opposed to it—so it is with Christianity. Its grandeur and truth are far best brought out *experimentally*; and the thing is, to make people see this.

But there is this difference between the religion of the Old Testament and Christianity. Of the religion of the Old Testament we can pretty well see to the end, we can trace fully enough the experimental proof of it in history. But of Christianity the future is as yet almost unknown. For that the world cannot get on without righteousness we have the clear experience, and a grand and admirable experience it is. But what the world will become by the thorough use of that which is really righteousness, the method and the secret and the sweet reasonableness of Jesus, we have as yet hardly any experience at all. Therefore we, who in this essay limit ourselves to experience, shall speak here of Christianity and of its greatness very soberly. Yet Christianity is really all the grander for that very reason which makes us speak about it in this sober manner,— that it has such an immense development still before it, and that it has as yet so little shown all it contains, all it can do. Indeed, that Christianity has already done so much as it has, is a witness to it; and that it has not yet done more, is a witness to it too. Let us observe how this is so.

II

Few things are more melancholy than to observe Christian apologists taunting the Jews with the failure of Hebraism to fulfil the splendid promises of prophecy, and Jewish apologists taunting Christendom with the like failure on the part of Christianity. Neither has yet fulfilled them, or could yet have fulfilled them. Certainly the restoration by Cyrus, the Second Temple, the Maccabean victories, are hardly more than the shadows of a fulfilment of the magnificent words: 'The sons of them that afflicted thee shall come bending unto thee, and all they that despised thee shall bow themselves down at the soles of thy feet; thy gates shall not be shut day nor night, that men may bring unto thee the treasures of the Gentiles, and that their kings may be brought.'[1] The Christianisation of all the leading nations of the world is, it is said, a much better fulfilment of that promise. Be it so. Yet does Christendom, let us ask, offer more than a shadow of the fulfilment of *this*: 'Violence shall no more be heard in thy land; the vile person shall no more be called liberal, nor the churl bountiful; thy people shall be *all* righteous; they shall *all* know me, from the least to the greatest; I will put my law in their inward parts, and write it in their hearts; the Eternal shall be thine everlasting light, and the days of thy mourning shall be ended'?[2] Manifestly it does not. Yet the two promises hang together; one of them is not truly fulfilled unless the other is.

The promises were made to *righteousness*, with all which the idea of righteousness involves. And it involves Christianity. They were made on the immediate prospect of a small triumph for righteousness, the restoration of the Jews after the captivity in Babylon; but they are not satisfied by that triumph. The prevalence of the profession of Christianity is a larger triumph; yet in itself it hardly satisfies them any better. What satisfies them is the

---

[1] Is. lx. 14, 11.
[2] Is. lx. 18; xxxii. 5; lx. 21; Jer. xxxi. 33, 34; Is. lx. 20.

prevailing of that which righteousness really is, and nothing else satisfies them. Now, Christianity is that which righteousness really is. Therefore, if something called Christianity prevails, and yet the promises are not satisfied, the inference is that this *something* is not that which righteousness really is, and therefore not really Christianity. And as the course of the world is perpetually establishing the pre-eminence of righteousness, and confounding whatever denies this pre-eminence, so, too, the course of the world is for ever establishing what righteousness really is,—that is to say, true Christianity,—and confounding whatever pretends to be true Christianity and is not.

Now, just as the constitution of things turned out to be against the great unrighteous kingdoms of the heathen world, and against all the brilliant Ishmaels we have seen since, so the constitution of things turns out to be against all false presentations of Christianity, such as the theology of the Fathers or Protestant theology. They do not work successfully, they do not reach the aim, they do not bring the world to the fruition of the promises made to righteousness. And the reason is, because they substitute for what is really righteousness something else. Catholic dogma or Lutheran justification by faith they substitute for the method and secret of Jesus.

Nevertheless, as all Christian Churches do

recommend the method and the secret of Jesus, though not in the right way or in the right eminency, still the world is made partially acquainted with what righteousness really is, and the doctrine produces some effect, although the full effect is much thwarted and deadened by the false way in which the doctrine is presented. Still, the effect produced is great. For instance, the sum of individual happiness that has been caused by Christianity is, any one can see, enormous. But let us take the effect of Christianity on the world. And if we look at the thing closely, we shall find that its effect has been this: Christianity has brought the world, or at any rate all the leading part of the world, *to regard righteousness as only the Jews regarded it before the coming of Christ.* The world has accepted, so far as profession goes, that original revelation made to Israel: *the pre-eminence of righteousness.* The infinite truth and attractiveness of the method and secret and character of Jesus, however falsely surrounded, have prevailed with the world so far as this. And this is an immense gain, and a signal witness to Christianity. The world does homage to the pre-eminence of righteousness; and here we have one of those fulfilments of prophecy which are so real and so glorious. 'Glorious things are spoken of thee, O City of God! I will make mention of Rahab and Babylon as of them that know me! behold, the Philistines also, and

XII GREATNESS OF CHRISTIANITY

Tyre, with the Ethiopians,—these were born *there!* And of Zion it shall be reported: This and that man was born in *her!*—and the Most High shall stablish her. The Eternal shall count, when he writeth up the people: This man was born *there!*'[1] That prophecy is at the present day abundantly fulfilled. The world's chief nations have now all come, we see, to reckon and profess themselves *born in Zion*,— born, that is, in the religion of Zion, *the city of righteousness.*

But there remains the question: *what* righteousness really is. The method and secret and sweet reasonableness of Jesus. But the world does not see this; for it puts, as righteousness, something else first and this second. So that here, too, as to seeing what righteousness really is, the world now is much in the same position in which the Jews, when Jesus Christ came, were. It is often said: If Jesus Christ came now, his religion would be rejected. And this is only another way of saying that the world now, as the Jewish people formerly, has something which thwarts and confuses its perception of what righteousness really is. It is so; and the thwarting cause is the same now as then:—the dogmatic system current, the so-called orthodox theology. This prevents now, as it did then, that which righteousness really is, the method and secret of

[1] Psalm lxxxvii. 3-6.

Jesus, from being rightly received, from operating fully, and from accomplishing its due effect.

So true is this, that we have only to look at our own community to see the almost precise parallel, so far as religion is concerned, to the state of things presented in Judæa when Jesus Christ came. The multitudes are the same everywhere. The chief priests and elders of the people, and the scribes, are our bishops aud dogmatists, with their pseudo-science of learned theology blinding their eyes, and always,—whenever simple souls are disposed to think that the method and secret of Jesus is true religion, and that the Great Personal First Cause and the Godhead of the Eternal Son have nothing to do with it,—eager to cry out: *This people that knoweth not the law are cursed!*[1] The Pharisees, with their genuine concern for religion, but total want of perception of what religion really is, and by their temper, attitude, and aims doing their best to make religion impossible, are the Protestant Dissenters. The Sadducees are our friends the philosophical Liberals, who believe neither in angel nor spirit but in Mr. Herbert Spencer. Even the Roman governor has his close parallel in our celebrated aristocracy, with its superficial good sense and good nature, its complete inaptitude for ideas, its profound helplessness in presence of all great spiritual movements. And the result is, that the splendid

---

[1] John vii. 49.

promises to righteousness made by the Hebrew prophets, claimed by the Jews as the property of Judaism, claimed by us as the property of Christianity, are almost as ludicrously inapplicable to our religious state now, as to theirs then.

And this, we say, is again a signal witness to Christianity. Jesus Christ came to reveal what righteousness, to which the promises belong, really is; and so long as this, though shown by Jesus, is not recognised by us, we may call ourselves Christendom as much as we please, the true character of a Christendom will be wanting to us, because the great promises of prophecy will be still without their fulfilment. Nothing will do except righteousness; and no other conception of righteousness will do, except Jesus Christ's conception of it:—his *method* and his *secret*.

III

Yes, the grandeur of Christianity and the imposing and impressive attestation of it, if we could but worthily bring the thing out, is here: in that immense experimental proof of the necessity of it, which the whole course of the world has steadily accumulated, and indicates to us as still continuing and extending. Men will not admit assumptions, the popular legend they call a fairy-tale, the metaphysical demonstrations do not demonstrate, nothing but experimental proof will go down ; and here is an experimental proof which never fails, and which at the same time is infinitely grander, by the vastness of its scale, the scope of its duration, the gravity of its results, than the machinery of the popular fairy-tale. Walking on the water, multiplying loaves, raising corpses, a heavenly judge appearing with trumpets in the clouds while we are yet alive,—what is this compared to the real experience offered as witness to us by Christianity ? It is like the difference between the grandeur of an extravaganza and the grandeur of the sea or the sky,—immense objects which dwarf us, but where we are in contact with reality, and a reality of which we can gradually, though very slowly, trace the laws.

The more we trace the real law of Christianity's action, the grander it will seem. Certainly in the Gospels there is plenty of matter to call out our feelings. But perhaps this has been somewhat over-used and mis-used, applied, as it has been, chiefly so as to be subservient to what we call the fairy-tale of the three Lord Shaftesburys,—a story which we do not deny to have, like other products of the popular imagination, its pathos and power, but which we have seen to be no solid foundation to rest our faith in the Bible on. And perhaps, too, we do wrong, and inevitably fall into what is artificial and unnatural, in labouring so much to produce in ourselves now, as the one impulse determining us to use the method and secret of Jesus, that conscious ardent sensation of personal love to him, which we find the first generation of Christians feeling and professing, and which was the natural motor for those who were with him or near him, and, so to speak, touched him; and in making this our first object. At any rate, misemployed as this motor has often been, it might be well to forego or at least suspend its use for ourselves and others for a time, and to fix our minds exclusively on the recommendation given to the method and secret of Jesus by their being *true*, and by the whole course of things proving this.

Now, just as the best recommendation of the oracle committed to Israel, *Righteousness is salvation*, is found in our more and more discovering, in our own history and in the whole history of the world, that it *is* so, so we shall find it to be with the method and secret of Jesus. That this *is* the righteousness which is salvation, that the method and secret of Jesus, that is to say, conscience and self-renouncement, *are* righteousness, bring about the kingdom of God or the reign of righteousness,—this, which is the Christian revelation and what Jesus came to establish, is best impressed, for the present at any rate, by experiencing and showing again and again, in ourselves and in the course of the world, that it *is* so; that this is the righteousness which is saving, and that there is none other. Let us but well observe what comes, in ourselves or the world, of trying any other, of not being convinced that this is righteousness, and this only; and we shall find ourselves more and more, as by irresistible viewless hands, caught and drawn towards the Christian revelation, and made to desire more and more to serve it. No proof can be so solid as this experimental proof; and none, again, can be so grand, so fitted to fill us with awe, admiration, and gratitude. So that feeling and emotion will now well come in after it, though not before it. For the whole course of human things is really, according to this experience, leading up to the fulfilment of Jesus Christ's promise to his disciples: *Fear not, little flock! for it is your Father's good pleasure to give you the kingdom.*[1] And thus that comes out, after all, to be true, which St. Paul announced prematurely to the first generation of Christians: *When Christ, who is our life, shall appear, then shall ye also appear with him in glory.*[2] And the author of the Apocalypse, in like manner, foretold: *The kingdom of the world is become the kingdom of our Lord and his Christ.*[3] The kingdom of the Lord the world is already become, by its chief nations professing the religion of righteousness. The kingdom of Christ the world will have to become, it is

---

[1] Luke xii. 32.   [2] Col. iii. 4.
[3] Rev. xi. 15. The Alexandrian manuscript is followed.

on its way to become, because the profession of righteousness, except as Jesus Christ interpreted righteousness, is vain. We can see the process, we are ourselves part of it, and can in our measure help forward or keep back its completion.

When the prophet, indeed, says to Israel, on the point of being restored by Cyrus: '*The nation and kingdom that will not serve thee shall perish!*'[1] the promise, applied literally, fails. But extended to that idea of righteousness, of which Israel was the depositary and in which the real life of Israel lay, the promise is true, and we can see it fulfilled. In like manner, when the Apostle says to the Corinthians or to the Colossians, instructed that the second advent would come in their own generation: '*We must all appear before the Judgment-seat of Christ!*'[2] —'*When Christ, who is our life, shall appear, then shall ye also appear with him in glory!*'[3] the promise, applied literally as the Apostle meant it and his converts understood it, fails. But divested of this *Aberglaube* or extra-belief, it is true; if indeed the world can be shown,—and it can,—to be moving necessarily towards the triumph of that Christ in whom the Corinthian and Colossian disciples lived, and whose triumph is the triumph of all his disciples also.

[1] Isaiah lx. 12.   [2] 2 Cor. v. 10.   [3] Col. iii. 4.

IV

Let us keep hold of this same experimental process in dealing with the promise of immortality; although here, if anywhere, *Aberglaube*, extra-belief, hope, anticipation, may well be permitted to come in. Still, what we need for our foundation is not *Aberglaube*, but *Glaube*; not extra-belief in what is beyond the range of possible experience, but belief in what can and should be known to be true.

By what futilities the demonstration of our immortality may be attempted, is to be seen in Plato's *Phædo*. Man's natural desire for continuance, however little it may be worth as a scientific proof of our immortality, is at least a proof a thousand times stronger than any such demonstration. The want of solidity in such argument is so palpable, that one scarcely cares to turn a steady regard upon it at all. And even of the common Christian conception of immortality the want of solidity is, perhaps, most conclusively shown, by the impossibility of so framing it as that it will at all support a steady regard turned upon it. In our English popular religion, for instance, the common conception of a future state of bliss is just that of the Vision of Mirza : 'Persons dressed in glorious habits with garlands on their heads, passing among the trees, lying down by the fountains, or resting on beds of flowers, amid a confused harmony of singing birds, falling waters, human voices, and musical instruments.' Or, even, with many, it is that of a kind of perfected middle-class home, with labour ended, the table spread, goodness all around, the lost ones restored, hymnody incessant. '*Poor fragments all of this low earth!*' Keble might well say. That this conception of immortality cannot possibly be true, we feel, the moment we consider it seriously. And yet who can devise any conception of a future state of bliss, which shall bear close examination better?

Here, again, it is far best to take what is experimentally true, and nothing else, as our foundation, and afterwards to let hope and aspiration grow, if so it may be, out of this. Israel had said: 'In the way of righteousness is life, and in the pathway thereof there is no death.'[1] He had said: 'The righteous hath hope in his death.'[2] He had cried to his *Eternal that loveth righteousness:* 'Thou wilt not leave my soul in the grave, neither wilt thou suffer thy faithful servant to see corruption! thou wilt show me the path of life!'[3] And by a kind of short cut to the conclusion thus laid down, the Jews constructed their fairy-tale of an advent, judgment, and resurrection, as we find it in the Book of Daniel. Jesus, again, had said: 'If a man keep my word, he shall never see death.'[4]

[1] Prov. xii. 28.
[2] Prov. xiv. 32.
[3] Psalm xvi. 10, 11.
[4] John viii. 51.

And by a kind of short cut to the conclusion thus laid down, Christians constructed their fairy-tale of the second advent, the resurrection of the body, the New Jerusalem. But instead of fairy-tales, let us begin, at least, with certainties.

And a certainty is the sense of *life*, of being truly *alive*, which accompanies righteousness. If this experimental sense does not rise to be stronger in us, does not rise to the sense of being inextinguishable, that is probably because our experience of righteousness is really so very small. Here, therefore, we may well permit ourselves to trust Jesus, whose practice and intuition both of them went, in these matters, so far deeper than ours. At any rate, we have in our experience this strong sense of *life from righteousness* to start with; capable of being developed, apparently, by progress in righteousness into something immeasurably stronger. Here is the true basis for all religious aspiration after immortality. And it is an experimental basis; and therefore, as to grandeur, it is again, when compared with the popular *Aberglaube*, grand with all the superior grandeur, on a subject of the highest seriousness, of reality over fantasy.

At present, the fantasy hides the grandeur of the reality. But when all the *Aberglaube* of the second advent, with its signs in the sky, sounding trumpets and opening graves, is cleared away, then and not till then will come out the profound truth and grandeur of words of Jesus like these: 'The hour is coming, when they that are in the graves shall hear the voice of the Son of God; and they that hear shall *live*.'[1]

V

Finally, and above all. As, for the right inculcation of righteousness, we need the inspiring words of Israel's love for it, that is, we need the Bible; so, for the right inculcation of the method and secret of Jesus, we need the *epieikeia*, the sweet reasonableness, of Jesus. That is, in other words again, we need the *Bible;* for only through the Bible-records of Jesus can we get at his *epieikeia*. Even in these records, it is and can be presented but imperfectly; but only by reading and re-reading the Bible can we get at it at all.

Now, greatly as the failure, from the stress laid upon the pseudo-science of Church-dogma, to lay enough stress upon the method and secret of Jesus, has kept Christianity back from showing itself in its full power, it is probable that the failure to apply to the method and secret of Jesus, so far as these have at any rate been used, his sweet reasonableness or *epieikeia*, has kept it back even more. And

[1] John v. 25.

the *infinite* of the religion of Jesus,—its immense capacity for ceaseless progress and farther development,—lies principally, perhaps, in the line of extricating more and more his sweet reasonableness, and applying it to his method and secret. For it is obvious from experience, how much our use of Christ's method and secret requires to be guided and governed by his *epieikeia*. Indeed, without this, his method and secret seem often of no use at all. The Flagellants imagined that they were employing his secret; and the Dissenters, with their 'spirit of watchful jealousy,' imagine that they are employing his method. To be sure, Mr. Bradlaugh imagines that the method and the secret of Jesus, nay, and Jesus himself too, are all baneful, and that the sooner we get rid of them all, the better. So far, then, the Flagellants and the Dissenters are in advance of Mr. Bradlaugh: they value Christianity, and they profess the method and secret of Jesus. But they employ them so ill, that one is tempted to say they might nearly as well be without them. And this is because they are wholly without his sweet reasonableness, or *epieikeia*. Now this can only be got, first, by knowing that it is in the Bible, and looking for it there; and then, by reading and re-reading the Gospels continually, until we catch something of it.

This, again, is an experimental process. That the *epieikeia* or sweet reasonableness of Jesus may be brought to govern our use of his method and secret, and that it can and will make our use of his method and secret quite a different thing, is proved by our actually finding this to be so when we try. So that the culmination of Christian righteousness in the applying, to guide our use of the method and secret of Jesus, his sweet reasonableness or *epieikeia*, is proved from experience. We end, therefore, as we began,—by experience. And the whole series of experiences, of which the survey is thus completed, rests, primarily, upon one fundamental fact,—itself, eminently, a fact of experience : *the necessity of righteousness.*

CONCLUSION

But now, after all we have been saying of the pre-eminency of righteousness, we remember what we have said formerly in praise of culture and of Hellenism, and against too much Hebraism, too exclusive a pursuit of the 'one thing needful,' as people call it. And we cannot help wondering whether we shall not be reproached with inconsistency, and told that we ought at least to sing, as the Greeks said, a *palinode*; and whether it may not really be so, and we ought. And, certainly, if we had ever said that Hellenism was three-fourths of human life, and conduct or righteousness but one-fourth, a palinode, as well as an unmusical man may, we would sing. But we have never said it. In praising culture, we have never denied that conduct, not culture, is three-fourths of human life.

Only it certainly appears, when the thing is examined, that conduct comes to have relations of a very close kind with culture. And the reason seems to be given by some words of our Bible, which, though they may not be exactly

CONCLUSION

the right rendering of the original in that place, yet in themselves they explain the connection of culture with conduct very well. 'I have seen the travail,' says the Preacher, 'which God hath given to the sons of men to be exercised in it; he hath made everything beautiful in his time; also, he hath set the world in their heart.'[1] *He hath set the world in their heart!*—that is why art and science, and what we call culture, are necessary. They may be only one-fourth of man's life, but they are *there*, as well as the three-fourths which conduct occupies. 'He hath set *the world* in their heart.' And, really, the reason which we hence gather for the close connection between culture and conduct, is so simple and natural that we are almost ashamed to give it; but we have offered so many simple and natural explanations in place of the abstruse ones which are current, that our hesitation is foolish.

Let us suggest then, that, having this one-fourth of their nature concerned with art and science, men cannot but somehow employ it. If they think that the three-fourths of their nature concerned with conduct are the whole of their nature, and that this is all they have to attend to, still the neglected one-fourth is there, it ferments, it breaks wildly out, it employs itself all at random and amiss. And hence, no doubt, our hymns and our dogmatic theology.

[1] Ecclesiastes iii. 10, 11.

Of our hymns we shall say a word presently; but what is our dogmatic theology, except the mis-attribution to the Bible,—the Book of *conduct*,—of a science and an abstruse metaphysic which is not there, because our theologians have in themselves a faculty for science, for it makes one-eighth of them? But they do not employ it on its proper objects; so it invades the Bible, and tries to make the Bible what it is not, and to put into it what is not there. And this prevents their attending enough to what *is* in the Bible, and makes them battle for what is *not* in the Bible, but they have put it there;—battle for it in a manner clean contrary, often, to the teaching of the Bible. So has arisen, for instance, all religious persecution. And thus, we say, has conduct itself become impaired.

So that conduct is impaired by the want of science and culture; and our theologians really suffer, not from having too much science, but from having too little. Whereas, if they had turned their faculty for abstruse reasoning towards the proper objects, and had given themselves, in addition, a wide and large acquaintance with the productions of the human spirit and with men's way of thinking and of using words, then, on the one hand, they would not have been tempted to mis-employ on the Bible their faculty for abstruse reasoning, for they would have had plenty of other exercise for it; and, on the other hand, they would have escaped

CONCLUSION

that literary inexperience which now makes them fancy that the Bible-language is scientific, and fit matter for the application of their powers of abstruse reasoning to it, when it is no such thing. Then they would have seen the fallacy of confounding the obscurity attaching to the idea of God,—that vast *not ourselves* which transcends us, —with the obscurity attaching to the idea of their Trinity, a confused metaphysical speculation which puzzles us. The one, they would have perceived, is the obscurity of the immeasurable depth of air, the other is the obscurity of a fog. And fog, they would have known, has no proper place in our conceptions of God; since whatever our minds *can* possess of God they know clearly, for no man, as Goethe says, possesses what he does not understand; but they can possess of Him but a very little. All this our dogmatic theologians would have known, if they had had more science and more literature. And therefore, simple as the Bible and conduct are, still culture seems to be required for them, —required to prevent our mis-handling and sophisticating them.

II

Culture, then, and literature are required, even in the interest of religion itself, and when, taking nothing but *conduct* into account, we make God, as Israel made him, to be simply and solely 'the Eternal Power, not ourselves, that makes for *righteousness.*' But we are not to forget, that, grand as this conception of God is, and well as it meets the wants of far the largest part of our being, of three-fourths of it, yet there is one-fourth of our being of which it does not strictly meet the wants, the part which is concerned with art and science ; or, in other words, with beauty and exact knowledge.

For the total man, therefore, the truer conception of God is as 'the Eternal Power, not ourselves, by which *all things* fulfil the law of their being' ; by which, therefore, we fulfil the law of our being so far as our being is æsthetic and intellective, as well as so far as it is moral. And it is evident, as we have before now remarked, that in this wider sense God is displeased and disserved by many things which cannot be said, except by putting a strain upon words, to displease and disserve him as the God of righteousness. He is displeased and disserved by men uttering such doggerel hymns as : *Sing glory, glory, glory to the great God Triune!* and : *Out of my stony griefs Bethel I'll raise!* and : *My Jesus to know, and feel his blood flow, 'tis life everlasting, 'tis heaven below!* or by theologians uttering such pseudo-science as their *blessed truth that the God of the universe is a* PERSON. But it would be harsh to give, at present, this turn to our employment of the phrases, *pleasing God, displeasing God.*

CONCLUSION

And yet, as man makes progress, we shall surely come to doing this. For, the clearer our conceptions in science and art become, the more will they assimilate themselves to the conceptions of duty in conduct, will become practically stringent like rules of conduct, and will invite the same sort of language in dealing with them. And so far let us venture to poach on M. Emile Burnouf's manor, and to talk about the Aryan genius, as to say, that the love of *science*, and the energy and honesty in the pursuit of *science*, in the best of the Aryan races, do seem to correspond in a remarkable way to the love of *conduct*, and the energy and honesty in the pursuit of *conduct*, in the best of the Semitic. To treat science with the same kind of seriousness as conduct, does seem, therefore, to be a not impossible thing for the Aryan genius to come to.

But for all this, however, man is hardly yet ripe. For our race, as we see it now and as ourselves we form a part of it, the true God is and must be pre-eminently the God of the Bible, *the Eternal who makes for righteousness*, from whom Jesus came forth, and whose Spirit governs the course of humanity. Only, we see that even for apprehending this God of the Bible rightly and not wrongly, letters, which so many people now disparage, and what we call, in general, *culture*, seem to be necessary.

And meanwhile, to prevent our at all

pluming ourselves on having apprehended what so much baffles our dogmatic friends (although indeed it is not so much we who apprehend it as the 'Zeit-Geist' who discovers it to us), what a chastening and wholesome reflection for us it is, that it is only to our natural inferiority to these ingenious men that we are indebted for our advantage over them ! For while *they* were born with talents for metaphysical speculation and abstruse reasoning, we are so notoriously deficient in everything of that kind, that our adversaries often taunt us with it, and have held us up to public ridicule as being 'without a system of philosophy based on principles interdependent, subordinate, and coherent.' And so we were thrown on letters ; thrown upon reading this and that,—which anybody can do, —and thus gradually getting a notion of the history of the human mind, which enables us (the 'Zeit-Geist' favouring) to correct, in reading the Bible, some of the mistakes into which men of more metaphysical talents than literary experience have fallen. Cripples in like manner have been known, now and then, to be cast by their very infirmity upon some mental pursuit which has turned out happily for them ; and a good fortune of this kind has perhaps been ours.

But we do not forget that this good fortune we owe to our weakness, and that the natural superiority remains with our adversaries. And some day, perhaps, the nature of God may be as

CONCLUSION

well known as the nature of a cone or a triangle; and then our two bishops may deduce its properties with success, and make their brilliant logical play about it,—rightly, instead of as now, wrongly ; and will resume all their advantage. But this will hardly be in our time. So that the superiority of this pair of distinguished metaphysicians will never perhaps, after all, be of any real advantage to them, but they will be deluded and bemocked by it until they die.

END OF VOL. VII